Dorothea Benton Frank

Carolina Girls

SIMON &
SCHUSTER

London · New York · Sydney · Toronto · New Delhi

A CBS COMPANY

First published in the USA by William Morrow, an imprint of Harper Collins Publishers, 2015
First published in Great Britain by Simon & Schuster UK Ltd, 2015
A CBS COMPANY

1 3 5 7 9 10 8 6 4 2

Simon & Schuster UK Ltd
1st Floor
222 Gray's Inn Road
London WC1X 8HB

www.simonandschuster.co.uk

Simon & Schuster Australia, Sydney
Simon & Schuster India, New Delhi

A CIP catalogue record for this book
is available from the British Library

Hardback ISBN: 978-1-4711-4963-4
eBook ISBN: 978-1-4711-4024-2

Printed and bound by CPI Group (UK) Ltd, Croydon, CR0 4YY

Simon & Schuster UK Ltd are committed to sourcing paper
that is made from wood grown in sustainable forests and supports the Forest
Stewardship Council, the leading international forest certification organisation.
Our books displaying the FSC logo are printed on FSC certified paper.

In Memory of
Tom Warner

If I can stop one heart from breaking,

I shall not live in vain;

If I ease one life the aching,

Or cool one pain,

Or help one fainting robin

Unto his nest again,

I shall not live in vain.

—EMILY DICKINSON

CONTENTS

CHAPTER 1

Meet Lisa St. Clair

June 2014

I hail from a very theatrical climate. Coming to terms with Mother Nature is essential when you call the Lowcountry of South Carolina home. At the precise moment I ventured outside early this morning, my sunglasses fogged. In the next breath I swatted a mosquito on the back of my neck. The world was still. The birds were quiet. It was already too hot to chirp. And, Lord save us, the heat was just beginning to rise. I thought the blazes of hell itself could not be this inhospitable.

But that was exactly how a typical summer day would be expected to unfold. The temperature would climb steadily from the midseventies at sunrise to the edges of ninety degrees by noon. All through the day thermometers across the land would inch toward their worst. Around three or four in the afternoon the skies would grow black and horrible. After several terrifying booms and earsplitting cracks of thunder and lightning, lights would flicker, computers reboot, and the heavy clouds burst as rain fell jungle style—fast and furious. Natives and tourists declared it "bourbon weather" and tucked themselves into the closest bar to knock back a jigger or two. Then suddenly, without warning, the deluge stops. The sun slowly reemerges and all is right with the world. The good news? The stupefying heat of the day is broken and the sun begins its lazy descent. The entire population of the Lowcountry, man and beast, breathes a collective sigh of relief. Even though every sign had pointed to impending catastrophe, the world, in fact, did not come to an end.

After five o'clock, in downtown Charleston, gentlemen in seersucker, linen, or madras, wafting a faint trail of Royall Bay Rhum, would announce to freshly powdered ladies in optimistic chintz that it appeared the sun had once again traveled over the yardarm. Could he tempt her with an iced adult libation? She would smile and say, *That would be lovely. Shall we imbibe on the piazza? I have some delicious cheese straws!* Or deviled eggs, or pickled shrimp, or a creamy spread enhanced with minced herbs from their garden. Ceiling fans would stir and move the warm evening air while they recounted their leisurely days in sweet words designed to charm.

By six or seven in the evening, across the city in all the slick new restaurants with dozens of craft beers and encyclopedic wine lists, corks were being pulled. Freezing-cold vodka and gin were slapping against designer ice cubes in shiny clacking shakers, with concoctions designed by a mixologist whose star was ascending on a trajectory matched with his ambition. Hip young patrons in fedoras and tight pants or impossibly high heels and short skirts picked at small plates of house-cured *salumi* and caponata. At less glamorous watering holes, crab dip was sitting on an undistinguished cracker, boiled peanuts dripping with saline goodness were being cracked open, and pop tops were popping.

An afternoon cocktail was a sacred tradition in the Holy City and had been as far back as the War. Charlestonians (natives and the imported) did not fool around with traditions, no, ma'am, even if your interpretation of tradition meant you'd prefer iced tea to bourbon. When the proper time arrived, the genteel privileged, the hipsters, and the regular folks paused for refreshment. If you were from elsewhere, you observed. We were so much more than a sea-drinking city.

But I was hours away from any kind of indulgence and it was doubtful I'd run into someone with whom I could share a cool one in the first place. To be honest, I was a juicer and got my thrills from liquefied carrots and spinach, stocking up when they were on special at the Bi-Lo. And I was the classic case of "table for one, please." Such is the plight of the middle-aged divorcée. I had surrendered my social life ages ago. On the brighter side, I enjoyed a lot of freedom. There was just me and Pickle, my adorable Westie. We would probably stroll the neighborhood later, as we usually did in the cool of early evening.

This morning, I finally got in my car and braved the evil heat baked into my steering wheel. I turned on the motor and held my breath in spurts until the air-conditioning began blowing cool air. My Toyota was an old dame with eighty-five thousand miles on her. I prayed for her good health every night. As I turned all the vents toward me I thought, Good grief, it's only June. It's only seven thirty in the morning. By August we could all be dead. Probably not. It's been like this every sweltering summer for the entire fifty-two years of my life. Never mind the monstrous hurricanes in our neck of the woods. I've seen some whoppers.

As I backed out of my driveway an old southernism ran across my mind. *Horses sweat, men perspire, but ladies glow.* Either I was a horse or I was aglow on behalf of twenty women. I'm sorry if it sounds like I'm complaining, which I might be to some degree, but during summer my skin always tastes like salt. Not that I went around licking myself like a cat. Even our most sophisticated visitors would agree that while Charleston could be as sultry and sexy a place as there is on this earth, our summers are something formidable, to be endured with forethought and respect. Hydrate. Sunscreen. Cover your hair so it doesn't oxidize. Orange hair is unbecoming to a rosy complexion.

It was an ordinary Monday and I was on my way to work. Oppressive weather and singledom aside, my professional life was what saved me. I've been a part-time nurse at the Palmetto House Assisted Living Facility for almost five years. The only problem, if there was one, was that I barely earned enough money to fulfill my financial obligations. But a lot of people were in the same boat or worse these days, so I counted my blessings for my good health and other things and tried not to think about money too much. I grew tomatoes and basil in pots on my patio, and I took private nursing jobs whenever they were available. I was squeaking along. And when I got too old to squeak along I thought I might commit a crime, something where no one got hurt, so that I could spend the rest of my days in the clink. I'd get three meals a day and health care, right? Or maybe I'd marry again. Honestly? Both of these ideas were remote possibilities.

My nursing specialty was geriatrics, which I'd gravitated toward because I enjoyed older people. Senior citizens are virtual treasure troves of lessons about life and the world. They hold a wealth of knowledge on a variety of subjects, many of which would have never been introduced to me if not for the residents of Palmetto House. The truth be told, those people might be the last generation of true ladies and gentlemen I'd ever know. They are conversationalists in the very best sense of the term. The time when polite conversation about your area of expertise was a pleasure to hear, I am afraid, is gone. These days young people speak in sound bites laced with so many references to pop culture that confuse me. The English language is being undermined by texting and the Internet. LOL. ROTFLMAO. BRB. Excuse me, but WTF? TY.

There was a darling older man, Mr. Gleason, long gone to his great reward, who would exhaust himself trying to explain the glories of string theory and the nature of all matter to me. To be honest, his explanations were so far over my head he could have repeated the same information to me like a parrot on methamphetamine and it never would have sunk into my thick head. But it made him so happy to talk about the universe and its workings that I'd gladly listen to him anytime he wanted to talk.

"You're getting it, you're getting it!" he'd say, and I would nod.

No, I wasn't.

I had a better chance with Russian history, wine, Egyptian art, astronomy, sailboat racing, the Renaissance, engineering—well, maybe not engineering, but there were Eastern religions—and a long list of different career experiences among the residents. Whenever I had a few extra minutes, it was a genuine pleasure to sit with them and listen to their histories. I learned so much. And just when things were running smooth as silk, believe it or not, there was always one man who'd have someone from beyond our gates slip him a Viagra or something else that produced the same effect. This old coot would go bed hopping until he got caught in the act or until the ladies had catfights over the sincerity and depth of his affection. Then Dr. Black, who ran Palmetto House, would have to give Casanova a chat on decorum even though his own understanding of the term might have been somewhat dubious. What did he care? The evenings would be calm for a while until it happened again. The staff would get wind of it and be incredulous (read: hysterical) at the thought of what the residents were doing. I'd get together with the other nurses and we'd all shake our heads.

"You have to admire their zest for living," I'd say.

Then someone else would always drop the ubiquitous southern well-worn bomb: "Bless their hearts."

Like many senior facilities we had a variety of levels of care from wellness to hospice and a special care unit for patients with advanced dementia. About half of our residents enjoyed independent living in small, freestanding homes designed for two families. They frequented the dining room and swimming pool and attended special events such as book clubs, billiards tournaments, and movie nights. They used golf carts to visit each other and get around. As their mobility and their faculties began to take the inevitable slide, they moved into the apartments with aides and then single rooms with nursing care where we could check on them, bring them meals, bathe and dress them, and of course, be sure their medications were taken as prescribed. For all sorts of reasons, our most senior seniors were often lonely and sometimes easily confused. But the old guys and dolls always perked up when they had a little company. It was gratifying to be a part of that. Improving morale was just a good thing. The other perk was that the commute from my house to Palmetto House was a breezy fifteen minutes.

This morning I pulled into the employee parking lot and kept the engine running while I prepared to make a mad dash to the main building. I spread the folding sunshade across my dashboard to deflect the heat and gathered up my purse, sunglasses, and umbrella. My shift was from eight until four that afternoon. The inside of my car would be steaming by then, even if I lowered my windows a bit, which I did. Otherwise how would the mosquitoes get in? If I didn't lower the window a bit I always worried that my windshield might explode, and who's going to pay for that?

I hopped out, my sunglasses fogged over again, I clicked the key to lock the doors, and I turned to hurry inside as fast as I could. I could feel the asphalt sinking under my feet and was grateful I wasn't wearing heels, though, to be honest, I hadn't worn heels since my parents' last birthday party.

The glass doors of the main building parted like the Red Sea and I rushed toward the cooler air. Relief! By the time I reached the nurses' station I was feeling better.

"It's gonna be a scorcher," Margaret Seabrook said.

Margaret and Judy Koelpin, a transplant from the northern climes, were my two favorite nurses at the facility. Margaret's laser blue eyes were like the water around the Cayman Islands. And Judy's smile was all wit and sass.

"It already is," I said. "The asphalt is a memory-foam mattress."

"Gross," Judy said. "I wanted to go to Maine on vacation this August, but do you think my husband would get off the boat to go somewhere besides the Gulf Stream?"

Judy's husband loved to fish and won one competition after another all year round.

Margaret said, "That's a long way to go for a blueberry pie."

"I love blueberry pie," I said.

"Before I die, I want to spend an August in Maine," Judy said. "Is that too much to ask?"

"I think the entire population of Charleston should go to Maine for the month of August," I said.

"Too far," Margaret said. "Besides, we'd miss the second growth of God's personal crop of tomatoes here! True happiness comes from what grows in the Johns Island dirt."

"Tomatoes and blueberries are not the same thing," Judy said. "And tomatoes are all but finished by August."

"I can make them grow," Margaret said.

"Yeah, and watch them explode in the heat," Judy said.

I laughed at them. They were always bickering about food, mostly to entertain themselves. Not because they really disagreed on anything.

"You're right," Margaret said. "But tomatoes are way more versatile than blueberries. By the way . . . Lisa?"

"Yeah?" I threw my things in my locker and picked up the clipboard from the desk that had notes on all the patients. "How was last night?"

"Not great. Dr. Black wants to see you."

"Oh no. Don't tell me. Kathy Harper?"

"Yeah, she had a terrible night. We had to start her on morphine."

Margaret's eyes, then Judy's, met mine. We all knew; morphine marked the beginning of the end. Kathy Harper was one of our favorite patients, but she was in a hospice bed fighting a hopeless battle against fully metastasized cancer. And she was the sweetest, most dignified woman I'd ever known. Her friends visited her every day and they always brought her something to lift her spirits. Brownies, tacos, granola, ice cream, a manicure, or a pedicure. The latest gift had been a documentary on the northern lights, something she had always wanted to witness. Sadly, a *National Geographic* DVD was as close as she would ever get.

"Are Suzanne and Carrie in there?"

"Yeah," Judy said. "God bless 'em. They brought us a box of Krispy Kremes. We saved you a Boston cream."

"Which I need like another hole in my head." I picked the donut up and ate half of it in one bite. "Good grief. There ought to be a law against these things." I ate the other half and licked my fingers.

"So, don't forget, Darth Vader wants to have a word," Margaret said.

"Can't be good news," I said.

"When is it ever?" she said.

His actual name was Harry Black but we called him Darth Vader and a string of other less than flattering names behind his back because he seldom brought tidings of joy. Harry was a decent enough guy. It seemed like he was always there at work. It couldn't be easy for him to watch patient after patient go the way of all flesh and to be responsible for all the administrative details that came with each arrival and departure. If there was one thing in this world that I truly did not want, it was his job. But we enjoyed some sassy repartee, making it easier to contend with the difficult moments.

I took a mug of coffee down the hall and rapped my knuckles on his door.

"Enter!" he said dramatically, as though I'd been given permission to come into his private and mysterious inner sanctum.

I smirked, even though I knew I was about to hear heartbreaking news, and pushed the door open.

"G'morning, Dr. Black," I said, walking in, and waited for him to tell me to sit. For the record, there was a half-eaten jelly donut on his desk between stacks of manila folders. Few humans I knew could resist the siren's call of a Krispy Kreme donut.

"Sit," he said. "Kathy Harper is failing. Pretty quickly. We have the unfortunate duty today of informing her friends that it's time to cancel the pedicures."

"Dr. Black? Did anyone ever accuse you of being overly sensitive?"

"Please. I know. But listen, you and I have been down this road a thousand times. She had a horrendous night last night. I had to sedate the hell out of her. She's sundowning for the foreseeable future."

"I am so sorry. I got the word from Margaret and Judy. The poor thing."

"Yes. God, I hate cancer."

"I do too. I don't understand why some people who are nothing but a pain in the neck live to a hundred and die in their sleep, never having needed anything more than an aspirin. And other people like Kathy Harper have to suffer and die so young."

"I know. It's terrible. Anyway, our job here is to make the end bearable not only for the patient but for the family and friends."

"Really? Dr. Black, I didn't know that. I just got out of nursing school yesterday. Do you want me to tell them?"

"Yes, but do you have to be so sarcastic?" he said.

"Do you have to be so condescending?" I said, and stood up. "Jeez. They're here, so I'll go talk to them now."

I stopped at the door, turned back, and rolled my eyes at him.

"Okay, okay. I know. I'm a jerk," he said. "But you know what?"

"What?"

"I'm gonna miss all those donuts," he said, and added in a mumble, "And the delicious legs on that little brunette."

"You're terrible," I said, and left thinking maybe gallows humor rescued us on some days. In any case, it clearly rescued Dr. Black. Not getting emotionally involved was obviously easier for him than for me.

I walked down the hall and turned to the right, making my way to Kathy Harper's room. It wasn't the first trip I'd made from Dr. Black's office with a message of this weight to deliver. Technically, it was his job to convey bad news but he hated doing it. And he knew I was very close with Kathy's friends, and truly, I wasn't going to tell them something they didn't already know. But I was going to tell them something they didn't want to hear. My heart was heavy.

I took a deep breath and slowly swung the door open. There was Kathy, peacefully sleeping in her bed, or so it seemed, with Suzanne seated on one side and Carrie on the other. Suzanne was checking her email on her smartphone and Carrie was flipping through a magazine. They looked up at me and smiled.

"Hey," I said quietly. "How are y'all doing?"

"Hey, how are you, Lisa?" Suzanne said in a voice just above a whisper. "How was your weekend?"

What Suzanne and Carrie did not yet know was that Kathy was not really asleep but drugged and floating somewhere in what I hoped was a pain-free zone in between sleep and consciousness. I knew she could hear our every word.

"Well, I took Pickle over to Sullivans Island and we had a long walk. Then I drove down to Hilton Head to check on my parents. My dad cooked fish on the grill. We had a nice visit. How about y'all?"

"I had three weddings and a graduation party!" Suzanne said. "Crazy!"

"I helped," Carrie said. "You know that Suzanne was desperate if she let me in the workshop."

"Oh, hush! I would never have been able to get it all done without you and you know it!"

Suzanne owned a very popular boutique-sized floral design business. June was her busiest time of the year, followed by December, when she decorated the mantelpieces, swagged doors and staircases, and hung the wreaths of Charleston's wealthiest citizens. Suzanne was a rare talent.

"Well, I was hoping to have a word with y'all. Should we step outside for a moment?"

"Sure," Suzanne said.

They stood and followed me to a small unassigned office that served as a private place for conversations not meant to be heard by the patients. It held only an unremarkable desk, three folding chairs, and a box of tissues.

Before I could sit Carrie spoke.

"This is really bad news, isn't it?" she said.

Carrie Collins had recently buried her husband in Asheville, North Carolina, and was enjoying an extended visit with Suzanne while her late husband's greedy, hateful children contested his will. And she had become great friends with Kathy while working at Suzanne's design studio. She'd told me that she arrived on Suzanne's doorstep with only what she could fit in her trunk.

"Well, it's not great," I said. "Kathy had a really difficult night last night. So the doctor ordered morphine for her and that's why she's resting now. He thinks it's time to begin administering pain meds on a regular basis."

"Is she already going into organ failure?" Carrie said.

Boy, I thought, for a nonprofessional she sure is familiar with how we die.

"Oh God!" Suzanne exclaimed. "She can't go yet! I promised her I'd take her out to the beach!"

"The minute I came in this morning I could smell death in every corner of her room," Carrie said.

"Don't be such a pessimist. She's just having a setback, isn't she?" Suzanne asked. "Do you think we can get her out to Isle of Palms? Maybe by next week?"

"To be honest?" I said. "Who knows? She has a living will that dictates the care she wants for herself, but when she's unable to make decisions, like now . . . You have her health care proxy. Her will says she does not want to be resuscitated or intubated."

"Yes. I know that," Suzanne said.

"Anyway, we feel the time has come to provide maximum comfort for her. Her living will also says, as I'm sure you know, that she asked for pain medication as needed."

"Are you asking my permission?" Suzanne said.

"Yes," I said.

"Is she in pain now?" Carrie said.

"She was last night, but as you can see, she's resting comfortably now," I said.

"Then give her whatever she needs," Suzanne said. "Please. God, I don't want her to suffer!"

"She won't suffer, will she?" Carrie said.

"We will do everything in our power to see that she doesn't. I promise," I said.

"Is this the end?"

This was the question every single person who worked at

Palmetto House dreaded. I gave her the best answer I could.

"Oh, Suzanne. If I knew the answer to that, I'd be, well . . . I don't know what I'd be. Einstein? The truth is that no one can precisely predict the hour of someone's death. But there are signs. As she gets closer to the end, things will change, and I promise I will tell you all I know."

Suzanne's bottom lip quivered and she burst into tears, burying her face in her hands. Carrie's eyes were brimming with tears too. She put her arm around Suzanne's shoulder and gave her a good squeeze. They were both devastated. I pulled tissues from the box on the desk and offered them. Even though I'd seen this wrenching scenario play through more times than I wanted to remember, this seemed different. It felt personal. And suddenly I was profoundly saddened. I had become involved. In my mind, seeing Kathy Harper's demise was like witnessing a terrible crash in slow motion.

"I'm okay. Sorry," Suzanne said. "It's just that this whole thing is so unfair."

"Yes. It is terribly unfair," I said, "But I can tell you this. Everyone around here has seen y'all come and go a million times since Kathy came to us. And every time you visit, her spirits perk up, and by the time you leave, she honestly feels better. Who could ask for better friends? Y'all have done everything that anyone could do."

"Thank you," Suzanne said, and then paused, gathering her thoughts. "Oh God! I really hoped, or I had hoped, that she'd get to a place where she could come to the beach to convalesce. The salt air would do her so much good."

"Well, for now I think we just take one day at a time."

"Yes," Carrie said. "God, this stinks. This whole business stinks."

"It sure does. But, listen. Keep talking to her, even when she appears to be sleeping," I said, "because she can probably hear you. She just can't respond. Y'all are helping her in ways you can't even imagine."

"And shouldn't we pray?" Carrie said. "Prayer can't hurt."

"That's right," Suzanne said to no one in particular.

"Prayer helps everyone. I've seen some pretty amazing things happen when people pray."

They looked at me and I knew they were hoping against reason that I was going to tell them I'd seen people miraculously cured. I'd heard of miracles, lots of them in fact, but I had not seen one. I was sorry. I wished I had. I wanted to give them hope where there was so very little, but I failed. I could not lie to them or give them false reassurance.

As the day crawled by, I became more and more disheartened. Every time I went by Kathy Harper's room, she seemed a little worse. By the time I got home, I was beside myself with dread and all sorts of claustrophobic and woeful feelings. But Pickle was at the door and all but swooned with happiness to have me back. Dogs were so great. I adored mine and could never resist her enthusiasm.

"Hey, little girl! Hey, my sweet Pickle!" I reached down and scooped her up in my arms and she licked my face clean. "Did you go outside today? Did John and Mayra come and take you to the park?"

Pickle barked and wiggled and barked some more. Apparently, John and Mayra Schmidt, my dog-loving next door neighbors, had indeed taken Pickle somewhere where she found something to roll around with or to challenge because she smelled like shampoo. They were retired and kept a set of keys to my house. Mayra spent a lot of time making note of the personal comings and goings of all our neighbors. She was always peeping through her blinds like Gladys

Kravitz on that old television program *Bewitched*. I loved her to death.

"What did you do, Miss Pickle, to deserve a bath today? Hmm? Did you find a skunk?"

Pickle loved skunks more than any other mammal on this earth. Maybe it was the way they moved in their seductive stealth, low to the ground. They held some kind of irresistible allure. That much was certain.

She barked again and I'd swear on a stack of Bibles that she said yes, she'd been rolling around with a dead skunk. But most dog owners thought their dogs spoke in human words as well as dog-speak. I took her leash from the hook on the wall and attached it to her collar.

"Let's go, sweetie," I said, and we left through the front door.

John and Mayra were outside getting into their car. I waved to them and they stopped to talk.

"Hey! How are y'all doing?" I said.

"Hey! Good thing we had tomato juice in the house!" Mayra said. "Our little Pickle ran off with Pepé Le Pew this morning!"

"Pickle," I said in my disappointed mommy voice.

I looked down at her and she looked at the ground, avoiding eye contact with me.

"So John baptized her with a huge can of tomato juice and then I shampooed her in the laundry room sink."

Mayra squatted to the ground and held out her hand. Pickle was so happy to be in Mayra's favor again that she pulled hard against her leash, yanking me forward.

"Thank you! She sure does love you," I said.

"We love her too. Little rascal. Good thing I went to Costco," John said. "I stocked up on enough tomato juice to make Bloodies for the whole darn town!"

John was famous for his Bloody Marys but refused to share the recipe. I had tried many times to figure it out and finally decided, because he grew jalapeños, that he must've been using his own special hot sauce. And maybe celery seed.

"Well, good! Call me when the bar opens! And thanks again for taking care of my little schnookle. She's like my child."

"Ours too!" Mayra said. "I love her to death. She gets me out of the house, and golly, she's good company."

"Thanks. I think so too. Come on, you naughty girl, let's get your human some exercise."

We walked the streets of my neighborhood, passing one midcentury brick ranch-style home after another. Some had carports and some had front porches but they all had a giant glass window in the living room. Some people parked their boats in the yard and others didn't even have paved driveways, so the cars were just pulled onto the property.

After my near bankruptcy—which is a story I'll tell you about how I wound up with boxes and boxes of yoga mats—I was basically homeless. Fortunately for me, my mother had elderly friends who owned this house, which is in the Indian Village section of old Mount Pleasant. My financial disaster coincided with their decision to move to Florida because our climate was too cold for them. I know. That sounds crazy, doesn't it? But it's true. Here I am swearing up and down that it's a sauna outside and someone else thinks it's too cold. Maybe it's my age. Hmm. Anyway, I do whatever maintenance there is to be done. I can mow the grass and turn on sprinklers with the best of them.

The house is an old unrenovated ranch constructed of deep burgundy bricks that would never win a beauty pageant. One bathroom is blue and white tile with black trim and the other is mint green with beige. The kitchen is completely uninspiring, and no matter how much I scrub the linoleum kitchen floor it never looks clean. It's pretty gross, but for the cost of utilities, five hundred dollars a month in rent, and a swift kick to the lawn mower, I have a roof over my head. And one for my daughter when she visits, which is, so far, not much. We're not speaking and I'll tell you about that too.

So Pickle and I walked around the block and she sniffed everything under the late-day sun while I looked at other people's landscaping, wondering how this one grew hydrangea in the blistering heat and why that one's dead roses weren't cut back. And I wondered how much longer Kathy Harper could and would hang on to the thinning gossamer threads between her life and the great unknown.

Later on, in the evening after a dinner of salad in a bag and half of a cold pork chop, I called my daughter. She didn't take the call. I thought about that for a moment and it made me feel worse. I didn't leave a message because she would know from caller ID that it was me who had called. Then I called my mother. It was either sit on the old sofa and watch *Law & Order: SVU* until I couldn't stand it anymore, do sun salutations to relax my body, or call my mother. I sort of needed my mom and some sympathy.

"Hello?"

"Hey, Mom. You busy?"

"Never too busy for my darling daughter! What's going on?" She put her hand over the receiver and called out. "Alan? For heaven's sake! Turn that thing down!"

"All right! All right!"

My father yelled from the background and I could see him in my mind's eye: pushed back in his leather recliner, fumbling with the remote to his sixty-inch television that had its own pocket in the chair opposite the cup holder that held his beer and yet another pocket for his reading glasses and the latest issue of *TV Guide*.

"I just wanted to talk for a minute. I had sort of a rough day."

"What happened? Gosh, it was nice to see you last weekend."

"You too. Well, we have this really sweet patient at Palmetto House who's got terrible cancer and it's like almost the end, you know?"

"Loss has always been hard for you to handle."

"Well, Mom, death is hard for most people to deal with."

"You spend too much time dwelling on the negative. Why don't you join a book club? Or an online dating thing? My book club is coming here this Thursday night. What should I serve them?"

"Oh, just go to Costco and buy a brick of cheese and a box of crackers. And I can't join book clubs and dating sites because that stuff costs money. You know that."

"Well, then, do the free things. Go for a walk! Take a book out of the library! Get interesting! Go back to teaching yoga, but in someone else's studio!"

"Mom! Stop!"

"I'll tell you, ever since Marianne moved to Denver and you closed your business, you've been on a big fat bummer and it's time for you to snap out of it! All this wallowing—"

"Mom!"

"I'm just saying that you'll regret your wallowing when you're my age. You'll get up one morning and every bone in your body will be killing you. You still have a lot of living left to do, so don't waste it!"

"Mom! Stop! I didn't call you to—"

"Here! Talk to your father! Alan! Come talk some sense into your daughter!"

"I'm busy! Just tell her I love her and to quit spending money!"

"Your father's right. Now, how's Marianne?"

"How would I know? She never calls."

"See? There you go again! Why can't you call her?"

If I told her why Marianne and I weren't speaking she'd have a heart attack. Somehow, I got off the phone, stared at it, and thought, That's all he ever says. And she's always telling me what's wrong with me! Then I had a terrible thought. What if one of my parents died and the surviving one wanted to live with me? Oh! God! No! I sort of said a blasphemous prayer, petitioning the Lord for my mother to go first because I could tolerate my father's company without every moment feeling like I was having a deep scaling in the dentist's chair. But my mother was overbearing and loud and frankly not very nice to me. We would kill each other! But living with Dad would be terrible too. First of all, I couldn't afford to take care of him. Second, having Dad in my house would obliterate any hope of an intimate life. (Yes, I still had hope.) And third, I might be a nurse but being a personal nurse to my father wasn't something I could easily do. We were both ridiculously modest and those personal moments of his hygienic routine would be so awkward. On top of it all, he was so set in his ways. He wouldn't be very happy if the refrigerator wasn't arranged by size and category or the spice drawer wasn't alphabetized. Worse, my stupid brother, Alan Jr., and his horrible wife, Janet, would want no part of my parents' care but they'd want quarterly expense reports on how this arrangement was affecting their inheritance. Oh Lord, please be merciful. Take Carol and Alan St. Clair home to heaven at the very same moment while they sleep.

On that night life seemed dreary, but when the sun came up in the morning, I was filled with irrational happiness. And it proved to be irrational. When I got to Palmetto House I found Suzanne and Carrie with Kathy as she took her final breaths. I cried with them. I couldn't help it. I'd had no idea she would die so soon.

"Listen," I said, as soon as I could speak without the fear of sobbing, "I can help if you'd like, with phone calls or arrangements. Just tell me how I can help."

My words hung in the air for a few minutes until the reality began to sink into Suzanne and Carrie's minds.

"There's no next of kin," Carrie said. "Isn't that terrible?"

"She wanted to be cremated and she wanted a Mass to be said," Suzanne said.

"And she didn't want flowers. She worked at a florist but she didn't want flowers," Carrie said. "No flowers at her own funeral. Oh God."

"But she wanted donations to go to a hospice of your own choosing. I'm sending flowers anyway. I couldn't live with myself if I didn't," Suzanne said, and collapsed in a chair. Then she sighed so hard that she looked ten years older. "How am I going to handle this?"

I said, "Don't worry. I will help you. We do this kind of thing here all the time."

CHAPTER 2

A Curious Requiem

THE *POST & COURIER*—OBITUARIES

KATHRYN GORDON HARPER

Born August 30, 1956; died on June 10, 2014, after a long battle with cancer. A native of Atlanta, Georgia, Ms. Harper adopted Charleston, South Carolina, as her home nearly twenty years ago after having spent many years in Minneapolis. Kathy, as she was known to her many friends, was a devoted volunteer of the South Carolina Coastal Conservation League. She was an avid history buff, a longtime volunteer for the South Carolina Historical Society in membership and the editor of their newsletter. For the past few years she was employed by the SGW Floral Design Team in Mount Pleasant. She held a master's degree in art history from the University of Georgia and a black belt in karate, and had a special interest in snuff bottles. She will be missed by all who knew her. Friends are invited to attend a Mass in her honor at the Church of Christ Our King in Mount Pleasant on Friday the twentieth of June at ten o'clock in the morning. In lieu of flowers please send donations to a hospice of your own choosing.

When I arrived at the church I was disappointed by the scant showing of cars. I had been hoping that Kathy had friends I'd never met, scores of people I hadn't seen visit her at Palmetto House who would come out of the woodwork to mourn her passing. In some ways the light showing was a reflection of my worries about my own demise. I mean, didn't we all wonder from time to time who would come to our funeral? Who would stop their day, cancel appointments, put on the appropriate clothes, get in a car, and drive to our funeral service? Who did we know who would stand or sit or kneel in a pew, hopefully recite a prayer for us, reflect on the life we had lived, and remember something good and worthy about us, some kindness we had shown them?

It was true what people said about life being too short and time going quickly. One lifetime was never enough to do all the things any person wanted to do. I was still trying to figure out what Kathy Harper could possibly have done to deserve this lousy karma. Nothing, as far as I knew. Nothing at all. There was just no logical reason.

I opened the door to the church and stepped inside. There were fewer than twenty people there, spread among the pews. Two baskets of gorgeous exotic flowers flanked the altar. They had to have been from Suzanne. The organist was playing something lovely that was probably Vivaldi or Bach. I never knew the difference, only that I liked both of them. Whatever the music was, it wasn't too maudlin or too liturgical. Kathy would not have wanted anyone to be maudlin, and though I was less sure about her feelings on religion, the music seemed appropriately dignified for the occasion.

I spotted Suzanne and Carrie, recognizing them by the backs

of their heads. Carrie was a tall, striking blonde and Suzanne, in contrast, was a beautiful, tiny sprite with long, shiny dark brown hair. They turned when they heard the echo of the closing door and motioned to me to come and sit with them. As soon as I sat down in the pew next to Carrie, Suzanne leaned over her to whisper to me.

"See that guy playing the organ?"

I looked around over my shoulder in perfect synchronization with Carrie and Suzanne. We must've looked like the Snoop Sisters.

"He used to date Kathy."

"Really?" I said.

"He was crazy about her," Carrie said.

"And she was crazy about him," Suzanne said. "He's a tree hugger."

I looked at him and thought he seemed like a nice enough guy. His blond hair was sort of long in the front and I liked his shirt. What was the matter with being a tree hugger?

"What's his name?" I said.

"Paul something—sounds like Glider," Suzanne said.

The service began then with the priest appearing on the altar preceded by an altar server who lit some candles. A large man in a dark suit, presumably from the funeral home, slowly and with great solemnity pushed a rolling cart, a tiny bier, up the aisle to the front of the church. On it stood a box covered in a beautiful lace-trimmed cloth and a single ivory-colored candle pressed into a heavy brass candlestick. In that box were the ashes of Kathryn Gordon Harper. The altar server came down from the raised altar and lit the candle. The gentleman from the funeral home turned quietly and walked back down the aisle, taking a seat in the rear of the church.

Suzanne, Carrie, and I looked at each other with startled expressions, each of us on the verge of tears with a similar question on our minds. How, exactly *how,* did Kathy's entire life fit into that tiny little box? Just then, as though he wanted to divert our attention, Paul the tree-hugger organist began playing "My Favorite Things" for a moment or two and then broke into a wild and rollicking rendition of "When the Saints Go Marching In." You would have thought we were in the French Quarter of New Orleans at a Cajun funeral. I felt a sudden piercing urge to get up and dance in the aisle. It wasn't until we were all smiling, and the priest had cleared his throat loudly several times and made some terrible faces and hand gestures indicating his displeasure, that Paul let the music die out. And he didn't stop playing all at once. He slowed down, dropped his left hand, slowly played a few notes with his right hand, and then let the final notes fade away entirely, without finishing the verse.

Clearly, Paul the tree-hugging organist was insulted. We could hear his shoes click across the floor. He took a seat in the pew right behind us.

"I was ready to join in," Suzanne said.

"Me too," I said, and looked at Carrie, who bobbed her head in agreement.

Paul leaned forward and whispered to us. Loudly.

"She loved that music," he said. "That priest is a stuffy old man."

Suzanne turned around and said to him, "You're right."

Then, sensing that wasn't enough to repair his embarrassment, Carrie turned and said, "Kathy would've loved your selections."

I turned to see him blush and smile and it appeared that the sting had been soothed. But in my peripheral vision I saw Suzanne roll her eyes, which seemed a little snide. I didn't know if I agreed with her position or not. Suzanne didn't suffer fools well and this Paul fellow was obviously a sensitive man. I didn't have to agree with Carrie and Suzanne on everything to be on good terms with them. Being a medical professional and one who had spent a great deal of time seeing to Kathryn's comfort gave me a space where I could hold my own opinions. Personally? In my experience, sensitive men were an unusual and beautiful thing. Unfortunately, they often played for the other team.

I felt a little bad for Paul. He was obviously affected by the death of Kathy. I wondered how close they had been. Had they been lovers? Whatever relationship they had known with each other must've ended some time ago because I could not recall ever seeing him at Palmetto House. But that didn't mean their relationship had been insignificant. Maybe he had thought they might reunite? Maybe he had thought there was time? Maybe he had never even known she was so ill? Or ill at all?

The priest was circling Kathryn's ashes and sprinkling holy water all over the place. It was an interesting service, filled with all the smells, bells, and drama that you always hear go on in the Catholic Church. I wondered if I should go to Communion for Kathy's sake, but then the priest made a small speech about who was welcome at the Communion rail and who was not. I was a "was-not." So were Carrie and Suzanne. In fact, the only people who went to Communion were Paul and a prim older woman who Suzanne said worked with them at her florist.

Suzanne leaned over toward me again.

She said, "He's a convert."

"Converts are the worst," Carrie said. "He used to be Jewish. But clearly not terribly devout."

Soon we were reciting the Lord's Prayer and being told to "go in peace." Kathryn Gordon Harper's Requiem Mass was officially ended. It was the strangest moment. I felt a chill travel from the bottom of my spine to the top of my head, and despite the heat, I shuddered. Not only was Kathy gone from the world but I realized then that I might never see Carrie and Suzanne again. I know that remark probably seems ridiculous. After all, they were Kathy's friends and I was merely one of the many people who saw about her care. But I knew I'd miss them.

Inside of an hour I had gone from a strong, independent, seasoned nurse to an insecure woman whose insides jiggled a bit over the thought of not having these two women for friends. Was I being pathetic or merely human?

The priest came down from the altar and removed the linen cloth that covered the tiny box which held Kathy's ashes. He folded it carefully so that it would not have to be reironed for the next ceremony and handed it to the altar boy, who turned and left. Then he spoke.

"To whom shall I entrust Kathryn Harper's remains?"

"To me," Suzanne said, and stepped forward. "I'm Suzanne Williams. Her friend and her employer. But mostly her friend."

"My condolences," he said disingenuously, and handed her the horrible box. He then turned on his heel with all the officiousness of a visiting bishop or perhaps a cardinal and simply walked away. *Ashes to ashes, dust to dust.* He probably sang it in the shower.

Suzanne just stood there with the box in her hands, looking at it.

"How terrible," she said.

"What?" I said, silently agreeing with her.

"Well, there was no wake, no reception, no nothing at all for our friend," Suzanne said. "Just this Mass with this cranky priest, and oh, I don't know, it just seems like . . ."

"She deserved more?" Carrie said.

"It's just over too quick," Suzanne said. "Everything, this service, her life . . . God. How awful."

"I know what. Why don't we go out for brunch?" I said, thinking I was ripe for an episode of purely emotional eating.

"I could go for pancakes big-time," Carrie said. "Or waffles. Well, just one."

"I could go for pancakes anytime," I said, but I did count carbs.

"Or an omelet," Suzanne said. "Maybe a mimosa or . . ."

We were walking outside and we paused near the door of the church to see an older woman approaching us. She was very chic and could possibly have been wearing vintage Courrèges or Givenchy, which was odd for Charleston, in the middle of the day, in the broiling weather. She didn't have a drop of perspiration on her and we were practically dripping. When she removed her oversized sunglasses I gasped, wondering how many times she'd had an eyelift. Then there was the alarming matter of her chin and neck to be considered.

"Excuse me," she said to Suzanne. "Are you part of Kathy's family?"

"No," Suzanne said.

"Oh. Well, did she have any family?"

"No. She was an only child. Her parents died years ago," Suzanne said. "No siblings."

"Who are you?" Carrie asked. She seemed uncomfortable and she whispered to me, "Who knows? These days?"

I nodded in agreement because sometimes suspicious people did turn up in the strangest places.

"I'm her landlady. Wendy Murray. I have to dispose of her earthly treasures. Will you ladies be helping me to do that?"

Suzanne and Carrie exchanged looks and said, "Sure, I guess. Of course."

"She left everything to me," Suzanne said.

This was news. I had wondered about Kathy's estate.

"What got her?" Wendy asked.

"Cancer," Carrie said. "She sure fought it."

"She was incredibly brave," Suzanne said. "And she never complained. Not one word."

"Humph, I knew there was something fishy going on. At first I thought she went on a long vacation, like a Carnival Cruise. She was always getting brochures from them in the mail. And then I had to read her obituary in the paper," Wendy said. "Sometimes I think the whole world has cancer."

"Seems like it, doesn't it?" Carrie said.

"We see so much of it," I said.

"Who's we?" Wendy asked.

Boy, I thought, this is one salty little old lady.

"I'm Lisa St. Clair. And I was one of her nurses at Palmetto House."

"What in the heck was she doing there?" Wendy said, and shook her bangle bracelets. "I thought cancer patients went to hospice."

Carrie cringed.

"She *was* in hospice," I said. "We have some hospice beds."

"Palmetto House, huh? That's where I want to go when my time comes! That's a swinging place," Wendy said with a wicked grin that stretched across her stretched face.

I figured she had to be seventy or maybe even eighty if she was a day. Well, I thought, she'd better hurry up and book a room if she wants to be part of the Palmetto House action. How long did she expect to live?

"After happy hour it can get pretty crazy." And, you'd better bring an antibiotic for STDs if you know what's good for you, I also thought but did not say. Party on, babe.

"So I hear," Wendy said, still grinning, and began digging in her purse, pulling out a pen and tearing the back from an envelope. She leaned on a car, scribbled her address and phone number, and handed the paper to Suzanne. "It's already the twentieth of the month. If you could get her stuff this week it would be great."

"I'll try," Suzanne said.

"I have to paint and try to rent the place out by the first," Wendy said. "Life goes on, you know?"

Wendy Murray turned on her kitten heel and proceeded to cross the parking lot to her car without so much as a "Gee, it was nice to meet you ladies" or "Wasn't Kathy such a sweet lady?" or even a "What a shame!"

We stood there together watching her get into her car and I think it's safe to say there was a collective feeling that we'd been on the receiving end of some very unsouthern and unladylike behavior.

"Here I am with my dear friend's ashes in my arms, practically warm, mind you, and her landlady wants me to hustle and get her belongings so she can rerent the apartment. What is this? New York?"

Carrie said, "Pretty cold, if you ask me."

"Terrible," I said. "I'm starving."

"Ravenous," Suzanne said. "Let's go to Page's."

"Excellent," I said. "Can't get there fast enough." I gave them a little wave and walked toward my car. There was no point in belaboring our departure given the heat.

Page's Okra Grill was where everyone went to eat great food at a great price in an unpretentious atmosphere with friendly service. It was the perfect choice. Also, it was a mere five minutes from the church.

The restaurant was packed with patrons of every size, shape, ethnicity, and age. There were families with tiny children drawing on placemats with crayons, teenage girls having lunch, taking selfies and comparing pictures while munching on shared french fries, and old geezers shaking their heads, discussing life with other old geezers while they enjoyed their one hot meal of the day. In the front of the restaurant, there were gigantic, delicious-looking cakes on display, and a counter with a dozen or so spinning stools in the rear. At the far end of the dining room there was a community table and racks of T-shirts for sale. On the other side was a bar that served alcohol because after all, one never knew when "bourbon weather" or sundown might arrive. The place was alive and thriving and it smelled like a beloved grandmother's kitchen during the holidays. I could smell bacon and gravy and sugar. What else could you ask for?

We must have looked grim, like we were coming from a funeral, because the hostess whisked us through the waiting throng and gave us a roomy booth.

"I'll be right back with your menus," she said.

We nodded and slid across the seats. I sat opposite Carrie and Suzanne.

"Well, here we are," Suzanne said. "I left Kathy's ashes in the trunk of my car. Doesn't that sound so weird to say?"

"Yes, it does," Carrie said. "So, Suzanne? Did you notice anything unusual about Kathy's landlady?"

"Besides her really extreme plastic surgery?" I said just to make myself a part of the conversation. "If she lifts her chin again she'll be able to tie her ears in a knot in the back of her head. Her face is stretched like Saran Wrap."

Suzanne and Carrie looked at me and giggled.

"Oh, I knew I really liked you," Suzanne said.

"Meow, me too," Carrie said, and looked back to Suzanne. "I meant, her bracelets. Didn't they look familiar to you?"

The hostess returned with menus and a waitress put glasses of ice water on the table in front of us.

She said, "Can I tell y'all about our specials?"

"I think we all want pancakes," I said, "with fried eggs on the side and an order of really crispy bacon to share and sweet tea? How does that sound, y'all?"

"Perfect. And a waffle for the table," Carrie said.

"And one well-done sausage patty," Suzanne said. "For me."

"I'll get that right into the kitchen for you," the waitress said.

"Bracelets? Bracelets?" Suzanne said, not making the connection, and then a lightbulb flashed in her brain. "Carrie! They were just like the ones you gave Kathy for her birthday last year. Weren't they?"

"How about they *are* the ones I gave Kathy for her birthday last year," Carrie said.

"Oh no!" I said. "How terrible!"

"Stealing from a dead person is about as low as you can go," Suzanne said. "Are you sure?"

"Absolutely certain," Carrie said. "Look, they weren't worth a fortune. I bought them in Asheville from some little artist's gallery. But they were one of a kind."

"You should tell her you want them back," I said.

"Oh, right," Suzanne said. "She'll just say Kathy gave them to her."

"Exactly," Carrie said. "I knew I didn't like that woman the moment I laid eyes on her."

"That's totally disgusting," I said, and suddenly a familiar face appeared across the dining room. "Wait! Y'all! Isn't that Paul, the tree-hugging, organist, sensitive guy Kathy dated?"

They both turned as inconspicuously as they could to verify the sighting.

"Yes. It's him all right," Carrie said. "Should we ask him to join us?"

"Oh, please, no," Suzanne said. "I'm already exhausted. I can't be nice to anyone new."

"To be honest? Me either," I said.

But I was already in the soup because Paul made eye contact with me. I smiled in a way that I hoped would say, *Glad to see you again but don't come over here.*

"He saw you, right?" Suzanne said.

"Yeah, but he's not moving toward us. He's sitting at the counter."

"Good," Carrie said.

I looked at them and wondered why they didn't like him.

Carrie, who was more sensitive, said, "I just want to be in my misery with you and Suzanne. I don't want to share."

"That's pretty much how I feel too," Suzanne said.

"So? Y'all? What about the landlady and the bracelets?" I said. "The thing that's bothering me is that if she'd take those, what else did she take?"

"It makes me ill to think about it," Suzanne said. "I think I'd better get over there pretty quickly or she'll have a yard sale with Kathy's personal possessions. Not that Kathy probably had much to leave behind."

"It's all so unbelievable," Carrie said. "Look, I can help you, you know. All I have to do with my time is fight with lawyers and my idiotic ex-stepchildren."

"Oh, them. Dear Mother. Any news?" Suzanne said.

"The little darlings had the judge freeze my bank accounts," Carrie replied.

"Why would they do that?" I said.

"Because they think they're entitled to every dime I have," Carrie said.

"Why do they think that?" I asked. I knew Carrie's husband had passed away recently but I didn't know all of the details, only that his children were giving her a hard time.

"Tell her, Carrie," Suzanne said.

Just then the waitress returned with our tea. A waiter followed her and put everything we had ordered in front of us. My mouth began to salivate. It was a Carb Fest.

Carrie broke off a piece of the waffle, popped the yolk of her fried egg, dipped the waffle into it, and took a bite.

I waited. Suzanne nibbled on her sausage patty.

"It's a rough story," Carrie said. "Why did I order all this food? Y'all go ahead and start. Cold pancakes aren't as good as hot ones."

I poured a liberal stream of maple syrup on and around my pancakes and took the biggest bite I could manage, hopefully without looking like I was going for some kind of competitive eating title.

"I lived with John for over seven years before we finally got married. He dropped dead on the altar."

I swallowed funny, nearly choked, and started coughing. With a totally straight face, Suzanne slid my glass of water to me, which I sipped while I tried to catch my breath.

"I told you it was a rough story. Heart attack," Carrie said. "You okay?"

"Fine," I said, recovering. "On the altar?"

"Yes. Can you imagine what that was like? All the kids were whipping out their smartphones and taking pictures? Oh God! But we had already signed our marriage license, so we were technically married."

"So then why is there a problem?"

"Because his kids are so greedy. I'm fighting for common-law rights. I mean, seven years is a long time. Right? His daughter is saying the marriage is invalid because it was unconsummated. She should only know the things I did to her daddy."

"Good grief!" I managed to say. I mean, what was the right response to that?

"Unfortunately, North Carolina doesn't recognize common-law marriage," Suzanne said, adding, "I could eat pancakes every day for the rest of my life."

"Me too. And weigh nine hundred pounds," Carrie said. "Anyway, there's an awful lot of money at stake and my lawyer says he's happy to litigate."

"I hate lawyers," Suzanne said. "They're always happy to litigate and send you the bill."

"Amen," I volunteered, even though my single experience with a personal lawyer was twenty-five years ago when my darling husband, Mark Barnebey, left me right after our daughter Marianne was born. Mark was in Montana now, living off the grid, building bunkers, preparing for doomsday. "Well, I can help you clear out Kathy's apartment too. If you'd like. We have a steady supply of boxes at Palmetto House."

"That would be great," Suzanne said. "You're right. We're going to need a lot of boxes, I'm sure."

"Maybe we should take a ride to Miss Wendy's after we eat and do an inventory, you know? So we can see how big of a job it's going to be?" Carrie said.

"Excellent thinking," Suzanne said, and looked at me. "Want to come?"

"Sure," I said, "why not?"

"I'll call her. I still can't believe she took—"

"Believe it," Carrie said.

Suzanne called Wendy, who said to come whenever, that she was home. Right after we ate, we paid the bill, got in our cars, and drove to Charleston.

Wendy's house was on Wentworth Street downtown, close to East Bay Street, in the historic section of Charleston. It was a classic Charleston single house, built over two hundred years ago of tiny handmade bricks, wide thick planks of wood, and other materials by hands with skills that no longer existed. The shutters with their scores of tiny louvers, the brass door knocker, and the doorknobs appeared to be original to the house because the shutters were so sturdy and the doorknobs were so low. But if they were reproductions someone had done an amazing job of making them authentic to the period. Her flower boxes were filled with bright green asparagus fern that tumbled out over the edges while pretty pink and white begonias poked their heads straight up through the needles and thorns stretching toward the sun for sustenance. What can I say? The witch had a nice house.

We were standing on the sidewalk, waiting for Wendy to answer the door.

"Maybe the doorbell is broken," I said when it seemed an inordinate amount of time had passed.

Suzanne nodded and used the large knocker several times, letting the heavy hammer fall against the mounded bed for all it was worth. It gave off a thunderous sound and I was sure that if there was a living soul inside, the door would open momentarily. It did.

"Sorry," Wendy said. "I was in the back of the house on the second floor and I didn't hear you. Come in!"

She had changed her clothes and was now wearing tan capri

pants, ballet flats, and a big white cotton shirt, à la Audrey Hepburn, Katharine Hepburn, or what's her name from *An American in Paris.* Leslie Caron! That's who. I wondered how many closets of clothes she had. The bracelets had been removed.

We stepped inside the dark foyer and it took a moment for our eyes to adjust.

"Come with me and I'll take you to Kathy's apartment. Would y'all like a cold drink of something? I have iced tea and, well, water, and that's it, I'm afraid. I don't get a lot of company."

Because you'd go through their purses when they're not looking, I thought.

"I'm fine," Suzanne said.

"Me too. But thanks," Carrie said.

"I'm fine too," I said. "We just wanted to get an idea of how much . . ."

She squinted her eyes at me, obviously debating saying something sharp.

"Of course!" she finally spat out. "Why else would you be here?"

What a stinker she was! She led us to Kathy's apartment, which was actually an ancient kitchen house that had been attached to the main house with a narrow hallway at some point in its history. There was a locked door on either end of the hall to allow privacy and I could see through the window that there was an outside entrance too. A few steps made of the same tiny bricks as the house led up to a narrow porch. It was completely charming.

"I'll just let y'all in. How long are y'all going to be? I have things to do."

"Just a few minutes," Suzanne said.

I thought, Wow, her mother must have weaned her too early.

Wendy opened the door and moved aside. We stepped into a

small living room with bare heart-pine floors, and an uneasy spirit permeated the space. It was too still. To the left there was a tiny, neat Pullman kitchen concealed by curtains, pulled back over hooks as though the cook had just stepped away. In the rear of the apartment was a sparsely furnished bedroom and bathroom. I was focused on the wrong things. Instead of trying to figure out how much time we needed to pack up how many boxes, I was riveted on Kathy's personal possessions. Her toothbrush in a cup. Her towels neatly folded over a rod. Her bathrobe hung from a hook on the back of the door. I had to turn away or I was going to lose it.

The spool-post bed was covered with a handmade quilt, probably a family treasure, and comfortable-looking pillows were piled high. Kathy's framed photographs covered tabletops and the mantelpiece. Books—scrapbooks and novels—were stacked on shelves and everywhere under tables and in corners. And snuff bottles. She must've had a hundred of them or more. Some of them were quite beautiful. All her furnishings were evidence of a life lived rather well. In a strange way it felt like Kathy would walk in the room any second, happy to see us all. We'd plop ourselves down and start talking about anything and everything. Except that she wouldn't.

Suzanne and Carrie seemed to be having similar thoughts, but after a few questions, the ever-practical Suzanne summed it all up.

"Well, if the furniture was hers I think we can do this with my van, two men, and three trips to the beach and back. We'll be back tomorrow? Are y'all free?"

Carrie said, "Well, you know I am."

And I said, "I can help after two o'clock."

We had a plan.

CHAPTER 3

Life Goes On

At one thirty, my cell phone rang. As always, I hoped it was Marianne. It was Suzanne.

"Are you still coming over this afternoon?" she said.

"Yep. I was just finishing up here. I was gonna run home and change and then meet y'all downtown? How does that sound?"

"That sounds perfect. And if you have boxes . . ."

"Got 'em! I'll load up my car."

Margaret and Judy had been stockpiling boxes for me. Needless to say, there was continuous headshaking among us over the terrible reality of Kathy's death.

"The poor thing," Judy would say. "I still can't believe it."

To which Margaret would add, "What a shame."

So when I asked them for the boxes they offered to help me carry them out to the car. We were standing in the parking lot then, my car jammed to the roof, and I was thanking them.

"Y'all are the best," I said.

"You're the one who's the best," Margaret said. "This is definitely above and beyond your job description to help her friends, but you know that."

I just shrugged my shoulders and looked up at the sky.

"It got personal," Judy said. "Didn't it?"

"Yeah, it did," I said. "Look, when somebody lives to a hundred and then they die, it's okay to go."

"And this ain't okay," Margaret said.

"You got it. It makes me really mad," I said.

"I agree," Judy said. "If helping them move her things can make you feel better, then go for it."

"I agree," Margaret said. "Hey, sometimes life just stinks."

"Yeah, it does," I said. "But not all the time."

"Thank the Good Lord for that," Judy said. "You working tomorrow?"

"No, not so far," I said. "Y'all call me if you need me, okay?"

I got in my car thinking that I could use the extra hours of work, but at that moment I was concentrating on trying to honor Kathy Harper's life, hoping to become the third wheel who was missing. I hated to admit it, but a part of me was doing this so I could get something out of it for myself. Did anyone ever do things completely altruistically? I thought for a moment and quickly decided yes. People did charitable things all the time. But if you acknowledged that being charitable made you happy, was it altruistic? Did personal satisfaction or a sense of pride negate the good that was done? Certainly seeking recognition for your good works seemed to devalue them on some level. But we were all only human. I'd been taught from the cradle of my parents' arms—such as they were—that we were all sinners, victims of the frailties of existence on this earth. There's no guilt like a parent's guilt. Carol and Alan St. Clair could teach a class at Notre Dame about it.

"Face it, babe," I said to myself out loud, "you're not a living saint."

So, I put my ego where it belonged and I resolved to help Carrie and Suzanne. If friendship evolved from it then so be it. That would be lovely. If it didn't, then at least I had done something to help. That's what I told myself. I used to be that girl who made friends so easily, never worried about a date for prom, and didn't sweat that some sorority would want me as a sister. But after a failed marriage and a colossally failed business to boot I counted my blessings and didn't torture myself wishing for things that would probably never come my way. Though I had to believe that friendship was not too much to want.

And my bankruptcy? Okay, here's the short story on that. Around ten years ago I had this idea for a business model that was just way, way ahead of its time. So I took out a home equity loan for the maximum they would lend me and rented space for a yoga studio and juice bar. I had been teaching yoga off and on for years and I began experimenting with juices because they made me feel amazing. And, it's probably important to share that I was seeing this guy who was vegan. He was a bass player in a wedding band and, well, inappropriate. But over time he encouraged me to stop eating animals, and slowly but surely I felt wonderful physically and crystal clear mentally. In fact, I felt the best I had ever felt in my entire life. It was hard to make an argument against the facts. I became quite the enthusiast for organic vegan food. I'm completely over that now. Aside from a little juicing now and then and a few planks and downward dogs, I had fallen back into a secular lifestyle.

Anyway, I spent the money building the interior of a gorgeous studio. We had locker rooms with showers that gave the experience of standing in a bamboo rain forest and a retro-looking juice bar with tables made of blond wood of Scandinavian design and pale blue chairs. I had newspapers from all over the country delivered every day and every magazine under the sun that related to yoga, fitness, and vegan living. I had charging stations for cell phones and mixes of whales singing, Native American drum recitals, and Peruvian flutes. You could take a class, shower up, have a fabulous juice, read the paper, and then be on your way. I offered every single service I could think of for the classic busy woman who wanted to get healthier. I hosted lectures and book signings. I had a registered nutritionist on call and I even had this sort of avant-garde doctor from the Medical University who would take hair samples from clients, analyze them, and tell the clients what vitamins they needed. And there was a kinesiology expert on call as well to realign your electromagnetic field and an astrologer to discuss your destiny. Basically, I built it, nobody came, and I went down the tubes. When my inappropriate boyfriend left me for a bartender, I went back to eating bacon. I should've opened a nail salon or a micro pub. Seriously. Now there were yoga studios all over the place.

Looking over the side of the Ravenel Bridge at the container ships below, I watched the sun-dappled water sparkle all around. It was very hot but the humidity wasn't too high, making the heat infinitely more bearable. I was still thinking about the fact that Wendy was wearing Kathy's bracelets at the funeral and I wondered if Suzanne or Carrie would say anything to her about it. Between them, Suzanne and Carrie had enough nerve to confront a starving grizzly bear on its hind legs. It was hard to believe that someone who looked as respectable as Wendy—minus the surgical adjustments and enhancements—could do something so downright sleazy.

I found a place to park on the street and walked the short distance hauling as many boxes as I could carry. I decided to use the kitchen house entrance that had been Kathy's instead of ringing Wendy's bell. There was less opportunity to knock something from a table and I didn't want to make small talk with her anyway. I let myself in. Suzanne and Carrie were there wrapping up Kathy's kitchen equipment in newspaper.

"Hey!" Suzanne said. "Boy. Did she ever have a lot of stuff in these cabinets! Let me take those from you!"

"Thanks," I said. "I'll go get some more."

I went back outside to my car and brought back another load of boxes. As I returned through the courtyard, I saw Wendy staring at me through the windows. She had a strange look on her face. I wouldn't say that her mouth was twisted into a snarl exactly, but it was the expression of someone defiant and angry, not a good combo. Her bitterness was showing. I had to ask myself how a woman who lived in such a beautiful home and who obviously enjoyed all the benefits that come with money and privilege could do something so low. I was convinced of her guilt. It bothered me so much then that I wanted to confront her about the bracelets myself. What was the matter with her?

I went back inside Kathy's apartment, where Carrie was struggling with a clear tape dispenser whose tape kept sticking to itself.

"Grrr! I hate these things," she said, shaking a wad of tape away.

"Yeah," I said, "you lose the edge of the tape and you can never find it again." I dropped the boxes to the floor. "Okay, so how can I help?"

Suzanne said, "Her clothes. I went through her closet and there's a ton of clothes in there with the tags still on them, including a pile of brand-new nightgowns. Why don't we take all the stuff that's used and put it in boxes and all the clothes that aren't used in others? You know, separate them?"

"Great idea," I said. "The used clothes, depending on how used, could go to a consignment shop or to Goodwill? Right?"

"Exactly!" Suzanne said.

Carrie asked, "Could you use the nightgowns at Palmetto House? Maybe someone might need them?"

I thought for a moment about all the really old people who were bedridden whose families rarely came to visit them. It would surprise the negligent relatives to find their grandmothers in fresh new gowns and let them guess where they came from.

"Absolutely! We have all these supersweet older ladies who would love a new gown!" I said. "I mean, it's not like their daughters visit too much or ever bring them anything useful."

"Are you kidding me?" Suzanne said, stopping and putting her hands on her hips. "Is that what goes on?"

"You have no idea. Listen, usually family comes on the weekends and they bring cookies or maybe some DVDs or magazines. Sometimes flowers. But not everyone shows up on a regular basis and a lot of them come empty-handed, with no concept of what their mother or grandmother might need. And they don't ask."

"Well, good grief," Suzanne said. "We've got clothes and books and all sorts of things here . . ."

Before Suzanne could finish, Wendy appeared through the door that joined the hallway and her part of the house.

"I thought it might be a good idea for me to put stickies on the few things that belong to me, you know, so there's no confusion."

"Good idea," I said, stepping across the living room but not making eye contact with her.

"We were planning on coming back tomorrow with two men and my van to take everything," Suzanne said.

There was the spool bed, an older slipcovered sofa with crocheted afghans over its back, and some throw pillows strewn about. A small coffee table, a club chair and ottoman, an end table and some lamps. But the prize pieces of furniture were a gorgeous chest-on-chest and a beautiful linen press in the bedroom. I watched as Wendy attached the sticky yellow squares to those exact two pieces and my eyebrows must have shot up to the ceiling. I said nothing.

"That's it," Wendy said.

She shot me a prissy smirk and left, closing the door behind her.

"Did you see that face she made?" I asked.

"I'll bet she knows we're onto her," Carrie said.

"I'll bet she doesn't," Suzanne said. "She's not that smart."

"I'll bet y'all five dollars that furniture isn't hers," I said.

Suzanne's eyes narrowed and she said, "You're on, but tell me what you're thinking."

"I don't know but I just can't understand why anyone would furnish a rental apartment with furniture that's so much nicer than what she has in her own house."

There was the briefest moment of silence while they pondered the question. Suzanne spoke.

"Why indeed?" she said.

"Because it isn't hers at all," Carrie said.

"You're right," Suzanne said, running her hand across the patina of the chest-on-chest. "I'm not a furniture expert but I'll bet you this is worth a pretty penny."

"Before they retired my mother and father were antiques dealers," I said, and pulled my cell phone from my purse. "I'm going to shoot a picture of this and the linen press and send it to them. They'll know if they're worth anything."

I was clicking away and Suzanne and Carrie were stunned.

Carrie was wide-eyed by then and said, "Ladies? We might have a genuine situation on our hands."

"I'll let you know what my parents think as soon as I hear back from them."

That evening I sent those pictures to my mother and she called me right away.

"Where did you find this furniture?" she asked.

"In a friend's apartment. What do you think?"

"Well, they are both English. Walnut. Nineteenth century. I'd say 1860. Maybe earlier. There's a lot of it out there, which brings the value down somewhat, especially these days when everyone wants new. I mean, what's wrong with people? I'd much rather have an old chest-on-chest like this one than some junk made from particleboard and faced with laminate."

"Me too. Do you think they're worth like a couple of thousand dollars or more?"

"Sure. They might be worth tens of thousands, especially if they are polished up and all the handles are secure and original and so on. You have to look at them carefully, the joints and everything. Why? Is she going to try and sell them?"

"I don't think so. She was just curious and so I told her I'd ask you."

I didn't want to tell her the whole story about Wendy and the bracelets and how we thought she was stealing from Kathy's meager estate. Even though I was all but convinced Wendy was a liar and a thief, I knew five minutes of full disclosure with my mother would result in an hour of inquiry. I didn't have the strength.

"Uh-huh, well good luck. The antiques market is deader than Kelsey's cow."

"No one has money anymore."

"Amen to that. Do you hear anything from Marianne?"

"Not a word."

"Well, it's very peculiar not to call your mother. Anything from her father?"

"Zero. I saw pictures of his new bunker on Facebook. He's trying to promote his business."

"Dear Lord, Lisa! What are you doing on Facebook? Aren't you a little long in the tooth for that kind of thing? And isn't it dangerous to put your life out there on the Internet?"

"No, and I don't know what you mean by 'that kind of thing,' but it's actually sort of fun to reconnect with old friends."

"If you say so. Here, you want to talk to your father? *Alan? Alan?* He was here just a minute ago. Where did he . . ."

There was a beep in my ear as the extension phone picked up and next I heard the voice of my father.

"Hi, princess!"

"Your daughter is inviting ax murderers into her life on the Internet."

"Hi, Daddy. No, I'm not."

"That's a good girl," he said. "We both know your mother likes to exaggerate things."

"I do not!"

"So how's life treating you? You coming down this weekend? I'm thinking about grilling a big bass. You can't grill a whole bass for two people, you know. It's too much work and it's a sin to waste food."

Last year, my father bought a small Green Egg grill and suddenly his evil twin "the Chef" was unchained and released into the world. He had become the guru on dry rubs and the various advantages of brining turkeys and all species of fowl. When he wasn't watching football or golf. And on a side note, I loved when he referred to me as a girl, something the rest of humanity did not do.

"I'll have to let you know because I might have to work."

"Well, the sooner you can tell us the better," he said.

"We could invite Copeland and Andree Bertsche, you know," my mother said. "They've had us for dinner three times."

"We could. We could. I like them. Co makes a mean martini."

"Well, let's call them!"

"Okay, you two," I said. "It sounds like you have an alternate plan. I'm going to go back to my laundry now. The washer just beeped."

"I really wish you had a man in your life," my mother said.

"Why?" I said. "Then I'd have more laundry."

There was silence from the other end as my parents wondered for the billionth time how anyone could survive without a partner who was sworn to love you and take care of you until death came creeping along to snatch one of you from the other. We hung up and I thought to myself, It wasn't that I had anything against commitment. I didn't. I just hadn't felt the pressing need or had the opportunity to change my life.

I called Suzanne.

"Hey! You busy?"

"Nope. I just got home from dinner. My grandmother Miss Trudie and I have a date at the Long Island Café every week."

"Love that place."

"Me too. She loves the flounder and it's easy for her to manage getting in and out of there with her cane. She still has her big white Cadillac from 1985. It only has thirty thousand miles on it. We use it to go out on the town, but I drive it. We call it Gertrude's Land Yacht."

We giggled because who wouldn't?

"I'd love a picture of that!"

"Yeah, it's a pretty crazy sight all right."

"How old is she?" I asked, even though it was none of my business, but who still had their grandmother at Suzanne's age?

"Ninety-nine and she still has all her beans. She's a pistol."

"She sure sounds like it. Most people that age have some kind of cognitive issues and usually some mobility issues too. She must be amazing."

"She is. She still has perfect hearing."

"You gotta be kidding me."

"Nope. She can hear a dollar bill drop across the room. Listen, back in the thirties she used to be a wildly popular chanteuse. She played piano and sang torch songs in the finest places in Charleston."

"Really?"

"Yep. We still have some of her newspaper reviews. She was a real character."

"That's unbelievable. So, does she live close to you?"

"I'd say so. I live in her house on the Isle of Palms."

"That's close!" I said, and laughed.

"Well, it's no palace but it's comfortable. She lives upstairs in three rooms, I'm across the hall if she needs me. It works out great. We put an elevator in like ten years ago. Carrie's ensconced in one of the guest rooms downstairs."

"Miss Trudie. Wow. I'd love to meet her sometime."

"Well, are you working Sunday?"

"Not so far."

"Great! Come over! I'm closed on Sunday, so I thought it might be a good time to start sorting through Kathy's stuff. I'll have it all here in a day or two. Hey, did you show the pictures to your folks?"

"Yep, and my mother thinks the chest and the linen press might actually be worth more than a few thousand dollars," I said.

"Wow. I think that Wendy's a lying sack of you know what."

"I couldn't agree more. We will get to the bottom of it somehow."

"I hope so. But even if we do find out that she's absolutely lying, then what?"

"We will figure that out too! Hey, how do you feel about dogs?"

"Love them. Why?"

"I've got one. I know this may seem nervy to ask . . ."

"How big?"

"She's little. Under twenty pounds."

"Does she bite, jump on you, or pee indoors?"

"Never. She'd rather die than embarrass herself."

"Then bring her! Miss Trudie will adore her! Is she pretty calm?"

"Oh, yeah. She's totally mellow." Unless she smells skunk, I thought.

"Then bring her! We'll have fun with her! And hopefully get through some boxes."

She gave me her address and we hung up. Well, I thought, I've been invited to join the Unpack the Boxes Club. And Pickle was welcome. Cool.

After breakfast on Sunday morning, I looked at Pickle, who had eaten one pancake and a strip of bacon. She had that worried look. I knew it wasn't in her best interest to eat pancakes and bacon but she loved them. So, on that rare occasion when I made them, I'd make tiny ones for her. But no butter and syrup. Or for me either, only because there was none in the house. I was waiting for coupons.

"Pickle? Let's brush your hair. We're going out to the beach! You want to go to the beach?"

She began her dance of abandon, a combination of running backward, stopping to run in a quick circle, and then a bark and more moving backward until we reached the spot by the back door where I hung her leashes. Then she sat quietly, waiting with a pounding heart while I attached the retractable one to her collar. Pickle was going to the beach and she was thrilled.

It was hot outside but what else was new? I'd given up looking at the thermometer. All it did was depress me. I turned over the engine of the car, blasting the air-conditioning, and got out again to let Pickle water the grass. She sniffed around and found a spot to leave her visiting card.

"Good girl!"

I would've sworn my dog was smiling when she hopped in the backseat and I looked at her in my rearview mirror. She was in the passenger seat opposite me with her tongue hanging out, panting a little but positioned like royalty in her special doggie seat. She was simply adorable.

We took our time driving slowly in the beach traffic across the causeway. Every weekend hundreds of people came to the islands for a swim and a megadose of vitamin D, and they slowed traffic to the point that travel time was easily doubled or tripled, especially if the drawbridge opened. But it was the kind of delay I didn't mind at all. Usually there were a few sailboats with their sails unfurled, gliding across the water. They were beautiful to watch. To my right and left were fields of sun-soaked spartina, as dense as the pelt of a mink, each blade long and green, drinking up the brackish water in the salt marsh where it grew. Great numbers of snowy egrets peeked in and out of the marsh grass. When they lifted into flight they looked like a band of angels. No, I didn't mind the delay at all.

Eventually I crossed the Ben Sawyer Bridge onto Sullivans Island. The fire department's sign announcing the date of their annual fish fry was to my right. And there was another sign warning about public consumption of alcohol and the fine you'd have to pay if you were caught. The fine was as wacky as the law was ill-conceived. Why one thousand and forty dollars? Why not eleven hundred or a mere one thousand? And truly, when it was over a hundred degrees, there was nothing in all this whole wide world more appealing than a freezing-cold beer. I guessed the Town Fathers felt Sullivans Island's society of residents and guests could no longer rely on their own common sense and decorum and that they must be policed. When I was a younger woman there was no such law and beer drinking never resulted in mayhem. In fact, the overserved usually dozed off and woke up sunburned. The island's dog laws were even worse.

I made a left on Jasper Boulevard behind a long line of cars and we inched along like an army of ants until we reached Breach Inlet and crossed another small bridge onto the Isle of Palms. I looked in amazement at all the expensive cars people were driving. Every third car was German or a superexpensive SUV. Not that I wanted either one but I couldn't help wondering how all these people could afford the luxury. Could they all be that successful?

"Nah," I said out loud, and then to Pickle, "they're probably in debt up to their eyeballs. They ought to know what I know about how your world can change in a flash with just a few wrong decisions. Right?"

Pickle barked in agreement.

"Well, at least we have each other," I said, and smiled.

Suzanne's house was right across the street from the ocean. I pulled up in the driveway, got out, put Pickle on her leash, and gave the place a good look. It was an old clapboard house, a classic island cottage with a deep screened porch and a red tin roof. This was my favorite style of beach house. The front steps were made of white-painted risers and thick boards that had been lacquered black. The simple handrails were forged of black wrought iron and the screen door had the silhouette of a loggerhead turtle incorporated into its design on the bottom, giving the entrance an old-fashioned Low-country signature.

I'd live with my grandmother too if she had a house like this, I thought.

The French doors that ran the length of the porch were all wide open and three ceiling fans were spinning on full speed, creating a breeze. Was it possible there was no air-conditioning? Suzanne must have heard my car door close because she met me at the entrance before I could ring the bell.

"Hey! I'm so glad you're here!" She leaned down and offered her palm to Pickle, who held back for two seconds and then leapt forward and licked it furiously. "Sweet girl!"

"Yeah, that's my dog playing hard to get."

"She's precious! Y'all come on in. Would you like a glass of iced tea?"

"More than anything on earth," I answered, and followed her into the house, through the living room, where there stood an old

Steinway grand piano, and finally to the kitchen, where a television was playing on mute. "Great house! When was it built?"

"Thanks. It's sort of falling down here and there. I think it was built around 1910. The house isn't worth much, but the dirt? The dirt under the house is pretty special."

The screen door slammed again and Carrie sailed in with a box of Krispy Kreme donuts.

"They're still warm!" she said. "Hey, Lisa!"

"Hey," I said. "I'm here to help sort through Kathy's stuff."

"Great! Who's this little lover?"

She put the box on the kitchen table and flipped it open. In there were six opportunities to commit the sin of gluttony.

"Stop bringing donuts! You know I'm trying to diet!" Suzanne said.

"I know. But the light was on. And I could smell them. And I'm weak. And I can still afford six donuts."

There was an infamous red neon light on the sign in front of the donut shop that they turned on when they had donuts fresh from the oven. And they had drive-thru service, a diabolical invention of entrapment.

"This is Pickle, my meaningful other. Pickle say hello. Go on. Say hello!" Pickle yipped and licked Carrie's outstretched hand. "Good girl. Okay. Let's just get it over with and eat them right now."

There was a distinct thumping on the floor from the room above us. Suzanne started to laugh.

"What's that?" I said.

Suzanne said, "That is my Miss Trudie's cane. She can smell sugar." She hurried to the stairway in the hall and called out. "I'll be right there!"

"How funny!" I said.

"Nothing wrong with her sense of smell," Suzanne said. She put two donuts on a small plate and turned to Pickle. "You want to go say hello to my grandmomma? Come on!"

Pickle looked at me for approval.

"Go on! Behave yourself."

And Pickle scampered out of the room and up the stairs with Suzanne.

"So, how's it going?" I said to Carrie.

"You know? Not so great. I've got that problem with John's children?"

"The darlings," I said.

"Well, I found out late Friday afternoon that they won and now I'm broke. The judge was as mean as John's kids."

"Aren't you going to contest the decision? Surely they don't want you to be destitute. I mean, how could this happen?"

"Because the judge is a sanctimonious asshole. He said under North Carolina law, since John died on the altar before the marriage could be deemed legal and be consummated, that we weren't married and his children should get everything. And the fact that John and I lived together all those years was of no interest to him. In fact, he seemed offended by me like I'm some kind of a Jezebel."

"Good grief. Didn't your lawyer object?"

"Of course! He went crazy! But it didn't matter. Judges can do whatever they want."

"Aren't you going to file a countersuit?"

"And get the same judge? And the same result? For what? And who'd take the case? A contingency lawyer? I'm sick of lawyers and courts and judges."

"So, what are you going to do?"

"Well, being that I'm practically a professional spouse, I guess I'll start looking for another husband. I just joined About Time."

Suzanne reentered the room.

"Professional spouse? Ha! That's rich! More like a black widow spider, if you ask me," she said. "She gets them in her web, has her way with them, and then zaps them!"

"Oh, thanks!" Carrie said, and laughed. "Sadly, it's true. I have been unlucky with husbands."

I didn't want to ask how many there had been but I knew because of what Suzanne said that I would be correct to assume that however many there had been, they were all dead. And what was About Time? One of those online dating sites?

"Where's Pickle?" I said, unsure of how to respond.

"Sitting on my grandmomma's lap watching old reruns of *Lassie.* You may never see her again."

"Oh Lord," I said, and laughed. "She loves *Lassie* like no other."

We started opening boxes and, once again, decided to categorize the contents by what the nursing home could use, what could go to Goodwill, and what should get ditched.

"Most of the clothes should go to Goodwill," I said.

"Probably," Suzanne agreed.

"Yeah, now that I'm looking at her clothes again," I said. "It's all pretty beaten up."

Suzanne was going through a box of Kathy's papers and came upon a pile of bank statements held together with rubber bands. She opened one and within a minute or two I could see the surprise on her face.

"Oh my!" she said.

"What?" Carrie said.

"She didn't even have five hundred dollars to her name!" Suzanne said.

"Really?" Carrie said. "That's worse than my situation!"

"Maybe she had other accounts?" I said, thinking how does a woman get along in the world with only five hundred dollars to her name? Not that I had much more, that was for sure.

"I'm digging," Suzanne said. A few minutes later she added, "Well, if there are other accounts they're not in this box. All I've got here are six years of statements from Wells Fargo. Thank goodness she had good medical insurance."

"Who can afford insurance these days?" Carrie said. "It's so expensive."

"You didn't sign up for Obamacare?" Suzanne said.

"Are you serious? Have you been to that crazy website? Forget that! Wait! Oh, gosh! I can't believe I forgot to tell y'all!"

"What?" Suzanne and I said together.

"Guess who was standing on Savannah Highway with a big old sign protesting Krispy Kreme using palm oil that comes from cutting down rain forests?"

Suzanne looked at me and arched an eyebrow as if to say, *How should I know?* I giggled because I didn't know anyone who protested anything. Ever.

"Boy, I have some dull life," I said. "I don't know *anybody* who would do that."

"Me either," Suzanne said.

"Yes, y'all do! It was Paul! That guy Kathy used to date! The organist from the church!"

"Holy Mother!" Suzanne said.

"Did you talk to him?" I asked.

"Come on, you know me. Do you think I could pass that up? I went over to him and said, So, Paul? What's going on? He gets all worked up and says in this very deep man voice, Well, I have a problem with child labor, destroying orangutan habitats, and driving Sumatran tigers to extinction. I was like, You've got to be joking! Sumatran tigers? Oh Lord! But I said, Oh! Of course! Me too!"

Carrie started laughing so hard and Suzanne laughed politely, but something about the way Carrie had been speaking didn't sit right with me.

"What in the world are you talking about?" I asked nicely even though I was irked.

"Remember I told you that guy was a tree hugger?" Suzanne said. "I mean, not that there's anything the matter with saving the planet."

"It's just that he's so adamant. I don't know. It's just a little undignified for a man his age to be out there raising hell at a Krispy Kreme. Aren't college students supposed to do that?" Carrie said. "It's weird."

"Maybe," I said, "but at least he's got some convictions. Every man I've dated in the last ten years, and I mean both of them? Their only convictions are that they don't want a committed relationship, and don't worry, you're not going to emasculate them by paying half the bill. Then they want to screw."

"Then give them half a screw," Carrie said, and her face turned scarlet.

Then we laughed, really laughed. It felt good.

CHAPTER 4

In the Dark

The late-afternoon horizon was dissolving into the jewel-toned colors of sunset. The temperature was finally dropping too, but the air was still warm and nearly wet. It would be as sultry an evening as any I'd ever known. We were gathered on Suzanne's porch sipping wine, picking at a wedge of Gruyère, nibbling apple slices and thin slices of a smoked sausage, and talking. Pickle was curled up at my feet. I was looking forward to meeting Miss Trudie. Suzanne and Carrie assured me she always appeared around the cocktail hour. And besides the much anticipated arrival of Miss Trudie, it was the most exciting hour of the day. The colors of the sky all around the horizon went completely berserk, sending out flashes of rose and purple and shades I could not name because there were no words for them. Even for the most hardened old salt, sunset was too spectacular to ignore.

"Miss Trudie likes to have a small glass of sherry with me," Suzanne said. "And then she goes in the kitchen and makes herself a martini in an iced-tea glass and she thinks I don't know. She eats the olives on the side. By the handful."

"Whenever you see her eating olives," Carrie said, "you can be about one hundred percent positive that there's gin in her glass."

"What happens when the gin runs low?" I asked. "And the vermouth and olives?"

"Well, I go to the liquor store, of course!" Suzanne said. "We just don't discuss it."

"No! Of course not!" I said.

Weren't they merely doing their part to live up to our hard-earned reputation as eccentric southerners?

And of course, the more wine we consumed, the more we revealed about ourselves. Going through Kathryn's clothes, papers, and books had once again been profoundly unnerving. We were all just wrung out.

"You know what was really strange?" Carrie said.

"What?" Suzanne said.

"Seeing what she read," Carrie said. "I'd bet you a tooth that I've read all the same fiction authors that she did. Ann Patchett, Anne Tyler, Anne Rivers Siddons, Anna Quindlen—all the Anns. But we never talked about books. Not even once."

"Well, she played her cards close," Suzanne said. "But she read lots of people. She always had a book with her."

"Didn't you think her clothes were like ultratailored? Almost to the point of being utilitarian?" I said. "So much khaki and so many little cardigans."

"Yes, she was pretty conservative," Carrie said. "Did you have a chance to get a good look at her china? Her dishes were ancient.

Probably from some relative. Her teacups were actually thin around the lip. I mean they were worn down!"

Suzanne said, "That's because she believed that drinking green tea would help push her cancer into remission."

"The poor thing. I read somewhere that you'd have to drink five hundred cups a day for green tea to make a difference," I said. "But what is *truly* interesting is that the Japanese get a lot less cancer."

"That's weird. I wonder why?" Carrie said.

"The only difference I could ever find in our diet and theirs was that they eat shiitake mushrooms like mad, a lot more fish, and way less gluten."

"And they drink green tea all the time," Suzanne added.

"Listen," I said, "we're all gonna go someday from something."

"True enough," Carrie said. "Nobody gets out of here alive. At least no one that I know of."

We smiled at that. Carrie was amusing even when she didn't know she was.

"Well, I'm not going to be happy until I can figure out why Wendy was wearing the bracelets you gave Kathy and what is up with her furniture."

And I liked Suzanne because she was so pragmatic.

"I say that the answer is somewhere in Kathy's boxes," I said.

"I sure hope you're right," Carrie said. "I really don't like that woman."

"She'd be hard to like," Suzanne said.

We rocked back and forth for a few moments, sort of mesmerized by the day's end.

"This is such an amazing place," I said. "How long have you been living here, Suzanne?"

"Oh, I don't know. Maybe fifteen years?"

"Really? Wow!" In my mind all I could do was quickly calculate and then wonder why Suzanne, who would've been about thirty-six at the time, would want to come and live with her grandmother, who would've been right at eighty-five. So I asked the question in the most diplomatic way I could. "Have you always lived in Charleston?"

Suzanne and Carrie exchanged looks.

Carrie said, "Oh, for heaven's sake, Suzanne. Tell her! It's not like you're protecting a matter of national security!"

Suzanne took a deep breath and refilled our glasses.

"Okay," she said, "did you ever make a bad judgment and totally screw up your life? And no matter what everyone told you, you just kept making one bad call after another?"

"You mean, like when I married Mark, who left me with an infant to go live in the deep woods in the Northwest to become a doomsday prepper and live in an underground bunker?"

Suzanne looked at Carrie and they burst out laughing. I joined in because what else could I do? It was just so ridiculous.

"That's a good one!" Carrie said.

"Yeah," Suzanne agreed. "*That* kind of bad call."

"And he never sent any child support except for twenty dollars and a lottery ticket at Christmas?" I said.

"Oh God," Suzanne said. "That's terrible."

"Awful!" Carrie said.

"And your own mother never fails to remind you that she told you so and that you're still an idiot?" I tossed a crouton into the salad just to emphasize how incredibly unlucky and naive I had been, and that in addition to the price I'd paid, I was, now and forever, the family dartboard.

Suzanne couldn't wipe the grin from her face. Her right hand was covering her mouth, and I could tell that the laughter she was holding back was in the tsunami range. She held her left hand in the air like a woman about to testify at a revival, took several gulps from the wineglass in her other hand, clunked it down on the table, and then she stood.

"Okay," she said, then whispered, "Before Miss Trudie shows up for her one ounce of sherry and her half pint of gin, I'll give you the short version."

"We're ready," Carrie said, and winked at me.

"So, after I got my MBA from Columbia—"

"You mean Carolina?" I asked.

"No, I mean Columbia University in New York," Suzanne stated.

What was I thinking? Of course she went to Columbia University in New York. She probably had an IQ of two hundred and fifty. I completed my nursing and nutrition courses almost right in my backyard and never went anywhere. And almost all of the people I grew up with went to a college in South Carolina. I wondered at what age I would stop being insecure about not graduating from Harvard, which I would never have had the courage to attend even if it was free and they were begging me to come. Which they weren't. Begging, that is, or offering me a free ride.

"Oh!" I said. "I thought so but I wasn't sure."

It was the tiniest of fibs.

"Anyway, I went to work for FTD in Chicago."

"You mean the flower delivery company?"

"Yep, that very one. Even then I was in love with flowers. I don't know why I thought Chicago winters would be fun, but I did."

"Because if you're from here you know what it's like to live and die in hell," Carrie said. "Freezing to death is an attractive alternative."

"Oh Lord!" I said, and giggled.

"Anyway, I worked like a beast, climbed the ladder very quickly, and caught the attention of all the managers and officers."

"And *one* in particular!" Carrie said.

Suzanne squinted at Carrie and put her hands on her hips. "Do you want to tell this story or am I telling this story?"

"Sorry," Carrie said, and made sort of an apologetic face.

"Naturally, he was married but he said he was going to leave his wife. It was textbook classic. I believed him. I was such a fool for that man it was pitiful. This went on for nearly ten years. He would leave her, she'd threaten suicide, he'd go back to her. It got to the point that it was just stupid. I was so worn out from his lies and the disappointing truth of it all that I quit my job, came home to Charleston, and had a little meltdown."

"That is so terrible!" I said.

"And opened my business. Well, it was especially terrible because by the time I untangled myself from him and got over it, I was almost too old to hope to safely bring babies into the world."

"He was a world-class shit," Carrie said. "That's what he was."

"Boy, I'll say!" I said.

"Look, there are worse ways my life could've played out than this," Suzanne said. "He didn't hold a gun to my head, you know. I have a pretty sweet business. I have the pleasure of my grandmother's company and I get the benefit of her wisdom every day. I'm healthy. I live in a magical place. I'm solvent and hell will freeze before I let another man in my bed. Maybe."

"That's right, sugar. Keep your options open!" Carrie said.

"With any luck," I said, with a smile as big as I could manage, "someday you might inherit this magical place!"

I never would've guessed that someone as brilliant as Suzanne would get caught in one of those messy affairs. Not in a million years.

"Are you kidding? I have two sisters, Alicia and Clio, both of them very wealthy with long marriages and tons of kids who are just waiting for Miss Trudie to go to that big cocktail party in the sky so they can get their share."

"I have a brother like that," I said. "Alan Jr., also known as Bubba, and his very annoying wife, Janet, have something to say about every dime my parents spend. You know, it affects their inheritance if my father buys a tire for his car or if my mother buys a new sofa."

"Don't you just love families?" Carrie asked.

And then we heard what had to be Miss Trudie's approach from a distance. Shuffle, *thunk*. Shuffle, *thunk*. The sound grew louder as she neared us. Suddenly the screen door swung open, hit the wall with a thwack, and there stood Miss Trudie, relying heavily on her tripod cane to propel her forward. Her thin white hair was swept back into a braid that began at the nape of her neck and extended down almost to her waist. She wore a gauze, embroidered Mexican wedding dress and slip-on canvas shoes with a Mary Jane strap. Her arms were bony and marked with the bruises and ravages of time but she had decorated herself with Native American bracelets and necklaces of beautiful turquoise and hammered silver.

"Not that I was listening, but families are the bedrock upon which this country was built. If it were not for women, this whole darn society of ours would have fallen apart ages ago!" She turned to me, ignored me, then turned to Pickle and grinned. "Darling baby!"

Pickle, of course, hopped up, scampered to her side, and sat obediently.

"Lisa? Meet my grandmother, Miss Trudie. Let me help you to your chair."

"How am I to sit in my chair if someone else has parked themselves in it?"

She glared at me but I knew she was teasing. Nonetheless, I got up promptly. She shuffled over and eased herself down into it with a rather dramatic flourish, exclaiming "Oomph!" as she sat.

"It is nice to meet you, Lisa. It is even nicer to meet your Pickle!" She laughed.

"Thanks! It's great to meet you too! And, I love your turquoise," I said. "Is it Zuni?"

"How should I know? I have had these baubles since before Woodstock!"

"Oh! Did you go to Woodstock?" I asked without doing the mental math.

"Do I look like a hippie to you?"

"No, ma'am!" I said, but thought, Yes, ma'am, you sure as hell do.

"Maybe I could have been a mother to a hippie, but my Gertie was a stick in the mud, God rest her soul."

Suzanne had yet to reveal what happened to her mother, but since Miss Trudie spoke of her in the past tense and prayed her soul to rest well, it was safe to assume she was among the dearly departed with all of Carrie's husbands.

"Oh!" I said, and sat in a Kennedy rocker across from them.

"Yes, sirree, Bob. It's still a mystery to me how she ever got a husband and where those three girls of hers came from. She never even went on a date, as far as I knew."

"Oh, Miss Trudie," Suzanne said. "You know that's not the truth. Momma dated all kinds of boys. She was a homecoming queen, for heaven's sake."

"She was? Now, you would think I would remember something like that," Miss Trudie said, and then she smiled at me. She looked back to Suzanne. "Well, if I am confused about the facts, it is probably because *somebody* has not given me my glass of sherry!"

"Oh, Miss Trudie! So sorry!" Suzanne said, and got up. She kissed her grandmother on the cheek before disappearing back inside the house.

"I have to keep her on her toes," Miss Trudie said to Carrie and me. "Otherwise our whole routine gets sloppy and goes out the window! Now tell me about yourself, Lisa. Who are your people?"

"Well, my parents are retired and living in Hilton Head. They're Carol and Alan St. Clair."

"St. Clair. St. Clair? Hmm. Did they own an antiques business on lower King Street?"

"They surely did. They finally sold it when those chain stores came to town. Big chains added to what you can buy on the Internet put a serious cramp in their sales."

"Well, darlin', the whole world is heading straight to hell in a handbasket, if you ask me," Miss Trudie declared. "And, how do they like living in Hilton Head?"

"They adore it," I said.

"Well, I'll be. I cannot stand the place. Every building looks the same. No landmarks. I'd get lost going to the grocery store. Anyway, you are awfully lucky to have parents considering how old you are. If my darling Suzanne's parents did not drive off a cliff in Italy they would be gone by now anyway. Or maybe not. But they would be almost my age!"

"Goodness!" I said because it was clear she was waiting for a response.

Then she started to fidget. "I am completely famished. I had tomatoes for lunch, so I think I am going to make myself a cream-cheese-and-olive sandwich."

Olive. The key word had been spoken.

Suzanne, who returned and handed Miss Trudie her glass, arched an eyebrow and smirked. Carrie nodded.

"My favorite," I said, adding, "or cream cheese and pineapple."

"Yum," Carrie said.

"Do we even own any olives?" Miss Trudie asked, and tossed back her shot of sherry like a frat boy swigging from a bottle of tequila.

"I just opened a new jar," Suzanne said. "It's on the second shelf in the refrigerator. Do you want a hand?"

"I think I can still manage a sandwich. I am not dead yet."

Miss Trudie looked from face to face to see if we were horrified, amused, or in agreement. Carrie gave her a smile, Suzanne shook her head, and I thought . . . well, I understood that kind of humor too well.

"You sound like a lot of our patients," I said, smiling.

"What? Are you a doctor?"

"No, I'm a nurse and I work at Palmetto House."

"Humph. I have heard that place is more fun than a barrel of monkeys but I like being in my own home. Even if the service is spotty."

"Miss Trudie!" Suzanne said in mock horror.

"Well," I said, "the current wisdom is that you're better off in your own house for a whole lot of reasons. As long as it's safe and you don't have any extraordinary medical needs."

"Please. Besides, I am not quite old enough for that joint. I still have all my own teeth," Miss Trudie said.

"Well, who else's would you have?" Carrie said, and then when she realized we were looking at her like she was cockeyed, she added, "Oh."

"So, well then, I will just excuse myself and my teeth and say good night. I just wanted to check on the young people and make sure y'all were behaving."

I loved Miss Trudie and I wanted a Miss Trudie of my own.

"I'll come say good night before I turn in," Suzanne said.

We watched her slowly rise, shuffle across the porch, and disappear inside the house. We listened to the rhythm of her footfalls as they faded. Shuffle, *thunk,* shuffle, *thunk.*

"She's amazing!" I said.

"*She* is the cat's mother," Miss Trudie called back to us, in a voice laced with insult.

We burst out laughing.

"Well, the cat's mother is some character," I said loudly enough for her to hear.

"She's really wonderful," Suzanne said. "Frankly, I don't know where I'd be without her."

"I need a Miss Trudie in my life. You know what's really terrible?" I said. Suzanne and Carrie turned to me, waiting for me to impart some new story. "I've made two decisions that have almost wrecked my life. I never thought I could get this close to disaster. I was the careful one, you know?"

They knew all about my yoga studio and remembered how it never quite took off.

Suzanne said, "Me too. Pick the wrong man and whammo! I've got no children, no husband to depend on. Really! And I was the whiz kid in the family. All my sisters did was sleep with the right guys. I didn't. As soon as Miss Trudie closes her eyes for the last time, I'm going to be homeless."

"Oh, Suzanne. Don't say that. Your sisters wouldn't throw you out," I said.

"You don't know her sisters," Carrie said. "They're some tough customers when it comes to money."

"Carrie's right. Both of their husbands are Wall Street types. One works for a junk bond firm and the other one is a day trader. They'll say, look, what's ours is ours and what's yours is yours and all we want is what's ours. Period. So I have my business, but even that was started with money from Miss Trudie. I'm going to have to repay her estate."

"Surely your business earns enough to live on," I said, knowing even in my fermented fog that the answer wasn't one bit of my business, but it was almost dark and we had just pulled a second cork. "My God! You're the best floral designer in town!"

"Thanks. Maybe it earns enough to live on," Suzanne said. "But not enough to live here. I mean, one of the reasons I'm so busy is that my rates are a lot cheaper than anyone else. So when I close my books each year there's not much left. And beach house properties are worth crazy money even if the house has seen better days."

"Look, after three husbands, you'd think I'd be rolling in it. I didn't even do that well," Carrie said.

"Carrie? Marriage is supposed to be more than a business transaction," Suzanne said.

"I *know* that! Well, theoretically. Seven years I gave that man!

Seven years! What did I walk away with besides the trauma of burying another man? I've got this ring, my diamond studs, a four-year-old Mercedes that doesn't even have Sirius or an updated satellite GPS and maybe fifty thousand in cash that I had stuffed in shoe boxes. That's it. And I've been down the aisle three times! You want to know why I'm on About Time all the time? I need Mr. Fourth *tout suite*!"

Her assets sounded pretty good to me. Fifty thousand in cash was a fortune in my book. I could live on that for a long time.

"How'd you get that much money into the shoe boxes?" I asked.

"Well, every time John and I did the wild thing, I'd take two twenties out of his wallet and stash them away."

I wasn't an accountant but a rough calculation in my head meant they had sex almost every other day. That was impressive.

"Which is way more sex than I'm interested in! And, Carrie? I think I'd keep that detail about being widowed three times to myself," Suzanne said. "Not to mention they were all named John."

What? I thought.

"You think?" Carrie said. "I'm just saying I need another husband. Preferably one without greedy children."

"Maybe we all do!" I said. "It sure would be wonderful not to worry about money for once in my life. I'm going to be working until I'm older than everyone at Palmetto House or until I drop dead. Whichever comes first. Remember when everyone was expected to retire at sixty-five?"

"Who can afford to retire? Listen. I can't even afford to change the oil in my Benz!" Carrie said.

"Now, that is a first-world problem!" Suzanne said, and shook her head. "I'm going to be working until I do the flowers for my own funeral!"

"Unless something gets us first like poor Kathy," I said.

We were quiet then for a moment. Was it worse to moan about no end of work in sight for us or worse to face an abbreviated life? Were we as ungrateful or hopeless as we sounded? No, we were just being honest.

"I'd rather work for another thirty years than die from cancer like Kathy did," Suzanne said. "She worked hard all her life and still never saw the northern lights."

"But she had really remarkable friends," I said.

"I hate cancer," Carrie said. "And I loved that girl like a sister."

"Me too. Lisa? Do you think processed food causes it? Cancer, I mean."

"Well, the nitrates in this sausage I'm devouring don't help."

"I know but I love it," Carrie said. "So how much of illness is caused by what we eat?"

"I wish I knew the answer to that. I mean, there's evidence to support the impact of diet. But the current thought is that we are what we eat. Not to mention environmental considerations like too much sun or exposure to asbestos and so forth. I mean, the only way to avoid cancer is great genes and raising your own food."

"That's probably true," Suzanne said. "If I were going to grow things, I'd grow flowers for my business. As it is, I have enough to do just trying to keep up with my lavender and my rosemary."

"I'd grow weed," Carrie said, and we stared at her, slack-jawed in surprise. "Why not? There's big money in pot. I used to smoke pot with my second husband—no, wait—maybe it was my first, and let me tell you sex was never better!"

I wasn't getting too deep into this topic, no matter what.

"I've heard that," Suzanne said.

"What?" I said.

"The part about sex and smoking weed and how, you know, it's supposed to be amazing," Suzanne said. "The sex, that is."

"Oh, yeah, sex. I remember sex. It's true," I said. "I mean, I'm not an expert on this stuff, that's for sure. But, well, years ago I used to see this guy that was well, really inappropriate . . ."

"What does that mean? Inappropriate?" Suzanne asked.

"He was younger."

"How many years?" Carrie said.

"More like decades," I said.

"Whoa!" Carrie said.

"Don't be so judgmental!" Suzanne said. "Your last husband was decades older than you!"

"That's different," Carrie said.

"Yeah, it actually is. I mean, I'm pretty sure sex with an older man must've been way different than spending the night with Surfer Boy!" I said.

Okay, yes, I had smoked the tiniest bit of pot in my past and as a nurse it wasn't something I was particularly proud of either. But I hadn't touched it in years and never would again.

"Lisa! You bad, bad girl!" Suzanne exclaimed, laughing.

"I told you he was inappropriate!" I said. "I was younger and stupid."

"Well, darlin'?" Carrie said. "Here's to inappropriate!"

"I'll drink to that," I said, and thought, Oh, boy, I sense a slippery slope in my immediate future if I continue to run around with these two.

"Kathryn loved pot brownies," Carrie said.

"What?" I said. I was surprised.

"I know. I had a problem with it at first too. But," Suzanne said, "she was terminal and she hurt all over. What's the harm there?"

"Honey," I said, "don't get me started. I'll tell y'all a story another time. Why we don't have medical marijuana for cancer patients is beyond me. But for now? I'm like Switzerland on this one. No judgments."

CHAPTER 5

Palmetto House

I went to work on Monday with boxes of Kathy's property and dropped two of them on the back counter of the nurses' station.

"What's all this?" Judy asked.

"Oh, DVDs, books, nightgowns. Kathryn Harper's contribution to our residents."

"Well, that's awfully nice," Judy said. "Is there more to bring in?"

"Just a couple of boxes," I said, heading back out.

"Do you need a hand?" Margaret said.

"No, I've got it," I said. "But thanks."

It occurred to me then, as it did from time to time, that helping other people was one of the things that made the world tolerable. Judy and Margaret were always ready to pitch in. I was too. It was in our nature and it's probably what led us to nursing in the first place. The reward of nursing was that it was satisfying to provide a little comfort or just to let a lonely patient know that someone actually cared about their well-being. The donation from Kathy's estate would bring hours of enjoyment to a lot of people.

I brought the rest of the boxes in, and when I got to the desk Judy and Margaret were already sorting through the books.

"I've been dying to read this," Margaret said, holding a book close to her chest.

"You're a pervert," Judy said.

"Yeah, that's me all right," Margaret said. "That's what everybody says."

"Oh, right. What is it?" I asked. Margaret showed me the cover and I almost fainted. "*Fifty Sh*—! No way! How did I not see that?"

"You tell me," Margaret said. "But I'm taking this home."

"And don't bring it back!" I said. "Good grief! Kathy Harper read erotica? Our beloved residents don't need any encouragement in that department."

"Boy, you can say that again!" Judy said.

Margaret and Judy looked at each other and cracked up laughing.

"Okay, y'all. What did I miss?" Something had obviously occurred over the weekend and I was about to hear what it was. "Spill it!"

"All right, so old Mrs. Richards in 317? She's had the hots for Mr. Morrison in 215 ever since Mrs. Morrison was part of a Celestial Recall?"

Celestial Recall was one of many terms we used for those who went to the light, dropped their body, or just flat-out flatlined.

"I'm aware," I said.

Mrs. Morrison's passing had been an uneventful surprise. She simply didn't wake up in the morning among the living. And Mr. Morrison's bereavement period had been remarkably brief. He had wasted no time in calling Ben Silver's, a lovely men's boutique in downtown Charleston, and ordering himself a new kelly-green sport coat and a blue seersucker suit. On Saturday nights, he wore one of these with white buckskins and a pink carnation in his lapel, that carnation being one that he removed from someone's floral arrangement at their bedside when they weren't looking. We called him Marty Robbins for some singer from the fifties who recorded a song about sport coats and boutonnieres. Anyway, among the octogenarians, he was The Dude.

"You're not gonna believe . . ." Judy said, with tears of laughter rolling down her cheeks.

"We caught them in the shower together," Margaret sputtered between laughs. "One of them accidentally pulled the emergency cord."

"Tell her what he said, Margaret! Lisa, you're gonna die when you hear this! Oh God! I haven't laughed this hard all year!" Judy leaned over and slapped her leg.

And Margaret, in that deadpan style of hers, said, "He said, 'Oh! Excuse me, I was just looking for my little rubber duck.' "

"Rubber duck?" I said, and opened my eyes wide in disbelief.

"Yes. On my mother's grave. His little rubber duck."

"Oh God! That's crazy! What did Mrs. Richards say?"

"She said"—Margaret paused to cross her heart with her finger—" 'Michael? I think it's time for you to go home! Here's your duck.' And I will not tell you where it was concealed but it wasn't where you think."

"Oh, my word! This place is getting wilder all the time," I said, thinking no matter where the duck was I really didn't want to know. "Does Dr. Black know about this?"

"Of course. The duck has been confiscated, sterilized, and is sitting on Dr. Black's bookshelf with his other trophies," Margaret said.

"Good grief. So did we lose anyone this weekend?"

"No, other than a rousing game of Hide the Duck, it was pretty quiet," Margaret said. "Mr. Child appears to be slipping away. His family was here this weekend pretty much around the clock."

"He's such a sweet man," I said.

"Yeah, he sure is." Margaret agreed.

"His wife, Lee, has been by his bedside for weeks. She says she just knows if she leaves the room he's gonna leave the world," Judy said.

"She might not be wrong," I said. "How many times have we seen that happen?"

"Too many to count," Margaret said.

"Personally?" Judy said. "I like the ones that sprinkle their comatose relatives with holy water and read the death psalm."

"That is so medieval," I said.

"Oh, hell yeah," Margaret said. "Let's pray Daddy into the grave! Good idea!"

"Remember that woman who said she saw her sister's soul fly up through the ceiling?" Judy said. "What was her name?"

"I can't remember," I said. "But hey, it's bad enough to have to go through someone else's illness and death one day at a time. I think people tell themselves what they need to hear. You know?"

"Yes, ma'am, I surely do," Margaret said.

"Hide the Duck?" I said.

"Can you imagine the look on my face?" Margaret said.

"I'll bet you didn't even raise an eyebrow," Judy said.

"Yeah, Margaret, you're a pretty cool cucumber," I said, and laughed.

"It was some sight, 'eah?" Margaret said, and shook her head. "You might want to check on a new resident if you have the time. Mrs. Brooks in The Docks. She's not too happy. Her husband has big-time Alzheimer's and a broken hip, so he's in the SCU and she took an apartment to be near him."

"Oh Lord," I said.

"She's not adapting well."

"Well, let me see what I can do," I said.

"Her family didn't think she should be driving back and forth from her house west of the Ashley all the way over here at eighty-six years old. So they took her keys, found this apartment, and convinced her to move in."

"And Mrs. Brooks didn't have a whole lot to say about it?" I asked.

"You got it. She probably feels like she got robbed of her life."

"I'm sure. I'll look in on her," I said.

Margaret gave me Mrs. Brooks's apartment number. Her first name was Marilyn. If she was resentful, I didn't blame her. But the greater truth was—and I knew this before I even met her—that she was far and away better off with us than alone at home.

I took all the DVDs to the media room and put them away. Next, I took the books to the reading room and put them on the shelves. Then I started doing rounds, delivering meds. When I came back to the nurses' station, my cell rang and I pulled it out of my pocket to check the caller ID. It was Suzanne.

"You busy?" she asked.

"Nope. I was just going to get some lunch."

"I won't keep you but a moment. Carrie and I were talking and we decided if we're going to keep eating donuts and drinking wine we've got to exercise. We just have to. My behind is growing at the speed of light. Carrie's on the prowl again and wants to drop some weight. The gym's too expensive. So we're going to walk the beach every morning except when it rains. Would you like to join us?"

"Why not? Sure! Thanks!"

"Bring Pickle too. How's seven tomorrow?"

"See you then!"

Pickle was going to love this. We liked to get up with the birds anyway.

Margaret said, "So, you made a new friend?"

I said, "Yeah, it looks like it. Suzanne and Carrie wanted to know if I wanted to get some exercise with them."

"Good for you! Those girls were amazing to Kathryn," Judy said.

"You can't place too high a value on friends like that," Margaret said.

"Absolutely," I said. "I think I'll grab a couple of turkey sandwiches from the kitchen and pay Marilyn Brooks a visit."

"Good luck," Margaret said.

I left the main building through the doors in the dining room that overlooked the swimming pool. There was a walking path that led to the group of apartments we called The Docks. They were surrounded by man-made lagoons that were visited by egrets and the occasional osprey. It was a very picturesque setting with benches along the banks. The fencing across the front lawns was fashioned of thick rope threaded through large holes in low columns of sun-bleached wood, giving The Docks a bit of nautical detail. I thought it would be peaceful to sit on one of those benches and read a book. Maybe someday I would. In January. Not in the dead of summer.

I found Marilyn Brooks's apartment and knocked on her door.

"Mrs. Brooks?" I called out. "It's Lisa St. Clair. One of the nurses? I've brought lunch?"

The door opened and there stood a tiny lady with thick white hair cut into a stylish bob. She was wearing a freshly starched white shirt and purple cropped pants. Large purple reading glasses hung from a matching chain around her neck. Her iPad, which was tucked under her arm, had a hot-pink Kate Spade leather cover. This lady had style.

"Hello. Can I help you?" She gave me a thorough appraisal and decided I probably wasn't there to do her any harm. She opened the door wider. "Come in. Please."

I stepped into her living room. It was furnished in authentic mid-century antiques, including a large Andy Warhol lithograph of the iconic Marilyn Monroe, a turquoise sectional sofa, and a tangerine velvet pouf. Her taste was the polar opposite of my parents', and frankly, I fell in love with her living room at first glance.

"Thank you! Wow! This is fabulous! It's so optimistic!"

"I've always liked strong colors," she said. "One should never be afraid to be bold."

"I see that! And I agree. Anyway, I heard from my nurse buddies that you'd just moved in, so I thought I'd just take a few minutes to welcome you."

"Well, that's awfully nice. May I offer you some iced tea?"

"Sure. Thank you. I brought sandwiches to share."

"What kind?"

What kind? Was she allergic or vegan?

"Turkey. Turkey on white bread with a little mayonnaise and lettuce. And cranberry sauce."

"Cranberries? Who puts cranberries on sandwiches?"

"It's actually pretty good. Are you allergic to something?"

"No, I was just being an old fussbudget. Come sit. I'll get us some plates and some tea."

"I'll help you."

"No. Please. Just have a seat. I can still pour a glass of tea. You know, my family thinks I'm an invalid or too decrepit to do anything."

"Children are deathly afraid of seeing their parents get older," I said.

She stopped and turned around to face me.

"Do you know what?" she said. "That's the first really honest thing anyone has said to me since I got here."

"I'm sure. It's a shame but it seems like there are just some things that families don't know how to say to each other."

"Truly." She turned back toward her kitchen and opened the refrigerator, taking out a pitcher of tea. Lemon slices and mint sprigs floated in the top. "And you know what else? They're not merely afraid. They're terrified. I thought my son had more spine."

She filled two glasses with ice, then handed me two plates and paper napkins. She moved back and forth deliberately and then with the halting gait of her years. Uncertain for a moment and then surefooted again. She should probably be using a cane for her balance when she leaves her home, I thought, but that was up to her doctor, not me.

I opened the bag and began unwrapping the sandwiches at her small dining table.

"Well, this is a very big change for you and your whole family," I said.

"You're telling me. Here's how this started. First my son, Alvin, and his wife, Connie, invited me to this Come to Jesus meeting."

I laughed at that.

"It always starts with a big talk. Was the car talk first or this place?"

"No, it really started because of Marcus, my husband of sixty years. Sixty years. Can you imagine how long that is? Marcus has terrible Alzheimer's."

"Yes, I heard that from the other nurses, Judy and Margaret. You'll like them a lot when you get to know them. But back to Marcus. I am so sorry to hear it. I really think Alzheimer's is the meanest disease on the planet."

"It certainly is. My poor sweet Marcus. Forgive me for speaking so plainly, but I don't like to play games." She sighed dramatically and sat down across from me. "Who knows? I could go any minute."

"No, you won't! I don't like to pussyfoot around either," I said, and smiled.

"Good. Anyway, it was obvious, even to me, that I couldn't take care of him by myself anymore. He'd put on three pairs of pajamas, leave the house, and take off for who knows where. I'd realize he was missing, get all upset, and call Alvin to go find him."

"And Alvin did what? Called the police?"

"Do you know my son?" She looked at me with an odd expression and for a moment I thought she was serious.

"No, I . . ."

"Please! I'm kidding! Alvin is just . . . well, dramatic. He always jumps the gun. Everything is a bother and a burden to him. He lives out in Summerville and I guess there was just one emergency phone call too many. I took care of my parents in my home for years but they didn't have Alzheimer's. Things were different in my day." She finally took a bite of her sandwich. "Say! This is pretty good! Cranberries. I'll be darned. I think I might be glad you came by."

At least she wasn't just complaining. Reasonable social skills could definitely work to her advantage.

"My pleasure. I like to know who's coming and going around

here." I smiled at her. "The kitchen is actually pretty good. They roast fresh turkeys every week. None of that 'cold cuts with nitrates' business. And the dining room is packed every night."

"Well, that's nice to know. Anyway, we had another episode of Marcus disappearing, and the next thing I know, Marcus's locked up in a ward. And me? I'm suddenly without my car and my home. It's all pretty depressing, I'll tell you. I'm not sick. Marcus is sick. And because of that, I can't even go to Belk's when I want to."

"I'm sure it's a pain in the neck but they try to make a shuttle bus schedule that works for everyone. Wednesday is seniors' day all over town. You can save some money at Publix. Five percent, I think."

"Well, that's something, I suppose. This move is just going to take some getting used to. I guess I just don't like change. At least I've got some of my favorite pieces of furniture and so on here with me."

"And they are lovely. You have the coolest apartment of anyone here."

"Do you think so?"

"Yes, I know so!" I reached across the table and patted the back of her hand in solidarity. "I know you think this place is a prison but I'm going to tell you something that you will most likely discover soon and it's the truth."

"What's that?"

"At some point? If we are all lucky enough to live long enough?"

"Yes?"

"It's our house that's the prison."

I looked at Marilyn's face. The sun was streaming in through the window on a particular slant that made her seem, in that moment, to be a much younger woman. And very beautiful. It was as though

I could see who she once was. Then a cloud must've passed over the sun because the illusion disappeared. Now she seemed to be on the verge of tears. Her eyes were rimmed in scarlet and her face held hundreds of tiny wrinkles.

"Is anyone ever happy to come here?"

"The truth? No. I mean, just as you said, it's an enormous change. As we mature, we like our routines more and more. And there's some comfort in really simple things, like knowing where all the light switches are. But unless I miss my guess, if you'll just give this place a chance, you'll be on the go and doing things with a whole lot of new friends."

"Maybe. I'll give you a maybe. We'll just have to see how it goes."

"Hmm. Well, I'm sure they've told you about all the clubs and so forth?"

"Oh, yes. I've got a welcome package that looks like a phone book from Atlanta."

"I know," I said, and took a bite of my second sandwich half. "It can be very overwhelming."

"And depressing. You know what I mean? I feel like I've given up too much of my personal life. I have a whole host of strangers—not of my own choosing, may I add—who know what medications I take. And Marcus? He doesn't know I'm here anyway. He doesn't even know me."

There was no response I could offer that would fix that. I wiped my mouth with my napkin and took a sip of tea.

"You know, Mrs. Brooks, I think I have a pretty good idea of how you must be feeling. There's nothing you can do for your husband except watch over him and see that he's being well taken care of. Which he will be. It's simply a terrible thing to see someone you've loved, for most of your life really, in this shape. And you know, no one can tell you whether Palmetto House is right for you except you."

"Tell my knuckleheaded son and his knuckleheaded wife that."

I smiled then and she did too.

"I will, if you'd like. They wouldn't be the first children I've told where the bear goes in the buckwheat. Anyway, what I'm thinking is that you seem like a pretty strong lady. You have a fabulous sense of style—"

"Thank you," she said, and brightened up a bit.

"And I don't think you'd let anyone really railroad you into something you really didn't want to do."

"Yes. I suppose you're right. You know what it is that has made me so unhappy?"

"No, ma'am. You can tell me."

"The love of my life has disappeared into oblivion. And I'm a bit frightened. As long as I was in my own home, I could tell myself that nothing had changed, that I wasn't this old. I could tell myself that maybe Marcus would snap out of it. You know, some days he'd tell me he loved me even when I wasn't sure he knew it was me he was telling. Now he doesn't even know his own name. And being here is hard evidence that my life is almost over too. It just makes me a little sad, that's all. I thought we would have more time together."

"Then you have to do what I tell other residents to do."

"What's that?"

"Make good use of every day."

She was quiet then while she considered my Pollyanna advice.

"You're right, of course. Right now, though, this is like wearing tight shoes."

"Yeah, you just need to break them in."

"That's right. I just need to break them in."

"Tell me; what are your favorite hobbies, Mrs. Brooks?"

"Oh, I don't know. I suppose a good book and someone to take a walk with. I like old movies. And I love live music of all kinds."

"For starters, why don't you go to the reading room, pick a book off the shelves, have a seat on our newly upholstered sofas, and see what happens?"

"Really? Just walk in?"

"Absolutely! We just got a huge donation of all sorts of novels and biographies. When the residents hear about it, they'll be gone in a flash. We have lots of book lovers here and several book clubs too."

"Well, maybe I will." She smiled and exhaled. "I guess I shall have to take charge of my own happiness. Right?"

"Yes! That's the spirit!" I drained my glass of tea and said, "I'd better get back to work."

"Thank you, Lisa. For lunch and . . . well, for this conversation."

"You're welcome for lunch. And I enjoyed the conversation too." I got up and took my plate to the sink.

"Just leave it there," she said.

I walked toward the door to leave.

"Mrs. Brooks?"

"Yes?"

"If you need anything at all, just call the desk and ask for me. Lisa St. Clair."

"Okay, Lisa St. Clair, on one condition." She was smiling.

"What's that?"

"That you call me Marilyn and that we do this again sometime."

"That's two conditions! Ha ha! But it's a deal!"

I left her then and I felt that her spirits were lifted a little. The transition from private life to fishbowl living could be almost impossible for your emotions to reconcile, especially if you were perfectly healthy. There was always some demoralizing price to pay. Loss of privacy. Condescending health care workers. Nosy residents. But my money was on Marilyn Brooks. She would adapt because she knew that she should give this new life some effort. It was only fair. And if she decided that she didn't like living at Palmetto House, she was free to leave and her son could go scratch his mad place, like my mother used to say.

Later that day, as I was walking out after work, I passed the reading room. To my surprise, there was Mrs. Brooks seated at the library table on one side and the frisky Mr. Morrison sat opposite her on the other side of the table, smiling wide. There was no evidence of a duck. I wondered if Mrs. Brooks would succumb to his charms and quickly decided she would never dishonor her marriage. However, if Marcus Brooks died, things might take another path. It was interesting to consider. It was just as important for me to remember, though, that familiarity with the goings-on of our residents and patients did not add up to a personal life for me. As friendly as I was with Judy and Margaret, they were wonderful professional colleagues, not really my personal friends.

That's exactly why I set my alarm for six the next morning and why I was in the car with Pickle, a bottle of water, and a to-go cup of coffee by six thirty. I needed a life of my own.

The sun was already climbing and it was going to be another hot day. Every year I had to get used to the heat all over again. Thank goodness my air-conditioning cooled the car down quickly. But by the time I reached Suzanne's house and got out of my car, the air felt thick and wet. Suzanne and Carrie were standing on the sidewalk, wearing leggings and running shoes, waiting for me.

"Hey! Good morning!" I called out to them.

Pickle pulled the leash to get closer to them, knowing there was some doggie love coming her way. Carrie was the first to scratch her behind the ears.

"I don't know about that but I'll never get a cute husband if I don't shape up," Carrie said.

"But your shoes should get you noticed," I said.

They were hot pink and turquoise with white trim.

"Precious, aren't they?" she said. "They divert attention from my other declining assets."

"Oh, come on, now," I said.

"Quit hogging the dog!" Suzanne said, bending down to talk to Pickle in a baby voice. "There goes Aunt Carrie again. We haven't even had breakfast and she's already talking about finding another man."

"Stop!" Carrie said, pretending to whine.

Suzanne stood up, handed me Pickle's leash, and said, "Let's get the misery over with."

We walked down the path and over the dunes, and happily for us, the tide was low, giving us plenty of room to walk. There was a breeze. A lovely breeze of salted air pushed my hair away from my face. Runners, groups of walkers, and dogs were all over the place.

"Can I let her run off her leash?" I asked.

Every island had its own laws about animals and the beach.

"Yep. This time of year, Pickle can run around until nine."

"Great!" I leaned down and unhooked the strap from her collar. Pickle took off with so much enthusiasm that we started to laugh.

"Look at her go!" Carrie said.

"This is fabulous!" I said. "Absolutely fabulous!"

"It kind of is, isn't it?" Carrie said.

"I hate exercise," Suzanne said. "But if you don't get some cardio, you can drop dead."

Carrie said, "Bull dukey."

"I haven't heard that term since fifth grade," Suzanne said. "Lisa? Tell Carrie what sitting around eating donuts does to your blood."

"Well, basically, it turns it into sludge," I said. "Then you get high cholesterol, high blood sugar, ingrown toenails, and hemorrhoids. Next thing you know you have a heart attack and a brain tumor and then you're finito. So, just get some exercise. We could do some yoga. And drink a lot of water."

"Nicely done," Suzanne said, and snickered. "And we should swear off donuts until further notice."

"I'll take the pledge," I said.

"Me too, okay? Y'all can giggle all you want about me being on the prowl for another husband," Carrie said, "but y'all will stop your giggling when I find us all one."

"One to share?" I said, and laughed.

"He had better be a manly man," Suzanne said in a deep baritone.

"Oh, brother," Carrie said. "Well, I'll have you know I've already had four inquiries from four very handsome gentlemen about sharing a glass of wine and or dinner."

"Jesus Lord, my Savior!" Suzanne exclaimed. "John's only been dead for ten minutes! And you sound like Amanda from *The Glass Menagerie* waiting on a gentleman caller."

"But life has to go on," I said. "It's okay, Carrie. When you find out where they intend to take you, let me know. Pickle and I will be close by if you need a getaway car."

"Thank you," she said.

"Better yet," Suzanne said, "make him pick you up and I'll have Miss Trudie interrogate him. You know, to see if he's worthy."

"What? Are you insane? Rule one of online dating—you meet somewhere where there are lots of people around. Like a busy bar or restaurant," Carrie said. "You never let them know where you live until you are absolutely certain that they're normal."

"Ted Bundy seemed normal," Suzanne said.

"Until he wasn't," I said, and chuckled.

"You're right," Suzanne said.

"Good grief," Carrie said. "Anyway, I'm meeting candidate number one at Rue de Jean tonight at six."

"I can't wait to hear all the details," Lisa said.

We walked a good distance in about twenty minutes and then turned around. Pickle was beside herself with happiness to be chasing seagulls and sandpipers as fast as her little legs would carry her. Without warning, she'd stop and sniff another dog and then take off again.

We said good-bye at eight, deciding to do it again the next morning.

"This was actually fun," Suzanne said.

"Sort of," Carrie said. "I mean, it's nice to be together and all, but I perspired."

"Oh! Not that!" I said, and laughed.

"God, what a princess!" Suzanne said. "Hey, y'all?"

"What?" Carrie said.

"What are we gonna do about Wendy? You know that furniture isn't hers," Suzanne said.

"But we have to be able to prove it," I said.

"There are still boxes of things we haven't gone through," Carrie said.

"True. Maybe we should all get together one night when Carrie isn't interviewing for her next husband and dig through them," Suzanne suggested.

"You're terrible," I said to her with a laugh. "I'll bring the wine."

"That sounds good," they said.

"And y'all?"

"Yeah?"

"There's some advantage to limbering up, you know, stretching out your muscles. We should do a few sun salutations before we walk."

"Good idea," they said.

"I've got mats. I'll throw them in the car."

Later on, after my shower, when I was dressing for work, I thought about how energized I felt. Endorphins. And, in addition to the challenge of solving the mystery of Kathy's furniture, it appeared that I had gained two new friends. On the way out of the house I looked for Pickle. I went from room to room, calling her name. Finally, I found her exhausted and fast asleep in her bed. She was snoring in tiny gusts. Running full throttle after birds was not the same thing as casually walking the neighborhood on her leash with me.

Sometimes, I told myself, change was good.

CHAPTER 6

Landscaping

The next morning Pickle and I returned to the Isle of Palms to walk with Carrie and Suzanne as planned. From the moment we made eye contact, I could tell Suzanne was thoroughly annoyed. In fact, they both looked pretty serious. I put Pickle on the ground and hooked her leash to her collar. Then I pulled three yoga mats from the backseat of my car and went up to the porch where they stood.

"G'morning," I said. "What's wrong?"

Suzanne pulled an envelope from her pocket and pushed it toward me. I took it and looked at it. It was a bill from Green Carolina, a landscaping company.

"Read it," she said. "Open it and read it. You won't believe."

"By the way, good morning," Carrie said. "Steady yourself."

"G'morning," I said. I unfolded the statement, which was billed to Kathy Harper. "Two thousand fifty dollars and thirty-eight cents? Are you kidding me? No way!"

"For work done at her landlady's house?" Carrie said. "It doesn't make any sense. Right?"

"Why would a tenant pay to landscape a rental property?" I said.

"My point exactly!" Suzanne said. "And the work was done after Kathy died?"

"First, it was the bracelets and then the furniture and now landscaping?" Carrie said.

"You've got to ask Wendy about this," I said.

"I can't deal with her. She really kind of scares me. I'm *not* kidding," Suzanne said. "She's a psycho."

"Yep. She sure is," Carrie said. "Who knows? She might stick a knife in between your ribs. That's the world we live in today, ladies. Sorry, but it's the truth."

"Wait a minute. Everybody hold the phone here," I said. I could feel my face getting hot. "I'm not afraid of that woman. Granted, she must be a little crazy to think she can get away with this. But, this is fraud. Fraud is a felony! She could go to jail."

What was I saying? I was the biggest sissy in the world! If Wendy scared Suzanne she terrified me!

"Let's not do yoga. Let's just walk this morning," Suzanne said. "I need to burn off some anxiety."

"Leave the mats," Carrie said.

"Sure!" I said, and we went downstairs to the sidewalk. "I only have about sixty of them at home."

Pickle was pulling me toward the beach, so I followed her across the street. Carrie and Suzanne were right behind me. We didn't need to waste the morning standing around. In seconds, we were over the white dunes and on the beach. It was low tide again. I liberated Pickle from her leash, and in the blink of an eye she was flying down the sand, chasing a Yorkie terrier that was chasing a ball. It was a wonderful sight to see my dog in a state of near rapture. I looked at the backdrop of gorgeous sparkling blue water and hard-packed silver sand. We began to power walk. Like yesterday, laughing seagulls swooped down, hopped a few steps, pecked at the shore for whatever critters lay there in hiding, and then lifted back into the sky cackling like mad. The closer we came to them, the faster they scattered. But happy dog, glistening water, and crazy birds aside, my mind was spinning about the landlady from hell. Was I choosing to do battle with a nut job?

"Suzanne?" Carrie said. "Lisa is right. This has to be dealt with. Psycho or not. That company is going to want their money."

"Why don't we just pay her a little visit?" I said. "I'll go with you."

"Me too," Carrie said.

What was the matter with me? Since when was I so brave? What if the landlady really *was* a psycho? What if she—I don't know—started screaming or something? What if she sued us or called the police?

"Would you all do that?" Suzanne said. "I could just call her but I think it's better to face her."

"Absolutely," I said.

"You bet," Carrie said.

I agreed wholeheartedly but the truth was that I hated confrontations of any kind. My stomach was already getting knots.

"Definitely," Carrie said.

"You know, I told her to send me any mail that came in for Kathy and I'd deal with it. I'd see the bills got paid and so forth. And obviously, I'd notify the various people who needed to know that she was deceased. You know, like her cell-phone company and the bank. I'm just so uneasy about this and I don't know why."

"Because anyone who would do something like this is definitely off their rocker," I said. "But take heart. I've dealt with all sorts of people who are confused about reality. It's part of my job."

No, it wasn't. There was a vast and maybe even an immeasurable difference between helping a very nice but really old lady find her way to wherever she was headed and taking on a raging mental case with possible sociopathic tendencies.

"Okay," Suzanne said. "Let's just take it up with her today after work and be done with it. I've got a crazy day ahead of me. Bridal showers and birthdays. And it's gonna be hot like hell. What time do you finish work, Lisa?"

Suzanne was so determined and this fueled my sudden but rarely seen burst of courage. That and a healthy distaste for the witch with the nice house on Wentworth Street who was stealing from the dead.

"Four," I replied. "Want to get together after that? I can zoom home to walk my dog and then we can meet somewhere and ride over there together."

"Sounds great," Suzanne said. "We can park in the Bottles parking lot. It's huge."

"That's settled," Carrie said. "Let's pick up our pace, girls. We're dwaddling."

"Is that even a word?" I asked, and moved a little faster to keep up.

"Probably not but my daddy used to say it all the time," Carrie said.

Carrie was really moving quickly down the beach. I struggled to keep pace.

"Dwaddling? Really? I say bull dukey to that," Suzanne said, catching up to us. "Boy, Carrie, you're on a mission today!"

Carrie's face was all red from exertion.

"I'm gonna be so thin y'all're gonna think I've been sick!" Carrie said, adding, "And excuse me. How come neither one of you asked about my hot date last night?"

"Oh! Sorry! I forgot! How was it?" I said.

"Sorry. I was a little distracted by the landscaping bill," Suzanne said.

"Not so hot," she said. "He was a lip licker. I hate that."

"Ew," Suzanne made a face. "That's worse than an eye roller."

"But not as bad as a toupee," I said. "I went out with a toupee once. He was really tall, so I couldn't tell it was a wig at first. But then, for some reason, it began to slide."

"Oh Lord! What did you say to him?" Carrie asked, laughing.

"Well, it was awkward. I think I said something like 'Honey, you might want to go to the men's room and make a small but critical adjustment.' He went to the men's room and I'm embarrassed to admit that I just sort of left. Really. My dating history is littered with moments I'm not proud of."

"I would've slipped out too," Carrie said. "Anyway, I've got another Mr. Possibility lined up for tonight. We're meeting at Cypress for a cocktail."

"You're wasting no time there, sister," Suzanne said, remarking on Carrie's pace.

"I don't have any time to waste," Carrie said. "My assets are dwindling."

"Oh Lord," I said, and I meant it in a prayerful way, asking the Lord to be merciful to all of us. What becomes of girls like us? Really, what becomes of us?

Later on that morning at work, I was startled by the sound of jackhammers.

"What's all the ruckus about?" I asked Margaret.

"Like we don't have enough to do? Now we're building a neighborhood of group houses out back. It's a Green House Project model."

"No kidding," I said. "How many?" More residents might mean more work for me. That would be great.

"Two for now but the plan is for eight," she said.

"Wow," I said. "They're supposed to be terrific. I've been reading all about it."

"Hey, you know we're on the cutting edge."

I giggled and said, "If you say so. But how did I miss this?"

"I don't know but you should go out there and see what's going on."

"Yeah, I might do that later."

The Green House Project was designed to provide group housing for seniors who didn't want or need to live in a nursing home environment but for one reason or another had decided to make a change. Each house had up to ten bedrooms, private bathrooms, a common living and dining area, and outdoor porches and patios with gardens. There were windows everywhere, so that on nice days sunlight could flood the rooms. And there was no typical nurses' station but an open office where a Shahbaz or two kept records and watched a light board. A Shahbaz was a friendly certified nurse's assistant dressed in street clothes and thusly dubbed with the Persian word for "royal falcon." If a light came on, it meant that a resident needed something and the royal falcon would sweep in to assist them. A registered nurse was also on staff. It was a far less exacting plan that allowed more independence for the residents and it encouraged social activity, which was especially good for those who had been lonely in their own homes. Loneliness was another curse of old age to add to the list.

Because I have too much time on my hands, I had been reading all about GHP online. Basically, it was the coolest trend in elder care out there. I just hoped it wouldn't prove to be one of those ideas that looked good on paper but in reality didn't make life one whit better for anyone. But having some Green House Project homes would make another level of care available for people considering life at Palmetto House. Why not? Here was one more option to deal with all the issues of aging.

When my shift ended at four I walked outside intending to take a look at the construction site. There were trucks everywhere and at least a dozen men in hard hats milling around, a few of them taping off areas like a crime scene and others using noisy chain saws that screamed and whined, cutting down a skimpy population of twiggy pine trees. In our neck of the woods, pine trees popped up and grew like weeds right in their own shadows.

Two tanned men in jeans with remarkable biceps were consulting with a third man in khakis and a knit shirt. They were looking over architectural drawings on the bed of a pickup truck. The guy in khakis looked familiar. I walked over toward them.

"Paul?" I said. Since when was I so brazen?

He turned around and smiled when he recognized me.

"Hey! I remember you," he said, walking toward me. "You were at Kathy's funeral, right?"

"Yes." I pushed my sunglasses up and let them act as a headband.

He took off his sunglasses, tortoiseshell Ray-Bans, for the record, and ran his hand through his hair. Was it my imagination or was he just one helluva lot better looking than the last time I saw him? But then, who looks good at a funeral?

"Funny meeting you here," he said, and paused, squinting in the brutal sun. "Um, you work here, I guess?"

"Yes, I'm a nurse. I've been here off and on for a few years now. So, you must be the architect?"

"Yep. That's me. This is going to be a Green Ho—"

"Green House Project," I said. "I actually know quite a lot about the whole deal. You know, ADA compliance and all that."

He had nice eyes. Brown. And warm. I've always liked brown eyes, for some reason. Especially if they're warm. And for no good reason in this entire world I felt myself wanting to take a short swim in them. Just a few laps around the chocolate pool. How stupid.

"You do, huh? I'm sorry. What's your name?" he said.

"Oh!" I said. "Sorry! I'm Lisa. Lisa St. Clair. Well, it was Barnebey, but after my divorce I started using my maiden name again. My daughter, Marianne, uses Barnebey, which she should since it's her name. At least I think she does. I haven't spoken to her in six months. She doesn't call much."

He was just looking at me, smiling. He wasn't smiling at me like I was a lunatic but it was a kind expression, so kind it made me want to tell him everything. But now he knew my name, that I was divorced, had one child, and that she was grown and probably not a burden. What in the hell was happening here?

"Why am I telling you all of this?" I laughed and shook my head.

"I don't know, Lisa St. Clair. Why are you?"

He was grinning from ear to ear like big cats do when they've got the little mouse cornered. He was going to taunt me and run me around before he ate my soul. I knew how this game worked. I didn't know how I got so off-kilter but I knew I had to get in my car and drive away from him or I was going to say something really stupid and then he would know what an idiot I really was.

"I just came out here to see what the jackhammers were doing. That's all."

Another pearl from me. Yeah, boy, those jackhammers are wild things.

"They're tearing up unnecessary macadam."

"Right. So, right, well, I gotta go. I gotta go meet some friends and solve a mystery." I was babbling like the proverbial brook. "Nice to see you."

"Nice to see you too," he said. "Come back and visit. Maybe you could consult?"

"Oh, right. Very funny. But I would like to see how this progresses. The whole concept is . . . well, I think it's great. So I'll be around."

"Great!" he said, and gave me a little wave as I turned to scurry to my car as fast as humanly possible without seeming like I was rushing from a crime scene.

Oh yeah, I'll come back and I'll bring donuts, I thought with glee, and then quickly realized I was in a situation. I was in a situation because for the first time in at least ten years I felt a powerful twitch south of the Mason-Dixon Line in my personal Lowcountry. That twitch was a profound warning. Part of my brain, the seductress cells that had been in mothballs for a decade, suddenly sang an aria and wanted to lure a man with food, decadent food. Sugar. Caramel. Chocolate. I was on the edge of falling right into a mine shaft of carnal desire. How shocking! But every experience I'd ever had with an adult male had proven to me that love, or whatever it really was, pheromones maybe, wasn't worth the trouble. I was going to get a grip on myself, and the next time I saw him, I'd be cool. Serene like Grace Kelly in a film with Cary Grant. That's who I'd be. Grace Kelly. Maybe I'd have a friendship with him. Nothing dangerous or too personal. Sure. Just friends. It might be interesting to see if I could have something platonic with a man. It would be a first. But I was older now. I could manage it. I could control myself. For heaven's sake, I could control myself.

I got to my house, walked my dog, and drove to the Bottles parking lot on Coleman Boulevard. I pulled in and parked next to Carrie's Mercedes. Carrie and Suzanne were standing there, waving at me. I got out of my car and clicked the key to lock it.

"The air-conditioning is running. Jump in! It's as hot as Hades out here," Carrie said.

"I don't know why the late-afternoon sun is hotter than it is at noon, but it feels like it," Suzanne said.

"It sure does," I said, and slipped into the backseat, moving a dozen empty water bottles to the other side with my foot.

"Sorry about all the bottles," Carrie said. "I keep forgetting to throw them out."

"No problem," I told her.

"So, how was your day?" Suzanne asked. "You want a bottle of cold water? We brought you one."

It wasn't unusual for Lowcountry residents to drink water or tea all day long in the summer.

"Sure. Thanks!" I took the bottle, unscrewed the cap, and took a long sip. "My day was fine. Hey! Guess what?"

"What?" Carrie said.

"I'm not sure my nervous system can take any more surprises, so tell me quick," Suzanne said.

"I saw that guy Paul. He's the architect on a new building project at Palmetto House."

"No kidding?" Carrie said. "How funny!"

Suzanne turned to say something to me and I must've had a really goofy expression on my face.

"Oh! God!" she said.

"What?" I said, and felt my face flush.

"You've got a thing for him!" Suzanne said.

"I do not!" I said adamantly.

I saw Carrie look at me in the rearview mirror and then she grinned so wide I could see her gums.

"Yes, you do," she said. "I'm an expert in the field, you know."

"Lord save us," Suzanne said, and giggled.

"Oh, brother. Listen, you two matchmakers, I don't have it going on for Paul or anybody else. It's just me and Pickle in my little world."

"And us!" Carrie said.

"Yeah," Suzanne said, adding, "and Wendy. Y'all? What are we going to say to her?"

Carrie made the left on East Bay Street. We were almost there. Somebody had better think of *something* to say.

"You've got the landscaping bill with you?" I said.

"Of course, but only a copy of it," Suzanne said. "And a copy of Kathy's last bank statement."

"I think we should just be nice, you know, let her think that we think the bill is a mistake," Carrie said.

"Yeah, there's no point in pinning her against the wall and calling her a liar," I said.

"Unless we have to," Suzanne added.

We pulled up in front of Wendy's house and got out.

"Did you call her, Suzanne?"

"No," Suzanne said.

"What if she's not home?" I said.

"Then I think we wait," Suzanne said.

"Or we can sneak in and get the bracelets back," I said.

"Not me, sugar," Carrie said. "I look terrible in orange."

"Would you really be a cat burglar?" Suzanne looked at me as if she were wondering in that moment if I had criminal tendencies.

"No, never. But I just feel like this horrible woman is so far over the line that I could somehow justify it."

"Nuh-uh," Carrie said, and rang the doorbell and banged the door knocker. "Not me. Too chicken."

The door opened and there stood Wendy, surprised to see us. Carrie turned turtle and quickly stepped behind Suzanne. I moved up, giving Wendy a little dose of stink eye.

"What do y'all want?" Wendy said, and not very politely.

"May we come in for a moment?" Suzanne said as sweetly as a saint.

"Well, all right. But only for a moment. I'm busy."

"Thank you," Suzanne said.

We followed Wendy to the living room and stood by two facing slipcovered sofas, waiting for her to sit down. She stood by the fireplace. Over the mantel hung an ancient sword, probably from the Civil War. It seemed she had no intention of offering us a seat or a drink of anything.

"So?" she said, pretty icily. "Would you like to tell me why I have the honor of this unexpected visit?"

Woo-hoo! She was a serious bitch, I thought. I mean, world class. More stink eye ensued.

"Well, I received this bill from Green Carolina for two thousand dollars," Suzanne said, holding the envelope in her hand.

"So?" Wendy said.

"Well, it's for landscaping done here *after* Kathy died," Suzanne said.

"She said she wanted to help me renovate the gardens as a birthday gift. They started the work when they did because they're very busy. It seemed like an extravagant gift to me but I didn't want to hurt her feelings," Wendy said.

"I knew Kathy from the time I was just a little girl," Suzanne said. "She was my babysitter. In all the years I knew her I never saw her do anything so over the top as this. I mean, this is obviously a mistake."

Suzanne was giving her the opportunity to save face but Wendy didn't seem to care about that. Her eyes darted all around the room and then settled evenly on Suzanne's face.

"What do you mean?" she said. "It's no mistake. She always paid the landscaping bills."

Suzanne's face turned red. She was getting angry.

"No, she didn't. I have all of her bank statements to prove it."

"Well? Maybe she paid them in cash. How should I know?"

"But a two-thousand-dollar bill? Are you serious?" Suzanne said. "She didn't have that kind of money to spend."

"She didn't? I thought she came from money," Wendy said.

"I don't know what made you think that she did. She died with less than five hundred dollars to her name. My grandmother and I paid all the funeral expenses."

"Good grief!" Wendy said.

"So, Kathy's estate cannot pay this bill."

Wendy gasped. "Well, then, I'll just have to call a lawyer. Won't I?"

"Are you threatening me with a lawsuit?" Suzanne said. Her voice was escalating and I could see we were heading for trouble.

"I never threaten," Wendy said evenly.

"Fine," Suzanne said, and dropped the copy of the bill on the coffee table.

Now this glass coffee table in between the sofas was covered in a collection of magnifying glasses and letter openers. They were beautiful pieces and one exquisite pair in particular caught my eye. I picked it up to look at it.

"Put that down!" Wendy said, nearly shrieking at me. "That belonged to my mother!"

"Sorry!" I said, and carefully replaced it on the table.

Carrie caught my eye. We knew something wasn't right. She started coughing and coughing. And then, as her coughing fit progressed, she became dramatic, waving her arms and pointing to her throat.

"Are you okay?" Suzanne asked.

Carrie shook her head back and forth. She was not okay.

"Now what?" Wendy said. "You want water? Good grief! Lord! Deliver me from these women!"

As soon as Wendy huffed out of the room to get a glass of water for Carrie, I whipped out my cell phone and started taking pictures of the letter openers and magnifying glasses, vases, figurines, and paintings. Suzanne, sensing I was onto something, did the same. She took pictures of mirrors, the rugs, the end tables—as many as she could in the narrow time frame we had. Carrie kept coughing. Hearing Wendy's footsteps cross the ancient heart-pine floors, we stopped clicking away and put our phones out of sight. Suspecting nothing, she came back to the living room and handed Carrie a glass. Carrie curbed her drama and took a few sips.

Carrie finally managed to speak. Her voice was raspy. "Thank you. Do you have cats?"

"Only Sylvester, my sixteen-year-old Persian. Why? You allergic?"

"Obviously," I muttered.

"Deathly. I'll just wait outside," Carrie said, wheezing a little.

"It's probably time for all of us to go," Suzanne said. She pointed to the paper on the coffee table and then looked Wendy straight in the eye. "Pay the bill, Wendy."

"I don't take orders from you," Wendy said.

Then I couldn't stand it another minute, so I jumped in.

"First, it was the bracelets. Now this. What else is going on here? Pay the bill and let's have no more nonsense from you."

"Get out of my house or I'll call the police," Wendy said.

I walked to the door and followed Suzanne and Carrie outside. Wendy slammed the door so hard it could've fallen from its hinges and it wouldn't have surprised me one little bit.

"She's a terrible person," Carrie said.

"She's a thief," Suzanne said.

"Something tells me that this isn't our last dealing with her," I said.

"Oh, please!" Suzanne said. "Make her go away!"

"By the way, I adore cats," Carrie said in a perfectly normal voice, and laughed. "The furrier, the better."

My jaw dropped and Suzanne said, "Please, the only things Carrie's allergic to are stepchildren."

CHAPTER 7

Still Searching

After our confrontation at Wendy's we were all pretty breathless. All the way back to Mount Pleasant we called her every name in the book. The plan was to go to Suzanne's house after I picked up my car. We weren't quite ready to call it a day and we decided some adult hydration was definitely in order to soothe our rankled nerves. And we shared a crushing need for a postmortem rehash. There was a lot to discuss.

"I'm glad we parked at Bottles," I said. "What's it gonna be, ladies? White or red? My treat."

"Anything, as long as it's alcoholic," Suzanne said.

"I have to be downtown by six. No vino for me," Carrie said. "Well, maybe a thimble."

"Okay!" I said, and got out of the car. "See you soon."

They pulled away and I walked across the steaming parking lot to the store's entrance. It was divided into two parts—one side sold liquor and the other sold wine. I'd had a twenty-dollar bill in my wallet that morning when I checked. I hoped it was still there. Money, in my life, had a way of disappearing into thin air. Inside, I walked to the wine side of the store and rested my shoulder bag on a counter to check for cash. When there are more receipts than money in your wallet it's time to clean out your whole purse. Obviously I wasn't going to start doing it then and there, but given the hoorah I'd just been through, it wouldn't have really surprised me if I had. My behavior that day was unusual, to say the least. Normally, I didn't talk too much or take sides in arguments. But that day I went from batting my eyes at Paul while giving him a verbal résumé, to giving the hairy eyeball to Wendy, letting her know we knew she had stolen the bracelets. What was next?

I walked the aisles of wine from all over the world thinking about Wendy and about Carrie's coughing fit and the pictures we took. How in the world were we going to prove anything? All of us knew Wendy was guilty, but without Kathy to confirm our suspicions, what could we do? Tell Green Carolina to come take back their boxwoods and azaleas? Maybe they would. Maybe I should suggest that to Suzanne.

I chose a Malbec from South America and a pinot grigio from Italy and took them to the checkout counter.

"That'll be eighteen dollars and thirty-two cents," the checkout man said.

"Here you go," I said, remembering the days when checkout personnel would ask to see some ID to prove I was old enough to buy booze. Now they wanted to give me the senior discount at the Bi-Lo. Maybe I needed a better moisturizer and a neck cream.

My car was a veritable oven, but I expected it to be one. I just blasted the air conditioner and backed out of my spot. I hurried home to get Pickle and she was thrilled to see me.

"Come on, sweet baby! We're going to the beach! You can watch *Lassie* with Miss Trudie! Yes, you can! Oh, you're such a sweet girl! Let's go!"

I'm telling you that my dog knew exactly what I was saying. I'd bet the ranch on it—not The Ponderosa, but my rental. It's a ranch style? I know, dumb joke.

We rolled into Suzanne's yard twenty minutes later. Suzanne, Carrie, and Miss Trudie were on the porch. Suzanne stood up to hold the screen door wide for me.

"I can open the wine," she said. "Should I?"

"God, yes!" Carrie said. She was dressed for the evening.

"Wow!" I said. "You look great!"

"Thanks!" she said.

"The white's cold," I told her. "But it would probably stand up to ice very well." Meaning, it was pretty cheap, so the colder it was, the better.

"Oh!" Miss Trudie said. "My little friend is back!"

Well, Pickle had to circle the porch and get her doggie love from each of the women and then she settled at Miss Trudie's feet. Suzanne put the wine bottles on the table.

She said, "I'll go get some glasses and a corkscrew."

"And ice," I said.

"And some olives!" Miss Trudie added.

"I've got y'all covered!" Suzanne disappeared inside the house.

"Sit! Sit!" Miss Trudie said. "I've been hearing all about this terrible woman. I want to hear what you think. Is she really a thief?"

"I think so," I said. "It surely seems like it."

"Well, this is very interesting. Not much happens in my life these days. So this is very exciting. How do you girls plan to resolve it?"

I said, "Well, that's the problem, isn't it? Kathy's not here to set the record straight. But I keep thinking we're going to find evidence at some point. Suzanne, as you know, inherited everything Kathy left behind. Somewhere in that pile of boxes is more information."

Carrie said, "I agree. At some point, we're going to have to get focused on that. We've all been so busy!"

It was true. We *had* been busy, but to be honest, I felt like we had to take our cue from Suzanne. If Suzanne wanted to spend an evening unpacking Kathy's things and going through them, I'd be glad to help. She knew that, I think.

"Miss Trudie? Did Suzanne and Carrie show you the pictures?"

"No, what pictures?" she said.

Carrie said, "We took pictures of some of the objects in Wendy's living room. When Lisa picked up a letter opener that was on her coffee table, Wendy nearly died! She actually yelled at Lisa!"

"What an odious woman!" Miss Trudie exclaimed. "She raised her voice to you?"

"Yes, ma'am," I replied. "I picked up the letter opener because it didn't really fit the style of the others. And because it was filigreed gold encrusted with a large stone on the end of its handle. There was a magnifying glass that matched it."

"Oh! I'd love to see that!" Miss Trudie said.

Carrie and I pulled out our cell phones and fiddled with them until we could find a picture of the whole collection on the coffee table.

"See this?" I said, handing my phone to Miss Trudie. "That's the one we're talking about."

"Oh my!" she said. "I see what you mean! There is a very big difference between this one and that one. This one looks like it belonged to some bigwig, like royalty or maybe Donald Trump. That one looks like it came from a yard sale."

"And some of the others are nice, but not even in the same ballpark as this one, right?" I said.

"Lisa? Do you think Wendy stole this from Kathy too?" Carrie said.

"I don't know, but I wouldn't trust her as far as I can spit," I said, and then thought better of my choice of words. "Miss Trudie? I don't spit."

"Of course you don't, sweetheart! It's unsanitary and you're a nurse!"

"Plus it's gross," Carrie put in.

"Exactly," I said.

Suzanne returned with the glasses and began pouring wine.

"Just a drop for me. I have to leave in a few minutes," Carrie said. "Well, not a drop exactly."

"Ahem!" Miss Trudie said.

Suzanne looked at her. "Oh! I've done it again! I'm so sorry!"

"Go!" I said. "I can pour!"

Suzanne scurried back into the house for Miss Trudie's olives. I suspected that the tumbler next to her seat was filled with gin. It was clear liquid for sure and I doubted that it was water. Suzanne quickly returned with a small dish of big pimento-stuffed Spanish olives.

"Thank you, dear."

"Here you go," I said, and handed a half pour to Carrie.

Then I poured a glass for Suzanne and for myself.

"Cheers!" I said.

They responded in kind and Suzanne said, "I've got to get to the bottom of this business with Wendy and Kathy's things. It's just not right. I know it in my bones."

"Well, I love y'all but I've got to go see a man about a future!" Carrie said. She drained her glass and stood. "Keep a light on for me. I should be home by nine at the latest."

We gave her a little wave and she left, wisely navigating the front steps with some caution considering the height of her heels.

"Have fun!" Suzanne called.

"Happy hunting!" I said.

Carrie got in her car and closed the door.

"She looks amazing," I said. "And you have to admire her tenacity."

"That's for sure. Watch her find some fabulous guy," Suzanne said.

"I hope she does," I said, and looked out across the water. "This sure is a mighty pretty place."

The sun was slipping away and the colors of the sky were just as insane as they were most nights. There was a large cloud over the water. It wasn't exactly cumulus. It was more like hundreds of huge cotton balls pushed together to make up a kind of openwork crocheted afghan. Streams of gold light slipped through the openings. The horizon itself was the reddest. As your eyes moved away from the sun, the whole vista seemed to be painted in diminishing shades of purple, rose quartz, and gold. It was stunning and mesmerizing at the same time. It wouldn't be dark until almost nine o'clock and the scene before us would continue to change until then.

"So, what do you think, Lisa?" Suzanne said. "Should we try going through some of Kathy's scrapbooks or a box of letters?"

"Why not?" I said. "George Clooney's married, so I've got time on my hands."

Well, what do you know, I thought. Progress. It takes a little time for minds to meet.

"We've got a bowl of peel-and-eat shrimp in the fridge," Miss Trudie informed us. "When you girls get hungry."

"Sounds like a perfect dinner!" I said. "Thanks!"

"I'll go get a box," Suzanne said. "The light is fading but we can still see well enough to look at photographs, don't you think?"

"Sure," I said.

Over the next hour, Miss Trudie went inside and Suzanne and I went through two photograph albums, sadly to no avail. There was nothing in Kathy's pictures that was currently in Wendy's side of the house. At least if there was, we didn't recognize anything.

"This is useless," Suzanne said. "And I feel sort of like an intruder."

"It's a little weird, I'll give you that," I said.

"Let's get a plate of shrimp."

"When in doubt, eat," I said.

We carried the albums and the wine into the brightly lit kitchen and I sat down at the table, continuing to flip through the pages. Suzanne was rumbling around in the refrigerator, pulling out lemons and cocktail sauce and, of course, a large mixing bowl filled with shrimp.

"Where are the shrimp from?" I asked.

"Simmons Seafood. They're local. In fact, they swore to me that these babies were swimming yesterday."

"They look gorgeous!" I said.

"Well, I'm no gourmet chef but I do know how to cook shrimp. Miss Trudie taught me."

"Can I help you do anything?" I asked.

"No, thanks. This is more like an all-you-can-eat-of-a-single-item snack than a serious dinner. Piece of cake."

She put plates on the table, poured the cocktail sauce in a small bowl, then added a plate of lemon wedges.

"Voilà!" she said. "Let's eat."

"Voilà!" I said, and giggled.

We clinked glasses and got down to the business of peeling the little devils. The scrapbook was open and there were two pages of photographs that appeared to be from around 1970. An older woman, maybe Kathy's mother or an aunt, was smiling in front of a Christmas tree. There were lots of pictures like that. I recognized Kathy as a little girl and as a teenager. But neither Suzanne nor I detected anything worthy of note. When we got to the pictures of a cemetery headstone I had to stop. I closed the album.

"Okay! That's enough!" I said.

"What was it?" Suzanne said.

"A headstone."

"Oh Lord."

"That's too morbid for me," I said. "I'm sorry."

Suzanne wiped her hands on her napkin. "Here, pass it to me. I'll put it back in the spare bedroom and we can look through them another time. I completely agree. Too bizarre." She got up and took the book across the hall, returning in seconds.

"It is one hundred percent peculiar to take pictures of somebody's grave unless it's the Taj Mahal or the Great Pyramids," I said. "And by the way, the shrimp are fabulous, Suzanne. So sweet and tender."

"It's my one culinary claim to fame. Usually people rubberize them. They boil 'em to death. The secret is to drop them in boiling water for just a minute and then pull the water off the heat. Wait a minute or two and try one. If it's how you like them? Drain them in a colander and cover them with a pile of ice to stop the cooking. That's it."

"What's the seasoning?"

"An Old Bay boiling bag, a lemon cut in two, and a heaping tablespoon of salt. That's it. Not too complicated."

"Gosh, I think even I can handle that."

"Darlin'? Don't you know you can't call yourself a Lowcountry girl if you can't fix shrimp!"

"Do I have to cook grits too?"

"Nah. But it helps. I'm always counting carbs unless we're going out for pancakes, but when Carrie brought donuts all bets were off."

"Me too."

Basically that meant we tried to watch what we ate but not to the point of fanaticism. It was a statement expressing exhaustion with the world's expectation of perfection in women. You can't go gray, gain weight, get wrinkles, sag anywhere, or age in general. If you do you will be overlooked by the opposite sex, seated in the back of restaurants, ignored in clothing stores, especially at makeup counters, and deferred to on a regular basis. If you, at my age, found yourself in one of many chain stores like Victoria's Secret or J.Crew, the salesperson automatically assumed you were shopping for someone else. So, you know what? Every now and then, girls like Carrie, Suzanne, and me ate the damn donuts and pancakes too. Go ahead. Live a little. Besides, I've done enough juice cleanses for all of us.

Later, when Pickle and I were home watching television, my cell phone rang. I hoped it was Marianne. It was my mother, who rarely called me on weeknights.

"Is everything okay?" I said, waiting for terrible news. "Is Dad all right?"

"Oh, yes! Don't worry! He's fine. I'm fine, but I've had a phone call from the Smiths."

The Smiths were my mother's friends who owned the house I was renting.

"Oh no! Are they coming back?"

"No, but their fifty-five-year-old daughter just lost her job. She's divorced and her husband isn't exactly consistent with his alimony payments and she needs a place to live that's free."

"How terrible! Wait. Does she want to live with me?"

"No, honey, I'm afraid she wants the whole house to herself. You're going to have to start looking for another arrangement. She's taking over August first."

"Oh my God. Okay, okay. That gives me a month. Don't worry, I'll find something."

We chatted for a few more minutes and I tried to keep the rising panic out of my voice. Then we hung up and I looked at Pickle.

"Bad news, baby girl. We're gonna be homeless in thirty days. Where are we going to find a house at this price that isn't a meth lab?"

Pickle clearly had no idea. My cell phone rang again. It was Suzanne.

"I just found Miss Trudie on the floor."

"Is she all right? Is she conscious?"

"Yes, she said she doesn't know what happened and she absolutely will not let me call 911. She is so pissed you can't believe it."

"I'm sure. What do you think happened? Do you have any idea what caused the fall?"

"No. But fortunately, she landed on carpet and I don't think anything's broken. I've asked her fifty times if anything hurt and she says she's fine. But she's so thin that I know she's going to be sore tomorrow."

"Is she on an aspirin regimen?"

"I think so," Suzanne said.

"Does she take Coumadin or any other kind of blood thinners?"

"No, I'm pretty sure about that."

"Well, look, if you want I can hop in the car and come take a look at her. It's no problem at all."

"No, but thanks. It's almost ten o'clock and I've already put her to bed. She was very upset with herself for falling."

"Well, pride takes a beating sometimes, but here's what I would do. I'd ice whatever she says might be hurting—twenty minutes on and twenty off. Use a gallon Ziploc or whatever you have, but wrap the bag in a linen towel."

"Okay."

"And then listen for her. If she's moaning, call 911. If she seems off in the morning? I'd toss all her meds into a bag, put her in the car, and take her to Dr. Durst on Sullivans Island. Let him make the decisions. By tomorrow she'll know if she broke anything. Her bones will be talking to her."

"I just hope she didn't crack her hip or something. But I have to say, she seemed pretty much okay. She was more shook up than anything else, I think."

"Well, thank the Lord. Listen, if you need me to come over, just whistle. Okay? I mean that!"

"Okay, thanks. And thanks for your advice. I guess I needed to tell someone."

"Carrie still out?"

"Yep."

"That Carrie!"

"Gotta love her!"

"Let's talk tomorrow. I'm off, so if you want help taking her to the doctor, let me know."

But when sunrise rolled around Suzanne called and said, "She's the bionic woman. She was up at six making eggs and bacon for us. You want to walk?"

"I'll be right over," I said, and looked at Pickle. "Will wonders never cease?"

CHAPTER 8

It's 4:20 Somewhere

My dog raced me up the front steps of Suzanne's house.

"You can't open it, Pickle," I said in my I'm-a-fool-for-my-doggie voice. "Only Mommy can do that."

Pickle responded with a frustrated yip and I knocked on the door. Moments later, Suzanne appeared and flipped the latch.

"Hey! Good morning!" she said. "Come on in. I have to get my sneakers on." She leaned down to scratch my dog behind the ears. "Hi, baby!"

Pickle gave her a lick. I followed Suzanne into the house. Miss Trudie was in the kitchen reading something on her iPad and the television was on but muted. When she put her iPad down I could see it was the obituaries.

"Hey! How are you feeling this morning?"

"G'morning! I'm fine. Right as rain!" she said. "Well, look who's here!" She held her hand out for Pickle, who tootled right over to give her a sniff and a lick. "You smell bacon, don't you?"

I was very relieved to see that she was all right.

"Who died?" I asked. "Anybody we know?"

"I was just checking to make sure *I* didn't!" she said, and laughed.

"Funny," Suzanne said, tying her shoelaces. "Don't even think about going anywhere."

"Listen, when you're my age, you read the obituaries," Miss Trudie said. "If people didn't drop dead I wouldn't have any social life at all! I never miss a wake. Of course, these days, most everyone I ever knew is already gone."

"Because you're crushing the actuarial tables!" Suzanne laughed.

"Where's Carrie?" I said. "Is she coming?"

Suzanne said, "She wanted to sleep in this morning."

"Oh! Okay! Well, let's go, then." I gave Pickle's leash the smallest little tug. Poor Pickle. I could see that she was torn between a beach frolic and Miss Trudie's lap with *Lassie*. She looked up at me as if to say, *What to do, Mom?*

"We are going to get some exercise, young lady! See you later, Miss Trudie!"

When we crossed the dunes I said to Suzanne, "So, are you going to tell me why Carrie is sleeping in this morning? Is she sick?"

I unhooked Pickle and she went flying down the beach toward some other dogs, terrorizing several seagulls along the way.

"Heck no! She's still sleeping because I think she just got home." Suzanne started laughing and so did I.

"Well, that little tart!" I said.

"I know. She's a bad girl. I said 'get up' and she said, 'Oh let me sleep!' She must have really liked the guy or she would've been home hours ago."

"I'll say," I said.

"She's lucky Miss Trudie didn't ground her," she said, laughing. "Did your daughter ever stay out all night?"

"Are you kidding me? Up until about a year ago my daughter was like a saint. She was a dream! Now we barely speak."

"Uh-oh. Can I ask what happened?"

I thought about it for a minute and then I decided to trust Suzanne with the truth. You can't claim someone as a friend if you don't trust them, right?

"Oh Lord. Okay, I haven't really told anyone this story because it's difficult to frame it from my point of view without sounding like an old biddy. And it's embarrassing. God knows, I wouldn't want anyone at Palmetto House to hear it."

"I'm listening. You can tell me anything. I won't say a word. I swear!"

"When I tell you this story you are going to think there's something seriously questionable about my judgment because this had to have sprung from my ex-husband's gene pool, not mine. If I had married anyone else in the entire world, she never would've done this."

"What? Is she in jail?"

"No! Of course not. But she owns and operates a tour company in Aspen for visitors who want to experience marijuana. How's that?"

"What? Oh my God! I've never even heard of that."

"She doesn't smoke it, so she says. Oh God. I did without nearly every pleasure in the world to put her through school, keep her healthy and safe, and keep a roof over our heads for twenty-two years. She earned a degree in business from the College of Charleston that I completely paid for with just a smidgen of help from my parents and nothing from her father. Next, her father, Mark—who, as you know, never called or sent money or remembered her birthday?—well, he finds her through Facebook and tells her how much he loves her and wishes he could see her. At first, I thought, Well, it's about time."

"Yeah, but I can see how you might have mixed feelings about him just jumping back into her life without checking with you first."

"I know and you're right. I did feel uneasy about that. But he's her birth father and it never occurred to me that he could influence her choices so easily. She's pretty stubborn."

"I don't blame her for wanting at least to know who he is, you know . . . did she look like him and all that."

"Right. That's reasonable. So, first there was a lot of chatter on Facebook, and then, out of nowhere, last January he bought her a ticket to come and visit him. She was twenty-three years old and she didn't know her dad and she wanted to, so, reluctantly and with a whole lot of trepidation, I let her go."

"I'm sure I would've done the same thing."

"Thanks for saying that but I can tell you it was a huge mistake for me to support it at all. She gets out there, and with his stupid ideas about opportunity knocking, he helps her set up this crazy business. It's called High Note Travel. I should've been smarter."

"High Note Travel? Please tell me you're kidding," she said.

"I wish. It's on the Internet and Facebook and all over the place. All anyone has to do is go on her site and click their way to an all-inclusive package to stay stoned for as long as you'd like."

"Oh, Lisa. This is terrible. You're not an old biddy one bit."

"Wait! It gets worse! The package includes airport transfers, pot-friendly hotels that have THC in the candy bars in your welcome basket, tours of dispensaries, tours to glassblowers who make these things you use to smoke—I mean, I'm a medical professional and my only child is practically a drug dealer!"

"But it's legal, isn't it?"

"I don't care if it is! I still think drugs are immoral. That's just how I was raised."

"Well, me too."

"Why can't she see how difficult this is for me to reconcile? Someone says, 'Oh! What does your daughter do for a living?' What am I supposed to do? Tell the truth? Then they'll say, 'Oh! How hilarious that you're a nurse and your daughter helps people get high.' It's just mortifying."

"I see your point. Gee, what a mess."

"Yeah. So, Mark Barnebey feels like Marley's chains to me. I can't shed them or him. And now he's got his ridiculous ideas in her head and she's making more money than all of us put together. And I'm the bad guy because I'm not proud of my daughter's success."

"This has to just break your heart," Suzanne said.

"Today's her birthday. She twenty-five today. After I practically starved to give her a life, this is my reward."

I had sent Marianne a card and a framed picture of us taken when she was little, but I would have given anything to be making a cake for her instead.

"Well, maybe this is just a fad. Or maybe competition will squash her. I can see lots of folks wanting to make money from this. I mean, what's to stop Expedia or someone like that from squeezing her out?"

"Honestly? I wish they would. Anyway, we have had so many terrible arguments about it that now we hardly speak. She doesn't answer my calls or texts or anything."

"What a shame," Suzanne said. "This is one of those situations that requires prayer."

"Or maybe a miracle. Now, look. In the case of medical marijuana? That's different. If somebody's hurting or having seizures or there's a condition that can be helped by it? Okay, I understand that. You know, like Carrie giving Kathy pot brownies. I get it. But I have to tell you, it's not legal in South Carolina. So it's probably best that y'all keep that to yourselves."

"It was Carrie's idea. I wouldn't know where in the world to find it."

"Ha! Ha! Poor Carrie! Under the bus! You okay, Carrie?"

"Okay, okay. I knew what she was up to. But she baked them, not me."

"Well, it doesn't matter now. Anyway, I cannot say that I am thrilled with my daughter. At all."

I leaned down and pried a sand dollar out of the wet mud. It was in perfect condition.

"Wow!" Suzanne said. "You hardly ever see those things whole."

"That's true." I slipped it in the pocket of my shorts. "You ever hear the story about the doves in these things?"

"Only a billion times. Why?"

"Well, one variation says the doves are the Holy Spirit. So I'm going to take this shell as a good sign. When I get home, I'll call Marianne and tell her I love her."

"Well, I'm no expert on children, but I do know you have to keep the door open."

We turned around and started walking back. I gave Pickle a whistle and she fell right in step with us.

"Miss Trudie seems fine to me," I said. "But if she falls again, she ought to let a doctor take a look at her."

"Oh, absolutely! Thank goodness she wasn't really hurt. I would have had to call my sisters and tell them about it because they'd pitch a fit if anything happened that they didn't know about. Not that they'd get on a plane and come visit. And it's not like they'd actually take care of Miss Trudie if she got sick. They stop in Charleston overnight on their way to Europe. You know, when it's not a terrible inconvenience for them."

"All families are dysfunctional. I don't know one that isn't."

"Boy, is that ever the truth."

"Where do they live?"

"Alicia's in Los Angeles and married to Giles. And Clio lives outside of Chicago and she's married to Ben. I wish we all got along better."

"I feel the same way about my brother and his wife. They think money is the only measure of success. They're idiots."

"My sisters' husbands think the same way. Like the fireman who pulls them out of a burning building isn't successful? Or the teacher who teaches their kids to love literature or math or history isn't successful? My sisters used to be nice, but over time Clio and Alicia guzzled their husbands' Kool-Aid. Now they're idiots too."

"It would be easier to like them if they didn't have so much money. Isn't that terrible?"

"Well, yeah! But, Lisa, that's not all there is to it. The very nature of how they go about their day has nothing in common with mine. Starting right here! You and I walk the beach. They have personal trainers."

"That's not the problem with my brother. He'd never spend the money on a trainer. He's so tight he squeaks when he walks. My poor sister-in-law. I can't imagine what it's like for her to live with him."

"Where do they live?"

"On a farm outside of Boone, North Carolina. Can you imagine? If she needs milk and bread she has to drive ten miles."

"I imagine the cost of living is less out in the country?"

"It's gotta be or they wouldn't be there. It's pitch-black dark at night. You can't even see your hand in front of your face. Not even a streetlight! I've been there. It's so quiet at night it scares me to death!"

"I think it would scare me too. I'm used to hearing the ocean and the occasional car whizzing by."

"I'm too social to live in the country."

"Me too."

Later, when I got home and showered, I waited until ten o'clock to call Marianne and wish her a happy birthday. My call went straight to voice mail. I felt my heart sink. She would see my number on caller ID and call me back, wouldn't she? I waited an hour and called her again, telling myself she couldn't take my call for any number of reasons. This time I left a message.

"Hi, sweetheart. It's just your mom calling to wish you a happy birthday. This is our special day, you know. I hope you got my gift. Now listen, I don't want you to think about the twelve hours of excruciating pain I suffered to bring you into the world. And I don't want you to think about everything I gave up in the last twenty-five years so that you would not have to pay off student loans. I just want you to know that I love you and I miss you very much. Happy birthday, baby!"

I pushed the "end call" icon and looked at my phone. Would my message make her mad? Probably. But when I told my secret to Suzanne she had agreed with me. I wasn't an old biddy after all. Nonetheless, Marianne was avoiding me and that wasn't nice either.

I decided to call my mother and see if she had spoken with Marianne.

"Hi, Mom! It's me. Got a minute?"

"Of course! Hold on just a second so I can turn the stove off."

I heard her put her phone down and walk away. Then I heard her footsteps coming back.

"It's Lisa! Yes! I said it's Lisa on the phone!"

"Mom? Are you wearing high heels?"

"I swanny to Saint Pete, your father is as deaf as a doornail! I keep telling him to put in his hearing aids and he says he can't remember where they are. This getting-old business is a pain in the derriere! Now, what did you say? Am I wearing what?"

"High heels?"

"Well, they're not that high. I'm going to a lunch at Andy Bertsche's house and I'm bringing my world-famous deviled eggs with chopped shrimp and minced chives. They are so good!"

"You do make the best deviled eggs, Mom. You surely do."

"Okay. What's going on? I can hear it in your voice."

"Have you spoken to Marianne? Today's her birthday, you know."

There was a short period of silence on the other end of the phone while she considered my question.

"I think it's time for you to tell me what the problem is between you two. I mean, I want the truth."

"Then you'd better tell Daddy to pick up the extension."

"All right. *Alan? Alan? Go pick up the extension! Lisa has something to tell us! Alan?*"

Dad picked up the phone and said, "I'm not deaf, Carol! I heard you the first time! Hi, Lisa. How's my girl?"

"Oh, I'm okay, I guess."

"Lisa is finally going to tell us why she and Marianne aren't speaking."

"Okay, I'm ready," Dad said.

"You know she owns a travel business that caters to high-end travelers?"

"Yes, and that she's very successful," my mother said.

"Well, what you have not put together until now is that recreational use of marijuana is legal in Colorado."

"So what does that have to do with my granddaughter?" Mom asked.

"I heard about that. People do crazy things everywhere," Dad said.

"Y'all? One of the reasons people go to Colorado is to smoke pot. Marianne has people who visit her website who want to get stoned and she makes it happen for them."

"What did you say? I don't think I heard you correctly."

"Yes, you did. She picks them up at the airport, she books a pot-friendly hotel for them with pot waiting for them in the room, and she takes them on tours of pot shops, and I have a problem with that."

"Oh, my dear Lord. I think I'm going to faint," Mom said.

"Get a grip on yourself, Carol. It's legal, isn't it? I mean, Marianne isn't doing anything illegal, is she?"

"No, it's not illegal but it's certainly not morally right," I said. "And she promised me that she's not smoking it herself."

"I've got to sit down," Mom said.

I heard a kitchen chair being dragged across the floor. Then I heard her sigh so hard it sounded like a gale of wind.

"All right, ladies. Here's what I don't understand," Dad said. "Nobody's getting hurt, are they?"

"Actually, there have been several instances, probably many but I only know of a few, where people have smoked too much pot and they had to go to the hospital. The problem is most people new to it don't understand its potency."

"Dear God," Mom said. "Please tell me this isn't true."

"Sorry, but you've been hounding me for an answer and here it is."

"So, help me get this through my head," Mom said. "How does she justify this?"

"Well, she says now that marijuana's legal, an entire new population of people are coming to Colorado to get high. And that the general public is better served if those people who are smoking pot for the first time have some supervision. Apparently, there are all sorts of pot that bring on different effects. Some make you hungry, some make you laugh. And while that may be true, as a registered nurse, I cannot condone the recreational use of drugs that are illegal here. She's so defiant you wouldn't believe it. She says it's a free country and she's not breaking any laws and I should be proud of her because she's running a successful business! Can you imagine that? Be proud of her? For facilitating drug use?"

"It's unbelievable to me," Mom said. "Shameful. This does not reflect the way you raised her, Lisa. It does not."

"That's right. It's the influence of her father. He could always justify anything."

"Wait a minute," Dad said. "Would you say the same thing if she had started a vineyard out in Napa Valley?"

"Of course not," I said. "That's an entirely different thing."

"Is it?" he said.

"I'm sorry, Alan, but I'm taking sides with Lisa on this one."

"Dad? Should I run down the street and brag about this? Should I brag about this to the medical staff at Palmetto House?"

"Of course not," he said. "It almost always pays to be discreet."

"Look, if prostitution was legal would that make it okay?" I said.

"It's legal in Nevada the last time I checked," Dad said.

"Well, don't tell Marianne or her father that. The next thing you know they'll be running houses of ill repute," I said.

"What were you doing checking on legal prostitution?" Mom said. "Is there something you want to tell me, Alan?"

"I think prostitutes are disgusting," Dad said. "The very thought of one repulses me." And then he started to giggle. "I've learned so much from Siri."

"Oh, boy," I said. "What is this world coming to?"

CHAPTER 9

Dreaming Green

Marianne never returned my calls yesterday. My only child who carries my blood in her veins made me cry on her birthday. I thought it was so mean to deliberately hurt me when she knew I loved her so very dearly. Surely there had to be a part of her, one brain cell perhaps, that realized the conflict I would have with the way in which she had decided to earn her living? I consoled myself a little with the knowledge that she was healthy, solvent, and probably having the time of her life when she wasn't faced with me. But I had really hoped that the picture I sent her would break down some barriers. She was so precious when she was a little girl. That picture of her grinning and riding her bicycle without training wheels for the first time was irresistible. I was in the background clapping my hands like the very proud mother I was. Could she be that hard-hearted? All she really had to do to make things right was just acknowledge my issue with her business and perhaps reassure me that it wouldn't go on forever, that she had other dreams too. Jesus, just throw me a bone!

It was early in the morning, and as soon as I finished watering my tomatoes and basil, I'd be on my way to work. The thermometer was expected to climb to one hundred sweltering degrees. Again. Throw in the humidity and the world would feel like a steam bath. The heat was just one more thing to deal with but at least it distracted me from dwelling on my disappointment with Marianne. I put the watering can back under the kitchen sink, begged the tomatoes not to explode, and filled Pickle's bowl with fresh water. I opened her food and filled her dish.

"It's just you and me and Bobby McGee, babe."

She was so excited to see breakfast she didn't respond.

I wished I could take her to work with me. I hated leaving her at home. But my consolation was that John and Mayra would look in on her several times during the day and they would walk her. I loved living next door to them. And I suspected she spent more time in their house than mine.

"It's like having a granddog!" Mayra always said. "She's a sweet baby!"

John and Mayra Schmidt, for whatever reasons, had never had children. And frankly, at that moment, having children seemed overrated to me. They were so affectionate with Pickle it always made me think what wonderful parents they would've been. I wondered what they would say if I told them the truth about my Marianne. They would probably faint dead on the floor. That reminded me that I had to start looking for a place to hang my hat. I sure would miss them.

I pulled into the parking lot at Palmetto House and began my routine of unfurling my sunshade across the dashboard of my car and gathering up my things. There was a tapping on my window and I turned to see Paul standing there smiling. I gulped, opened my door, and got out.

"Good morning! Where were you yesterday?" he said.

"Good morning! Oh, I don't work every day."

We were standing face-to-face then and he looked at me curiously.

"You don't?"

"No, just part-time."

"You okay?"

"Oh, sure. I'm fine." He had the same molten chocolate-brown eyes as he did the last time I saw him. I realized then that his lips also carried some sensual promise. There was the hint of an adorable dimple in one of his cheeks. I must be losing my mind, I thought.

"It's not me, is it?"

"Oh! Goodness no! I just—"

"Somebody took the wind out of your sails, didn't they?"

"Yeah, I guess. Sort of. It's okay."

"Listen, I have an excellent idea. When do you finish for the day?"

"At four this afternoon."

"You need cheering up. Why don't we take a ride over to Sullivans Island and try the gelato at BeardCats? Then we can go upstairs to The Obstinate Daughter and get a bowl of pasta? I've been wanting to go there."

"Eat dessert first?" I said.

"Why not? Life's short, right?"

I started to giggle. He was absolutely irrepressible and it was contagious.

"You don't have to tell *me*. Okay. Wait! Is this a date?"

His face became very serious and he said, "I don't know. Why?"

"Because then I'd have to wash my hair. I haven't been out on a date in at least five years."

"Please. It's not a date. Don't go to any trouble. I just want to talk to you about compliance with the Americans with Disabilities Act."

"Why do men always want to talk about the ADA with me?"

"Because you're so well versed in the nuances. Now tell me where you live and I'll pick you up at six?"

"Oh, you can't pick me up! What if you're a psycho killer? I'm told it's very dangerous to give someone your address if you don't really, really know them."

"Okay, so if I text you my résumé and you find it acceptable, would you reconsider?"

"Maybe. No, wait. Yes."

"Okay, so then may I please have your cell number?"

He pulled his iPhone from his pocket and I dutifully recited my number while he entered it. My phone rang. I answered it.

"Excuse me for a moment," I said, and stepped away. "Hello?"

Duh. It was Paul calling.

"Guess who?" He was laughing so hard. I thought, I am a total nitwit. I started laughing too. "Eventually I will have your home address and I will pick you up at six. Is that okay?"

"Yes," I said, and thought, Oh no! I have a date!

"Okay, then. I'll see you later. Don't forget to check your messages. My résumé?"

"Right." I felt woozy. And I don't think it was heat-induced. It was, God help me, hormonal. "See you later."

"Yep, you will."

Later on, after I had delivered the prescribed medicines to our patients, I was back at the nurses' station. Sure enough, Paul texted his résumé to me. What had I done? I started reading. Then I started talking to myself out loud.

"Undergraduate work at Cornell. Not bad. Graduate work at Yale. Okay, so he's a genius . . ."

"What are you reading? Who's a genius?" Margaret said.

"Oh! I didn't see you there! This guy Paul." I showed her my smartphone. "Glazer? Glicer? I can't pronounce his last name. He's a complete brainiac. How do you pronounce this?"

"I don't know. Gleicher? Boy, I sure can sneak around in these shoes. You wouldn't believe what I run into."

"Oh, yes I would."

"Who's Paul?"

I looked up and there stood Judy and Margaret, waiting for an answer.

"He's Kathy Harper's long-lost flame, though, and he's super-smart and nice. And he's actually the architect who's building the Green House Project houses."

"No kidding? You sure have a funny look on your face. What's going on?" Margaret said.

Judy said, "Heck, I know that look. She's been bit by the Love Bug!"

"And you don't even know how to pronounce his last name. Come on, Lisa. You've got to do better than that," Margaret said.

"I'll find out. We're going out tonight," I said, deciding Cornell and Yale were beyond my expectations and I should at least find out who he was. I mean, who was I kidding? It wasn't like there were throngs of men lined up to take me out to dinner.

"We'll be expecting a full report in the morning," Margaret said.

When I was leaving for the day I passed the card room. Marilyn

Brooks was playing a game with Mr. Morrison and Mrs. Richards. All of them were smiling and chatting. That did my heart an awful lot of good. Whatever awkwardness may have lingered after the duck-in-the-shower incident had apparently dissipated to the point that no one seemed embarrassed. Or maybe Mr. Morrison and Mrs. Richards had decided to forget it ever happened. I'd take a guess that Marilyn Brooks had not heard the story. I decided to say hello.

"Well, good afternoon!" I said. Mr. Morrison started to get up. "Please don't get up! I'm just saying hello. How are y'all doing?"

Marilyn said, "I have to tell you, Lisa. I was saved by a turkey sandwich with cranberry sauce." They looked at her like she was crazy. "And a very nice nurse."

"The turkey here is sprinkled with a little Lowcountry magic," I said, and smiled.

"It must be!" Mr. Morrison said. "Mrs. Richards and I have been looking for a good cardplayer for the longest time. And our Lowcountry magic delivered up our Mrs. Brooks!"

"We might start a poker club," Mrs. Richards said.

A nightmare of these rascals playing strip poker ran through my head and I pushed it away. Surely they wouldn't be able to cajole someone as dignified as Marilyn Brooks into something so risqué. But the persuasive powers of Mr. Morrison were legendary and I decided to keep an eye on them.

"That sounds like fun!" I said. "See y'all later!"

I got in my car, texted Paul my address, and drove home. Every so often I'd say "I have a date" to the thin air and laugh out loud. It was so silly really and I knew it, but hey, I had a date. I opened the front door and my dog all but tackled me.

"Hey, sweet girl! How's my baby?"

Lick! Lick! Lick!

"Oh, now I definitely need a shower, and as long as I'm in there I may as well wash my hair. Did I tell you I have a date tonight?"

I showered and blew out my hair. The big problem with chemically enhanced blond hair is you get dark roots pretty fast. Dark roots might be trashy but white roots are old. I didn't have time to do my color and I wasn't even sure I had things like eyeliner and mascara. I probably did have some makeup somewhere because I had used it for my parents' party, but was it contaminated? Would it give me sudden-onset conjunctivitis? That would be attractive.

What in the world was I going to wear? I checked the website for the restaurant and it looked pretty casual. Most of what I owned was uniforms. I managed to dig around my closet and found a pair of white pants and a pink linen shirt that was reasonably new. I had white sandals but no recent pedicure. So, this might sound really cheesy, but I found my nail polish and just painted over what was already there. Two coats. It didn't look bad at all and it wasn't like Paul was going to get out a bottle of nail polish remover and discover that I had, horror of all horrors, painted over an old pedicure. I found the mascara, sanitized the brush with alcohol, and applied it only to the tips of my lashes. I sharpened my eye pencil so it had a fresh tip and used it along my upper lids. I sprayed some cologne on my neck and wrists and gave my lips a swipe of a rosy gloss. Then I looked in the mirror. Well, I decided, I'm still tall and I'm not too fat and my hair's clean and he'll be able to see I made some effort in the cosmetic department.

"Not too bad," I said, and the doorbell rang.

Pickle, of course, started going insane. We were unaccustomed to company. I hurried to get her away from the door before she ate her way through the wood trying to protect me. I picked her up in my arms.

"It's okay, girl," I said. "It's Mommy's friend."

I opened the door.

"Hi!" I said to Paul, who had showered and put on fresh clothes too. "This is my crazy sweet baby, Pickle." I put my dog on the floor and she stared at him.

To his credit, he leaned over slowly and extended the palm of his hand for her to sniff. When she decided he was a benign presence she gave him a slurp.

"You look so pretty, Lisa," he said.

"Oh! Gosh!" I didn't know whether to slam the door, run to my room, and hide under the bed, but I sure felt a wave of panic course through my veins. Somehow I managed to say, "Thanks! I'll just get my bag."

He stepped inside and my little Westie just sat by his feet, looking up at him, waiting for some adoration. He leaned over and scratched her behind her ears and Pickle made a funny little guttural noise. At her stage in life, if a human didn't just almost drool on her, there was something wrong with the human. But that guttural noise was one she saved for states of bliss.

"Let's go," I said to him. "I think she likes you."

I closed the door and locked it. I could hear Pickle yipping as we walked to his car as though she was telling us, *Hey! Come back! You forgot me!*

"Cute dog," he said, and opened the passenger-side door.

"She's not a dog," I said, and slipped into the car as demurely as I could.

"Oh no? What is she, then?"

"She's a teenaged girl," I said.

He laughed and closed my door and came around to the driver's side, getting in.

"Named Pickle. As I understand it, teenaged girls can be petulant, demanding, sulky, and an all-around pain in the butt."

"Some are worse than others," I said. "With me? I just give her everything she wants. So she's a little bit rotten."

As he backed out of my driveway, I saw Mayra peeking through her venetian blinds, so I gave her a little wave. The blinds quickly closed. We turned toward Coleman Boulevard.

"I had a golden for fourteen years. His name was Jake. Best friend I ever had. When he died, I died."

"I can't even imagine life without Pickle. My daughter, on the other hand?"

"Oh, does she give you a run for your money?"

"You have no idea."

Soon we were sitting on a bench outside of BeardCats, lost in the wonders of Italian gelato, a gift from all the gods to us to remind us of the heavens. And although it was early evening, the gelato was melting quickly. We ate with alarming speed. Well, I did. It was just about the best ice cream I'd ever tasted.

"I would never have thought you could make gelato with olive oil and sea salt and that it would be this delicious!"

"I know! Here, taste this. It's just pistachio but it tastes just like it's supposed to. This reminds me of the gelato vendors on the Ponte Vecchio in Florence."

Despite the possibility that I might contract an infectious disease, I leaned in and took a lick. "Wow!" I said. "That's amazing! Do you mean Florence, South Carolina?"

"Italy. Florence, Italy."

"I'm kidding, Paul." No, I wasn't. Geography was never my thing. And who memorizes the names of bridges? Architects! Not nurses. Thank you.

"Of course you are. Anyway, way back when, during my junior year I spent a semester in Italy, trying to learn about all the great cathedrals and so on. But what I really learned was how to appreciate gelato and pasta and local wines. And this really ancient bridge, the Ponte Vecchio, has all these tiny shops right there on the bridge. You can eat gelato, go next door to buy a pair of Italian leather gloves, go next door and get some earrings or a chain, and then go to the next store and have more gelato."

"That must've been a fabulous experience," I said.

"Well, it was a long time ago, but yeah, I still love Italy and gelato and pasta. And when I go there, I always drink the local wines. Have you ever been to Italy?"

"No, not yet. I haven't really traveled too much. Oh no! This is dripping down my arm!" He handed me a napkin and I cleaned up. "Thanks! Colorado a couple of times but that's about it. And I've been to the islands a few times."

"Well, where would you go if you could go anyplace in the world?" he asked.

"Hoo! Loaded question! Well, a few places come to mind. Italy, definitely. And as long as I'm already in Europe, I'd try to go to France. And England for sure! But I'd also like to see to some other places, like India."

"India? Why?"

"Yeah, and Thailand. Because they're exotic to me and I was into yoga for a long time, which fed my curiosity about Hinduism and Buddhism. I mean, didn't you ever ask yourself how is it that all these really poor people in India are so happy? I'd love to see that for myself. And I love Thai food and Indian food."

"So do I but is there any really authentic Thai food in town? I mean, I love Basil's like the rest of the world, but I'd like some un-Westernized Thai."

"Yeah, there's actually a really good Thai restaurant west of the Ashley. I'll get the name for you. I'm pretty sure it's called Taste of Thai."

"Hey, I'll tell you what. If we're still speaking after tonight, I'll take you there!"

I looked at him and his sly grin. Then I stood up and threw the remains of my cone in a trash can. I was practically full from the gelato but I wasn't ready to go home. Oh, hell no. I liked him and I loved Thai food.

"That sounds like a deal," I said.

We climbed the stairs to the restaurant and stepped inside. It was very slick with baby-blue bar stools that reminded me of the ones I had in my yoga studio. And it was packed. Regrettably, I was probably not their target customer. But as I looked around while Paul spoke to the hostess, I saw that people my age were there, couples who would be contemporaries of my parents, families, and young hipsters. That was a great relief. Suddenly I felt at home. Why should the young and hip have all the cool restaurants to themselves? I liked The Obstinate Daughter right away. In fact, it might become my favorite. Wait a minute, I go out to restaurants maybe twice a year. Diners were my specialty. Still, it could be my favorite.

A young man with a well-groomed dark beard led us to our table. He didn't seem old enough to grow one much less be wearing a wedding ring, which he was. I was getting old. He was probably thirty but he looked like a baby to me. That's what happens as you age. While everything is starting to sag, your judgment goes to hell. Paul and I slid into a booth and sat opposite each other. The young man handed us menus.

"I'm Jonathan Bentley, one of the managers. Have you dined with us before?" he said.

"No," Paul said, "but I've wanted to come here and see what y'all have done. Gosh, it didn't look like this when it was Atlanticville. Not even a little bit! This is just gorgeous. Y'all are a certified green restaurant, aren't you?"

"Yes, we are."

"I'm a LEED architect, which is—"

"No kidding? No, I know all about it. My undergraduate degree is in environmental studies. But yeah, over half of what's here is either reclaimed or sustainable. And most of it's from within a five-hundred-mile radius, except the blue glass backsplash. That's all recycled and from France. It's pretty cool, right?"

"No kidding," I said, properly impressed.

Here was a whole new world for me. Sustainable? What was that? LEED? Lead who? Suzanne and Carrie might think Paul was a nerd but didn't nerds rule the world?

"It's wonderful," Paul said.

"Well, thanks! I'll pass that along. Can I get y'all started with a beverage?"

"Lisa?" Paul said.

I loved Paul's manners.

"I think I'd like a glass of wine, maybe a pinot grigio?" I said.

"You'll have to show me some ID, ma'am," Jonathan said, and grinned.

"Adorable," I said, and I knew we were going to have a wonderful time.

Paul ordered the same and in the blink of an eye our wine was placed before us.

"Cheers!" he said. "Now tell me why you've never been to Italy?"

"Well, I guess because until recently I was a single parent putting my daughter through college. It's not easy you know."

"I can imagine."

"You have kids?"

"No. I was married once to a certifiable head case. No kids. She's remarried and lives in Tokyo."

"Tokyo! Wow!"

"She had friends there. She married some textile guy and I never heard from her again."

So, there was no ex-wife or stepchildren to contend with. Very good.

"Oh. Anyway, I had no one to go with. I don't think Venice or Florence is somewhere I'd want to go alone. Does that sound silly?"

"Of course not. In fact, I agree with you. Sometimes business takes me to the most beautiful places and I'm always so sad to be there by myself."

"And what exactly is a lead architect?"

"What? Oh, LEED is an acronym for Leadership in Energy and Environmental Design. It means I'm a certified green eco-friendly guy."

"That's wonderful! I didn't even know there was such a thing." I looked at the menu again. "Do you know what you're going to have?"

"I want everything," he said with a laugh. "This menu is one temptation after another."

We ordered Geechie fries with salsa rosa, Mepkin Abbey mushrooms, pappardelle with sausage and tomatoes, and the special fish of the day.

"Can we share?" I said.

"Of course!"

"There's something else I wanted to ask you."

"My life is an open book. Ask away."

"You were close with Kathy Gordon, weren't you?"

"How much time have you got?"

"I've got the rest of my life," I said, and thought, Oh, the poor guy had his heart broken.

"So I met Kathy about six years ago. We met in the lobby of the Palmetto Grande movie theater in Towne Center."

"She loved going to the movies," I said, and had no idea if I was right or not. But who didn't like the movies?

"Well, it was pouring rain like you couldn't believe and I had an umbrella. She didn't. Still, it was raining too hard to go outside even *with* one. So we stood there with a lot of other people waiting for the weather to improve."

"Ah! The old damsel-in-distress situation."

"Exactly. So we were talking and I said something like 'Where are you parked?' And she told me she was parked in the same vicinity I was. Behind Belk's. Anyway, we really hit it off and the rain continued. It was a huge scary thunder boomer."

"We have some very memorable storms around here."

"No lie. Well, eventually the rain and the pyrotechnics calmed down. We wound up running across the street to this little pub and having dinner and talking for hours. She was one of the nicest women I have ever known. I miss her a lot."

"Did you know she was so ill?"

"I didn't have a clue. I would've come to see her. I felt terrible when I read the obituary. I just happened to see it. No family. Nothing. At one point, I even wanted to marry her. I even converted to Catholicism for her. Good thing I don't have any family around here. My parents would sit shiva. Anyway, these days I guess I'm more agnostic than anything."

"Where are you from?"

"New York. Anyway, out of nowhere, she broke up with me."

"Good grief!" I wasn't sure if I'd change my religion for anyone. "Why did y'all break up? Did you fight?"

"No. Never. We got along great. She just said she didn't want to commit."

"Maybe she had an inkling about her cancer."

"She never said a word if she did. Somehow, as wonderful as she was, I always felt there was something she wasn't telling me."

The server, an adorable girl with straight brown hair, put the Geechie fries in front of us. They were really fried grits rolled in eggs and seasoned flour and served with salsa. To be honest, I liked fried anything. Who didn't? I know, I know. I'm a nurse who eats fried food. But listen, I ate enough tofu for half the planet when I was Yoga Girl.

"Maybe she did have a secret that she never told anyone. Who knows?"

"Anyway, I really loved her."

"I thought the world of her too. She had such grace," I said.

"Yes. She did," Paul said, and looked across the room, remembering her. "Hey! Would you like another glass of wine?"

I had drunk my whole glass while I listened to him talk. His glass was still half full.

"Sure! Thanks!"

He caught our server's eye and ordered more.

"Now, tell me some more about you."

"Oh, gosh! Next to your life? Mine's going to put you to sleep!"

Forty minutes later I had delivered a sketch of my life to him that included my parents' story, my brother and his long-suffering wife, my ex-husband and his bunker business, my yoga studio fiasco, and finally, my daughter's venture into the world of legalized marijuana. All the while I was describing my adventures and those of my family we were wolfing down some of the most delicious food I'd ever eaten. And I was having a ball watching his eyes grow, especially when I got to the part of the story about Marianne.

"Your story is not putting me to sleep," he said.

"Yeah, I don't live in a cookie-cutter world."

"So, forgive me. We have to go back for a minute. I must have misunderstood you. Your ex-husband thinks it's perfectly fine for his daughter to squire a bunch of stoners around Aspen?"

"Yes. He says somebody's going to make money with this and it might as well be Marianne. Unbelievable, isn't it?"

"And Marianne's justification is?"

"That her business keeps stoned tourists off the road. She says they don't know where they're going because they don't know the area and they get too high because the pot is superpowerful and it's going to be a real problem for everyone's safety."

"Well, she's probably right about that. But I know how you feel. If she was mine I'd want to lock her in her room. Is she smoking it too?"

"No. Well, she says no. And unfortunately there are laws about holding adults against their will. It's called kidnapping. But I know what you mean. Anyway, medical marijuana? I get it. People going to Colorado to get toasted? I just can't. I don't know. I think there's not enough medical research that gives guidelines on how to use pot safely and wisely."

"I think it's stupid to smoke *anything* unless you're terminal or have some other circumstance that actually warrants the risk," Paul said.

"Thank you!" I said. "Thank you! So, Paul? Can I ask you something that might seem like an odd question?"

"Sure."

"Did you ever visit Kathy when she lived in a guesthouse on Wentworth Street?"

"Yep, all the time."

"Did she ever tell you where her antiques came from?"

"No. Why?"

"Because . . . well, there's a strong suspicion that her landlady stole a big chunk of her estate."

"Really? Good grief. That's terrible. Let's go to her house and get Kathy's stuff."

"It's not that simple. Did you ever visit her when she lived anywhere else?"

"No. But I still say let's go give this woman a little hell and tell her we'll call the police."

"Oh my goodness. Where have you been all my life?" I said, and laughed.

"Working on being green. It's not easy, you know." He grinned and his dimple appeared.

"Being green?"

"Yeah."

"I've heard that."

I was falling in like (maybe) with Kermit. Great.

CHAPTER 10

On the Sofa

My last thought before I went to sleep last night was that I was excited to tell Carrie and Suzanne about my evening with Paul. It felt so nice to have met someone, a man, who was sane, age-appropriate, and talented. And appealing. But when I woke up in the morning I knew there would be no beach walk that day. Rolling nickel-colored clouds covered the skies, hanging low and dark. It was raining like crazy, hard and fast blinding rain. But the wheels of the Lowcountry still had to turn, and so we were all going to get wet. Running shoes were going to squeak, hair was going to go haywire, and T-shirts were going to cling. That's just how it was.

Driving in this kind of weather gave me anxiety. It was gloomy and the roads would be slick. Drivers unaccustomed to flash flooding would hydroplane, flipping over into ditches when they slammed on their brakes. It happened all the time.

"Ugh," I said to Pickle as I opened the back door for her to go out.

She looked up at me as if to say, *Really? You want to send me outside into a hurricane for my morning constitutional?* She turned around, trotted back into the kitchen, and hopped into her bed underneath the table. She was having no part of it.

"I don't blame you," I said. "We can try again later."

I was reluctant to fill her water bowl or to feed her, for obvious reasons. I knew her well enough to know she couldn't hold it forever. At some point, she'd go out.

My shift was from ten to four that day. Maybe the storm front would move through quickly, as they often did in the summer months. I flipped on the television to catch the news. The weather report was not pretty. It was going to pour off and on all day. As I watched the ebullient child meteorologist telling us what to expect for the balance of the day and week, I wondered when it became appropriate to show cleavage at seven thirty in the morning. When I was a young woman, showing cleavage was trashy unless you were Sophia Loren.

I decided to do a load of laundry. It was one of the less pleasant household tasks on my weekly list but it had to be done. As I was dropping lingerie into the machine it occurred to me that if Paul called it might be a sign that I should invest in some underwear that actually matched. At some point, I'd consider it. I had no budget for that kind of indulgence these days. Maybe I would start clipping Victoria's Secret or Belk coupons or watching the newspapers for a sale. The very thought of having sex made me shudder and feel really self-conscious. It wasn't like I was exactly a hot babe anymore. In the next breath I told myself to keep my bloomers on and get over myself. I'd had one dinner with him. Okay, it was the best dinner and the most fun I'd had in so long I couldn't remember, but it was still only one dinner. But hadn't he said it was a blast too? Yes. But one mutually felt blast did not translate into impending nakedness.

"Pickle? Mommy's losing her mind. Want to try again?"

I opened the back door and she flew out, squatted, and very quickly zipped back in. She ran right to me and the towel I held because she knew the drill.

"Good girl!" I said, and ruffled her furry round little body until it seemed like enough and then I fed her.

She was on that bowl of food so fast I wondered how she didn't make herself sick. But she never did.

It was getting close to nine by the time I put my clothes in the dryer and an armful of towels in the washer for a second load. My delicates were really pathetic. Maybe I'd actually do a little preemptive shopping even if Paul didn't call. Heaven forbid I got in an accident with my current inventory of unmentionables. At a quarter of ten I threw the towels in the dryer and left the house, throwing caution to the wind. Am I not the wildest thing you've ever heard of, to leave the house with the dryer running?

It was still raining cats and dogs when I reached Palmetto House. As soon as I got to the nurses' station, there stood the jury.

Margaret said, "So are we going to have to wait all day for you to tell us how last night went?"

Judy said, "Must've gone pretty well because she's blushing."

"All right, you two," I said. "It was really, really fun."

"Where'd you go?" Judy said.

I gave them the pertinent facts but I was smiling so much I knew I seemed like a schoolgirl, smitten for the first time. I didn't really care.

"He sounds like a really nice guy," Margaret said.

"Yeah," Judy said. "In my day, we had to go bar hopping hoping against hope to find a decent guy who was halfway sober. Or you had to wait for someone to fix you up. And you met this one at a funeral!"

"It's called fate," Margaret said. "So? Did he put the moves on you?"

"Margaret Seabrook! What a thing to say!" I said. Is that how it was described these days?

"Well, did he?" Judy said.

"Sadly, no. Maybe next time," I said, and giggled. "If there is one."

"Hey, Judy? I'll bet you five bucks he calls," Margaret said.

"You're on," she said.

"I'll let you know. Now, I've got to administer all these medications to our patients. Oh, by the way, I could use some extra hours this month."

"What's going on?" Margaret asked.

"I need a new place to live, so I'm going to need security-deposit money and all that," I answered. "And if you hear of a rental nearby I'd love to know."

"Let's see what we can do," Margaret said. "If you get desperate let me know. I've got a sofa bed in my den."

"Thanks," I said, and hoped I'd not have to call her. I wasn't a fan of sofa beds.

Later, just as I was going to lunch, my cell phone vibrated. I looked at the caller ID hoping it would be Paul. It was Suzanne.

"Hi!" I said. "Good day for the ducks, right?"

"Yeah, the ducks are swimming all over the streets. Listen, Miss Trudie's had another fall. This time she grabbed a curtain on the way down to the floor and somehow she twisted her shoulder."

Falling down was very bad but especially at her age. You break a hip and it's the beginning of the end. Although, she was ninety-nine. Not to be insensitive, but no one lasted forever. She was so with it mentally, it made it hard to believe she was that old.

"Oh no! Is she in any pain?"

"She says not, but you know what a stoic she is. I can see her wince when she reaches out, like to open a door or something."

"She probably has a wrenched muscle. Make her an ice pack. Just like I told you the last time she fell. Pray it doesn't go into spasms. Spasms are miserable. I'd hate to think of her in that kind of terrible pain."

"Me too. Okay."

"If her pain worsens maybe someone ought to take a look at her. I can get a recommendation for an orthopedist if you'd like."

"Thanks. I'll keep an eye on her and I'll let you know."

"It's probably time to make some changes around the house. I mean, I don't want to overstep the boundaries."

"Like what? A ramp out the front door to the street? She says the day there's a ramp in this house she'll check herself into a nursing home!"

"No, no, I don't think she needs ramps, but there are lots of little things you can do to make the house safer for her."

"Like what? Dilute her gin? I've already done that."

I couldn't help but laugh at that.

"Oh my goodness! You are too much! Listen, why don't I swing by after work? I'm out of here at four."

"That would be great. Obviously, we could use some direction here."

By four o'clock that afternoon, the rain had subsided to intermittent drizzles and the sun was struggling to push through the remaining clouds. First, I stopped at home to change clothes and to walk my dog. The door was unlocked. That wasn't right. I always checked the door to be certain the house was secure. I opened the door slowly. From where I stood I could see that there were suitcases across the entrance to the kitchen where Pickle was. When she saw me, she started barking her head off and leaping into the air behind the luggage. Confused, I stepped into the living room and turned on the overhead light. There was a woman sleeping on the sofa. I nearly fainted from fright.

"Turn the light off!" she screamed.

"Who are you and what are you doing in my house?" I screamed back, leaving the door open in case I had to grab my dog and run. "I'm calling the police!"

She got up from the sofa and stared at me. She had a swollen lip that looked like someone had punched her. Her black hair was filthy dirty and she looked like she hadn't slept in a week.

"No! You listen to me. This is my house! I'm Debbie Smith, Roy and Mary Anne's daughter? I just drove here the whole way from Akron, Ohio. I'm exhausted!"

"I thought you weren't coming until August first?" I said.

What did this mean? Did I have to move this afternoon?

"Yeah, well, I had to get away from my ex-husband. He's fucking crazy."

"Oh!" I didn't really need an explanation.

"So I'm here early. I'm sorry, but you've got to pack your stuff and get out of here today. I'm too old for a roommate."

"But I have an agreement with your parents!"

"Not anymore you don't. And take your dog too. It smells."

I gasped. My dog did not smell like anything other than a clean dog. Who did this hateful person think she was talking to?

"Oh, great," I said, and thought, What am I going to do? "Okay, look. Give me a couple of hours. I don't have much here. I have to go get boxes. I am supposed to be somewhere right now to see about my friend's very elderly grandmother who had a fall this morning."

"So go see the old lady and go get boxes, and when you come back you can pack and get out. I'm sorry but I've been going through some . . ."

She sank to the couch, put her head in her hands, and began to cry. Suddenly I felt sorry for her. My phone vibrated. I took it out of my pocket and checked the caller ID. It was Paul. Boy, if there was ever an inconvenient time for someone to call, this was it. Against my better judgment, I took the call.

"Hey, Paul!"

"Hey, Lisa! I just wanted to tell you what a wonderful time I had with you last night."

"Best first date ever!" I said. "But listen, I'm sort of in the middle of something. Can I ring you back a little later?"

Debbie Smith with the skank hair and fat lip began to bawl her eyes out. I was positive Paul could hear her.

"Yeah, sure. Is everything okay?"

No, I'm homeless, I wanted to say. But I didn't.

"Just a little snag in my rental agreement but I'll get it sorted out. Call you later, okay?"

"Okay," he said. His voice sounded uncertain and slightly alarmed. "You sure you're okay?"

Debbie Smith continued to wail. Loudly.

"Yep. I'll call you back in a few minutes."

"Okay, then . . ."

"Bye bye!" I said, and touched the end call key. "Good grief." I called Suzanne. "I'm on my way to your house now."

Debbie continued to blubber.

"No problem. I just got home from work. Is everything okay?" she said.

"Oh, sure," I said. "Everything's fine."

I ended the call and thought, Oh, brother. No, everything's not okay. What am I going to do? I've got almost no money and nowhere to go. I hooked Pickle's leash to her collar and started back toward the front door. Debbie was blowing her nose with all the majesty of a foghorn. I stood there and stared at her, waiting for her to stop. Maybe I'd call Margaret and ask for that sofa bed after all.

"What are you staring at?" Debbie said, wiping her runny black Tammy Faye Bakker mascara away with the back of her fingers.

"I'll be back in a couple of hours," I said.

"I knew that."

I wanted to say, *You've got some nerve to march in here like this telling me to get out. Thanks for nothing.* But I didn't because she was so wretched. Maybe I was temporarily homeless but I had a lot more going for me than she did. She was the poster child for that old saying about there's always someone worse off than you are. Well, it's true. Besides, it's just not nice to kick someone when they're so down. But Lord in heaven with all His saints, she didn't have an ounce of grace to her name.

Pickle and I got in the car and began the drive to Suzanne's. I decided to call my mother to tell her what happened.

"Mom?"

"Hi, honey! What's going on?"

"Well, when I came home from work this afternoon, guess who was sleeping on the sofa?"

I told her the whole story and she was flabbergasted.

"Holy Mother Church! This is terrible!" she said. "What are you going to do?"

"Well, I thought about calling this woman I work with to see if I can stay there for a bit until I find something."

"Well, if you can't Daddy and I can help you. Maybe you could stay in one of those extended-stay motels for a week or so? I can send you the money but you know it would have to be—"

"I know, deducted from my inheritance. That's understood."

"I'm sorry, darling, but that's how it is. You should hear the lecture I got from your brother for spending money with my dermatologist."

"He's a horse's ass." Did my brother think my mother was too old to see a dermatologist?

"No, he's not."

"Yes, he is. I'll let you know about the money," I said. "Thanks for the offer."

"We're always here to help," she said.

We hung up and I thought, She thinks that's help? Oh, boy—which I seemed to be saying with some frequency—if I ever win the lottery, I'm just going to give it all away with no strings attached.

Then I called Paul. We chatted for a few minutes about how much fun we'd had together and he stepped up, asking for the next date.

"So, what are you doing Saturday night?"

"Well, hopefully I'll have a place to live by then," I said.

"Why? What happened to your midcentury brick façade ranch?"

"Listen to this."

I told him the story and he offered me the other side of his bed.

"I mean, I know we've only been on one date and this may seem somewhat forward, but I promise I wouldn't . . . you know, you can trust me."

He was laughing so hard and I thought, He sure is quick on his feet.

"Yeah, that's a great idea! I'll be right over!"

Men.

I told him that I was on my way to Suzanne's to help her figure out what to do to keep Miss Trudie safe and that I'd call him as soon as I knew where I'd be staying. My face was hot. I was really looking forward to seeing him again more than I'd admit. Suzanne and Carrie were wrong about Paul with the last name that had a curious spelling that in my opinion didn't match the pronunciation. Was he a nerd? Yes, if the definition of nerd was well educated, successful, interesting, and funny. And apparently he got my motor going. This was a curious developing story in the long-dormant Department of Moufky Poufky. I think you know what I mean.

I pulled into Suzanne's driveway and got out. Pickle watered the grass and then she lunged, dragging me up the front steps. She knew Lassie was in the house. I rang the doorbell. A few minutes later I rang it again, and just as I was pressing it, Suzanne appeared.

"Come in! Come in! Sorry it took me so long. I was deeply engrossed in one of those reality shows on weddings. It was the segment on the flowers, and I didn't hear the bell until just now. I keep forgetting I can watch everything online."

"Oh, it's no problem. I do the same thing."

I stepped inside with Pickle and unattached her leash. She made a beeline for the kitchen, where she thought Miss Trudie and Lassie might be found.

"Miss Trudie's upstairs in her room, darlin'!"

Don't you know Pickle turned around and headed straight for the stairs? My dog was a genius.

"Too bad she doesn't know how to make herself at home, right?" I said. "She's too shy."

Suzanne giggled and said, "Let's get us a glass of iced tea."

I followed her to the kitchen.

"Where's Carrie?"

"She wanted to stop by Bits of Lace before they closed."

Bits of Lace was a high-end boutique that sold beautiful lingerie.

"Really? I had similar thoughts this morning."

"Honey, she's a woman on a mission. You know that last guy she met from that dating service? You won't believe this. His name is John."

"Another John?"

"Well, he goes by 'Mike,' but his middle name is John. The poor thing doesn't understand he's doomed. Anyway, he's all she talked about all day long. She'll be home soon and I'm pretty sure you're going to hear the whole story about him. So, what's new with you? How was your day?"

She handed me a tall glass of tea.

"Thanks. Well, I had dinner last night with Paul."

Suzanne's eyes grew large.

"Tell me this minute! How was it?"

"Really pretty wonderful, to be honest. I mean, I like him. We went to The Obstinate Daughter . . ."

I gave her all the details about dinner and of course I told her about Paul's relationship with Kathy and why it ended. And that he would be useless in trying to solve the mystery of Kathy's estate. She was just smiling and listening.

"I'm seeing him again Saturday night," I said.

"Well, good! But this is very interesting. You know, I've been thinking. I wonder what Kathy was hiding?"

"Hiding? What do you mean?"

"Things just don't add up. I mean, along comes a really smart guy who's supernice. Not my type, mind you, but the kind of guy who would appeal to most women."

"What's your type?" I said.

"Oh, please, I only like men who are more trouble than they're worth, as you know. Anyway, he has some money and he adores her. He even converted to Catholicism, and shortly after that, just when he's ready to pop the question, she dumped him. And they didn't even have a fight? Why did she break up with him? It just doesn't make sense."

"He says she had a phobia about commitments. But who knows."

"You're right. Who knows?"

I said, "Well, like my mother says, in time, all will be revealed. Want to take a walk around to see what we can do for Miss Trudie's safety?"

"Let's do it. You want more tea?"

"Sure," I said.

We refilled our glasses. We went from room to room, picking up small throw rugs, moving ottomans from the end of club chairs and putting them against the walls. I pointed out extension cords and door saddles that could be potential hazards. We went upstairs and stopped at Miss Trudie's room.

“Miss Trudie? Lisa’s here. Can we come in?”

“Of course! Since when do you need an invitation on a silver platter?”

“Please! I just wanted to give you warning,” Suzanne said, and shook her head. “You might be watching a naughty movie or something.” She winked at me and I smiled.

“Hey, Miss Trudie!”

“Hey there, Lisa.”

As we stepped farther into her sitting room, Pickle looked up from Miss Trudie’s lap. Then she put her head back down. Miss Trudie, who was running her hand over my dog’s back, smiled up at me. My dog was mesmerized.

“Lisa offered to have a look around and help us make the house safer.”

“Why? You think I’m too old to walk now? That I can’t see where I’m going?”

“No, ma’am,” I said, jumping in. “But if the house is safer for you, Miss Trudie, it’s safer for everyone. Now tell me, what’s the matter with that?”

She stared at me, the skin all around her eyes pleated with decades of memories, and her initial anger melted into a sort of resignation. She sighed deeply.

“I may as well face the facts. I’m ancient,” she said. “Every bone in my body knows how old it is and they all creak and complain like a choir singing off-key. To be honest, even getting up from the—well you know, the place where we *sit* in the bathroom. Even that can be a risky event.”

“Well, then we are going to do something about that,” I said. “You know, there are very simple devices that can make life a whole lot easier.”

"Like what? Those horrible-looking metal bars you grab to rise from the throne? Not in *my* bathroom, thank you very much!"

"They're not all like the ones you find in a handicap bathroom at Burger King," I said.

"What were you doing in Burger King?" Suzanne said.

"Eating a Whopper Junior and washing my hands," I said. "About once a year I give in to—"

"Temptation," Miss Trudie said. "Whopper Juniors and Krispy Kreme donuts are the work of the devil."

"Yes, ma'am, they are," I said.

"All right," Miss Trudie continued. "Just nothing institutional-looking, okay?"

"I'll show you everything first," I said. "How's that? In fact, some of these companies make beautiful things."

"Fine," she said.

In Miss Trudie's bathroom we confirmed the fact that her shower had no grab bar and there were none near the toilet either. And I knew from experience that she should have lever faucets to make turning the water off and on simpler. And the bath mats were slippery.

"Probably better to get her ones with nonslip rubber backing. They sell them anywhere. I'll get some catalogs of grab bars and other things."

"That would be great," Suzanne said.

"Let's look at the soles of her shoes," I said, "because she shouldn't be wearing anything that can slide, causing a fall."

"Right! Gosh, I'm so glad you know all this stuff."

"Me too."

We checked out Miss Trudie's shoes and she had several pairs of sandals with leather bottoms.

I took a pair and went back to Miss Trudie and sat down next to her. I put my hand on her chair and Pickle moved toward me and gave my knuckles a lick.

"Thanks, baby," I said.

"Who are you calling baby?" Miss Trudie said. "Not me, surely."

I had to smile then.

"No, ma'am. My dog's my baby. Miss Trudie, I have to ask you to do something for me, okay?"

"What's that?"

She and my Westie were thoroughly lost in whatever old television show they were watching.

"Well, you see these shoes?"

"Of course I do."

"Well, until further notice, I don't think you should be wearing them."

I told her why, and when I was finished explaining her mouth and jaw were tight. She was annoyed.

"Do you know what old people worry about?"

"No, ma'am. You tell me."

"They worry about losing privileges. First, nobody wants you to drive. Then the doctor tells you he needs to run a test on this and a test on that. Every time I turn around somebody in the doctor's office wants blood. Now it's my shoes?"

"And long dresses too."

"Why?"

"Because you've taken a couple of spills. When you lean forward your long skirts and dresses drag on the floor."

"But my legs are so ugly. I don't like to look at them."

"I don't like mine either. But! It's better than looking at them in a cast, though, isn't it? Listen, you're lucky that you didn't get hurt, you know? Okay, you're a little banged up, but you didn't break a hip or have a head injury. Those kinds of accidents are very bad news."

"Oh, ho! You think I don't know that? They can be a one-way ticket to the Pearly Gates!"

"That's true. So what I want is for you to understand the advantage of certain kinds of footwear and clothing. Leather bottoms, bare feet, and socks don't create enough friction on bare floors. If you'll just consent to wearing rubber-bottom shoes, you'll increase your safety by over thirty percent."

I spoke to her as sweetly as I knew how, in the same voice and with a dose of humor that I would've used with my own grandmother. She didn't respond, so I continued, hoping she was processing what I was telling her in a positive way.

"Get Suzanne to take you shopping for some cool linen pants and comfy shirts. There's great stuff out there. Eileen Fisher is a brand that makes a bunch of things I think you might like. Not terribly expensive if you catch a sale and it's very fashionable, like you!"

I smiled at her. She was quiet for a moment. Then she smiled and winked at me.

"Suzanne? Come in here!"

Suzanne was still in the closet.

"Yes, ma'am?"

"I want you to take all my long dresses and all my leather-bottom shoes over to the Goodwill in Mount Pleasant first thing tomorrow. Then I'd like you to go shopping for some new clothes and shoes that won't break my neck. I intend to see my hundredth birthday, if that's all right with everyone."

"Sure! That will be fun!" Suzanne said.

There was nothing wrong with Miss Trudie's cognitive skills.

"And, Miss Trudie," I said, "our handyman from Palmetto House can install pull bars and replace door saddles for you. He's a retired policeman and very good with his hands."

"A policeman? Well, at least I won't have to hide my candlesticks! Suzanne, please bring me my pocketbook, sweetheart."

Suzanne handed Miss Trudie her purse, and Miss Trudie took out her wallet.

"Now, I don't want to hear a word about this," she said, handing Suzanne her MasterCard, "but I want you to take Lisa and yourself out to dinner anywhere you want to go. Where's Carrie?"

"She should be home any minute," Suzanne said, looking at her wristwatch.

"Well, take her too! My treat."

"Why?" Suzanne said. "You know you don't have to—"

"Because you girls are so nice to me and I'd like to do something nice for you. *Capisce?*"

"She dated an Italian count when she was a young chick," Suzanne said.

"I certainly did," Miss Trudie said, smiling. "He was a hunk too! Now you girls run along and let me and my little friend enjoy my show."

"Thanks," I said.

Suzanne and I went downstairs to the kitchen to refill our glasses.

"Well, thanks, Lisa, for all your great ideas. You probably just added another year to her life."

"My pleasure. Maybe more. She's really great, you know. Anyway, I'll be glad to help you get her organized. We should probably change her faucets too. You know, to swing arms?"

"Oh, gosh! Good idea! She's got some evil-looking knuckles. It must hurt like holy hell to try to turn the faucets."

"That was my thought. Anyway, you don't know of anyone looking to rent an apartment, do you?"

I told her what happened with my rental and Debbie Smith and my whole tale of woe.

"That's terrible!" she exclaimed when I was done.

The front screen door slammed and there was the distinct rustle of shopping bags. Carrie had returned.

"What are you going to do?" Suzanne said.

"I'm going to find a place to stay, that's what. One of the other nurses at Palmetto House has a sleeper sofa. She offered it to me until I can find something."

"You can't sleep on a pullout bed! You'll ruin your back!"

"Well, it would only be temporary."

Suddenly Carrie was there in the kitchen, almost bursting with exuberant smiles.

"Hey! Y'all! How're you, Lisa?"

"Great!" I said. "How're you?"

"I'm in love again! Isn't the world such an amazing, wonderful, magical place?"

Suzanne rolled her eyes and I giggled.

"What'd you buy?" Suzanne asked.

"It's not an indulgence so much as an investment," she said, pouring herself a glass of tea, gulping half of it down nonstop. "Lawsa! I was so parched! Want to see?"

She put her glass on the kitchen counter and pulled something from a large glossy shopping bag. It was wrapped in layers of carefully folded and pleated tissue paper, an exercise in origami. There was no doubt she had spent a lot of money, because what store does that anymore? She held up an aqua lace bra and panties and a matching garter belt for us to consider. They were exquisite pieces of lingerie, but a garter belt? Who even wore stockings?

"Holy hell, Carrie! This is serious!" Suzanne said. "Are you really going to wear stockings in July?"

"I won't be wearing them for long. Listen, I'm gonna tell y'all about something that's gonna blow y'alls minds. I have discovered the secret to falling in love!"

"Really?" I said. "Lingerie?"

"Oh, dear," Suzanne said. "This is going to be good. Let's talk about it over dinner. Miss Trudie's treating us to dinner anywhere we want to go."

"Wow! That's nice!" Carrie said. "Isn't she coming?"

"She's dog sitting," Suzanne said. "Anyway, give me two minutes. I'm gonna go tell her that we're leaving and see if maybe she wants us to bring her something."

"Okay," Carrie said. "So, Lisa, I met this guy last night, Michael John . . ."

"Another John," Suzanne said, over her shoulder, and of course I already knew this fact.

"I met someone too," I said.

CHAPTER 11

Keep Moving

"So, where do y'all want to go?" Suzanne asked.

"I'm okay with anywhere," I said, knowing I still had to go home that night and collect all my stuff. But to be honest, I was so irate with Debbie Dirty Hair Smith. I wasn't going to ruin my evening over her drama. I'd have dinner and then I'd deal with finding a bed.

"What about Coda?" Carrie said.

"Great choice!" I said. "I love that place."

Coda del Pesce was a very popular oceanfront Italian seafood restaurant on the Isle of Palms that had opened about two years ago. The food was delicious and fairly priced. I'd been there once and I loved it. Better yet, it was close to Suzanne's house, which made the evening's full agenda more efficient.

Soon we were seated at a table. The restaurant was full but still we somehow managed to land at a table by the windows. We ordered wine and were perusing our menus.

Suzanne said, "Now listen, y'all. Before Carrie tells us the secret to finding true love, I talked to Miss Trudie and she wants Lisa to stay with us."

"What? Wonderful!" Carrie said. "What happened?"

"Long story," I said. "Suzanne, I can't impose on you like that!"

"No arguments!" Suzanne said. "Here's why it's a good idea. Pickle won't have to be alone when you're at work. It doesn't have to be forever, of course. And you can help me keep an eye on Miss Trudie because I know that she's . . ."

"Getting frail," Carrie said. "It just breaks my heart, y'all. It truly does."

The waiter put our glasses of wine in front of us.

"Thanks," Suzanne said. "So, Lisa? What do you say?"

"Oh Lord," I said. "Well, it's unbelievably nice of you, so okay, thank you. Just until I find something. Ugh. After supper I have to get my things."

"Is anybody going to tell me what happened?" Carrie said.

I regurgitated the awful story of Debbie with the fat lip, and Carrie was visibly disturbed because the story hit too close to home.

"You see? This is what can happen to women like us! This is just like what John's kids did to me. One day I'm a bride, marrying millions, and that afternoon, I'm a broke widow."

"Because we don't have enough security," I said.

"Humph. We don't have any. I'd like to yank Debbie's hair right out of her head," Suzanne said. "I don't understand why people just can't be nicer to each other. What's the matter with a little personal consideration?"

"Gosh, is that ever the truth. Listen, Lisa, we can help you get your things," Carrie said. "Moving is my specialty!"

We started to laugh.

"And so you know?" Suzanne said. "Moving you in was Miss Trudie's idea. Don't let me forget to bring her an order of fried calamari. She'll have my head."

"Thank you and here's to Miss Trudie, who saved the day!" I said.

We raised our glasses and clinked the edges.

"She's a helluva girl," Carrie said.

"Yes, she surely is!" I said in agreement. "So, Carrie? What's the secret to love?"

Carrie's eyes began to sparkle. She took a deep sip of her wine and leaned in across the table to be sure we could hear her.

"Okay, y'all. Did you ever hear of a guy named Arthur Aron?"

We shook our heads.

"Well, he's a famous psychologist up in New York City."

Suzanne and I shook our heads again.

"Okay, so about twenty years ago he devised this experiment where two people who never met each other got together in a lab. They asked each other a series of questions that took a couple of hours to answer and then they stared in each other's eyes for like four or five minutes. It's called gazing. Anyway, six months later they tied the knot!"

"No!" I said. "No way!"

"Yes, they did! I'm not kidding!"

"That is unbelievable. I heard you talking about this earlier today but I was too busy to really pay attention," Suzanne said.

"I know," Carrie said, pretending to be miffed.

Suzanne leaned in then. "Not that I want to fall in love with anyone, but what kind of questions are they?"

"See? I knew y'all would want to know. Well, they start out with really basic things, like, if you could have dinner with anyone in the world, who would it be? Then they get deeper and more personal as they go along. Y'all, there are only thirty-six questions. We are only thirty-six questions away from the possibility of everlasting love."

"It's got to be based on some premise, like if people really talked to each other they'd be closer. Do you have a copy of these questions?" I asked.

"You know I do. I made a copy for y'all." She leaned down to her purse and pulled out some papers. "It's how I fell in love with Michael John Kelly. And you know what?"

"What?" Suzanne and I said.

"He's in love with me," Carrie declared. She sat back in her chair and looked at us, smiling. "Y'all? These questions are a daggum gold mine!"

Suzanne looked at me. "Go through them with Paul and let's see what happens! I dare you!"

"Oh, I don't know. I'm not sure I want to hear his answers. Or mine."

"Who's Paul?" Carrie asked.

"Remember back at the house I told you I met someone too?" I said.

"Oh my goodness, you surely did! And here I am running my mouth about me! I've got the me-me's tonight. I'm so sorry!"

"No, it's okay," I said, and thought, okay, she's a little self absorbed sometimes but she had taken a recent beating from her ex-stepchildren and buried three husbands so who could blame her?

I looked at the list of questions again. They seemed so innocuous.

"What's the worst thing that could happen?" Suzanne said to me. "You'll fall in love with a successful architect and be happy for the rest of your life? Besides, I'm telling you, when Miss Trudie goes to that big gin joint in the sky? We're all on the street!"

"You keep saying that and I hope you're wrong," Carrie said.

Suzanne was right. I had nothing to lose. I was going to give it a whirl.

"So who is Paul?" Carrie said again.

"The tree hugger," Suzanne said. "The guy Kathy used to date."

"There's more to him than meets the eye," I said.

"Hell, honey, Suzanne and I want the best for you just like we do for each other. Ask him the questions and you'll find out more about him in one night than you would in a year. I'm not kidding."

"I just might do it," I said. "But I don't believe I need a man to survive, do y'all?"

"Obviously not," Suzanne said.

"I sort of do but I wish I didn't," Carrie said. "Who can live on a schoolteacher's salary in the south?"

"Anyway, after dinner we can all go to your house with all our own cars and load them up," Suzanne said. "Do you think we need more than one trip?"

"I don't think so," I said. "I hope not. The less time I have to spend with that woman the better."

An hour later we were leaving my old house, our trunks and backseats loaded to the hilt. Carrie stopped in the driveway.

"You know what?" she said.

I threw another two armloads of hanging clothes in the back of my car and closed it.

"What?" I said.

Suzanne walked back to Carrie's car after she closed her trunk at the same time I did.

Carrie lowered her voice. "Listen, we might not have it so great, but that poor thing? Lord help her. She's a mess."

She was referring to Debbie, who was sitting on the sofa drinking cheap beer and eating a bag of bacon rinds while she watched some terrible reality show about fat people.

"No, she's pitiful," Suzanne said. "We are way better off than she is."

By ten thirty that night the move was complete. I was to occupy the extra bedroom on the first floor that apparently doubled as a storage room. The air inside was still and slightly musty. I didn't care. We opened the windows and pulled the chain on the overhead fan. In minutes, salted night breezes filled the room. Every trace of stale air was a thing of the past.

"Sorry about this little mountain," Suzanne said, referring to the dozen or so cardboard boxes that held the last of Kathy Harper's possessions. "I just haven't had the time to sift through it all."

"Well, you do have a business to run," I said.

"Yeah, there is that," she said. "You'll have to share a bathroom with Carrie. I hope that's okay."

"Gosh, I don't mind that at all," I said.

"I'm cleaning out half of the medicine cabinet!" Carrie called from across the hall.

"Thanks!" I called back.

"Can I get you anything?" Suzanne said. "Towels? Sheets?"

"No, believe it or not, I have sheets and towels. Good thing I did the wash this morning."

"Sorry the bed's not queen-sized. It's ancient but it was my mother's bed. We have a hard time giving up anything that was hers. In those days people had full-sized mattresses, if they even slept in the same bed. Remember watching *I Love Lucy*?"

"Twin beds. Yeah, I remember. The censors thought it was immoral for married people to be seen sleeping together on television," I said, and hung some clothes in the closet.

"Well, that sure didn't bother Hollywood movie makers. Remember *From Here to Eternity* with Deborah Kerr and Burt Lancaster? That scene on the beach? That must've driven the censors crazy. I mean, for its time, it was practically porn!"

"Oh gosh! I remember that! Must've been different censors. Yeah, it was pretty sexy. You know, Suzanne, I can go through some of this stuff if you'd like. It would be awfully nice to solve the riddle of Kathy's landlady, wouldn't it?"

"Be my guest," she said. "I've got three weddings this weekend and two next week."

"Let's see what I can find," I said.

Carrie came in and said, "Y'all, I keep thinking about that poor woman. Lisa, I'm so glad you're out of there. She's a complete train wreck."

"She needs to wash her hair," Suzanne said. "She must have had to escape something terrible."

"That's what I'm thinking," I said. "I hate drama."

We all said good night to each other. Pickle wandered in and got hugs and scratches from everyone. She hopped in her bed on the floor next to the dresser and curled up in a ball. The last two things I remember thinking about before I fell asleep were that my bad luck must have turned around because, even if it was temporary, I was falling asleep listening to the sounds of the ocean. And I wondered if the questions truly worked, did I want them to work on Paul Gleicher?

The morning came with strong sun streaming in through the windows and the chirps and chatters of hundreds of tiny birds in the live-oak tree right outside my room. It was all new music. I smelled coffee and bacon. Suddenly I was ravenous. After the fastest shower on record, I dressed and followed my nose.

Everyone was in the kitchen, including my dog.

"Morning! Pickle's already been out," Carrie said.

"Thanks! Good morning!" I said, and poured myself a cup of coffee.

Miss Trudie was scrambling eggs and stirring a pot of grits. Carrie was buttering toast. Suzanne was setting the table. Crispy bacon strips were piled high on paper towels. It was only seven o'clock and the house was already jumping.

"Good morning," they all said.

We peppered each other with the usual polite questions of how did you sleep and how are you feeling this fine day. Everyone seemed to have a plan. It was Saturday. Suzanne and Carrie had to dash off to work early because of the weddings. I was excited to call Paul and tell him where I was staying. I had promised to go search for ADA-compliant fixtures. Miss Trudie was going to dog-sit.

Miss Trudie spooned the creamy grits into a serving bowl, dropped in a slice of butter, and covered the bowl with its lid. Suzanne arranged the steaming scrambled eggs in the center of a platter and surrounded it with bacon. Carrie put all the buttered toast in a linen napkin that lined a sweet-grass basket. Pickle was nearly delirious from the food perfume. I filled her water bowl and fed her. She danced and danced until the bowl was put down on the floor.

"Lord love a duck!" Miss Trudie said, watching Pickle inhale her food. "She is too cute!"

"Thanks," I said. "I think she knows it."

We sat down to eat.

"Now that I have a little charge to see about, my life has new purpose!" Miss Trudie said. "Will you please pass the jam, dear?"

She nodded toward the elaborate cut-crystal jar. A small sterling-silver spoon protruded through an open notch in its lid. I passed it to her wondering if they ate like this every morning. It was just breakfast around an old kitchen table in a timeworn beach house, but it was genteel and unpretentious at the same time. I felt perfectly at home.

"It's so pretty," I said.

"Thank you," she said. "It was a wedding gift from a million years ago."

"It's so civilized to use a jam jar on the breakfast table, isn't it?" Carrie said. "Hardly anyone does this anymore."

"Because the world is no longer civilized," Miss Trudie said.

"It's true," Suzanne said. "Most people wouldn't know a jam jar if it jumped out of the bushes and bit them on the nose."

"Maybe I'll make biscuits tomorrow," Miss Trudie said. "After all, Sunday meals should have a little something extra, don't you think so, Lisa?"

"Miss Trudie, until this morning, my idea of a great breakfast was something out of my juicer, like a carrot and celery juice. For a really over-the-top, fabulous breakfast, I'd throw a little piece of ginger in the juicer along with the other stuff. This is like Christmas morning!"

"Breakfast is the most important meal of the day for me," Suzanne said. "I'm usually too busy to eat lunch and eating at night makes me gain weight."

"That's why we really chow down in the morning," Carrie said.

"Did you bring your juicer with you?" Miss Trudie asked. "I've never had a drink of carrots and vegetables except from a can of V8."

"It's still in my car but I'll bring it in. I'll make you some tomorrow morning," I said.

"Thank you," she said.

I made a note to pick up tons of things that could go in the juicer. Maybe lots of healthy juice would help Miss Trudie regain some strength. It always made me feel reenergized.

"Let me do the dishes," I said. "I'll see y'all tonight at some point."

"Would you really?" Suzanne said. "I'm starting to have a panic attack about being on time for the first wedding."

"Stop worrying!" Carrie said. "It's all set up! Besides, we've got four extra girls coming to help us. We'll be fine. But let's get going."

"Go! Go! Y'all have a great day!" I said.

I began to clear the table and run the hot water. Miss Trudie got up to leave the room. I understood then that they all liked to cook but they didn't like to clean. Neither did I, but someone had to do it. And I was better at cleaning than cooking anyway. It was a very fair trade.

"Thank you for breakfast, Miss Trudie. It was really wonderful."

"You're welcome. Don't throw out the grits. I'll make Geechie french fries with them tomorrow. Just spread them in a brownie pan, okay?"

"Where's a brownie pan?" I said.

She told me where to look. Pickle padded out of the room right behind her and I scoured all the pots and pans. It felt good to be in a bright, sunny kitchen. For the first time in I didn't even know how long, I felt calm.

Then Marianne crossed my mind. My relationship with her was the most troubling thing on my heart.

If only she would come around and see the immorality of what she was doing. She wouldn't even take my phone calls. Maybe I should call Mark and tell him that she wouldn't speak to me. Mark was a mule but he understood parental respect. Even though he hadn't done much to help me in all those years, he was grateful for my sacrifices and told me so on the rare occasion that we spoke. I couldn't decide. It didn't feel right to pick up the phone and call him. Not then and not about this. Not yet.

As soon as I was satisfied with the state of the kitchen, I called Paul.

"Hey! I'm staying with some friends on the Isle of Palms until I can find something else," I told him.

"Great! So, where are you? The address, I mean."

I told him and he said, "I'll pick you up around six?"

"That sounds great," I said. "Where are we going? You know, I have to figure out what to wear."

"Well, actually, I was planning to cook for us, if that's okay with you."

"I think that sounds fabulous. What are you going to make?"

"Spaghetti. I make killer spaghetti, if I say so myself." I could feel the laughter in his voice.

"Well then, if we're going to your place, why don't I just drive myself there?"

"Because the gentleman comes calling for the lady. At least that's what my momma always said."

"Is your momma gonna be there to chaperone?" I giggled.

"No, unfortunately, she'll be watching us from heaven. Don't worry. I promise not to try any funny business."

"Then maybe I *don't* want to come over and eat spaghetti," I said. What the hell was I saying? Since when was I so flirtatious?

There was a lengthy pause.

"Oh, come on, Paul! I'm just messing with you!"

"Um . . ." he said. "This is going to be fun."

I couldn't have agreed more.

I told Miss Trudie I was going to the store and asked her if she needed anything.

"Yes!" she said. "I need shoes and clothes. Remember?"

"Of course. Well, would you like to come shopping with me?"

"Are you kidding me? I'm ninety-nine years old, for heaven's sake. I don't need to be shuffling around a shopping mall bumping into people and their nasty germs! Besides, Pickle and I are watching a Snoopy movie at ten this morning. I already promised her."

"Oh, okay."

She gave me her sizes and said, "Bring me my purse." I got it for her from the closet. She took her Belk card from her wallet and handed it to me. "If they want me to authorize a purchase, tell them to call me. Suzanne shops for me all the time."

"Okay. See you later! Pickle?"

Pickle looked up at me.

"Be a good girl, okay?"

I have to admit my head was spinning, between thinking about shopping for Miss Trudie and getting tossed out of my house. I really had to do something to stabilize my life. The very idea that someone could just walk in my house and throw me out with no warning was not only demoralizing, it was horrifying. But was a man the answer? It just seemed like prostitution somehow. Unless I found a man who made me a better person, someone I didn't want to live without. And what were the odds of that?

I went through the sale racks at Belk's and chose a number of things I thought Miss Trudie might like. Pull-on linen pants with pockets, loose shirts and tank tops that matched. And in the shoe department I found some adorable sandals that looked comfortable and cool for the hot weather and a pair of athletic shoes and low socks for chilly nights. If she liked what I bought she could keep it, and if she didn't I'd return it. I just have to say, I never thought a crusty ninety-nine-year-old lady would be my shelter from a storm. I was so happy to be able to do something for her.

I paid for everything with her card without a problem and next I went to Lowe's. The plumbing supply houses were closed on Saturdays. I thought I'd just have a look at what they had in stock. I roamed the aisles as though I was walking a labyrinth, awed by the mountains of merchandise. Five hundred kinds of lightbulbs, hundreds of colors of paint, countless chandeliers and ceiling fans, doorbells, ladders in every size. I finally reached the bathtubs, toilets, and sinks and knew I was getting close. I spotted the fixture aisle a mere football field away and hurried over.

"Not too bad," I said out loud to no one.

Of course they had the utilitarian big fat grab bars made from PVC to every combination of chrome and brass you can dream up. I tried to remember if Miss Trudie's cabinet pulls were silver or gold and brushed or polished, and of course I could not. But I looked at the prices and decided they were very fair. It wasn't a wasted trip. At least now I knew that we had options.

Next I went to Publix and bought fruit and vegetables to make juice. I passed on the kale and opted for spinach instead. I hated kale and I didn't care who knew it. And I knew there wasn't a cavernous refrigerator back at the house, so I tried to be judicious regarding the bulk of my choices, thinking it would be best to see if the others even liked raw juices.

Suddenly I was getting shaky. I looked at my watch. Two thirty. Good! I had an excuse to buy a piece of Publix's chicken, which is so good it makes my mouth actually water when I think about it. I ate it in the car with the engine running and the air-conditioning going full blast. If my car smelled like chicken for a week it would be okay with me. The smell of fried, baked, or roasted chicken was my Chanel No. 5.

By the time I got back to the Isle of Palms and unloaded the car, it was almost time for me to shower and dress for my date with Paul. But I knew that out of simple courtesy I should show Miss Trudie each garment, wait for her to try them all on, and see what she thought. So I did.

"I look like a red-hot momma!" she said, looking in the mirror, grinning from ear to ear.

"That's your color, Miss Trudie. You should wear aqua all the time. It will look so great with your turquoise jewelry."

"I think you're right," she said. "I love all the clothes but I can't tell you that I love these sneakers. I mean, I understand why I need them. But I don't love them."

"Well, good. We'll take that for now. It makes me very happy that you like the clothes."

"I do. Thank you, Lisa. Pickle and I had a grand time while you were gone. And . . . well, it's awfully nice to have you here."

"Thank you," I said. "For everything. Yesterday wasn't exactly—"

"Lisa? There are bumps in everybody's road or else you're not really living."

"I think that's right. I'm just saying I don't know what I would've done if you and Suzanne hadn't stepped in to help me."

"It's all right now. So, don't you have a date tonight?"

"I sure do," I said. "At six."

"Well, then shouldn't you be getting ready? Or doing something?"

I started to laugh and she did too.

I showered and blew out my hair and made some attempt at cosmetic enhancement. By five forty-five I had the thirty-six questions in my purse and I was ready. Suzanne and Carrie weren't home yet, but I knew they'd had a very long day in front of them. I was sitting on the porch with Pickle and Miss Trudie when Paul pulled into the driveway. Miss Trudie sat up in her chair and looked over the banister. She gave him the once-over as he got out of his Audi.

"Good car," she whispered.

"Yeah," I said, and stood up.

He saw me.

"Hey there! Don't you look nice? You ready to go?"

"Yes, but come meet my friend!"

"Sure!" he said, and came up the front steps onto the porch.

Pickle, of course, ran to him and sat waiting for his praise and a little love. Paul immediately leaned down and gave her a good tousle and some sweet words.

"That's such a sweet girl!" he said in a baby voice. "Yes, she is!"

"Pickle, give Paul some breathing room," I said. "Paul, say hello to Miss Trudie. Miss Trudie? This is my friend Paul Gleicher."

"Hello, Miss Trudie," Paul said. "It's a pleasure to meet you."

"It's very nice to meet you too," she said. Then she smiled. "Lisa? Would you be a dear and bring me some olives before you go?"

Olives. That glass of clear liquid next to her was gin. And she wanted a moment alone with Paul. I wondered why.

"Sure! I'll be right back."

I hurried inside and scooped a handful of olives into a little dish and brought them to her.

"Here we are," I said, and put them on the table next to her. "Okay, so I guess we'll see you later?"

"Try to get home at a decent hour," Miss Trudie said. "I don't want the neighbors to talk."

I knew she was just teasing me, so I said, "Well, if we start running late should I stay out all night?"

She looked at me and laughed. "Yes, you certainly should! I don't want the neighbors to think I'm running a cathouse!" She paused for a moment and added, "Go have fun. And have fun for me too!"

"Okay! We will!"

We got in the car and Paul started backing out of the driveway.

"She's a character," he said. "Do you want to know what she said to me while you went to the kitchen?"

"I sure do."

"She said, 'Now you listen to me, young man. Lisa is a nice girl and I don't want to see her get hurt, so you'd better mind your p's and q's.' "

"Oh! That is just about the sweetest thing I've ever heard! My mother would've said, 'I don't understand why you're not taking me with you. I'm more fun than my daughter!' "

"Really?"

"Yeah, definitely. What does 'p's and q's' mean? Do you know?"

"Actually I do. Well, this isn't the only explanation. But there was an expression that came from seventeenth-century English taverns referring to a method for how the bartenders calculated the alcoholic consumption of their patrons by counting their pints and quarts. Or it might have been for figuring out the tab. But today it just means, 'you'd better behave.' "

"That's what I thought," I said. I most certainly had not ever heard that explanation and I wondered how he knew all these weird things. "If we ever play Trivial Pursuit, I want to be on your team. So, you live downtown?"

"Yep, I have a loft on Chisolm Street. It's a great location but it's probably too small for more than one person. I bought it a long time ago with the intention of flipping it, but I can work from home, so it's pretty convenient."

"Well, I can't wait to see it," I said.

We made pleasant conversation for the remainder of the fifteen-minute ride to his house. Not to sound too sappy but there was definitely some voodoo in the air between us. I thought I was too old for my hormones or pheromones to start itching for a scratch. Nonetheless, I had this ridiculous smile on my face that was more than a smirk and less than a full-on gum-baring grin. So did he. I think the term is "giddy." Yep. That's it. We were giddy.

What can I say about where Paul lived? It was one hundred and eighty degrees different from anyplace I'd ever called home; that was for sure. The loft was open and airy and very modern. It was a tiny industrially finished man cave. Exposed pipes crawled the walls and expanding tubular silver ductwork was draped through the air like the dragons that appear during Chinese New Year celebrations. No amount of fabric, artwork, or rugs could hope to soften this place. Nope. You could bring in trees and ceramics until the cows came home with the sheep and I'd still swear that no woman I'd ever known would want the credit for the decor. Its one redeeming furnishing was a gorgeous, lacquered black piano.

"So, what do you think?" he said, spreading his arms out and turning around.

"I think it's . . . um, it's sort of incredible!" I smiled and hoped I had sounded complimentary.

"It could probably use a woman's touch, right?" he said.

I shrugged my shoulders. "What do I know? I like the openness of the space. It's very different."

I walked all around the living area and peeked into a powder room. It was spotless, I'll say that much. There was a dining table near the front window and it was set for two people. And there were candles on the table, although darkness was hours away.

Paul went over to the stove in the kitchen that was smack-dab in the middle of the living area and lifted the top of a pot, peering inside. He turned on the gas under it, presumably to reheat the spaghetti sauce. I sat on a stool at the breakfast bar. He turned on the heat under another large pot, probably filled with water for pasta.

"Well, I had all these plans to decorate it but I've just been so busy and I travel too much. Basically I'm here to sleep and do a little work. Otherwise, I'm in my office or on a job site. Would you like a glass of wine?"

"Sure. Thanks. So you play the piano, I assume?"

"Not as much as I'd like to. Too busy. I hated practicing when I was a kid, but now I'm glad I learned to play. Music soothes the savage beast, you know."

"Oh, dear! Are you, you know, a savage beast?" I pretended to be horrified.

"Um, no."

He pulled the cork from a bottle of some kind of Italian red wine and filled two goblets a little less than halfway.

"Here's to you, Lisa, and to getting to know you better!"

He raised his glass in the air between us.

"And here's to you too! Thank you for this lovely evening!"

We touched the rims of our glasses. The gentle clink produced pleasant echoing notes, like slight movements of tiny crystal wind chimes. We took a sip. It was really delicious. Not sweet and not sour. I guessed it probably cost more than ten dollars, because even at room temperature it didn't make me draw up my cheeks like I had just sucked a lemon. And it didn't need ice.

"This is probably the most delicious wine I've ever tasted," I said.

"It ought to be!" he said, and laughed. "It's an '83 Barolo. I've been saving it for a special occasion."

"And I'm a special occasion?"

"Yes, ma'am."

Wow, I thought, I'm a special occasion. There was a first time for everything.

CHAPTER 12

The Fix

In the end I decided that I liked the fixtures I had seen at Lowe's better than what I saw anywhere else. I bought what Miss Trudie needed, including a little teakwood bench for her shower so she could sit down to wash her feet. The handyman from Palmetto House gladly installed the grab bars and faucets for a modest fee and Miss Trudie was tickled pink, especially with the bench.

"I never thought about putting a bench in my shower. What a wonderful idea," she said.

"They even have walk-in bathtubs now. With Jacuzzis! Maybe you've seen them on television?" I said.

"Yes, I have, but let me ask you this. You go in there in your birthday suit, correct?"

"I imagine so," I said.

"And then you have to wait around for the fool thing to fill and you have to wait for it to drain. You could get pneumonia with all that waiting around," she said. "I'll stick with my bench, thank you. That's plenty of excitement for me."

"Me too!" I said.

We both laughed and I realized again that it was still possible to make new friends. Even at my age and even at hers.

My date with Paul last Saturday night had gone really well. He had not oversold his spaghetti. It had simply been the best Bolognese sauce I'd ever eaten. Ever.

"What's in this?" I'd said. "There's something different."

"I can't tell you," he said.

"Why not?"

"Because it's a secret."

"Then I'll have to squeeze it out of you."

"That's what I was hoping for," he said.

"You bad boy," I'd said, and thought, Wow, it's okay to be silly!

I'd forgotten how much fun it was to tease and just give in to having fun. What a dreary woman I'd been. And for far too long. Of course I didn't have a crystal ball to see far into the future and find out if Paul would still be there. It didn't matter. We just liked each other and he brought out the girl in me. I was glad to know the girl was still there. We never got to go through the thirty-six questions because we were too busy talking about other things. But I told him about the experiment and he thought it was sort of incredible.

"I might be up for that," he said. "Why don't we have dinner on Tuesday and give it a whirl? There's a new restaurant on Shem Creek I want to try. It's where The Trawler used to be. Remember The Trawler?"

"No Thai food?"

"Ah! You're right. I promised you Thai food. We'll go there another time? Is that okay?"

"Of course. That sounds great," I said. "I haven't had a decent piece of fish in a while."

So Tuesday evening he picked me up at seven and very soon we were being seated in The Tavern & Table on Shem Creek. The dining room was beautiful in a rustic and inviting way.

"Gosh! Somebody spent some money on this place, didn't they?" I exclaimed.

"They sure did," Paul said.

"I remember it from another incarnation, after The Trawler. It was pretty sticky and disgusting, but they still had people lined up out the door and into the parking lot."

"That's when hole-in-the-wall eateries were chic. Now they're just holes in the wall or maybe I just got old and picky."

I thought, Wouldn't it be wonderful to afford being picky?

The young server approached our table, poured water, and recited the specials. Paul ordered some white wine—a bottle of Château de Sancerre—and we looked over the menus again. Eric, our server, had a deep golden tan, longish sun-bleached straight hair cut better than mine, and I suspected that when he wasn't waiting tables he was riding waves and chasing skirts. This suspicion was more or less confirmed when he replied to Paul's wine order.

"Awesome," he said, "great choice."

But then he stunned us when he continued.

"That particular Sancerre has truly piquant citrus notes that totally enhance the experience when it's paired with seafood, but the floral finish complements without being overpowering. The 2014 is total child abuse but the 2009 is pouring really well."

You could have knocked us out of our seats with the flick of a finger.

"I think I need a moment to give this menu the consideration it deserves," Paul said.

"Awesome," he said again, bobbing his head like a wonton just dropped into a steaming bowl of hot soup. "Totally take your time. I'll get that bottle right away."

Eric stepped away to be awesome in the wine cellar. I caught Paul's eye and we laughed.

"Nothing like a totally awesome studly sommelier to make me feel like a totally decrepit old dude," Paul said.

"Totally," I said, and giggled. "I guess he's smarter than he looks."

"Never judge a book . . . Okay, so before we ask each other the now infamous thirty-six questions that will change our lives? I'm thinking of ordering the shrimp beignets and a T-and-T charcuterie plate, and I'm hoping you'll share the whole fish with me. How does that sound?"

"As long as I can have the salted caramel *panna cotta* for dessert?"

"You'll give me a bite?"

"Of course!"

We closed our menus and looked at each other. It was that dreamy time of evening when the ambient light softens, when you need to turn on a few lights, so you do, but you use a dimmer switch. You don't want to re-create midday. You want to relax . . . And as for me, I was ready to let the Lowcountry begin its seductive magic.

I still found myself feeling too shy to peer into Paul's eyes for more than a few seconds, but I was going to have to do exactly that as a part of the thirty-six-question experiment. I hoped that by the time we reached that point it would seem comfortable. As though he read my mind, he reached across the table and covered the back of my hand with his and squeezed.

"Lisa? May I say something and will you tell me if I'm out of line?"

"Why not? Of course."

"I've been thinking about you and your daughter since you told me the story and I had a few thoughts about it. A different point of view."

Eric reappeared with the wine, so we stopped talking. He pulled the cork in a swift movement, placing it on the table in front of Paul. This kid was slick. He poured an inch or so of wine into Paul's glass and stood back. Paul gave it a swirl and a sniff, took a sip, and smiled.

"It's delicious," he said.

"Very good, sir," Eric said, filling my glass to the halfway level, and then finished pouring for Paul. "Have you made a decision about your meal? May I answer any questions?"

We told him what we'd like to have and he knitted his surfer-boy eyebrows in concern.

"Is something wrong?" Paul asked him.

"No, no. I was just thinking it would be perfecto if you had the pork-belly steamed buns to round everything out. You know, a little bit of Hong Kong meets Lowcountry? But that's your call. They would just balance all the flavors, that's all."

"Well then, bring on the pork-belly buns," Paul said, smiling.

"Yes, sir! I'm gonna bring it!" Eric laughed.

"He's a very good waiter," Paul observed when Eric was out of earshot. "He didn't even write anything down."

"I'll bet he remembers everything. No flies on him," I said. I took a sip of my wine. "You were going to tell me something about my daughter's excellent career path?"

"Yes," he said, looking pensive. "Okay, here's my thought. I think you have to take the long view on her business, and here's why. I did some Googling and it turns out that the legal marijuana business is about the fastest-growing business in the country, up to something like three billion in sales last year. That has some mighty powerful implications."

"Such as?" I said.

"Well, for one thing, every time there's a new trend, big money figures out how to get involved. Look what Home Depot and Lowe's have done to mom-and-pop hardware stores. Big money has crushed independent businesses in almost every category and I predict they will do it here too."

"Good grief. Suzanne had a similar thought but I haven't really thought it through."

"And although pot's legal in Colorado, it's still in violation of a whole pile of federal laws. So my next prediction is the timing. If the federal government decides to decriminalize the use of recreational marijuana? That's when the big guys will make their move. Could be a year, could be two. Who knows? And I'm sure they already have people in place laying the groundwork."

"So, what do you think?"

"I think you should get her on the phone and tell her to consider the fact that this might be a short-term business. Tell her she should save her money and plan to reinvest whatever she nets in something else. You know, tell her, 'Marianne? Let's be practical about this.' Tell her that while free enterprise is at the foundation of capitalism, at some point she's going to get pushed out by bigger players. There's precedent in every sector of the market. Books, furniture, clothes, food."

"You're brilliant. Do you know that?"

"That's highly debatable. Listen, it's easy for me to step back and look at this differently. Number one, she's not my child, so I don't have an emotional investment. And I completely understand why this is so offensive to you."

"It really is."

"Well, my mother always said that when I did something stupid she didn't take it personally. That's the thing. You can't take this personally."

He was one hundred percent right. It was a eureka moment of true revelation. I had personalized my daughter's choices when it was not about me at all. Marianne had not ventured into the World of Weed to offend me. She wasn't that kind of girl. She had done this with her father's support, and to be honest, that one fact infuriated me as much as anything else. She set out primarily to make money and maybe she ignored the moral questions because she simply believed her business was a legal means to a lucrative end. At least I'm sure that's what her father told her. But was she becoming a man-pleaser? Was she so deprived of a father's love that she'd do anything he told her to do?

"What about the moral aspect?" I said.

"Well, that's the issue, isn't it?"

"Yes, and there's also the fact that there's not enough medical research yet to show that weed is harmless," I said. "I just read something about a recent study that said pot can trigger psychosis in people who have paranoid personalities. Getting involved with that whole scene just seems stupid to me."

"Me too," he said. "I was just thinking you could approach this from another perspective, that's all. This angle might catch her off guard and at least get the conversation going again."

"I'm a little worried that she's doing this because her father suggested it and she's desperate to please him."

"I'm sure there's some of that in the mix," he said. "But it's not the end of the world if she is. That would be normal, given the circumstances."

This was the moment when I realized why women need men for reasons beyond procreation, carrying heavy things, killing large creepy bugs, taking out the garbage, and making our coats shiny. We need another perspective and men really do have a remarkable capacity to look at things differently. Men are just different. *Vive la différence.* Really.

"You are right. Absolutely, totally, and completely right. I'm going to call her and leave a nice message and I'm going to e-mail her too. Thank you, Paul."

"For what? I didn't do anything."

"Yes, you did. You were thoughtful."

"Well, you're welcome. I have this funny little sign on my wall in my office that quotes the Dalai Lama. It says, 'Give the ones you love wings to fly, roots to come back to, and reasons to stay.' I just always loved that."

"I love the Dalai Lama," I said.

"Yeah," he said, "me too."

Eric our waiter returned and placed the beignets in front of us and another dish too.

"These are some wicked good lobster and cheese wontons. Compliments of the chef. Enjoy!"

"Thanks!" Paul said. "Where are you from?"

"Maine, sir. Home of wicked good blueberry pie and Stephen King."

Eric refilled our glasses and left. I popped a beignet in my mouth. It was insanely good.

"Well, that was nice," I said, thinking I should ask Eric to send me a pie for my friend Judy.

"It sure was," Paul said. "Even if the food's only marginal, I'm definitely coming back here."

"It's way better than marginal. Try the beignets. So, did you ever think about becoming Buddhist?"

He took a bite of a beignet and his eyes grew wide.

"Wow! Is that good!"

"Told you!"

"No, but of all the religions and philosophies that are out there, I think I like Buddhism best. You can sum its core up in three words. *Do no harm.*"

"Good grief!"

"What?"

"I might already be a Buddhist!"

"Me too," he said, and we laughed.

"Oh! It feels good to laugh, doesn't it?" I said.

"It sure does," he said. "Now, as soon as I stuff this last beignet in my mouth, let's look at the questions."

"Sure," I said, "why not? Meanwhile this wonton is delicious."

I had brought two sets of the questions, one for each of us. And the questions themselves were divided into three sections, becoming more revealing and personal as they went along. At the end we were supposed to stare into each other's eyes for four minutes. I explained everything to Paul and we began. I went first.

"And we have to tell the total truth. Okay, so, given the choice of anyone in the world, whom would you have as a dinner guest?"

"What a question! Male or female? Living or dead?" he said.

"It doesn't matter," I said.

"I don't know. Present company excepted?"

"Of course," I said.

"Maybe John Adams. Or Carl Sagan. Or Pope Francis?"

"You only get one."

"Okay, then I'd choose John Adams."

"Why? Wasn't he supposed to be a really cranky guy?"

"I think so, but wouldn't you love to know what it felt like to be a founding father of a nation? I mean, there were no trains, no telephones or e-mail, the winters were brutal, and all the odds were against them. Nonetheless, the patriots prevailed and John Adams was in the middle of the whole thing. I'd just like to have that conversation about their amazing strength of perseverance and what it felt like to be willing to die for your convictions. I think. Now it's your turn. Whom would you choose?"

"Give me a minute."

"Sure. Are you going to eat that?"

There was one lonely wonton on the plate between us.

"No. You have it." I was going to say Jane Austen but suddenly she seemed too tame. "How about Mary, the Mother of Jesus?"

"Okay! Big name! And why?"

"Well, it had to be a very strange experience to have angels appearing and miracles happening all over the place. And obviously, I'd like to know what it was like to raise a boy who tells you he's the son of God. Her life must've been a nonstop roller coaster."

"Yeah, throw in a virgin birth and an actual physical ascension into heaven. That had to be wild."

"Paul, you know the rest of the Christian world is still unconvinced on those two points. Right?"

"Yeah, but I figure if God's possible, so is anything else."

"I've heard that said. Okay, next question. Would you like to be famous and in what way?"

"Oh my. Um, well, I think being famous probably isn't all it's cracked up to be. But I would like my life to have meant something. I'd like to, you know, leave a legacy?"

"I agree. I feel exactly the same way. Are you ready for another?"

"Shoot!"

We continued asking each other questions through the charcuterie plate and the fish. Finally the bottle of wine was empty and the *panna cotta* was consumed. Dinner had been a feast. A delicious beautiful feast.

"We're not quite finished with all these questions," he said.

"No, we're not. Why don't we ask some more in the car and then finish up on Miss Trudie's porch?"

"That's a good idea. Or we could take a leisurely stroll along the moonlit dock outside. Hmm?"

Was he saying there was romance to be had in the moonlight?

"Let's do that! Great idea."

Carrie was right about the questions. I learned so much about him that night, things that would've taken years to know. One of the questions was about naming three things we thought we had in common. I was delighted by his answer.

"Innate intelligence, a good sense of humor, and loyalty."

I said I thought our three common traits might be "curiosity and willingness to learn new things, that we were reasonably flexible by nature, and that we were both personable."

"We left off kind. We're both kind, don't you think?" he said.

"I think we might have a lot of things in common but the test only gives us three choices."

"Well, that's pretty anal-retentive, if you ask me."

"I agree," I said, and smiled. "I'll e-mail Arthur Aron in the morning."

"The guy who dreamed up this experiment?"

"Yeah, that guy."

"Well, give him a piece of my mind," he said, and laughed.

There were questions about the future and what you thought it might bring. There were questions about your greatest accomplishment and greatest regret. There was even a question about how close you were to your mother.

"I knew I couldn't get away without talking about her," I said.

Paul threw back his head and laughed so hard that I began to laugh with him.

"Wait until you hear about mine!" he said. "She was a guilt trip and a half!"

We finally got to the eye-gazing part of the experiment. We were sitting on a bench near the water. I set the timer on my phone for four minutes and we began. Well, they say the eyes are the window to the soul and I think it just might be true. For the first minute it was hard to settle down and keep looking at him. I felt very self-conscious. And then the experience moved me from self-consciousness to a place that was interesting, and finally I felt like I was in a hypnotic state. I felt transparent, as though he could see all my flaws and weaknesses but that he didn't care. My shortcomings became irrelevant, yet still I felt vulnerable. And as wacky as this may sound, I could feel understanding and affection radiating from him in waves of something not overpowering but as something warm and invited by an involuntary longing deep inside of me. Simply put, he seemed to know what my heart needed and he was happily giving it to me. I found myself giving it back to him. Everything between us changed then. I don't know if, at that moment, I would've called it love, but I was filled with a powerful desire to protect him. It was not a parental feeling. No, ma'am. I knew he felt the same way. I didn't want this part of the night to end. Then my timer began to ping. I tried to mash the end bar without taking my eyes away from Paul, but I couldn't, so it just kept making the most annoying high-pitched peppy noise. It was all I could do not to throw the thing into Shem Creek.

"I have to look at my phone to make it stop," I said.

"Okay," he said. "Time to come back to earth."

"Too bad," I said, and dropped my phone in my handbag. I started to stand up.

"Wait," he said. "We have to kiss."

"We do? Why?" I said, and he pulled away. "Wait! I don't have any objection. I'm just wondering why."

"To see what it feels like, you silly girl! Don't you want to know?"

"Roger that," I said. Since when did I use shortwave-radio lingo? "I mean, yes, you're right." God, I was such a dork.

Well, so what if I was a dork? He kissed me, and, honey, there was seismic activity in the Netherlands. So to speak.

"How's that?" he said, moving away after the kiss that was heard around the world. Thankfully, he was a bit of a dork too. I mean, who asks, "How was my kiss?"

I started to laugh and somehow sputtered out, "Pretty damn fabulous." And then he laughed too.

"Yeah," he said, "fucking inspired."

"Excuse me! Word order!" What was the matter with me?

"You're a very naughty girl," he said, still laughing.

"Well, I've never been called naughty but I think I sort of like the sound of it." Get a grip, Lisa! "Um, do you think we could do that again just to be sure the first time wasn't a fluke?"

"Sure! Come over here!"

It wasn't a fluke. When we opened our eyes, Eric our waiter was sauntering by.

"Dude!" he called out, and gave Paul a big thumbs-up.

"Awesome!" Paul responded.

Then we really laughed like two teenagers. I felt so alive then, more alive than I'd felt in years. What did I have to do to keep feeling this way? I know, go to Belk's and buy some decent underwear sooner rather than later.

Paul drove me back to the house on the Isle of Palms. Suzanne's and Carrie's cars were parked in the driveway. It was nearly ten o'clock. I wondered how long they'd been home. I imagined that they'd be inside with their feet up. The three weddings they had had over the weekend must have worn them both out.

Pickle was on the other side of the screen door waiting. She danced and hopped with happiness to see me and I wondered if she thought I had abandoned her. I leaned down and ruffled the fur behind her ears.

"Hey, little Pickle! Were you a good girl?"

She licked my hand over and over and then turned to Paul to receive the homage she felt was her due. He leaned down and whispered some doggie sweet nothings to her and she sat right down by his feet, practically purring.

"Call you tomorrow?" he said.

"Sure. Hey, thanks for a wonderful night! It really was incredible, you know."

He laid his lips on mine and then once again for good measure. Pickle barked.

"Hush, girl!" I said in my dog-mommy stern voice. "Mommy's having fun."

"Yeah, it was. It was great," he said. "Now, don't you yell at that dog. She's my new girlfriend."

"Go on home, boy," I said. "It's a school night."

He left me there on the porch and walked down the steps to his car. Then as though he knew I was still there watching him he turned and blew me a kiss. When he pulled away from the curb I went into the house.

"Come on, miss," I said. "I want a glass of water and then I'll take you out."

My dog followed me to the kitchen. Carrie and Suzanne were there at the table, looking somber.

"Hey!" I said. "What's going on? Is something wrong?"

I took a glass from the cabinet and filled it with water.

"We came home about an hour ago and I found Miss Trudie in a heap on her bedroom floor," Suzanne said. "She had fallen out of bed. She's okay, I think, because she fell on carpet. But one of these days she's going to really hurt herself."

"Did she say what happened?" I asked.

"She says she doesn't remember," Carrie said.

"This stuff scares the hell out of me," Suzanne said.

"Of course," I said. "It's not easy to find anyone on the floor, much less someone you love."

"I told Suzanne I think Miss Trudie needs someone to be with her, Lisa. What do you think?"

"Well, in-home care adds up very quickly," I said. "And from what I know of her, I don't think she'd be very happy to have a sitter following her around all the time. Does she check her blood pressure at home?"

"Never. You're probably right about a sitter. But there must be something I can do to see that she's safe and happy," Suzanne said.

Then I had an idea.

"Listen, Suzanne, why don't you come and talk to Dr. Black, Harry Black at Palmetto House. This guy is an encyclopedia on eldercare. There is not one possible family issue or situation he hasn't dealt with. I know he would give you some good advice."

Carrie said, "It's worth a shot."

"Maybe," Suzanne said. "I'll think about it. I know she really needs to be in assisted living or have an aid. But you're right, Lisa. She has too much pride. She'd never agree to either one."

"Probably not, especially if the idea came from a family member," I said, "but she might listen to someone like Harry Black."

"Do you think it's okay to just call him, out of the blue?"

"I'll tell him to expect your call. How's that?"

The next morning at work I put my head into Dr. Black's office.

"Do you have a moment?" I asked.

I gave him the story on Miss Trudie and Suzanne and he said in a highly animated voice I hadn't heard come from him in ages, "Are you talking about that little raven-headed spitfire with the donuts?"

I nodded.

"Tell her my door is open. Anytime."

"Thanks!"

If I didn't know that Harry Black had sworn off love years ago, I would've said that he was attracted to Suzanne. Nah. Not him. He was a living heart donor. A great doctor, mind you, but freezing cold. I sent Suzanne a text and told her to call Dr. Black and gave her his direct number.

She must have called right away because around lunchtime I caught a glimpse of her heading down the hall toward his office. I had my hands full, so I couldn't stop and call out to her, but I figured I'd catch up with her when I was finished administering meds and checking on our patients' well-being.

As it turned out, we nearly ran over each other at the nurses' station.

"Hey!" Suzanne said. "I was just coming to see you."

"And I was just going to Dr. Black's office to see if we had a hostage situation. How long did he keep you in there?"

"Well, he brought in sandwiches, which was very nice. Can you walk with me to my car?"

"Of course!" I turned to Margaret, who was there reading charts, and said, "I'll be right back, okay?"

"I imagine we can hold the place together," she said, deadpan as always.

Suzanne and I walked quietly until we reached the front doors.

"I have a secret," she said.

"We all have them," I said. "What are you not telling me?"

"I have a date with Harry Black. He asked me out to dinner and I accidentally said yes. Is that terrible? What am I going to do now?"

"No kidding!"

"He wants to take me to the Peninsula Grill this Saturday night. I said yes but I could cancel it."

"Why? Go! Let him take you out to dinner, for heaven's sake. What's the harm?"

"I don't know. I haven't had a date in ten years. I wouldn't know the first thing to say."

"Well, you just spent an hour and a half with him, so apparently there's something to talk about!" I started laughing.

"Wow! Was it an hour and a half?"

"Yeah, it was. Was he helpful about Miss Trudie?"

"Gosh, yes! He was supersensitive and caring—"

"Are we talking about Harry Black?" I could hardly believe . . . I mean, I had never heard a single soul describe Harry Black as sensitive or a good listener.

"Yeah, why? He's not sensitive?"

"You know what? I don't know! I mean, I think the work we do around here can desensitize anyone. This is just . . . well, a side of him I've never seen. He must really like you, Suzanne."

Suzanne blushed deeply.

"Good Lord," she said.

Later, when I returned from work, Suzanne, Carrie, and Miss Trudie were all sitting around the kitchen table. The room was dead quiet, except for the whirring of the overhead fan. Something was wrong. But if something was wrong, why were they all shaking their heads and smiling?

"Okay," I said. "Who did what to who?"

"Do you mean *to whom*?" Miss Trudie said.

Suzanne said, "How about we got another bill from Green Carolina and I just got off the phone with the owner. I called him and told him the whole story about Wendy and Kathy and he was steaming mad. You want to hear what he said?"

"There's just no telling," I said.

Carrie blurted out, "He's going over there tonight after midnight and pulling all the boxwoods and azaleas right out of the ground. I love him."

"Who's telling this story, madam?" Suzanne said. "And you can't love him. His name is Howard."

"Sorry," Carrie said. "I couldn't help myself."

"Can you believe it?" Suzanne said.

"Yes, but how weird! I had the same thought a few weeks ago when the first bill came in. Does he want help?" I said.

"I'd even pitch in for that one," Miss Trudie said.

"We can dress like ninjas," Carrie said. "Wouldn't that be fun?"

"Now you've really lost it," Suzanne said.

"Hopefully, this is the last you hear from Wendy," I said. "But you know it won't be."

"I smell real trouble," Carrie said.

"Remember when she threatened to sue me?" Suzanne said.

Miss Trudie spoke up. "That woman's full of some bodacious bull."

"Same thing as bull dukey," Carrie said.

"Yes," Miss Trudie said. "Except worse."

CHAPTER 13

Labor Day Approaches

Every other day there seemed to be some new speculations about tropical depressions that were going to ruin Labor Day weekend, which was still two weeks away. No, they wouldn't. Everyone with a brain in their head had a Plan B in place. But familiar with the tumultuous climate as I was, it was still remarkable to live through and witness the sudden changes in the ocean, the temperature, and the air. It was such a grand departure from the norm that it defied memory. The ocean sprang to life in crazy ways, twisting with choppy eddies, slapping itself with relentless whitecaps in the harbor, and on the horizon there were dozens of swirling water spouts. Swimming would be ill advised.

The good news about impending hurricanes was that they cooled the air. It was drizzling, small-craft warnings were in effect, and the skies looked ominous. It wasn't pretty but it was cooler. As you know, in the Lowcountry, the weather has a spectacular range like any other diva. Lowcountry natives are born with internal barometers. We feel changing weather in our bones.

Nonetheless, Suzanne, Carrie, and I decided to walk the beach Friday morning. We crossed the dunes with my dog in tow, but in one glance we knew the beach was too wild. Only a few people were out there, a couple of stalwart surfers and two determined joggers. The sand was running with the brisk wind, leaving wavy scars across the beach, and even from where we stood, it stung our ankles like thousands of tiny needles. Pickle had no desire to play. She stood on her hind legs leaning against my knees, squinting up at me. I picked her up so the sand wouldn't hurt her eyes or go up her nose.

"I think it's not a beach day for my pup," I said.

"And for me either," Carrie said. "This is ridiculous."

"Let's go get some breakfast," I said. "This lemon ain't worth the squeeze."

"Pancakes," Suzanne said. "Must have pancakes."

"Uh-oh," Carrie said as we hurried to get back to the house. "Somebody has anxiety! Is this date-related?"

"Well, hell yes, it is! Like, what am I supposed to wear?" Suzanne said. "Maybe the wind will pick up and they'll close the bridges."

I started to laugh. The weather was foul but it wasn't nearly bad enough to close anything. Although, I was pretty sure no one was playing golf or tennis or going out in their boat this day or the next. And parasailing was probably a bad idea too.

"You'll see," Carrie said. "Dating is just like riding a bike. You never forget. I should know."

"You sure should," Suzanne said, and giggled.

"Wear your navy linen dress," I said. "It looks great on you."

"You think?" Suzanne asked.

Carrie said, "I'll lend you my tan straw woven clutch. It would be perfect with that dress. And I have a great necklace you can wear."

"Make sure you have on good underwear," I said, and they stared at me, surprised that I might think that Suzanne would even consider diving into the sheets with Harry Black on their first date. "What? What if you get in a, heaven forbid, car wreck? Why are y'all looking at me like that?"

Suzanne shook her head and Carrie snickered.

"I need coffee," Suzanne said as a way of changing the subject.

"Yeah, and a new push-up bra," Carrie said.

We burst out laughing and hurried back to the house, heading straight for the kitchen, where Miss Trudie sat at the table sipping coffee and reading something in her large-print copy of *Reader's Digest*.

"Could've told you this was not a good day for the beach," she said. "My knees woke me up."

Miss Trudie had joint pain. I wondered what she took for it.

"G'morning! It's not a beach day. That's for sure," I said, and opened the pantry closet. "Okay, pancakes. Now, where do y'all hide the Bisquick?"

"Bisquick?" Suzanne said. "I don't think we have any."

"Suzanne? Even I know you can't call yourself southern if you don't have Bisquick in the pantry," Carrie said.

"In this house I cook from scratch," Miss Trudie said. "You girls want pancakes? Get me the canister of flour, Lisa. I'll have a batter made in five minutes." She got up and took milk, eggs, butter, and maple syrup from the refrigerator and put them on the counter. She was amazingly spry for her age.

"Carrie? Make yourself useful and give me a big bowl from the cabinet," Miss Trudie said. "Bisquick indeed. I need the canola oil too, hon."

"Maybe I'll fry a pan of bacon," Suzanne offered. "Y'all want bacon?"

"Are you kidding? I always want bacon. I'll set the table," I said.

"Well, I'm going to soft boil an egg for myself," Carrie said. "I've finally lost enough weight so that my leggings don't give me reflux anymore."

"You're the only person I know who would accuse her exercise clothes of such a thing," Suzanne said.

"Well, it's true," Carrie said.

We had breakfast and began what I thought would be an unremarkable day. After we ate, I washed the dishes as the others went on to what they had lined up for themselves. That was becoming the routine and it suited me fine. They cooked, which was always a time-consuming, messy process. Occasionally, I got out my juicer and made juice for everyone. But it was one thing to make a batch for one person—fresh juice for four turned the kitchen into a war zone. So they cooked and I washed the dishes, which was over in a flash, or so it seemed to me.

One of the nice things about dish duty was that there was a window over the sink. Outside, little Carolina wrens sang and hopped from one branch to another in a crepe myrtle tree. The birds were sweet to watch and they lifted my mind to a contemplative state once everyone had left the room. For some reason, Kathy Harper was on my mind that morning, almost as though she was nudging me. I knew, for some inexplicable reason, that the only way I would get the nudging to stop was to get to the bottom of her story. Who was she really? And what had been her true purpose in this world? And what had her life meant?

After I wiped down the stove, I went to my room to dress for work. The tower of Kathy's boxes was staring at me in the face, taunting me.

"Okay! I surrender!" I said to the thin air.

I decided I would go through some of Kathy's things that afternoon when I got home. Either that or live with a high-rise of cardboard where Palmetto bugs (cockroaches) would eventually make their home. I don't know why bugs love cardboard but they do.

There was a rapping on my bedroom door.

"Come in," I said.

"You decent?"

It was Suzanne.

"Yeah, sure. Come on in."

She entered the room and sat on the end of the bed.

"I've been thinking about something," she said.

"Shoot."

"Well, when I was talking to Harry, he mentioned to me that he was going to be cutting back your hours."

"Are you kidding me? Oh God!" I dropped to the hassock that stood in front of the armchair. "I can barely make ends meet now!"

"I know. But that Green House Project is eating his budget alive."

"So Paul's going to be earning my salary instead of me?"

"In a roundabout way, I guess that's sort of true."

"Well, that really, really stinks."

"I agree. Remember, we're basically all in the same boat. Anyway, I was thinking that instead of you trying to rent an apartment, why don't we swap some eldercare for rent?"

"What do you mean?"

"Just what I said. Look, you said yourself that if I brought in someone to look after Miss Trudie that she'd throw them right out on their ear, and I think you're right. She already likes you. This is a no-brainer."

"Yeah, but she needs someone all the time, Suzanne. I can't be with her all the time."

"I realize that. You've got an architect coming around here with high hopes, parents in Hilton Head who presumably like to see you once in a while, and a daughter and stuff going on, like the job you have. No, I get it. I was just thinking, though . . . here, look at this. I did the math."

She showed me a piece of paper with a rate multiplied by hours that would bring my workload up to thirty-eight hours per month. I'd still be trading hours for rent at a rate I'd never find in the marketplace. It was the deal of the century.

"Carrie and I can work our big important social lives around yours so that there's almost always someone here. On those occasions when Miss Trudie has to be alone, I'm going to strongly suggest that she wear a personal alarm device."

"What if she won't?"

"Then I don't know. But I can't keep worrying about her like this."

"Listen, Suzanne, I'm happy . . . no, I'm *thrilled* to offer my time in exchange for a place to stay, but you know this still isn't going to fully protect her. You can't ever fully protect anyone."

"Yeah, I know. But you could keep her meds straight. I mean, that is the toughest one for me. She hates the intrusion. Anyway, I just want to be able to say that I did my best. Can you help me get one of those alarms?"

"I can bring you some examples this afternoon," I said. "And Suzanne?"

"Yes?"

"Thanks," I said.

"No, thank you! Like I said, we're all in the same boat. Anyway, I'll see you tonight."

"Yep. Have a great day."

I wondered why she didn't ask her sisters for help with a full-time person. But maybe they didn't have control over their family's money. It had sounded like that when she talked about them some time ago. Maybe asking for money might start trouble between her sisters and their husbands. That was probably the reason. Suzanne didn't want to start trouble. They all stood to inherit the house, but they couldn't finesse the care of their benefactress. How stupid. I told myself for the thousandth time that I'd never give control of my finances to another person. I might not have had much, but what I had was mine.

I looked at the box of Kathy's ashes that was on the floor next to the chest of drawers and I sighed hard. Is this all there is?

I decided then that before I went to work I was going to compose a text to Marianne, and I did. If my daughter never spoke to me again it would be her choice. I was not going to give up on her. She was my child.

Marianne, I wrote, *my heart is so heavy with sadness from not hearing from you. I can hardly bear it. Whatever differences we may have doesn't change the fact that I'm still your mother and I love you with all my heart. Please take a moment to let me know you are all right.*

I looked at my words for a few moments and thought well, it was my heart reaching out for hers. If this didn't work, I'd do it again and again until I could find the right words to unlock her anger. I hit the send button.

I wrote my phone number on a piece of paper and went upstairs to check on Miss Trudie and my dog before I went to work. The door to her sitting room was open.

"Miss Trudie?"

She came into the room from her bedroom. Pickle was right behind her.

"Oh! I thought you'd left for work!"

"Well, I'm leaving now, but I just wanted to see if you needed anything before I go."

She smiled at me.

"No, sweetheart, you go have yourself a good day. If I need anything I'll call you."

"Okay," I said. "I'm going to put my phone number right here next to your phone, so if you need a single thing just call me, okay?"

"Well, that's awfully nice," she said. "Did you know that I've learned how to steam PBS on my iPad?"

"Do you mean 'stream'?" I said, smiling.

"I imagine so. 'Stream'? 'Steam'? Doesn't matter one fig to me. Except that Miss Pickle and I are going to watch season four of *Downton Abbey* today, aren't we, sweetie?"

My dog looked at me, made a whiny sound, and then she looked up at Miss Trudie and yipped.

"Well, I guess that settles that." I laughed. "See you later!"

I gave my furry little love a ruffle on her neck and left.

The day, as I had hoped, was uneventful. But I stopped in Dr. Black's office to confirm what Suzanne told me about my hours.

"Is it true?" I said.

"So she told you? I've never met a woman who could keep a secret. Well, I probably should've told you first but you know how I hate delivering bad news. Anyway, it's only temporary, for a few months, until we can start renting some of the new space. All the nurses are taking a haircut. It's better than laying anyone off."

"Right. But I've already had a haircut on my hours, and I think I would rather have heard this from you."

"Well, I'm sorry about that."

No, he wasn't.

"It's not the end of the world," I said.

"Good. Hey, you know I'm taking Suzanne to dinner tomorrow night. Did she tell you?"

I couldn't help but smile. He was as animated as I'd ever seen him.

"Yes, and she's looking forward to it too." Though only the Good Lord knows why, I thought. "Try to behave yourself, okay? She's a really nice person."

"What do you mean? I'm *not*? Come on, St. Clair! The milk of human kindness flows through these veins. You know that."

"That's exactly what I always say about you." I wagged my finger at him and left his office.

Judy gave me samples and the accompanying literature on alarm devices and I put them in a Palmetto House tote bag. And I picked up a blood pressure cuff at CVS. At some point over the weekend, I'd get together with Suzanne and Miss Trudie and walk them through the details.

The next night I was on the porch with Miss Trudie and our jointly held dog waiting for Dr. Black to arrive. The weather had cleared up somewhat and it was nice to sit in the fresh air. Suzanne had blown out her hair and tried on ten different outfits before she finally settled on the dress we'd all told her to wear in the first place. Carrie had done her makeup and accessorized her, and she looked great. So did Carrie, who had a date with Mike. Suzanne came out on the porch with Carrie to join us.

"Wow! You look beautiful!" I exclaimed.

"Thanks!" she said.

"Doesn't she clean up good?" Carrie said.

"Get back in the house this minute!" Miss Trudie said.

"Why?" Suzanne said. "It's not like I'm sixteen and going to prom."

"Oh, I know that," Miss Trudie said. "I just want to make him squirm a little. Can't I have some fun too?"

"Carrie? Lisa?" Suzanne said, rolling her eyes. "Do y'all have ten milligrams of something I might swallow to unrattle my nerves?"

"Yes," Carrie said, "you know I do. But if you take it you can't drink any wine."

"Oh, fine! God! I wish we hadn't given up donuts!"

Suzanne disappeared inside the house and let the screen door slam behind her.

"She's just nervous," Miss Trudie said. "Can't blame her. She hasn't had a date since George Bush Senior was in office."

"Junior!" she called back from inside the house.

"Aren't you going out tonight?" Carrie said to me.

"No," I said, "I'm seeing Paul tomorrow. He's working tonight, getting caught up on some stuff."

Harry Black's car pulled into the driveway. When he got out, Miss Trudie sat up tall so that she could see over the porch banisters. She gave him the once-over and turned to me.

"Handsome!" she whispered, arching her eyebrows.

"Meh," I replied, and shrugged my shoulders.

He rapped his knuckles on the screen door. Pickle hurried to the door ostensibly to protect us from the Dark Side and Darth Vader.

"Hi!" he said. "Can I come in?"

"Hello, Dr. Black," I said, thinking, Use the Force, Pickle! "Come meet Miss Trudie and Carrie."

"Call me Harry, Lisa. No formalities tonight," he muttered, and then brightened up, extending his hand to Miss Trudie. "Miss Trudie! My word! Suzanne has done you a great disservice!"

He smelled like the entire men's fragrance counter at Dillard's. And he ignored my dog.

Miss Trudie pulled back and said, "And how is that?"

"She did not tell me how regal you are," he said, and bowed a little. "You remind me of Maggie Smith."

I wanted to barf right on his shoes. Regrettably, I did not.

"Regal? Really? Maggie Smith? I adore her," Miss Trudie said. "Will one of you girls tell Suzanne her handsome date is here?"

"Oh, yes, ma'am! 'Regal' is the only word there is to describe you." He turned to Carrie. "And you're Carrie? I remember you from when you came to visit . . ."

"I'll go get her," I said, although no one heard me.

"Kathy Harper," Carrie said. "It's nice to see you again."

"Yes! That was her name. Well, it's nice to see you too. Who's the lucky man?"

"What do you mean?" Carrie said.

"Well, surely, you're going somewhere special because you wouldn't dress up to sit on the porch, would you?"

"Oh! My! Well, yes. Mike Kelly, we're . . ."

I slipped around them and went inside the house. Suzanne was in the living room, listening to everything.

"How's it going?"

I wanted to say, *Well, the disingenuous son of a bitch has them eating out of his hand and he makes me want to throw up and cut off my ears from listening to his bull.*

Perhaps that seemed harsh, so I didn't say it. Of course.

Instead I said, "Fine. It's going fine."

"Should I go out there?"

"If you want to keep your date with him, yes, I expect you have to."

My smile was involuntary. Suzanne was so excited and nervous. It was just completely priceless to see her this way. Usually, she was a take-charge-and-everyone-get-out-of-the-way kind of woman. But Harry Black had unnerved her? I just couldn't help how I was feeling about Harry. I wasn't wild about him at the moment.

"Okay, okay. My hair's okay?"

"Oh, for Pete's sake, go on out there and go have some fun. No worries. I'm in all night."

"Thanks!" she said, barely able to contain herself.

Suzanne went to the porch and I heard Harry say, "Wow! You look gorgeous!"

"Oh! Really? Wow, thanks! And you look great too!" Suzanne said.

Oh, brother, I thought, and then decided maybe superflowery compliments weren't the worst thing in the world.

I went out to tell them to have a good time just as Mike's car was pulling up to the curb.

Mike came up on the porch and scratched Pickle's ears. She was satisfied with that and went back to Miss Trudie's side to sit. He said hello to everyone, but when he looked at Carrie I could see this guy was completely taken with her. It was genuine. And lovely.

Finally, they all left with their unbridled enthusiasm and pheromones and it was just Miss Trudie and me. Pickle walked in a tiny circle, checking her territory, and then lay down next to my chair.

"How'd you like Harry Black?" I said.

"He's full of it," she said. "But on the other hand, it's not like I get that many compliments. Maggie Smith indeed. What do you think of him?"

"Well, I only know him professionally. At work he's not that friendly, but he's got a tough job and he keeps his professional distance, which is the right thing to do. He's a great doctor."

"Well, you could light a small village with the spark between them, don't you think?" she said.

"There's something icky about thinking about my boss that way," I said. "But what do I know?"

"Me too. So that's that. Want to order a pizza?" she said.

"Sure, why not?" I said. "It's Saturday night. We should live it up."

"The menu's in the kitchen junk drawer. Get whatever you like. My treat. And if it's not too much trouble?"

"Olives?" I said.

"You're such a dear!"

"A *dear*?" I narrowed my eyes at her. "Who's full of baloney now?"

She chuckled to herself and took a sip of gin, realizing I knew it wasn't Evian in her glass.

I called for a pizza with pepperoni and mushrooms and a house salad. They said they'd deliver within the hour.

I said, "Great! Thanks!" and hung up the phone.

After a gourmet dinner of mediocre pizza, salad, and iced tea, Miss Trudie excused herself for the evening.

"I want to help you get settled upstairs. Is that all right?"

She looked at me curiously, as though I might be on the verge of invading her privacy or overstepping my bounds. But then, probably because she remembered I was a geriatric nurse, she said, "If you want to see how an old dame piles her bones into bed, be my guest!"

We rode up together in the elevator.

To break the ice I said, "You know, I just thought it might be a good idea for me to give a little attention to how your bed is made."

"I don't mind if you do. Do you think I like to wake up on the floor?"

"No, ma'am. I'm sure you don't."

The elevator stopped and I held the door for her to get out.

"Old age is like this. Your brain is still fifty but your body betrays you whenever it feels like it. If it wants to throw you out of bed, it will."

"Well, let's see what we can do to hold back the beast," I said.

"Good idea."

When we reached her room, I pulled down the covers on her bed. There was a bottom sheet, a top sheet, two blankets, a blanket cover, and a spread. A quilt was folded over the bottom of the bed in case she got a chill.

"Miss Trudie? *I'd* break my neck with all these linens. What you need is a bottom sheet, a summer-weight duvet inside a duvet cover, and that's it."

"You know, I get so cold at night, even though it's as hot as Hades," she said.

"Most people your age have the same complaint," I said. "It's circulation. If you can make it through the night without killing yourself, I'd be glad to go to Bed Bath & Beyond first thing in the morning and straighten this all out for you."

"You would? Then I'll be careful." She leaned against the doorframe. "Thank you, Lisa."

"Get some sleep and I'll see you in the morning," I said, and left her for the night.

Back downstairs, I wrapped up the leftover pizza, threw out the box, and washed the dishes. I took Pickle out for her evening stroll. When we got home I decided to tackle a box of Kathy's things.

The first one was all linens. As was the second one. They were in decent shape but not anywhere close to new. We could cut the towels up for cleaning rags. So I shoved them back in their boxes and set them aside. The third box had scrapbooks, much like the other ones I had seen. I began flipping through the pictures and nothing there jumped out at me, even though I wasn't sure what I was looking for, beyond the furniture, magnifying glass, and letter opener that Wendy claimed were hers. It was too late in the evening to scrutinize photographs from someone else's past. I reached back into the box and pulled out a Bible. From the cracks in the leather cover, it was clear that Kathy had spent a good amount of time in its pages. That made sense to me, as it seemed like something someone like Kathy would do—take some time to read the Bible. I began flipping through it and came upon an official-looking document folded in thirds. It was a marriage license. I took it over to the bedside table lamp to give it further inspection. Kathryn Gordon Harper had been married to a man named David Harper. I sat down and thought about it for a few minutes. Maybe Carrie and Suzanne knew that but I never did. Wait! They couldn't have known because they would've said they knew Kathy had some family somewhere when she died. They would've notified him. I went back to the Bible. There I found one more document. It was a divorce decree.

I thought, How terribly sad. Oh, Kathy Harper, is this what you wanted me to find?

It was as though I could hear her in my mind saying, *Yes, it was.* And for no good reason other than my unreliable intuition, I felt like there was more to discover.

When Suzanne and Carrie came in later that night, I told them the news. I was positively gushing. They were stunned. We sat around the kitchen table going over and over the documents.

"Lisa! This is an awesome discovery," Suzanne said. "I had no idea. None whatsoever."

"Me either. This calls for a glass of wine," Carrie said.

"It definitely does," Suzanne agreed.

I got up and opened the refrigerator door. There was a bottle of white wine we had opened a few days ago. It was nearly full, which was unusual. I took three juice glasses from the cabinet and poured some in each one. Juice glasses go into the dishwasher. It was too late to hand-wash goblets.

"Here you go," I said, handing a glass to each of them. "Somewhere out there in the world might be Kathy's ex-husband. He might want Kathy's ashes."

"Here's to Kathy!" Carrie said. "God bless you, baby, wherever you are!"

We raised our glasses together and then took a sip.

"Wait! Suzanne? How was your date with Harry?" I asked.

"He's a little on the weird side," she said, "but I liked him."

"How was dinner?" Carrie asked.

"It was out of this world. He's sweet," she said. "We'll see."

"Is he worthy of the thirty-six questions?" I prayed she'd say no.

"Too soon to tell," Suzanne said.

"Well, if anybody cares, Mike's taking me to Bermuda for Labor Day," Carrie said.

"What? Lisa and I certainly hope you'll have separate rooms," Suzanne said.

"Of course we will or I won't go!" Carrie said, and winked at me.

"I wouldn't either," I said, and didn't mean it any more than she did.

"God, I hope Mike Kelly has plenty of life insurance," Suzanne said.

"Very funny," Carrie said. "He goes by 'Mike,' not 'John.'"

"Let's hope that brings him luck. Not to change the subject but you're right, Lisa. Somewhere out there might be Kathy's former husband and he might want her ashes and he might know things," Suzanne said. "Y'all! I'm so glad I didn't spread them around my rosemary bushes, but I just couldn't bring myself to do it. I know she said she wanted me to but—"

"It's okay, Suzanne. It really is. Poor Kathy!" Carrie said. "She must have really had her heart broken if she never told us she was married."

Maybe Marianne wasn't speaking to me but at least I knew she was alive. I still had hope of restoring our relationship. Kathy was gone.

"We have to try and find him," Suzanne said. "He might be able to answer some other questions too."

"Oh! Speaking of the evil one who thinks she owns the furniture?" Carrie said. "Mike and I took a ride by her house and guess what?"

"I'm not sure I have the strength for any more surprises tonight," Suzanne said.

"Well, she doesn't have any boxwoods or azaleas!" Carrie laughed.

"What? You mean the landscapers repo'd them?" I started laughing. It was just about the funniest thing I'd ever heard.

"Yes, see?" She showed us a picture she had taken on her phone. Wendy's yard, no shrubs. "That yard's as naked as a jaybird."

"I love it!" Suzanne said. "Finally, an ounce of justice!"

Later on, when I was getting ready for bed, I plugged my phone into its charger. I had a text message. It was from Marianne.

It said, *Love you, Mom. I'm so sorry.*

"Thank you, Lord. Thank you," I said to the heavens above.

That was all I needed for now. I sat on the side of the bed and tears of joy began to flow. It was a start. In fact, it was more than I expected.

CHAPTER 14

A New Groove

The first thing I did Sunday morning was reread Marianne's text. I'd never delete it. I read it over and over sitting on the side of my unmade bed. Here's why I thought my text message worked when the others had not. In those words I had laid my anger aside. My daughter's career choice really and truly was not a personal attack on me, and, in fact, it really didn't have a blooming thing to do with me. It was Paul who'd pointed that out, and once I let the idea rattle around in my head for a while, I came to see things another way. In fact, by viewing Marianne's choice as a personal attack, I had been throwing the proverbial baby out with the bathwater over and over again.

The wood floors felt cool beneath my bare feet and I noticed that overall the room was cooler than normal. And I was relaxed for the first time since my last horrible fight with Marianne, proof positive of the connection between comfort and anxiety. I should have taken my blood pressure because I was sure it was normal for the first time in months.

And now I had to answer her. I wanted to respond in words that would bring her back to me and make her want to stay. This too was something Paul had ever so gently pointed out to me via the Dalai Lama. I decided the best way to do this was to suggest that we talk about other things besides her business. And her father too. He was anything but neutral territory. But there were many safe topics, weren't there? Movies? Books? So, I composed a text to her that said, *You have no idea how happy your message made me. There have been some changes in my life I'd love to share with you. Let's not talk about business for now. Let's just talk about other things and try to get close again. I miss hearing your voice and about your friends and I don't even know if you have someone special in your life. Can I call you at eleven my time? Love you, baby. xxx*

I hit the send button and knew because of the time difference that I wouldn't hear from her for a couple of hours.

I could smell onions cooking in butter. There was nothing to compare except when you added garlic to the pan. I dressed and went to the kitchen, which, of course, was bustling with breakfast preparations. My little dog was there, ever vigilant, just praying for a piece of bacon or toast to fall to the floor.

"G'morning!" I said. "How'd y'all sleep?"

"Dog's been for a walk," Carrie said. "She did what she was supposed to do."

"Really? Thanks, Carrie." I fixed Pickle's food bowl and gave her fresh water.

"She's growing on me," Carrie said. "I might get a little dog myself . . ."

Everyone stopped what they were doing and stared at her.

"When I get married again! Don't worry!"

Did she really think she was getting married again?

"Whew! Well, I slept great! Lisa, we just told Miss Trudie about what you found last night," Suzanne said. "Here, you want coffee?" Suzanne filled a mug and handed it to me.

"Thanks," I said.

"Cream's on the table," Carrie said as she continued slicing strawberries.

I helped myself. "What are y'all making?"

"Coddled eggs, toast, and fruit salad," Suzanne said as she stirred the onions around in some butter.

"What exactly is a coddled egg?" I asked.

"It's like a tiny omelet steamed in a cup with a lid," Miss Trudie answered.

"A steamed omelet. What next?"

"See? Here's the cup." Suzanne held one out for me to see. It was a simple ceramic cup with a lid that screwed on and a loop of stainless steel on the lid that had some purpose I was sure to see.

"My mother taught me to make coddled eggs. But who cares about that? My goodness! We have a real mystery on our hands, don't we? This is the most peculiar thing that's happened around here in decades!" Miss Trudie said. "Lisa? I want to hear what you think."

"I think it's kind of miraculous, if you want to know the truth," I said.

"Miraculous? Why?" Miss Trudie said.

"Because between Suzanne, Carrie, and me, we decided Kathy's landlady was stealing from her estate. Until last night, we were stuck at a dead end. We couldn't prove it. This is our first shred of evidence. Well, not evidence, really. But we know that Kathy had secrets."

"And," Suzanne said, "he might be able to help us."

"The only satisfaction we've gotten out of this whole mess was seeing Wendy's yard without the bushes she tried to say were a gift from Kathy," Carrie said.

"That was some bull," Suzanne said.

"What are you talking about?" Miss Trudie asked.

"I'll explain it all to you in a minute," Suzanne said.

"Anyway, we didn't know of anyone who might confirm our suspicions," I said. "Now suddenly we have a real possibility of putting this to rest, if we can find her ex-husband."

"How are you going to find him?" Miss Trudie asked.

"Internet, Facebook, I don't know," I said. "We'll start there. What do you think, Suzanne? I'll set the table."

I went to the cabinet where the dishes were kept, took what we needed, and began placing them around the table.

"White pages on the Internet?" Suzanne said.

"If he's got a landline," Carrie said. "Hey! Here's a thought. If we can find out where he went to college he might belong to an alumni association. And don't forget about Match.com and all the others. I can search those. I've already paid the membership fees."

Carrie was right. Not too many people had landlines anymore. And she did belong to every Internet dating site there was. Every single one.

I watched Suzanne assemble the coddled eggs. She just cracked a raw egg into each cup, gave them all a bit of salt and pepper, a teaspoon of sautéed onions and minced ham, and about a tablespoon of grated cheese. She screwed on the caps and into the water they went for just five minutes.

So, over fruit salad, toast, and coddled eggs—which were delicious, by the way—Suzanne, Carrie, and I brought Miss Trudie up to date. Miss Trudie was completely flummoxed and annoyed to a degree I'd never seen in her before.

"Someone ought to give that insufferable woman a good slap right across her lying mouth!" she exclaimed. "She's a crook!"

I said, "I know. Isn't she terrible?"

Suzanne said, "Don't worry, Miss Trudie. We'll nail the bitch."

Miss Trudie flinched at Suzanne's choice of words but still she said, "Good!"

When the meal was finished, Miss Trudie went to her room to read and Suzanne, Carrie, and I cleaned the kitchen together. No one was rushing anywhere. It was Sunday, the one day of the week when we all slowed down. Somewhere between the scraping of plates and loading the dishwasher, I told Suzanne and Carrie that I had heard from Marianne. They were delighted.

"This must be such a relief for you," Suzanne said.

"I just love her so . . ." I choked back tears and they threw their arms around me.

"It's okay, it's okay," Suzanne said.

"It's going to be fine!" Carrie said.

I finally got a grip on myself and said, "Things are looking up slightly, but this is going to be a process."

"You have to fight for everything that's truly of any value," Suzanne said.

"It sure seems like it, doesn't it?"

"Even Kate Middleton," Carrie said.

Suzanne and I crossed our arms and dropped our heads to one side, looking at her as if to say, *Have you lost your mind?*

"Well? She had to stay thin and keep her mouth shut to get the green light to marry William, didn't she?"

"She's going to have to do that for the rest of her life," Suzanne said.

"Good point," I said, hanging up my dish towel to dry. "I'm going to drive over to Bed Bath & Beyond. Anybody want to join me?"

"Good luck finding parking," Carrie said. "You couldn't pay me to go to Towne Centre on the weekend."

"I'm going to take apart another box," Suzanne said. "It's weird that the marriage license didn't give her husband's middle name. Not even an initial. So I'm going digging."

"I'll help you when I get back," I said.

Half an hour later I was in the Towne Centre parking lot, and, as predicted, riding around and around, looking for a place to park. I finally found a spot by Barnes & Noble, which was a good long walk from Bed Bath & Beyond. But I needed the cardio, so I pulled in and checked my messages. There was a smiley face from Marianne. It was just a few minutes shy of eleven. I called her.

"Mom?"

"Yep, it's me, baby. How are you?"

"I'm good. I'm fine. You?"

"Well, there's a lot going on."

I told her about Debbie Smith showing up and how I'd had to move out of the house in one day. And I told her about Suzanne and Carrie and, of course, about Miss Trudie and how nice they all were to take me in. She asked about Pickle and I told her our dog was now everyone's darling and watching television all the time. She laughed and my heart melted. I didn't know how much I had missed the sound of her laughter until I heard it.

"I wish I could see you," I said.

"Well, we could FaceTime," she said.

"No, I mean in person. FaceTime makes me look like I'm in a fishbowl."

"It makes everyone look fat and weird," she said. "So, Mom?"

"Yes?" I said. God, it was just so wonderful to be talking to her again.

"I've met someone, a guy."

"That's wonderful! Who is he? Where's he from?"

"Well, his name is Bobby and he's really sweet. I think you'd like him. Well, I do."

"I'm sure I would."

"He's from a little bitty town in South Carolina right by York called Smyrna. Population forty-five. It doesn't even have a grocery store."

"Some of the best people come from tiny towns," I said. I wasn't just listening to my daughter's voice; I was listening to the sound of my daughter in love.

"His family grows pecans and peaches," she said. "Isn't that amazing?"

"Farmers know the best dirt," I said, and giggled.

"Oh, Mom! That is so lame!"

"I know, I know. Okay, just tell me that you're fine."

"I'm fine and I've never been happier in my life."

"Good, baby. That's all I really wanted to hear."

"And you're okay too?"

"Yes. I am doing remarkably well. Maybe we should do this next Sunday?"

"Sure. Same time?"

"Yes. That's fine. I really love you, Marianne. You know that, don't you?"

"You have to love me. You're my mother!" She laughed and I did too. "Love you too, Mom."

We hung up and I stared at my phone. I'd straighten her out but it was going to take time. At some point you can no longer insist that your children do this or that. I had learned this lesson the hard way. You have to let them fall down and then you can help them get back up. But you have to let them become adults. Still, it was not easy to silently stand by on my high moral ground while she continued on this road that was so problematic for me. High Note. What a stupid name for a stupid business.

I quickly bought what Miss Trudie needed and popped into Belk's to see what they had on sale. Well, don't you know there was a huge pre–Labor Day sale in progress? Everything was marked down and that included the lingerie department. Here was my dilemma. I wanted to buy something that didn't scream "whore." I didn't want to buy anything that screamed "matronly." I was looking for a middle road that said "she's a lady but she's sexy and she's not trying to pretend that she's in her twenties." No thongs and no garter belts. Thank you.

Sorry, Carrie, I thought.

I went for Donna Karan because in real life she was in the zone of my actual age. Call it a decision of designer confidence, not consumer confidence. And I saved some money. Now, I don't want anyone to think that tonight was the night I was going to let Paul wander into my secret garden, but I'd been around enough to know that kissing was a gateway drug. For the duration of the relationship I'd be prepared for car accidents and close inspections. Although, I have to say, I had always carried a suspicion that most men could care less about your underwear. Maybe a few viewed it as wrapping paper, but I'd bet twenty dollars that the majority of them never even noticed.

I hurried back to the house with three huge bags. Carrie and Suzanne were in my room going through scrapbooks and manila envelopes filled with papers. Pickle was curled up and fast asleep.

"Hey!" Suzanne said. "You're back! That didn't take too long."

"I got lucky," I said. "I'm going to go upstairs and fix Miss Trudie's bed."

"You are so sweet to do this for her," Carrie said.

"I may be a lot of things, but sweet ain't one of them." I laughed.

I thought about that while I was climbing the stairs. No, I wasn't sweet. But I was reliable and honest and surely I had some other redeeming qualities. I was reasonably smart and I had a decent sense of humor. But next to Paul, I certainly wasn't very worldly and sophisticated. Did that matter to him? Well by now, surely he realized what I was and wasn't. But what did I bring to the table for a guy like him? Even though the thirty-six questions had shown we had a lot in common, the same basic principles, and we liked a lot of the same things, the depth and breadth of his experiences were vastly greater than mine. I decided as I began unpacking the duvet and its cover that I would probably be smart not to invest too much emotionally until I knew more about his feelings. On the other hand, he had given thought to my dilemma with Marianne and it was his guidance that brought us together again . . . well, got us on speaking terms.

I pulled all the linens from Miss Trudie's bed except for the bottom sheet and folded them in a neat pile. Then I pushed the duvet into the cover and buttoned up the opening. I rolled it out across the mattress and restacked her pillows. It looked like a bedroom in a spa hotel.

"So is this my new bed?"

I nearly jumped out of my skin. I was so deep in thought I didn't hear Miss Trudie's shuffle or her cane's thump.

"Oh! I didn't . . ."

"I know, I'm wearing my new tennies! See? Aren't they dreadful?"

She was referring to her athletic shoes.

"They're not so bad."

"If you say so. But now I can sneak up on everyone!"

"Oh! Well, good for you!" I stood back so that she could enjoy the full view of her bedroom's updated look. "So, what do you think?"

"My goodness! It looks like something out of a magazine!" she exclaimed. "It's fresh and it's inviting. I might dive right in. Thank you, Lisa. I really appreciate this."

"It's my pleasure. It really is. It makes me want to make a white bed for myself!" I said. "Well, for wintertime. I get too warm at night to sleep under a duvet in the summer."

She looked at me and squinted. "I remember those days. My husband used to call me the furnace!"

"Ha ha! That's hilarious. Now, did you get some lunch?"

"Oh, no. I'm not hungry today. We had such a big breakfast."

I said, "Miss Trudie, you know it's not about appetite. You have to eat for other reasons, even if it's just a little bit."

"Give me a good reason," she said.

"Blood sugar. Blood pressure. If it dips, you can get dizzy and fall. Eating helps to keep you upright."

Miss Trudie pulled her lips together in a straight line and gave me some stink eye. She knew I was right and she wasn't too happy about it.

"That's an excellent reason. I'll have whatever you're having."

"Egg salad on white toast. How does that sound?" I actually made a pretty darn good egg salad, if I said so myself.

"Delish!"

"Okay. I'm on it."

In the kitchen, I put a dozen eggs in a pot of salty water to boil and stopped by my room to see how Suzanne and Carrie were doing.

"How goes the war?" I asked.

"Pretty good but I can't say we're finding anything that helps us," Suzanne said.

"Wait!" Carrie said excitedly. "Y'all! Look at this! Is this the chest-on-chest in this picture?"

We all stared at the photograph.

"It might be!" Suzanne said.

"Y'all, let's take this out to a better light," I said.

"That's right, you know antiques better than we do," Carrie said.

We took the scrapbook into the bright light of the kitchen and laid it on the table. The timer went off for the eggs, so I moved the pot from the flame to a cold burner and covered it, resetting the timer.

"Let me see that picture," I said, and sat at the table.

Carrie and Suzanne pushed the scrapbook over toward me.

"What do you think?"

I gave the picture careful scrutiny. It had to have been taken decades ago with Kathy's husband. Who was that baby? Were those other people her parents? Those details didn't matter. I compared it to the picture of the chest-on-chest in my phone. There was no doubt. It was the exact same piece of furniture.

"Ladies and gentlemen?" I said. "No more calls. We have a winner."

"Woot woot!" Carrie said.

"High five!" Suzanne said.

Much high-fiving ensued and then we settled down and got serious.

"One mystery is solved, but how are we going to get it out of Wendy's possession?" Carrie asked.

"Good question," I said.

"It would be so great if we could find a picture of the linen press too," Suzanne said.

The timer went off at the same time Suzanne's cell phone rang. She stepped away to answer it.

"What are you making?" Carrie said.

"Egg salad," I said as I ran cold water over the eggs. "There's plenty for everyone."

Suzanne returned.

"If it was anything more exotic than egg salad I couldn't eat it," Suzanne said. "My stomach is doing flips. That was Harry Black."

"Really?" I said.

"Yeah, he wants me to see a movie with him tonight."

"What did you tell him?" I said.

"I said yes. Before I even thought it through. Am I really this impulsive?"

"It's not impulsive," Carrie said. "Go! Have a good time, for heaven's sake. You need a social life outside of the three of us! Besides, when I get married again, I won't be able to hang around with y'all as much. You know how husbands are."

We were quiet then and for every reason.

"You sound pretty sure about marrying this guy. Are you?" Suzanne said.

"Honey? I can smell marriage coming along the same way you all smell coffee in the morning."

I'll be damned, I thought.

After lunch, the rest of the afternoon passed quietly as we continued going through Kathy's boxes.

"You know what we need?" Suzanne said.

"No, what?" I asked.

"We need a document or something with Kathy's ex-husband's middle name or even an initial. I've been all over the Internet and there are literally thousands of David Harpers in the world. We need something to narrow the search."

"I still can't believe she had a husband and never told you," Carrie said.

"She never even so much as hinted at it," Suzanne said.

"Yeah, it's a little unbelievable but her silence tells us something about the powerful depth of her pain," I said.

"You should've been a shrink," Carrie said.

"Ha! That's what they tell me, but I thought I'd make more money as a geriatric nurse! Shows you what I know, doesn't it?"

Suzanne left at five, and when Harry Black arrived to pick her up I stayed in the house. His cologne announced his arrival. Besides, I enjoyed a sufficient amount of the pleasure of his company during the week. Cutting back my hours, was he? And was Suzanne so deaf in the nose that she couldn't smell what he smelled like? Anyway, I wanted the time to figure out my hair and what I was going to wear.

"I've got Miss Trudie duty tonight," Carrie said, standing in the doorway of my bedroom. "Gee! Don't you look nice!"

"You think so? Not too virginal?"

I was wearing a white linen tunic with rolled sleeves over simple white cotton pants.

"Ha! Look in the mirror! You're not a virgin, honey bunny. You're smokin' hot!"

"Who me? You're nuts."

I looked in the full-length mirror. I saw a middle-aged woman, tallish, on the lean side, with blond hair blown out straight. My hair just hit my shoulders. All the beach walking had given me something of a suntan, which I'd never had in my whole life.

"Huh!" I said. "Maybe I don't look so bad!"

"Stay right there," Carrie said.

A few minutes later she came back with a handful of costume jewelry. "Here. Put this on and let's see."

She handed me a wide, coral-encrusted silver cuff bracelet with matching earrings and a chain necklace of large silver links.

"Wow!" I said when I looked in the mirror again.

"I've got the perfect lipstick. Stay put."

She dashed out of the room and seconds later she dashed back in.

"I cleaned it off with alcohol," she said.

"You're so funny," I said. "I'm not afraid of your cooties!"

The pale coral lipstick brought my face to life. I was grateful then to my mother for making me wear my retainer every night. At least I had straight teeth.

"Take it with you," she said.

"Thanks! You've got my cell number, right?"

"Yep. Don't worry. I'd call you right away if anything happens," she said. "Meanwhile, I'll keep digging."

"I'm not really worried about Miss Trudie. But I'm excited that we're unraveling Kathy's past, so call me if you find anything."

"Promise," she said.

Paul was right on time. He practically bounced up the front steps. I opened the door for him.

"Hey you," I said.

"Hey yourself," he said. "You ready to go?"

"Yep," I said. "Where are we headed?"

"Well, first we're going to Grill 225 for nitro-tinis and then we're heading over to Hall's for steaks or chops or whatever you want. How does that sound?"

"It sounds too fabulous! And, um, Paul? What's a nitro-tini?"

"You'll see," he said, and opened the passenger door for me.

Thirty minutes later we were seated on beautiful leather bar stools staring at the massive foggy fumes of a cocktail that came with a warning label taped around the stem of the martini glass. Mine was a chocolate-themed concoction. His was a cosmo. I loved that he didn't feel emasculated by a pink drink.

"Are you sure this is safe to drink?" I asked.

"Yes," he said, and laughed.

"I'm taking a picture of these babies." I whipped out my phone as quickly as I could and took pictures of our drinks.

I'm embarrassed to admit it but my chocolate nitro-tini slid down the hatch very smoothly.

"I could drink ten of these," I said, looking at the bottom of my empty glass.

"And I'd have to carry you out of here over my shoulder," Paul said.

"You're probably right. My dignity would take a vacation."

He laughed. "You're funny. Do you know that?"

"Oh, shucks, Paul. You're making me blush. Anyway, I'm not used to real alcohol but this is delicious! Once again, we're having dessert first."

"I think we always should," he said. "So, tell me what's new?"

"Well, I spoke to my daughter today. That's my really big news."

"That's wonderful!"

I told him how I decided to impose a moratorium on discussing her business, and that we agreed that we would talk about other things. He said that was brilliant, that the most important thing was that we talked.

I said, "It's not like we don't love each other. We just have a major difference of opinion on a few things."

Then out of nowhere, he looked at me with *that look*. You know the one. It's the one that says, *I've been thinking about what you look like naked. I might like to ravish your bones.* There was no doubt whatsoever.

"Holy shit," I said, without meaning to say it out loud.

"What?"

"Nothing," I said, lying.

"No, come on now. Tell me why you said that." He was smiling.

"Okay," I said, emboldened by a chocolate martini and his gorgeous brown eyes, "you're thinking about sex. You and me and sex."

"What's the matter with that?" He laughed.

"I don't know! Nothing?" I started laughing too.

I mean we weren't twenty-one years old. What were we saving ourselves for?

"Do you still want dinner?" he said.

"What's *that* supposed to mean?"

"Sorry. I was just kidding. Let's get our check."

He signaled the bartender, paid the bill, and we left with smirks on our faces.

There was a pedicab waiting on the curb.

"Hall's is pretty far from here," he said. "Should we ask this young man to haul us over there?"

"Why not?"

We climbed in and made the trip over to King Street and he held my hand the entire way.

"The steak is probably better at Grill 225, but Hall's has music and I love that," he said.

"I love music too."

"I miss playing my own piano. These days I don't have the time. But I played at Kathy's funeral, remember?"

"How could I forget that?" I smiled. "That priest was an old poop."

"He sure was. I was just playing music Kathy loved. If I'd played 'Ave Maria' or something like that, everyone would have been weeping."

"I totally agree," I said.

We climbed out in front of the restaurant and went inside, excited to see what the rest of the night would bring.

CHAPTER 15

Finders Keepers

All I'm admitting to is that second martini slowly sipped at Hall's and a lot of dessert. The rest is nobody's business but mine and Paul's. He managed to get me home before eleven, which was quite a feat because I was very comfortable at his condo. How did it happen? He played "Unforgettable" for me on his piano. Then he played "The Way You Look Tonight." That was it. The shoes came off and then he peeled away my clothes like the proverbial skins of an onion, taking his sweet time. At one point I was sure I was going to die. But I didn't.

I thought I looked pretty innocent when I walked into the kitchen and found Suzanne and Carrie at the table, combing the Internet.

"Hey! How're y'all doing?" I said, dropping my handbag on the table. "How was your evening?"

"Well, we found a man's monogrammed shoehorn," Carrie said. "Now we're looking for a David I. Harper."

"That's great!" I said.

Suzanne looked up, gave me the once-over, and commented, "Well, *somebody* had a big night!"

She said it like *I had sex* was written across my forehead in red lipstick.

"Oh Lord," I said. "Well, he started it. How could you tell?"

Carrie looked up and gave me an inspection from head to toe and a large grin grew across her face.

"Oh, sweetie! Because look how *relaxed* you are!" she said. "Was it fun?"

What a question!

"Oh. Hell. Yeah. It was fun," I said. "It was unbelievable. How was your date with Harry?"

"Well, obviously not as exciting as yours, but it was better than our first date," Suzanne said, and giggled. "We went to see *The Giver,* which was actually pretty interesting."

"Dating's awkward," Carrie said. "Suzanne? Download the app and use the questions on him to see if you're gonna really like him or not. I mean, be honest, you can only hold out for so long."

Now there's an app for the thirty-six questions? Good grief! There was an app for everything!

"She's right about saving it," I said. "Anyway, use it, girl! It's perishable!"

"That's your medical advice?" Suzanne said, and shook her head.

"Yep. If you don't use it, you lose it."

We laughed. It was 2014. Of all the possible offenses and perversions that were plastered across television, film, print, and the Internet, the news flash that two middle-aged adults had consensual sex without the sanctity of a church's blessing was just about the most boring thing in the world.

"So, look at this and tell me what you think?" Suzanne handed me the shoehorn.

I held it to my temple. "I'm getting a male, thinning hair, about six feet tall . . ."

"Oh, now we've got Uri Geller in the house," Suzanne said, and laughed.

"Very funny," Carrie said. "Y'all, there are fifty-six bazillion men named David I. Harper. We're gonna need something more than this shoehorn."

It was true.

"You're right. What's the latest on the hurricane?" I said.

A special advisory alert band was running across the bottom of the television screen but the sound was muted. I picked up the remote and restored the volume.

"Well, there's something brewing off the west coast of Africa," Carrie said. "I sure hope it doesn't ruin our trip to Bermuda."

"We just have to keep an eye on it," Suzanne said.

"Well, I'm going to turn in," I said, and remuted the TV. "Maybe I'll grab a shower."

"Take your time," Carrie said. "I'm still searching for David I. Harper."

"Did you narrow your search?" Suzanne said.

"Yes," Carrie said, "I'm in Minneapolis and St. Paul and still nothing."

"Maybe he moved to Kansas City," I said over my shoulder. " 'Night, y'all!"

In the morning, I shared a good walk on the beach with Carrie and Suzanne. The skies were gray but the beach was quiet. It was the classic calm before the storm. But the prediction for the day was just rain and some wind. It would be a week before anything close to the magnitude of a hurricane could reach our shores.

On the way to work I called my parents to see how their weekend went.

"Did the Bertches come over?" I asked.

"Oh, yes, and we had a wonderful time! You father grilled a big fat fish and I made a salad. We just laughed and talked the night away."

"That's great! And I'm staying with some friends on the Isle of Palms until I find something. Remember the young woman I told you about who died? Well, one of her friends is living in a big old beach house with her ninety-nine-year-old grandmother. They said I should stay, so I said okay."

"Sounds dull to me."

"Well, it's not. Mom?"

"Yes?"

"I don't think I've told you this, but, actually, I've been seeing someone."

My mother started screaming.

"What? Alan! Hurry up! Pick up the extension phone! Hurry!"

"Mom! Stop! Calm down! I'm not getting married or anything like that!"

"I need water! I'll be right back!"

My father picked up the phone.

"What's all the excitement about?" he asked.

"Don't tell him a thing until I get back!"

I heard the phone hit the kitchen counter.

"I guess we can't talk yet," I said.

"Your mother is very bossy."

"I heard that, Alan St. Clair! Ooooh! Men. Now, Lisa, tell us everything."

I told them what I thought they needed to know.

"He sounds wonderful," my mother said.

"Yeah, I think he is," I said.

"I gotta go," my father said. "Tiger Woods is playing golf. Don't forget to invite me to the wedding."

He hung up. My mother was still on the line.

"Lisa?"

"Yeah, Mom?"

"I want you to know that I'm one hundred percent on your side with this terrible business about Marianne."

"Well, that's actually the other reason I'm calling you. You know, it has been months since we've spoken, and we're finally in touch with each other again. I talked to her over the weekend."

"You did? What does she have to say for herself? I hope you told her that her grandmother is not happy with her."

"No, I didn't. I decided to come at this problem from an entirely different angle."

I explained to my mother that I had decided that Marianne's business wasn't something I should take personally, that it had nothing to do with me. And that I just wanted us to be talking again. So talking about her business or her father was going to be off-limits until we could figure out how to discuss those two topics without having a knock-down, drag-out war of wills. I told my mother I was sure that in time Marianne would see that this was all wrong.

"She has always been a wonderful daughter," I said. "She never gave me a moment of worry. Not one. She'll come to her senses."

My mother was quiet.

"That's quite a vote of faith," she said. "I'm not sure I would be that sanguine about it. If it were you, I'd beat your behind."

"She's an adult, Mom. Can't do that. Besides, whaling on someone's backside really never did anyone any good."

"You think so? I've got a good mind to pack my bags, go to Colorado, and do it myself! You just can't let her carry on like this. This is the most undignified behavior I've ever heard of in my life! She's working for the cannabis industry, Lisa, whether you like it or not. If my friends found out I can only imagine what they'd say!"

Mom was irate. And she had learned the term "cannabis."

"Well? I guess it comes down to do I want to have a relationship with my only child or do I want to show her who's the boss?" I said.

"You and your father think you're so smart. I've got a good mind to cut that child out of my will! And I'll do it too!"

May I inject just a few words here to say that I was completely surprised to know there was any kind of a provision for my daughter in my mother's will?

"Well, go on and do what you have to do, Mom."

I heard her gasp.

"I miss my daughter and I'm not going to fight. I do not approve of what she's doing, but I have to believe that the values I instilled in her and the culture in which I raised her will prevail over this craziness."

"Well, I'm going to call her. This is absurd, Lisa. Decent people don't help tourists do drugs."

"It's a very shady business. I agree. But it's just not nice to turn your back on someone you love."

There was silence.

"Mom?"

More silence.

She had hung up on me. Now that was a first.

I was at work by then. I spread the visor over my dashboard and got out. The sky was the color of tarnished pewter and growing darker by the minute. We were going to get a helluva soaking before the day was done. Little gusts of wind began kicking out of nowhere, shaking and rustling tree branches, sending leaves and other debris sailing across the parking lot.

I rushed inside to the nurses' station and put away my bag. Margaret and Judy were there talking about the hurricane and Labor Day.

"I guess I'm gonna start shopping this weekend," Margaret said.

"G'morning!" I said. "Shopping for what?"

"Morning," Judy said. "Margaret's shooting *The Ten Commandments* in her house on Labor Day."

"Oooh! Can I be in it?" I asked.

She meant that Margaret was having a Labor Day barbecue of epic proportions.

"You coming and bringing your cute boyfriend?" Margaret asked.

"I'm not so sure he's my boyfriend," I said. "But I'll invite him. What day is it?"

"Labor Day's still on Monday," Margaret said. "Isn't it?"

"As far as I know," I said, and smiled. "What are you cooking?"

"Everything," Judy said. "I'm making blueberry pies because I'm still dreaming of Maine. But I'm also making peach cobblers and maybe cold fruit tarts."

"And I'm making tomato pies, maybe deviled eggs, corn on the cob, hot dogs and burgers on the grill, and maybe ribs," Margaret said. "I haven't decided."

"They've got those premarinated baby backs on sale at Costco," Judy said.

"I like to make my own marinade," Margaret said. "That pre-mixed stuff has too much smoke in it. It tastes like chemicals. But their macaroni and cheese is great."

"My dad likes to make his own marinades too," I said. "So, can I bring something?"

"Sure!" Margaret said. "How about chips and salsa? And I heard a rumor that Dr. Black is bringing Suzanne, so why don't you ask that other friend of y'all's? Ask her to come too."

"Sure! That's awfully nice but I'm pretty sure she's going to Bermuda with her new beau. How'd you hear about Dr. Black bringing Suzanne?"

"He's got a picture of them on his desk," Judy said. "So I asked about it."

"He's besotted," Margaret said.

"Good grief!" I said, and wondered how that happened. And then I knew—a selfie and a cheap frame from CVS. "How many people are you having?"

"Half the planet," Judy said.

"If the weather's good? Probably somewhere around a hundred. If it's a full-on hurricane, probably not as many."

She said these things with a completely straight face and she just cracked me up. Judy and I burst into laughter. I couldn't pinpoint why Margaret was so funny but she was. It was probably all in her deadpan delivery.

That night, I was sitting around the kitchen table having supper with Suzanne, Carrie, and Miss Trudie. Miss Trudie had made baked pork chops with apples, mashed potatoes, and salad.

"This is so good I can't believe it," I said.

"This is why I can't lose any weight," Suzanne said.

"You girls are all just a bag of bones," Miss Trudie said. "Would you please pass the dressing?"

Suzanne passed the cruet to Miss Trudie and she doused her salad with the vinaigrette.

"Well, if any one cares," Carrie said, "I've lost eight and one half pounds since we started walking."

"I walk the same distance you do and I haven't lost one single ounce," Suzanne said.

"I gave up donuts," Carrie continued.

"I knew I was missing out on something," Miss Trudie said.

"Well, so did we all, didn't you, Lisa?" Suzanne said.

"Haven't had one since we swore off them," I said.

"Yes, but I also gave up the ones you didn't know about," Carrie said. "That's what love does to me."

We all just shook our heads. I was so tempted to tell Suzanne that Harry had a picture of her on his desk but there was something a little creepy about it. First, they'd only had a few dates. And second, for some reason, I knew Suzanne wouldn't like to know it. I knew she liked him but she didn't seem to be as enamored with him as I was with Paul and she was nowhere near what Carrie seemed to feel for Mike. Telling would be like stirring the pot. So I kept it to myself, deciding to turn the conversation back to Carrie.

"Well, I think you look great!" I said. "Tell me about your trip to Bermuda. You must be so excited!"

"No, you look great!" Suzanne said.

"Thanks!" Carrie visibly brightened up, becoming enthusiastic. "Well, we're staying at the Southampton Princess and Mike has made all sorts of plans. We're going to really great restaurants and we're going deep-sea fishing. And there's a special dinner where we can dance right on the beach, which is the most exciting part of the trip to me."

"Gosh! Dancing on the beach!" I said. "That sounds like the most romantic thing in the world!"

"Watch the weather," Suzanne said. "It could be dangerous."

"You know what, Suzanne?" Carrie said.

"I know," Suzanne said. "I sound like a worrywart. But watch the weather, okay?"

Carrie and Mike left on Thursday afternoon. Carrie was super-excited and I didn't blame her. Even though the weather didn't look so great. The hurricane had been downgraded to a tropical storm, but with winds over fifty miles per hour and nothing but rain in the forecast, would you go to a beach resort?

The rain and howling wind started in earnest on Sunday in Charleston, and by Monday the city and all the outlying islands had grown lakes everywhere you looked. I called Margaret on Sunday and she said her barbecue was still on.

"I have to admire your grit," I said.

"Oh, girl? I have so much porch it's not gonna matter. My sweet brother put up these canvas curtains last year. So he's just going to spread them out and we'll tell ourselves they're walls. Besides, it's supposed to clear up tomorrow in the early afternoon."

"I hope so," I said. "Paul and I will be there around one."

"Great!" she said. "We're looking forward to having y'all!"

I called Paul.

"Get your galoshes out!" I said.

"Listen, we'll make the best of it. Are Suzanne and Harry coming?"

"Yep. And they're bringing Miss Trudie."

"No kidding! Well, that's awfully nice. I imagine she doesn't get out a lot."

"No, she really doesn't. We got her this personal alarm device that notifies the fire department if she falls, and she hates it. So she's doubly thrilled because she's going to a party *and* she doesn't have to wear this ugly thing around her neck."

"Anyone hear from Carrie? I saw some weather report that said bands of this storm are just hovering over Bermuda."

"Well, Carrie's a clever girl. She'll figure out how to pass the time."

We snickered and I knew we were both thinking the same thing. Somewhere in Bermuda there was a mattress that was taking a terrible pounding.

I had spoken to my mother again and she was calmer but still adamant.

"I am sorry I hung up on you. I just couldn't listen anymore. Somebody in this family needs to have some common sense and find the courage to stand up to Marianne," she said.

"I did," I said. "And all it did was bring me misery and pain for months on end."

And I called Marianne at eleven.

"Hi, sweetheart. How's it going?"

"Great," she said. "I had a really busy week and I saw Dad. Oh, wait! We're not supposed to talk about him, right?"

"It's probably best if we don't. There are so many other things we can discuss, aren't there?"

"Yeah, definitely. Like I'm in love. I really am."

"Well, how's this? I might be in love too!"

"What? No way! You're kidding me, right?"

"Nope."

"Who? How did this happen? Who is he? What are his intentions? I mean, is he a good guy? Does he have a regular job?"

I laughed and so did she.

"Listen to yourself!" I said.

"I know. I sound like your mother now!"

I told her all about Paul, and she was completely blown away to even entertain the idea that I might not be checking into Palmetto House myself quite yet.

"I'm not dead yet," I said just as I'd heard Miss Trudie say once.

And she was fascinated by Paul's work.

"He's a green architect, huh?" she said. "Now, *that's* something I'd like to learn about."

"Well, if you come for a visit I'm sure he'd be delighted to tell you everything. He's always looking for souls to convert."

"So, you're okay living with two single women and a really old crone?"

"Actually? Yeah. And Miss Trudie's anything but an old crone. You'd love her."

"Awesome," she said.

I wanted to say no, *awesome* is a sunset on this island, *awesome* is a triple rainbow, *awesome* is the Mormon Tabernacle Choir singing Handel's "Hallelujah Chorus," *awesome* is holding your newborn child in your arms for the first time . . . oh, what was the point? I just let it go. When Marianne wanted a teachable moment she'd probably let me know.

So, I just said, "Well, happy Labor Day, sweetheart! Let's talk next week?"

"Sure!"

We hung up and I thought, Well, this is a good sign. She's interested in something else besides her ridiculous business that's probably keeping designer clothes on her back and who knows what else.

Maybe I needed to tell my mother to stay out of Marianne's business but I wasn't really too worried. My mother was really all bluster. In fact, I'd be floored if she said a word to Marianne about it.

I was wandering around the new Harris Teeter on the island to buy pita chips and salsa. I picked up a large container of guacamole too. Everyone loved guacamole, didn't they? It was still raining like mad. I thought, Well, at least Margaret had the good sense to ask me to bring something that didn't involve a stove.

Monday morning, I looked outside the window at the property around Miss Trudie's house. It was pockmarked with pools of standing water like the craters on the moon. The ground was soaked to its ultimate capacity and could not absorb another drop. Unless the temperature soared, soon there would be an epic invasion of mosquitoes. Flying jaws. The water would give rise to thousands of tadpoles. The appeal of life outdoors would be greatly diminished.

I encouraged Miss Trudie to wear her athletic shoes because they were waterproof and I'd had a thought that the floor of Margaret's porch might be damp and slippery. But when I saw her dressed and ready to go, she was wearing a pair of leather-bottomed sandals.

"I thought we agreed on rubber bottoms?" I said.

"I'll be fine," she said. "I'm not going to a party in those clodhoppers."

"Well, if they start a conga line, don't even think about getting on it!" I said, and she laughed.

"A conga line! Do people still do that?" she asked.

"Honestly? I have no idea."

What could I do? Put her in time-out?

Paul picked me up at noon right about the time the last drops of rain fell. Harry arrived just as we were leaving. For once he didn't smell like a whorehouse.

"See you there?" he said.

"You bet!" I said.

"You look pretty," Paul told me as he opened my car door.

"Thanks! You don't look so bad yourself," I said. "I missed you!"

"I missed you too!"

He had been up in Columbia, the state capital, for a few days, working out the budget details on a new project to build a mixed-use space. There was an old mill that would be converted into retail spaces on the ground level, some hotel rooms on a few floors above, and then condos on the higher floors. We talked about it on the drive over to Margaret's house on Johns Island.

"I'm excited to show the plans to you. For one thing, it's going to have thermostatically controlled skylights."

"In English?"

"Sorry. What it means is when the lobby interior temperature reaches eighty-two degrees, the skylights open, allowing the warm air to escape."

"Well, that's a piece of genius," I said.

"Yeah, it really sort of is. And we're putting a whole series of photovoltaic panels on the roof to capture energy from the sun and convert it into electricity."

Like I knew what he had just said?

"Well, if there's one thing Columbia's got, it's lots of sunlight, and Lord knows, I think summer is hotter there than here," I said. "If that's possible."

"That's the truth. And we're using pneumatic elevators. How cool is that?"

"I wouldn't know. It sounds like they need an antibiotic," I said.

He laughed so hard it gave me the giggles. We were so silly sometimes.

"Oh! You're going to make me run off the road!" he said. "No, they're not ill. Pneumatic elevators work on air pressure from pumps and vacuums so they don't need cables and pulleys. They're really an aesthetic choice more than anything else, but they don't need petroleum products. So, that's good for the environment. Anyway, they're slower, but I just like the whole George Jetson feel of them."

"Aha!" I said.

"Anyway, the lobby is going to have polished concrete floors and we're going to use lots of salvaged lumber and bricks. It's very cool. So what did I miss while I was gone?"

I told him about my conversation with Marianne and how my mother was poised to do battle in the name of human decency. And I told Paul that Marianne was fascinated with what he did for a living.

"Really? You know what, Lisa?"

"What?" I said.

"Give your girl a chance. It sounds like she might already be getting bored with what she's doing now."

"Wouldn't that be God's blessing?"

We knew which house was the party house from half a block away. There were dozens of cars parked on the side of the road on our left and right. We parked, got out, and began walking.

"Here," Paul said. "Give me that."

"Thanks!" I said.

It was enough for me to navigate the puddles, so Paul carried my bags of pita chips and dips.

Margaret's house was bursting with people. Adults laughed and chatted with each other over the din of children playing and running in between them. The bartender on the porch was as busy as anyone I've ever seen. We scooted through the crowd to deliver our contribution to the kitchen and Margaret was there.

"Hey, Margaret! I even brought two big bowls," I said. "They're plastic but they'll get the job done. You can just toss them or not. Your call."

"Well, thanks! And you must be Paul," Margaret said.

"I am," he said, and put the sacks on the counter. "Lisa speaks so well of you. It's such a pleasure to meet you at last."

Margaret took a step back and appraised him from head to toe. Then she nodded and smiled.

"I like him, Lisa," she said, and her eyes actually twinkled. "Now, y'all go on and mix and mingle. Judy and I can put the chips out."

"Okay," we said.

By the time we worked our way through the crowd to the back porch, I spotted Suzanne. She was leading Miss Trudie to a deep wicker chair with overstuffed cushions, probably so she wouldn't be run over by some well-meaning but undisciplined youngster. Miss Trudie sat with her trademark "oomph!" From where I stood it looked like Suzanne was asking her a question. Most likely she was offering her a drink and a plate of food. Suzanne had so much love for her grandmother, and her grandmother's affection for her was nearly palpable.

I didn't see Harry. I assumed he had dropped Suzanne and Miss Trudie off as close to the house as he could and that he was looking for a place to park, which was what a gentleman would do. I know Harry irked me sometimes, but he did have decent manners. Miss Trudie certainly didn't need to walk down the muddy road.

Suzanne waved at Paul but motioned for me to come over.

"I'll go get us a drink," Paul said. "White wine?"

"Club soda or iced tea, if they have it. Thanks!"

So Paul went in one direction and I went in the other.

The mood was just right. Everyone was smiling and telling stories and eating. There were four long tables covered in red-and-white-checked cloths begging for mercy under the weight of all the food. There was a platter of fried chicken, another piled high with baby back ribs, and burgers with all the fixings in large white ramekins. There were deviled eggs, hot dogs, a slow cooker of chili (these used to be called Crock-Pots), another of baked beans, a pot of red rice, a platter of corn on the cob glistening with melted butter. And of course there were Margaret's tomato pies, Judy's fruit pies, and a huge pan of peach cobbler. There was a cooler nearby that I decided must be holding the ice cream. I lifted the top to peek inside. Yep. Two gallons of vanilla were nestled in five pounds of cracked ice. Too bad there was nothing to eat.

The banisters of the porch were draped with red, white, and blue bunting and a huge, sopping-wet American flag hung from a pole. And, thank you, Lord, the sun was coming out. That would get the kids out of the house and into the yard, where they could scream their little heads off and get all muddy but their noise wouldn't bother anyone. I finally reached Suzanne's side.

"Hey! Is everything okay?"

"No," Suzanne said. "Harry is driving me crazy."

"Why, what happened?"

"He's being too kissy."

"Kissy? What does that mean?"

"I mean, in the car he was trying to kiss me in front of Miss Trudie."

"Kiss? You mean like open mouth with tongue action or a peck?"

"More than a peck but less than France, if you—"

"I got it!" I said. "Men can be so stupid. He just needs a refresher lesson in situational awareness."

Miss Trudie, whose hearing was still in the range of what dogs can hear, said, "He can't help himself!"

"What?" Suzanne said with a look of horror on her face. "What do you mean?"

"He's crazy about you!" Miss Trudie said.

"Well, that's stupid," Suzanne said. "We've only been seeing each other for five minutes."

"That's where you're wrong, Suzanne," I said, knowing this was the moment to make her understand what had been going on at Palmetto House. "All those visits you paid to Kathy Harper? I saw him mooning over you all the time. He feels like he's known you for months and months!"

"Good grief," she said. "Well, he's going to have to back off or I'm done."

"Poor Harry," I said, and laughed. "Miss Trudie? May I fix you a plate of food?"

"I was just going to do that," Suzanne said. "Let's help ourselves together."

"I'll fix a plate to share with Paul. Otherwise I'm going to eat everything in sight. It all looks so delicious."

"Yeah, to be honest, this is my favorite kind of food."

We walked to the other end of the massive but crowded porch, where the buffet was set up. A line had formed, so we had to wait a few minutes. I turned to see Harry coming onto the porch at the same moment Miss Trudie stood up from her chair, took one step, tripped, and fell flat on her face.

"Oh! Oh no!"

In what seemed like the exact same moment Harry zoomed through a mass of people straight to her side, scooped her up in his arms, and rushed her into the house. I could see through the windows as he turned left and right looking for a sofa. Suzanne and I were on the move, rushing to get to her. People were excited, saying, *What happened? What happened? Someone fell! Move back!* We finally got inside the door and to her.

We watched as Harry handed her his white linen handkerchief. Miss Trudie's lip was split and bleeding. Harry was standing over her saying, "Miss Trudie? I'm right here. Let me see now." He took away the handkerchief and inspected the wound. "No stitches. You are perfectly fine. I just want to check a few things."

"Are you okay?" Suzanne said.

Harry gently rotated Miss Trudie's ankles and felt the bones in her feet.

"I want my clodhoppers," she said, and shot me a guilty look.

I smiled. "I'll get an ice pack."

As I headed to the kitchen I heard Harry say in the sweetest voice I'd ever known to come from him, "Miss Trudie? I'd just like to get a look at your knees. Do you mind if I raise your pant legs a bit?"

What a sweetheart! This was a new and improved Dr. Harry Black. I really liked this one a whole lot better than the old one.

Paul appeared with two glasses of iced tea and I explained to him what happened.

"What a shame. Should we take her home?" he asked. "Is she all upset?"

"I say we let her make the call," I said.

To my surprise Miss Trudie wanted to stay. I saw her whispering in Harry's ear now and then and I watched him laugh. And in between icing her lip, she gobbled up every crumb of a slice of tomato pie, two deviled eggs, and a slice of blueberry pie with ice cream.

Judy and Margaret were back and forth every few minutes making sure Miss Trudie was okay.

"Who made the tomato pie and the blueberry pie?" she asked them.

"I did," they said in unison.

"Well, I want you to know it was the most delicious tomato pie and blueberry pie I've ever had in all my ninety-nine years!"

Judy and Margaret just beamed.

"I'll get you some to take home," Margaret said.

By five in the afternoon we were all gathered at Miss Trudie's house on the Isle of Palms. We were just rocking back and forth in our rockers, enjoying a cool drink, and chatting when Carrie and Mike arrived.

"Hey!" Carrie called out to us from the driveway. "Guess what?"

"What?" Suzanne called back.

Carrie turned the back of her left hand to us as she hurried up the steps. Mike was right behind her with her luggage. Something shiny on her finger was catching the light.

"We're gonna have us a wedding!" she said.

"How do you like that?" I said to Paul. Then I called to Carrie as she came onto the porch, "Congratulations!"

Miss Trudie said, "Well, like my momma used to say, butter my butt and call me a biscuit. This takes the cake."

CHAPTER 16

Wedding Belles

Carrie and Mike were beside themselves with excitement. Mike dropped Carrie's suitcase and tote bag to the floor of the porch and shook hands with Harry and Paul. Those two lovebirds were actually getting married. Suzanne and I hugged them. Even my dog, sensing happiness in the air, got on her hind legs and hopped a few times.

"This is wonderful!" I said.

"Let's see that ring!" Suzanne said.

Carrie extended her hand for us to see her engagement ring in all its intricate detail. It was absolutely lovely. I would've guessed it was a little over a carat but I'm not an expert when it comes to those things.

"This is so exciting!" Miss Trudie said. "Come let me see it too!"

Carrie hurried to Miss Trudie's side and showed her the ring.

"Well, isn't this the prettiest diamond I've ever seen! Tell me, isn't this a little sudden?"

"I don't think so." Carrie gave her a pretend pout. "What happened to your lip?"

"I had a little chat with the floor," Miss Trudie said. "I'm fine."

"Oh. Well, thank the Lord for that! Look, Miss Trudie, it's not like this is the first time for either of us. Besides, when we met each other we just *knew*! And so if you *know,* then why wait? Isn't that right, Precious?"

"Yes, Peaches! That's right!"

Nicknames. Precious and Peaches. Suzanne and I caught each other's eye. I expected to see her eyes roll all the way back in her head like Regan in *The Exorcist*.

"Oh! Mike! We forgot the champagne! It's in the car. Should I run and get it?"

"No, Peaches! Let me do that. Maybe you can get some glasses?"

"This is a champagne moment if ever there was one," I said.

"I'll help you," Suzanne said.

Mike went outside and down the steps quickly, and before Carrie and Suzanne could even step a foot into the kitchen, he was back on the porch with a fancy-looking bottle of champagne with a French name I couldn't pronounce to save my life.

"When's the wedding?" Paul said.

"Next week," Mike said. "We were thinking Saturday afternoon. We hope y'all will be there."

"Holy crap," Harry said. "You're not pregnant, are you?"

We all had a good laugh at that. What do you know? Harry could be fast on his feet. Suzanne and Carrie came back with champagne flutes.

"I had to rinse them!" Suzanne said. "We haven't used them since the millennium!"

"I'm sure they'll work just fine," Miss Trudie said.

"I have to say, I am slightly stunned myself. I know it seems impulsive and I've never done anything impulsive in my entire life," Mike said. "But we couldn't be happier. Isn't that right, Peaches?"

"Yes, it is, Precious," Carrie said, and gave him a polite smooch.

"Okay, enough with the Precious and the Peaches. I need insulin," Suzanne said.

"Oh, poop! You spent too much time in Chicago, Suzanne," Carrie said. "Those winters made you cold."

She was kidding, of course, but she hit a raw nerve. What happened to Suzanne in Chicago had surely made her leery of romance and all its nuances. And everyone on the porch knew it.

"I don't know about that, Carrie," Harry said, saving the moment. "In fact, I strongly disagree. Can I help you with that bottle?"

"Sure," Mike said. "Thanks!"

"Perhaps nicknames," Miss Trudie said with a pause, "are better used privately."

Carrie blushed and Suzanne said, "Oh, please! It's no big deal! I was just giving you a little heat."

The pecking order among the men was interesting. Harry was the most aggressive, Paul was quieter, and Mike deferred. Harry popped the cork and handed the bottle to Mike, who began to fill the glasses. Miss Trudie hooked her finger to Harry, indicating she wanted to have a private word with him.

He went to her side and leaned down.

I heard her whisper, "Just give her some time. I know my granddaughter."

Then Miss Trudie looked straight at me.

"Lisa?"

"Olives?" I said.

"Thank you, sweetheart," Miss Trudie said.

I went to the kitchen thinking about Miss Trudie and what she probably had rolling around in her head. Carrie had landed a man, and judging by his car and the ring, perhaps of some means, and suddenly her future seemed secure. Miss Trudie was working on Harry to be patient with Suzanne and I knew that she had told Suzanne not to let Harry get away. For all sorts of reasons that I couldn't find fault with, Miss Trudie was right about Harry. He was a catch.

And I knew Suzanne well enough to know that she was taking her time because she had been burned so badly by the only man she had ever loved. Who could blame her for that? Besides, it wasn't in her nature to be impetuous any more than it was in mine. And Paul and I seemed to have found a comfortable stride. Interestingly, none of us were staying at the men's houses overnight. We all came home to Miss Trudie as though she was the queen bee of our hive, which in many ways she was. All of us, the men included, wanted her approval. She was a very special lady, so generous to us, and she commanded and received a lot of respect for her common sense and insight. So she drank a nightly jumbo martini with a fistful of olives. So what?

I put some olives in a dish and took them out to her. Her glass of gin was empty.

"Can I refresh that for you?" I said.

"No, no. I'm going to have champagne," she said. "It's not every day that someone gets engaged."

"That's true! I'd like to propose a toast!" Mike said. "Here is to my beautiful bride-to-be. Thank you for saying yes. You've made me the happiest man in the world!"

"Oh, Mike! I love you, sweetheart!" she said.

"Here, here!" we all called out. "Congratulations!"

"Bride-to-be" and "sweetheart" were decidedly easier on the ear than "Peaches" and "Precious."

We raised our glasses and took a sip. It was delicious champagne. I made a guess that I could probably buy more than a few bottles of André for what that single bottle cost.

"So, Mike?" Harry said. "What kind of work do you do?"

It struck me then that I had no idea what this fellow did for a living. Carrie had never told us.

I looked at Carrie and whispered, "What does he do?"

"I have no idea," she said. "He tried to explain it to me but pheromones got in the way."

Suzanne threw an eye roll my way and I giggled.

"I own a small PR firm," Mike said. "I have about twenty accounts that are steady business and then a number of others that come to us for rebuilding market share and image or for lobbying services."

"Do you ever come to Columbia?" Paul said. "I just started a pretty big project there."

"Oh, yeah. Carrie told me about it. I'm there all the time. Actually, I'm from Greenville," Mike told him. "And I have a woman who just came on board who lobbies with the legislature on behalf of NORML."

"What's normal?" I asked.

"That's the question of the day," Carrie said, thinking Mike meant "normal" as in "the usual." "Sweetheart? I thought you were from Spartanburg."

"Simpsonville, actually. It means National Organization for the Reform of Marijuana Laws," Mike said.

Oh. God. Please. No.

"Do they want to decriminalize recreational use or make it legal for medical use?" Suzanne asked.

"Both," he said.

Harry piped up. "You know, I read somewhere that in 2012 there were over seven hundred and fifty thousand arrests in this country for possession. In 2013, there were fewer, around seven hundred thousand. Any way you slice it up, that's a crazy number."

"I guess you have to ask if this is the best use of our legal system," Mike said. "The court calendars are always jammed."

I said nothing. I wasn't about to join in a debate on the topic with my boss standing right there. So I changed the subject.

"Carrie? Tell me, what are your plans for the ceremony?"

"Oh my! Well, we were thinking we'd get married right across the street on the beach. We just have to find someone to officiate. Like a notary."

"I'm a notary!" Paul said.

"Wonderful!" Carrie looked at Mike to see if he had any objection.

"That's great! Would you do us the honor?" Mike asked, and squeezed Carrie's hand.

"The honor would be mine!" Paul shook hands with Mike.

"You're a notary? How come?" I said.

"Because early on in my career, the firm I worked for needed one. I just kept renewing my license. It comes in handy all the time," he said. "Like now."

"Oh! This is going to fall right into place," Carrie said. "Now, we need two witnesses. Suzanne, will you and Harry do the job?"

"Of course!" Suzanne said.

"I'd be so honored," Harry said.

"And then," Carrie continued, "I thought we'd go out for brunch at Langdon's in Mount Pleasant."

"This all sounds very nice," Miss Trudie said. "I'll have to go up to the Harris Teeter and get a new beach chair. I'm going to be part of the congregation with Lisa and Pickle."

"Let's get two chairs and I'll decorate them!" Suzanne said. "I've got miles of wedding ribbon in my studio! And, of course, the flowers are on the house."

"Would you like me to arrange the brunch?" I said.

"Would you?" Carrie said. "We've got so much to do! We need to get our marriage licenses and I've got to figure out what to wear."

"I'm happy to do it!" I said.

"Oh!" Carrie said. "Suzanne?"

"What?" Suzanne said.

"Can I have next Saturday off?"

"Um, okay," she said, and laughed. "As it happens, next weekend is the first weekend in three months that I don't have a big event on my calendar."

"We'll take that as a good omen," Carrie said.

So the rest of the week we were caught up in Carrie's wedding plans, decorating the beach chairs, and finding a selfie stick for our smartphones so we could take pictures of all of us at once. Did Suzanne and I believe that Carrie was deeply in love with Mike Kelly? We were less than certain, but I'd say that the affection they demonstrated seemed genuine and so did the love they proclaimed to feel. So? Why shouldn't it work? How much of falling in love was a decision? Maybe the fourth time was the charm? I just hoped no one would call him "John" and jinx it.

Saturday morning was clear and beautiful. The tide would be low at eleven, which was when Carrie and Mike decided to exchange their vows. Suzanne left early in the morning to put together a bouquet for Carrie and something for Mike. When she came home at ten with a long box it was obvious she'd made more than a boutonniere for Mike. And I had a bottle of champagne and a pitcher of orange juice on the table with glasses. Just for old time's sake I had slipped out and brought home a dozen Krispy Kreme donuts and paper cocktail napkins decorated with silver bells.

"I dropped off the flowers for the table at Langdon's," Suzanne said to me. "And guess what? Fox Music House was delivering a piano! Guess who's going to play music during brunch? Oh, you devil! Donuts?"

"Yeah. I was feeling sentimental. And mimosas?" I said, then added, "Darius Rucker?"

Darius Rucker was a huge celebrity who lived locally and actually played guitar. He was also the principal vocalist for Hootie & the Blowfish before he switched genres from R & B to country.

"Yeah sure, nice as he is, Darius Rucker's got nothing else to do on a Saturday morning."

"You're probably right."

"No, it's Paul! Paul rented a piano and a little dance floor and he's going to play so that Mike and Carrie can have a dance together. Isn't that the sweetest thing? That's his gift to them!"

"Wow! That is so nice!"

"Plus he's officiating? I'd say so!"

"I got them a crystal salad bowl. Not very original but very practical."

"I'm sure it's beautiful." Suzanne opened the flower box and carefully lifted out a lei made of orchids and pink roses and a crown that matched. Then she held up a small collar of flowers that was tied with a pink ribbon. "The lei is for our groom, the crown is for Carrie, and the collar is for Pickle!"

"How stinking cute is that?" I said.

On a rare splurge, I had taken Pickle to the groomer. She was going to look adorable.

Carrie had been locked in the bathroom since eight o'clock doing her hair and makeup. When she came out and into the kitchen, she looked so beautiful she literally took our breath away. She was wearing a white linen sundress and flat white sandals. It was very simple and pretty, although the wearing of virginal white was questionable, but I wasn't bringing it up. No, ma'am.

"Wow!" Suzanne said, handing her the crown of flowers and ribbons. "Try this on your pretty head!"

"Oh! Suzanne! It's gorgeous!" Carrie placed it on her head and it made her look like an angel. "Thank you so much!"

Then Suzanne handed her a small bouquet, tightly wrapped in the same ribbons that were in her hair.

"Just beautiful," Carrie said.

Suzanne shrugged. I could see that her eyes were misty. Weddings, however elaborate or intimate, had a way of bringing all sorts of complicated feelings to the surface. The sorrow of lost loves, unrequited loves, and the entire gamut of love, regrets, and disappointments run through your mind, wreaking havoc with your composure.

Miss Trudie came into the room all dressed for the ceremony. She was wearing the aqua linen outfit I'd bought her at Belk's and a large straw hat.

"I don't want to get a sunburn," she explained.

"Miss Trudie? You look so glamorous!" I said.

"You sure do," Suzanne said.

"Thank you. Now, Carrie? I want to give you a little bedroom advice," she said.

Miss Trudie giving bedroom advice to Carrie was enough to make the room go dead quiet.

"Sure! What?"

Then Miss Trudie started to laugh and we joined her because the idea that Miss Trudie knew more about the bedroom than Carrie was just so ridiculous.

"Well, I was just going to say to get in there and have the time of your life, but I suspect you know that."

"Well, we all know this is my fourth wedding, Miss Trudie, so I'm not unfamiliar with what goes on behind closed doors."

"Yes. I imagine so. But what I really mean is life's short; so have fun. As much as you can."

"I will, Miss Trudie. I promise I will."

She hugged Miss Trudie, and watching them made me feel as though we were all suspended in time. Carrie's wedding would change everything. The countdown had begun. After today we would never be the same. Our sorority was losing a member. I tied the collar of flowers around Pickle's neck and I promise you my dog preened.

"I have a flower dog!" Carrie exclaimed.

"So cute!" Miss Trudie said to Pickle, setting Pickle's tail in perpetual motion.

Over the next half an hour, Paul arrived with his Bible. Next Mike and Harry appeared in the kitchen. Paul and Harry were wearing the classic Charleston linen shirt from Ben Silver in pale blue and Mike had on the same shirt in lavender. Everyone had a mimosa and at least half of a donut. When Suzanne slipped the lei over Mike's head, it became real. I took a few pictures and saved them.

"Let's do this thing!" Mike took Carrie's arm.

Down the steps and across the dunes we went. I carried the

chairs and set one up for Miss Trudie and the other for myself. Carrie and Mike arranged themselves facing Paul. Suzanne stood to Carrie's left and Harry stood on Mike's right. Everyone was smiling wide as Paul conducted the ceremony. Pickle, whose experience on the beach was that it was a place to run and play, wanted to run and play.

She jerked her leash and I gave her the stern face and said, *"Shush!"*

She settled down. I took tons of pictures of Carrie and Mike from every angle as they said their "I do's."

"You may kiss your bride!" Paul said.

It was all over in ten minutes. After hugs and handshakes, we went back to the house. We poured the rest of the champagne and toasted the newlyweds.

"Congratulations!" we all called out.

"Thanks!" they said.

"Hey, Carrie?" Suzanne said. "Are you taking Mike's last name?"

"Of course! I always do!" she said, and there was a burst of laughter. "Well, if you can't laugh at yourself, you may as well hang it up."

Brunch at Langdon's was lovely. There was no strict brunch menu but the manager and I had chosen some very nice dishes from the dinner menu. They served seared foie gras over tempura-fried shiitake mushrooms to begin. It was an odd combination that turned out to be absolutely incredible. That was followed by a salad of arugula, goat cheese, and pears in a bacon shallot vinaigrette. And for the main course there was a choice of orange-soy grilled salmon or rack of lamb. And of course the pastry chef baked a small wedding cake and decorated it with a tiny bride and groom on the top. Somehow we consumed five bottles of champagne.

Paul played the most romantic music and Mike danced with

Carrie over and over. Of course, Suzanne danced with Harry, who to my complete surprise was a great dancer. Suzanne was giggling and making faces as he twirled her around and dipped her too.

"The doctor can really cut a rug," Miss Trudie said, and we giggled together.

Finally, Miss Trudie got up and said to Paul, "Go sit with Lisa. It's my turn to play."

So Paul got up and gave Miss Trudie his seat. And Miss Trudie removed her hat, and took her place on the bench, surveying the keys, her old friends.

She said, "Now listen to me, y'all, the last time I touched a keyboard was twenty-five years ago in the lobby of the Francis Marion Hotel, so I might be a little rusty. Bear with me."

She played some scales to get the feel of the piano and then she launched right in with "Autumn in New York," "Night and Day," "More," "You're the Top," "So in Love," and then she brought it on home with a saucy rendition of "Let's Do It." She missed a few notes here and there, but overall we were amazed by her. We snapped pictures, jumped to our feet when she stopped, and applauded her like mad. Even the maître d' stopped to listen and clapped loudly, stunned by her.

Before she stopped, we all waltzed to "So in Love" and Paul whispered in my ear, "I love you, Lisa."

"Yes," I said, "and I'm so very happy that you do. I love you too. But you know that."

"Yes, but it's still great to hear the words."

Words matter, I thought. They really do. It was so funny. Paul had this effect on me. He made me feel stronger. And somehow I felt like I was a better person around him.

After Carrie and Mike cut their cake and we all had a slice, I went to the ladies' room with Suzanne. We were reapplying our lipstick and saying what a perfect little wedding it had been. My cell phone rang. To my great surprise, it was Marianne.

"Hi! Sweetheart! How are you?"

"I'm actually in Charleston? I can't believe this, but I never asked you for your address! How stupid is that? I wanted to come and surprise you but I forgot to ask you where you live!"

"Oh! This is wonderful!" I said, and wondered what was going on.

"Yeah, and guess what else?"

"I can't begin to guess. What?"

"Grandma and Grandpa are here too! They're staying at Shipwatch in Wild Dunes. It's supposed to be a surprise but we're here for your birthday! We're gonna meet for dinner at the Water's Edge on Shem Creek at five."

"But my birthday is in October," I said, clearly confused.

"I know, but we couldn't come then, so we're here now."

"Well, wonderful! Do you think we could move dinner to seven? I'm actually at a wedding and we've just eaten ourselves into a complete stupor."

"Mom! We're starving now! Just meet us at five, okay? And, that's when Grandma and Grandpa wanted to eat."

"Okay," I said. "Well, I can't wait to see you!"

We hung up and I thought, This is very fishy.

"What was that all about?" Suzanne said.

"Well, my daughter is here and so are my parents," I said. "It's all a little bit confusing to me. Why didn't they tell me they were coming? She said they're all here to celebrate my birthday, but my birthday's in October."

"We'd better get you a double espresso," Suzanne said.

"Maybe two!"

We went back to the table, where everything was winding up. Mike had already paid the check. The manager took some more pictures of us and he even made a toast to Carrie and Mike.

"To happiness and good health and a wonderful life together!"

"Cheers!" we all said.

"Paul?" I said.

"Yes?"

"How'd you like to meet my parents and my daughter at five o'clock?"

"Holy cow! Sure, of course! I'd love to meet them. But this is obviously a surprise?"

"Yes. Totally."

"Hmm. And you think there's some mischief afoot?"

"Correct," I said.

"You know what? Life with you in it is anything but dull."

After brunch we all went back to Miss Trudie's house except for Carrie and Mike. He had reserved a room for them at Charleston Place Hotel as the last celebration of the day.

"It's just a junior suite. I want to sleep late and have a lazy Sunday," he said, and we all agreed that it was perfectly understandable after the whirlwind week they'd had.

"You were a really beautiful bride," I said to Carrie as we were leaving. "I don't think this wedding could've been any nicer if we'd had a whole year to plan it."

"Thanks, Lisa. I think so too. Now, what's this I heard about your daughter being here?"

"I know. Thanks for the warning, right?"

"Well, if it was any other night than this, I'd be right there with you," she said.

"It's your wedding night. I understand." We giggled and then we hugged. Then she pressed her bouquet into my hands.

"What?" I said.

"I want you to have them," she said. "They might bring you some luck!"

"They're so pretty," I said. "Thanks."

I was thinking about putting the flowers in a vase on the dining room table at Miss Trudie's while I was on the way to the car. Suzanne and Harry were walking ahead of Paul and me with Miss Trudie leaning heavily on Harry's arm. I watched them. I was struck by the thought that Miss Trudie's gait was less deliberate than usual. Then I thought, Oh, come on, it's hot and this has been a lot of hullabaloo for her to endure in one day. She's tired. In fact, we all were.

It was after three then and Paul and I decided it was pointless for him to go back downtown and then come all the way back to pick me up before five.

"There's one tiny problem, Peaches," he said, and made a face.

"What's that, Precious?" I said, and made a face back at him.

We laughed and he said, "My shirt is all wrinkled. I can't meet your folks looking like this."

It was true. As beautiful as the linen was, the shirt that was picture-perfect at eleven that morning now looked like he'd slept in it. My father and mother would surely have some sassy remark to say. I didn't want to hear it.

"Oh, dear Lord! I'm about to iron a man's shirt!" I said.

"You don't have to! I'm perfectly capable of doing it myself. Just give me an iron."

"No way," I said.

I went to my room, came back to the kitchen, and gave him a big T-shirt that I slept in sometimes.

"Just give me your shirt and nobody gets hurt," I said.

Around twenty minutes to five, reironed and freshened up, we were leaving for the restaurant to meet Marianne and my folks. We stopped on the porch, where Suzanne and Harry were chatting away.

"Paul! We were just saying what a great job you did—between the service and the piano—wow! You are something else!" Suzanne said.

"I think so too!" I said.

"Oh, come on, now . . ." Paul said.

"Where's Miss Trudie?" I said.

"She's upstairs in her spa bed snoring like a little baby bear. I had to help her take her shoes off!" Suzanne said. "Too much action."

"Listen, this was a big day for her," I said. "Big day for all of us. I won't be too late tonight."

"You kids have fun!" Harry said.

"Thanks," I said.

We were pretty subdued on the way to the restaurant. For my part, I was trying to garner what energy I had left so that I could have a civilized conversation with my family. And I could see that Paul was whipped.

"If I'd known I was meeting your parents this evening I probably wouldn't have had that glass of champagne."

He wasn't much of a drinker and neither was I.

"You and me both," I said. "It's fun in the moment and then later all you want to do is put your head on the table and sleep for a little bit, right?"

"Yes, ma'am."

"Well, no alcohol for me tonight."

"Me either," he said.

We pulled into the parking lot and found a spot right away. It was still early for people to be at the restaurant in the droves that would surely arrive over the next hour and a half. Inside the restaurant I spotted my parents on the enclosed porch by the windows that overlooked some docked shrimp boats. The Water's Edge was one of the most picturesque dining spots in the entire Lowcountry and directly across the creek from The Tavern & Table, the fabled locale of Paul's first kiss. The hostess led us to their table.

My father stood to shake Paul's hand.

"I'm Alan St. Clair," he said.

"It's very nice to meet you, sir." Paul gave my father's hand the classic macho solid one-two shake. Then he turned to my mother, took her hand in his, then covered hers with his other hand and said, "Now I know where Lisa gets her great beauty."

Well, that was it. My mother began to gush and I thought I would die of mortification listening to her go on and on.

"Oh my goodness! You sit right next to me! Aren't you a handsome devil? Yes, you are! Sit, sit! I want to hear every single solitary thing about you. Your childhood, your family, where you went to school—"

"Mom!" I said, and looked at Dad for help.

"Carol?" Dad said, signaling the waiter.

"Oh, sorry," Mom said to Paul. But then she did the strangest thing. She reached over and pinched him. "I just want to see if you're real." Then she snickered and the ice was broken.

"Oh, Mom! You're incorrigible!" I laughed.

"No, you're not!" Paul said to her. "You're wonderful."

It was then I realized we were seated at a table for six. They didn't know I was bringing Paul, which meant Marianne was bringing someone. Moments later I felt someone standing right next to me and my father stood. I looked up into my daughter's face.

"Mom? I want you to meet my husband, Bobby Floyd Jones!"

"What?" I bounced to my feet to hug my daughter and tried to process what she had just said to me. "You're . . . married?"

I took a good look at Bobby Floyd Jones and felt my blood pressure rise. He was wearing sunglasses indoors, a baseball hat on backward, a T-shirt printed with a picture of a cannabis leaf under a plaid cotton shirt, shirttail out, sleeves rolled up, and he was chewing gum. He was at least thirty. Maybe thirty-five. Did I mention the ponytail and the tattoos?

"Mom!" he said, and held his arms out to me.

"Merciful Mother of God," I said, and let him give me a very watered-down hug, then I fell back down into my chair.

"Your mom is like . . . hot! I mean, *awesome,*" he said to Marianne, who for some idiotic reason was grinning from ear to ear. And my daughter had a wedding band of hammered silver that might have cost him five dollars at a flea market.

I looked at my mother. For once in her life she was speechless. I looked at my dad. I knew that expression. He was lockjawed and his brain was going a thousand miles an hour, trying to stop the nightmare that was unfolding right in front of his eyes.

Paul—and this is why I love this man—stood up and shook Bobby Floyd Jones's hand and then Marianne's.

"I'm Paul Gleicher," he said to them. "Y'all have a seat."

"So this is really not about my birthday, is it?" I said.

"What? Your birthday isn't until October," my mother said.

"I know! I know!" Marianne said. "But I just wanted you to know I got married before you saw it on Facebook!"

Good idea, I thought, thank you for your consideration.

"When did you get . . ." I couldn't even bring myself to say the word.

"Last weekend," Bobby Floyd Jones said. "Her old man flew us to Vegas on his private jet with his biker babe, who's a trip and a half. Elvis did the ceremony. Not the real Elvis. Yeah. Mark Barnebey is one righteous dude. Totally."

My eyebrows were in the stratosphere and I could scarcely breathe.

"Mom? Did you know that Dad has his own reality show on Bravo now? It's called *Going Out in Style*. Have you seen *Doomsday Preppers*? It's like that except he renovates bunkers. It's like *The Property Brothers* sort of combined with the Apocalypse. He's making so much money he doesn't know what to do with it."

"Clearly," my mother said.

"But, so are you, babe!" Bobby Floyd Jones said. "You must be so proud of your daughter. She's a real ganja-preneur! Look what she bought me for a wedding present!" He pulled up his sleeve and there on his scrawny arm hung a Rolex the size of Big Ben. "And! She bought me a brand-new Ducati 1199 Superleggera!" He scrolled the pictures on his phone and showed the motorcycle to me. It was twice as big as he was.

"Vodka," I managed to whisper to Paul. Now I'd have paranoid fantasies about Marianne flying off the side of a mountain on a super-powerful motorcycle.

"You got it, sweetheart."

"If they have Bombay gin on the bar," my father said. "Dry? Rocks? One olive?"

"Me too. Thank you," my mother said.

"Hold tight. I'll be right back with fortifications," Paul said, and got up.

The waiter appeared with menus and passed them all around

while regaling us with descriptions of all the specials for the night. I didn't know what to do.

Paul returned and said, "The waiter is bringing our drinks. I didn't want to make a scene in public. I'd never made a spectacle of myself in my entire life, but I sure was on the verge of a verbal atomic explosion.

I wanted to call my ex-husband on the phone right then and read him the riot act. How could he let our daughter get married without me knowing about it?

And I wanted to throttle my daughter. What was the matter with her? Didn't she want her mother to be with her when she got married? Didn't she want a gown and a veil? She got married by an Elvis impersonator? Did she think getting married was a joke?

And to the completely vulgar young man who was my new son-in-law? There were no words. I wanted a rewind button on everything that had just happened.

We ordered dinner. Well, to be honest, Paul ordered crab cakes for me, asking if I'd share with him. I just nodded. Drinks appeared and were consumed, several rounds in fact. Marianne was oblivious to the fact that we were careening from her choices once again. But in this department of oblivious romance, however, she was operating at a strict disadvantage. She'd always been a bookworm and was not at all experienced in the ways of romance.

At some point during the meal, my father asked Bobby Floyd what he did for gainful employment.

"I'm a partner and a cannabis chef in a bud and breakfast in Aspen," he said. "Basically I run the place and I have all these choice señoritas that do all the real work. I'm *el jefe*."

"You're what?" my father said.

"Yeah, I know. Cool, right? We keep the bong burning for you. Ha ha! You know like in the morning, I make this special granola?

We call it wake and bake. It goes down smooth with a little Sativa strain and freshly brewed coffee. Then, of course, at precisely four twenty in the afternoon we offer cocktails and cannabis. Three different varieties. They're all perfectly paired to each other."

"Is that a fact?" I said.

"I read somewhere," Paul said, "that people who grow pot in their homes sometimes blow up the whole house. Is that true?"

"Oh, man, I know exactly what you're talking about. Bummer. Those guys are total idiots! You see, what they're trying to do is to extract the hash oil from the bud. It's not safe. Not safe at all. It's butane vapors that are the problem. They build up, the walls start bulging, and then, boom! The whole place just blows. They think they're like in *Breaking Bad* or something."

He stood and threw his arms open wide and said, "BOOM!"

People were staring at us. I was a little drunk by then and no longer able to remain quiet.

"Bobby Floyd? You sure are one weird and loquacious son of a bitch," I said quietly. "Why don't you show some manners and take off your hat and sunglasses?"

"Bobby? Don't you dare," Marianne said. "Mom? You can't talk to my husband like that."

"You've made a mockery of marriage, Marianne. I don't know what's happened to you," I said.

"Take me back to Wild Dunes," my mother said to my father. "I can't eat another bite."

"Right away," he said. "Lisa? Walk outside with us, okay?"

"Excuse me," I said, and left with my parents.

"Wow," I heard Bobby say. "That was intense."

In the parking lot my father said, "Has the entire world lost their minds?"

"Looks like it," I said.

"I don't know what to say," my mother said. "This is terrible! Terrible!"

"Me either," I said. "Here's the worst thing. I think that man married her for her ill-gotten fortune!"

"Let's hope she has a prenup," my father said.

"I have to go back inside. I love you. I'm sorry."

Then, and this is perhaps stranger than having Bobby Floyd as a son-in-law, my mother threw her arms around me.

"I'm so sorry, Lisa! You don't deserve this kind of disrespect. You are a good mother."

Then my dad opened her car door, she got in, he closed it, got in his side, and they just drove away.

When I returned to the table Marianne and Bobby Floyd were gone. Somehow they'd left and I didn't see them in the parking lot.

Paul was shaking his head and signing the check.

"We could've sold tickets to that," he said.

We left and began the drive back to the Isle of Palms. I started to cry. Paul turned the car around.

"You're coming home and spending the night with me," he said. "This is too much for you to handle alone."

"God, I love you, Paul Gleicher."

I texted Suzanne and told her I'd see her the next day.

Around six in the morning my cell phone rang. It was Suzanne.

"What's wrong?" I said.

"It's Miss Trudie. She's dead. Apparently, she died in her sleep."

"I'll be right there."

CHAPTER 17

Answers

We reached the Isle of Palms as quickly as we could. I wasn't surprised that Miss Trudie had passed away, as much as I was saddened to know it happened. There had been so much turmoil in our lives lately, beginning with my homelessness. Then there was Marianne, her sorry excuse for a business, and even sorrier excuse for a husband, Bobby Floyd. Next there was my unforgivably rude reaction to him. I felt like weeping. And any chance I had of restoring my relationship with Marianne had completely unraveled when I said those horrible words. My heart was just broken into a million pieces. What had I done?

"I'm never going to see my daughter again," I said in the car. "I ruined everything."

"No, you didn't, and yes, you will," Paul said. "Wait and see."

"Why couldn't I keep my mouth shut?"

"I think if you hadn't said something your parents would have. And believe me, Lisa, you only said what we were all thinking. Even me. That guy is bizarre. There's no better word to describe him."

"I'm not crazy?"

"No. You may be a lot of things but crazy isn't one of them."

"Oh God. I've lost my daughter for good now."

"Lisa, listen to me, okay? What kind of a young man comes to Charleston, which is one of the most buttoned-up places in the country, to meet his wife's mother and grandparents wearing what he had on, talking like he did, and acting like a stoner?"

"Someone who doesn't care about convention or what his wife's family thinks. And he wasn't acting."

"That's right. He deserved a lot more than you gave him. I suspect he doesn't care what *anyone* thinks."

Probably including Marianne, I thought.

"And there's poor Marianne in a pair of cheap jeans and a terrible shirt, looking as if she's been camping in the woods. I mean, fashion was never her thing, but she used to care more about grooming. Do you think she really loves this . . . this man?"

"Babe? I'm sorry to say this but I think she's in love."

We pulled up in front of Miss Trudie's house. There was an ambulance there and a couple of other cars.

"Her body is still in the house," I said. "You stay with Suzanne, and I'll go to the EMS workers. I'll have them take Miss Trudie out from the back of the house. Suzanne doesn't have to see that. It's the stuff of nightmares."

"Good call," Paul said. "That's the kind of image you can never get out of your head."

Suzanne was standing on the porch. I hurried up the stairs to her. I could see she had been crying. Pickle was pacing the porch from anxiety and she was whimpering, trying to tell me what I already knew.

I put my arms around Suzanne and she began to shake with

gulping sobs. Paul leaned down and gave my dog the attention she wanted. And needed.

"It's okay, sweetie," I said to my dog, and she gave me her famous worried look. "Oh God, I'm so sorry. It's okay, Suzanne. I'm here. Paul's here too. Go ahead, baby, let it all out."

"The room was so still," she said. "I knew she was gone before I even checked to see."

"I know," I said.

If I had a dollar for every time I'd put my arms around someone brought to tears over the death of a loved one, I'd be a very rich woman.

"I'm so sorry, Suzanne," Paul said. "Miss Trudie was a great lady."

Suzanne nodded.

"Thanks," she said in a whisper. "Yes, she was."

"I'm just going to go inside and see about a few things," I said. "I'll be back in a few minutes."

Upstairs, I took a deep breath and went into Miss Trudie's room. Her corpse was already in a body bag and on a gurney. It was a terrible sight but I knew it was only her remains. Her soul had already flown to heaven. At the risk of sounding like Carrie, I have to say there is nothing more dead than a dead person. I spoke to the doctor who was there and the EMS workers. They agreed with me that it was a more considerate plan to remove the body from the back of the house.

"No reason to further upset anyone," the doctor said. "These things are hard enough."

"I'll go bring the ambulance around back," one man said.

"I'll show you where the door is," I said.

"Thanks," he said. "And I think that elevator is too small."

"Just use the front stairs. I'll keep her granddaughter out on the front porch until y'all are done."

I showed him where to go downstairs. In the kitchen I pulled the chairs away from the table to give the EMS workers extra room to pass through. Then I started a pot of coffee and went back outside to Suzanne.

"How're you doing?" I said. "We'll have coffee in a few minutes."

The driver got into the ambulance and started the engine.

"Where's he going?" Suzanne said.

"I told them to go out through the kitchen door because you don't need to see her."

"You're right," she said. "Thank you. I was dreading that."

"Did you tell them where you wanted them to take her?"

"McAlister's in Mount Pleasant," Suzanne said.

"Okay. Good. Have you called Carrie and Mike? Or Harry?"

"No. I decided to let them all sleep for a while. If I call them later on, the story will still be the same. And my sisters. It's four in the morning in California."

"I'll go get us some caffeine," I said.

I put three mugs, a creamer of milk, a sugar bowl, packets of fake sugar, and the coffeepot on a tray and took it back outside to the porch. I laid the heavy tray on the table and began filling the mugs.

"Here you go," I said, handing a mug to Suzanne with the creamer and another to Paul and finally I took one for myself, stirring in a little cream. "So, from here on in, Suzanne, we just have to make a series of decisions."

"No, we don't. About six months ago Miss Trudie gave me a manila envelope. In it were all her plans for her own funeral. McAlister's bill is already paid. So is her plot in Mount Pleasant Memorial Gardens. And her headstone. We just have to give them today's date. She knew what music she wanted and she even wrote her own obituary."

"Well, I'll be darned." I shook my head, smiling. "Isn't that something, Paul? That's so like her."

"She was a helluva gal," Paul said.

"The only thing she didn't specify is what she would wear on the glory train. I guess she thought it would depend on the season. Right now I'm thinking we ought to run that aqua linen outfit she wore yesterday through the dry cleaners and bury her in that. She loved it so."

"That color was beautiful on her," I said. "I can take it to the dry cleaners and pick it up when it's ready. And I can deliver it to McAlister's too, if you'd like."

"Okay. Would you?"

"Of course!"

"Then let's do that. Do you remember what she said when she put that outfit on?"

"No—wait, yes! She said she felt like a red-hot momma!"

"Saint Peter's going to say the same thing," Paul said.

Suzanne called Harry at eight thirty. We didn't want to stand there and listen to her side of the conversation. Paul and I went into the house to give her some privacy. A few minutes later she came inside.

"He's on the way," she said, wiping her eyes.

"He's a good man," Paul said.

We called Carrie and Mike at nine, figuring they'd be awake by then. One thing to know about downtown Charleston is that on Sunday mornings you don't need an alarm clock. You can hear the peal of the church bells that ring from every quarter of the peninsula off and on all morning long. And, just as we thought, the newlyweds were up having breakfast in their room.

"We lost Miss Trudie," I heard Suzanne say to Carrie. And then she said, "Okay, thanks."

"They were awake?" I said.

"Yes, they're coming over right now."

Then, a little later, Suzanne called her sisters. They said they'd call her back as soon as they had travel arrangements confirmed.

"They're going to want to stay here," she said.

"Suzanne, that's not a problem. I can stay with Paul. Paul, can I stay with you?"

"Of course!" he said. "And bring the princess too."

"Thanks, baby. I'll just change the sheets and clean up the bathroom."

When Carrie arrived we explained the logistics of the bedrooms to her.

"And I guess I'm supposed to move in with my husband anyway, aren't I?" Carrie said, and we laughed. "I mean, it's a studio apartment but we can make do, can't we?"

Mike said, "Of course! So there you go! Problem solved."

"Yeah, but here's the terrible part," Suzanne said. "I'd rather be with y'all than them."

"Oh, sweetheart," I said. "I know just how you feel."

I didn't tell them that Marianne had shown up with an unacceptable husband or any of the details from the night before. When Suzanne wanted to know what had happened, she would ask. As deeply upset as I was, this was not the time to discuss it. Right now we had a job to do and that was to give Miss Trudie the send-off she had wanted and deserved.

Tuesday afternoon Paul and I met up with Mike and Carrie at McAlister-Smith Funeral Home for Miss Trudie's wake. Harry was there wearing a dark suit. He looked properly somber and I had a thought then that I was happy for him. Maybe he had fallen into the same trap that I had by thinking that work was my only life, that there was nothing else for us. Both of us obviously needed more than what we had been pretending made us feel complete. I liked the fact that he was there for Suzanne. I could only imagine that it was the magic of love that had humanized him. Paul had certainly softened my heart.

The open casket was at the far end of the room flanked by two gorgeous sprays of flowers, and a blanket of roses was draped over the bottom half of the coffin. No doubt Suzanne or the others who worked for her had done the flowers. And there was a basket from Carrie and Mike, and another from Paul and me that we ordered from her studio. Whether Suzanne had arranged the flowers herself or not, they surely had her signature style. Later I would discover her sisters had sent nothing.

I hated wakes. I really didn't want to see Miss Trudie's body lying in a coffin. Intellectually I knew it wouldn't be her anyway. But still. At every single wake I'd ever attended the body never looked like the living person. I would never have said, "Oh, she looks like she's sleeping!" It was like I was looking at the shell of that person, which, in my mind, it was. But I always went up to the casket anyway, knelt on the prie-dieu, and said a prayer for the family and for the departed. But, believe me, I kept my eyes focused on the lid of the casket and fought the urge to look at the deceased. It was just way too creepy for me. And I never understood how open caskets were supposed to be a comfort to the family and friends of the deceased.

As I understood it, the next day there was to be a religious graveside service performed by an nondenominational minister. Miss Trudie had given up attending church when she was eighty-five. One afternoon not long ago we got on the subject of religion.

"I'd like to think that God will understand. And if He doesn't, we'll talk about it when I get there. If He wanted to see me in a pew every Sunday morning, He shouldn't have given me arthritis. So sometimes I watch church on television and read my Bible. It's the best I can do."

I remember saying something like "Oh, Miss Trudie! I doubt that God takes roll call on Sundays. I think He'll probably judge you on how much joy you gave others and how much love. That's if He judges at all. If He's got any wrath, I like to think He saves it for guys like Hitler and Saddam Hussein."

"I hope so too."

I remember how she smiled then. She smiled so peacefully.

I was standing beside Paul, so lost in a memory of Miss Trudie that I didn't even see Suzanne approach with Harry.

"Hey," I heard Paul say. "How're you doing?"

"Oh, I'm all right, I guess. Come. I want to introduce y'all to my sisters."

"Suzanne's doing great. Considering," Harry said.

Well, *that* meant something I was sure we'd hear about later.

Suzanne led Mike, Carrie, Paul, and me to her sisters.

"Y'all? This is Alicia and her husband, Giles. And this is Clio and her husband, Ben."

"It's nice to meet y'all," I said. "I'm so sorry for your loss."

Paul shook hands with the men.

"We really loved Miss Trudie," Carrie said.

"Thanks," Alicia said. "Suzanne tells us that old Gertrude really liked all of you too."

I flinched when she called Miss Trudie that.

"Hey, how about the airlines don't give bereavement fares any-more?" Clio said to Suzanne and Alicia, ignoring us. "Ben threw a fit."

"Yeah, that's why I didn't bring the children," Alicia said. "Giles wasn't too happy about having to pay full fare either."

"Wow," Carrie said. "Bless your hearts, I'm sure that must be a terrible hardship for y'all. Is that why y'all didn't send flowers?"

"We're the bereaved," Clio said as though Suzanne's flowers were inappropriate.

I could not believe Carrie said what she said but the larger implication went right over the others' heads.

"Well, we loved your grandmother too," I said. "She was a wonderful woman who had an extraordinary life. How long will y'all be in town?"

Alicia was checking her e-mail on her smartphone, so her husband spoke up. "We've got a flight out tomorrow right after the reading of the will."

Now we knew why they had come at all.

"So do we," Ben said.

I had not even considered the will. The document that might put Suzanne on the streets. And me. Well, I was accustomed to my place of residence being fluid but Suzanne wasn't. I knew she had to be worried about it. I looked in Suzanne's direction and she slightly shrugged her shoulders.

"It's just going to be what it is," she said privately later on. "I'll figure it out."

"And I'll help you. You know that," I said.

The only visitors to the wake besides us were Margaret and Judy and a few of the women who worked for Suzanne, and those employees gave Suzanne a hug, said a prayer, and left. But Judy and Margaret stayed for a while.

"I'll bet if Miss Trudie had a last wish it would've been to take your tomato pie and blueberry pie to heaven with her," Suzanne said to them. "I can't remember seeing her enjoy herself more than she did at your house."

"Except for . . . well, obviously her fall," Harry said.

"It was just an accident," I said.

Harry looked at me and nodded in agreement.

"We just wanted to stop in and offer our condolences," Margaret said.

"She was such a sweet lady," Judy said. "What happened?"

"The doctor said her heart just stopped sometime during the night. She would've been one hundred years old in January," Suzanne said.

"Well, we're awfully sorry. I know you were very close," Margaret said.

Suzanne's eyes filled with tears and her sister Clio pursed her lips and shoved a box of tissues in front of her.

"Thanks," Suzanne said, pulled one, and wiped her eyes.

There was an upright piano in the room.

"What do you think?" Paul said. "Should I play some of Miss Trudie's repertoire?"

"Why not?" I said.

"Suzanne?" he asked, looking for her permission.

"Go for it," she said.

Paul took his place on the bench, ran scales up the keyboard and played "What a Wonderful World." When that failed to bring a single tear to the eyes of Alicia or Clio, I just shook my head. Next he played "At Last," "Stardust," and finally "Somewhere Over the Rainbow," during which they began to discuss over the music where they wanted to go for dinner. Paul politely stopped playing and closed the cover on the keyboard.

By the end of the funeral the next day none of us cared if we ever saw Suzanne's sisters again. She had been right in her description of them. They were a difficult pair, and when combined with their husbands, they were practically insufferable. Harry was going to drive Suzanne to the lawyer's office to be with her for the reading of Miss Trudie's will. She was talking to her siblings by the grave site and we had walked a short distance away from them.

"I don't think she should have to go through reading the will alone," Harry said.

"That's awfully thoughtful of you," I said. "I agree."

"I keep telling you what a nice guy I am," he said, and smiled.

"Yeah, and weirdly, I'm starting to believe you!" I laughed and he smiled.

Carrie said, "Well, the first thing I want to do is scour every trace of those people from Miss Trudie's house. Lisa? Want to go back to the house with me and decontaminate the linens?"

"Sure. I'd love to. Besides, I want to be there when Suzanne comes home from the lawyer's."

Paul said, "Me too. Why don't I cook dinner?"

"That's a great idea," I said.

"Mike? Why don't you and I go to the grocery store?" Paul said.

"Great idea," Carrie said. "By the time Suzanne's through with the will and Harry brings her home, we can have clean sheets on the beds and dinner on the table."

Paul said, "I'm thinking gumbo? Corn bread? Salad? Maybe some gelato from BeardCats? And I'll swing by my place and pick up the baby."

He meant my dog, of course.

"Thanks, sweetheart," I said.

"That sounds like a plan," Mike said.

"This is really nice of y'all to cook and all that," Harry said. "Suzanne shouldn't have to worry about supper."

"Let's hope for good luck for Suzanne with the will," Carrie said.

"No kidding. Okay, then," I said. "We'll see y'all later."

I gave Paul a kiss on the cheek. Harry returned to Suzanne's side. Carrie and I took Mike's car and Paul and Mike took Paul's car.

"You realize the will could be devastating to Suzanne's stability, don't you?" Carrie said in the car as we headed toward the connector bridge.

"She says that, but I don't think Miss Trudie would have left Suzanne in desperate straits, do you?"

"I don't know how much money is involved. I figure the house is worth a million because of the location, but beyond that, I don't have a clue what other assets there might have been."

"Well, we're going to find out soon enough," I said.

When we got back to the house I said, "I'll wash all the sheets and towels and run the vacuum." I paused for a moment and added, "Gosh, I miss Miss Trudie already."

"Me too. The house is so empty without her. Okay, so I'll do the bathroom and give the kitchen a good wipe-down so the boys can come in here and wreck it," Carrie said.

"Isn't that always the way? That sounds great."

I pulled all the sheets and pillowcases from the beds where Clio and Alicia had slept with their husbands and put them in the washer, setting the load to hot water and extra time. I wanted to boil their DNA out of the linens. If you want to find out which of your relatives are crazy, have a funeral. Then I went looking for Carrie with a question. She was in the living room, standing with a roll of paper towels, a bucket of cleaning supplies, and her jaw dropped.

"Look," she said to me, and pointed to the piano. "It's open. I haven't seen it open since I've been here. Ever."

"Well, maybe Clio or Alicia played it or one of their husbands did." I closed it. "There's no point in inviting dust into it."

"Oh. My. Goodness. I sure didn't think much of them, did you?" Carrie said.

"You know, it isn't very polite to say this, but no, I didn't think much of them at all. One thing is for sure: they weren't particularly broken up over Miss Trudie's death."

"Not even a little bit. Maybe that's why I didn't like them."

"It would be a good reason. You know, I haven't told you or Suzanne this, but remember I told you my daughter was in town last Saturday? What I didn't know then was that she had a husband."

"What? A husband! Oh, dear. You don't look very happy about this."

"He's a perfectly dreadful overgrown child and I said some terrible things to both of them. Paul was with me and so were my parents."

"What did Paul say?"

"He said he didn't blame me and I haven't even spoken to my parents about it yet. I'm sure my mother's been in bed on Xanax ever since that night. Basically I can't go back to The Water's Edge for a really long time. I think we made an awful scene."

"You want to talk about it?"

"Sure." I told Carrie how the whole disaster unfolded, starting with the story of Marianne's business, which I'd only told Suzanne. She seemed like she was going to cry. "Don't get upset, Carrie. This is my cross to carry. Just pray that we find a way to bring my daughter to her senses."

"Oh, Lisa, you are such a wonderful woman. You certainly do not deserve this nonsense."

"Thank you and thank God Miss Trudie died without knowing all of this. You know, Paul was the one who told me that Marianne's decision to go into her crazy business had nothing to do with me and I was beginning to see it that way. But what mother doesn't want to be a part of her only daughter's wedding? Since Marianne was just a little girl, I've had this fantasy of attaching a beautiful white veil to her hair. Now I never can."

"Oh, honey, come on now. I wore white and a veil in at least two of my weddings. And I wore a white pillbox hat à la Jackie Kennedy with John the third and flowers with Mike."

"Jeez, really? Well, I was there for the flowers."

"Yes. Lisa, I'm not saying I hope there's a divorce. I'm just saying there might be other opportunities."

"Yeah, like he could drive his Ducati off the side of a mountain. Look, here's what I don't understand. How could my ex-husband be so heartless to steal that tiny reward from me? Why didn't he pick up the phone and call me and tell me what was happening?"

"Because he's thoughtless and irresponsible and he knew you wouldn't approve of Bobby. Then he'd be the bad guy for supporting the marriage."

"Mark *is* the bad guy."

"I agree. He probably thought you'd try to stop them. And if you stopped them from getting married, Mark might look weak to Marianne. She'd think a lot less of him, his judgment. Everything."

"But what about all those years that I limped through life without his support? The sacrifices I made?"

"Honey? Don't you know they don't matter to him because he didn't see them happen."

"Great. Now he's got a reality show and a private jet? And he allows our daughter to enter into holy matrimony with an Elvis impersonator as the officiant? What's the message there?"

"Girl? He's the same man you divorced for good reason."

"It's too much, Carrie. It's really too much." I leaned against the wall and wiped my eyes with the back of my hand. "Oh God. Do you know where the vacuum cleaner might be?" I looked at her and I knew she could see the enormous heartbreak in my teary eyes.

"I'm so sorry, Lisa. This will get better, I swear. The vacuum is in the hall closet upstairs. I'll be in our bathroom. Some men totally suck."

"They sure do."

At that moment I loved that she still called the bathroom ours even though she was now married to Mike. It always struck me as funny that it took us a while to let go of ownership of a thing or to get used to new positions in life. Some changes made us very sentimental and we clung however hopelessly to the past.

Soon car doors were slamming in the driveway and I knew the boys were back. I put the vacuum away and I hurried downstairs to throw the sheets in the dryer. I pushed the towels into the washer with extra soap and hot water.

Paul and Mike bustled through the door and down the hall to the kitchen carrying four bags apiece.

"Y'all need a hand?" I said.

"Nope, we got this!" Paul said.

An hour or so later, the table was set, the towels were folded, the sheets were back on the beds, and dinner was ready. Still, there was no sign of Suzanne.

"Let's open a bottle of wine," Paul said.

"Good idea," Mike said.

Paul opened a bottle of something white from New Zealand, filled four glasses halfway, and handed one to each of us.

"Want to sit on the porch?" he said. "We sure earned this glass."

"I'll say," Carrie said.

"Sure," I said, "there's a nice breeze."

"Wait! Let me get the boiled peanuts," Mike said. "We stopped at the GDC in Mount Pleasant and bought a couple of pounds. You know that guy who sells them in the parking lot out of his truck?"

"Yeah," Carrie said, "but do you know how fattening those things are?"

Paul said, "What else is new? All the good stuff makes you fat."

"You're not listening to me," Mike said. We all stopped and looked at him. "He takes MasterCard."

"Come on! You're kidding! That guy?"

"That's the high-tech world we live in, y'all," Mike said. "Yep. A guy doing business out of a Styrofoam cooler takes MasterCard. I liked to have died laughing."

I said, "Next thing you know he'll have a website!"

"Truly," Carrie said.

After we had settled into rocking chairs on the front porch and devoured many boiled peanuts, Harry's car pulled up next to ours. He and Suzanne got out looking somber and I noticed Harry sort of struggling with the weight of a cardboard box.

They came up to the porch and I said, "How did it go?"

"Anybody want to help me with this box?" Harry said. "Champagne's heavy!"

Suzanne started to smile and high-five us.

"Miss Trudie left me the house," she said. "And all her furnishings. And all of her cash except for twenty thousand dollars that she gave to my miserable sisters. She left her silver and turquoise jewelry to Lisa because she knew you liked it."

"Oh my goodness!" I said.

"And she left her land yacht to Carrie. The will said that Carrie was the only woman she knew who was theatrical enough to appreciate it."

"Oh my!" Carrie said. "How sweet! But how did it end with your sisters?"

"It was a little rough, to say the least. In her will, Miss Trudie said she was leaving her worldly possessions proportionate to the loyalty and affection reflected in her family's behavior. That popped their party balloons. They literally sank in their chairs because they knew right then she had left almost everything to me . . . when they had told me earlier that they were getting a third of everything. They left without saying good-bye. Let's hope time will heal the wounds."

"How terrible!" Carrie said.

Paul said, "Wow. Amazing. Well? Are y'all ready for some dinner?"

"You cooked? Paul! You didn't have to . . ." Suzanne looped her arm through Harry's and we all went inside.

Throughout dinner we would get up from our seats to hug each other and to toast Miss Trudie. Champagne corks kept popping, and for the remainder of the evening we laughed and told sweet stories about Miss Trudie that she would've loved to hear. This night was the wake Miss Trudie should have had. We were like her chosen family. Maybe chosen family was better, more reliable. It was surely something to ponder.

"The only thing is," Suzanne said, "she didn't really have a huge amount of cash. Running this place comes with a big overhead."

"Raise your prices!" I said with conviction. "Seriously! Do it!"

"She's right," Carrie said. "And Mike and I have been talking, Suzanne, and we were hoping you'd consider renting Miss Trudie's rooms to us until we can find a bigger apartment."

"Basically," Mike said, "I have a three-hundred-and-fifty-square-foot box with one closet. It's so small I get on my own nerves."

We laughed our heads off at that.

"That's a great idea!" Suzanne said.

I was seized with worry again because Miss Trudie's death meant it was time for me to move too. It must've shown on my face.

"What's the matter?" Carrie said.

"What, me? Oh, nothing. I mean, I guess it's time for me to try and find—"

Reading my mind, Suzanne said, "I don't want to hear a word of that kind of talk! Real friends don't let their friends live like Blanche DuBois, relying on the kindness of strangers! We are going to keep things just as they are, and Mike, you're welcome to be here anytime and so are you, Paul, and Harry is too."

"This is truly excellent news," said Harry, who had yet to spend one night in the house.

"As Miss Trudie would've said, the neighbors are going to think you're running a cathouse!" I said, and we all laughed.

Suzanne said, "Let them think whatever they want."

CHAPTER 18

Guess Who's Coming?

On Thursday I went back to work. I had the eight-to-four shift. As soon as I got to the nurses' station Margaret said she had a message for me.

"Marilyn Brooks was over here first thing this morning. She says she has something important for you."

"Really? Well, that's *awfully* nice. I'll go see her when I'm done handing out my morning meds."

By ten thirty I put my cart away, took a walk over to The Docks, and knocked on Marilyn's door.

"Hey!" Marilyn said, all smiles. "Come right in!"

"Thanks! Well, don't you look snazzy?"

"Thanks! I got this outfit at Anthropologie downtown. And, thanks to you, I'm doing just great! Would you like a glass of iced tea?"

"Thank you. That would be great. It's as hot as the dickens outside, but what else is new?"

She walked toward her kitchen to get our drinks. I knew enough about her pride to let her handle the task alone.

"Well, at least now it's starting to cool off a bit. It *is* late September after all. I think I'm going to take that trip to Asheville in October with some of the other residents here."

"Yes! I saw the sign-up sheet for that. Asheville is so gorgeous when the leaves turn."

She came back into the living room with two tall tumblers filled with iced tea, and mint sprigs too. I took a glass from her.

"Cheers!" I said.

"Cheers! Sit, sit! Marcus and I used to go there every year for at least one weekend. Poor Marcus."

I made myself comfortable on her very cool midcentury sectional, took a sip of the tea, and placed my glass on a coaster on her Lucite coffee table.

"How's he doing?" I said.

"Not great. I'm afraid he's not long for this world. The disease has stolen him from me completely now. It's so sad."

"I know, and I'm so sorry."

"What can I do? Anyway, the reason I wanted to see you, other than to say hello, was because I took a book from the library and I found something inside of it. I didn't know what to do with it. And I know you better than the other nurses. I had not read *Gone with the Wind* in a thousand years, so when I saw it there on the shelf, I said to myself, Why not? It's a nice big saga that will keep me busy and out of trouble for a few days."

My heart skipped a beat, and quite literally, I gasped.

"What did you find?" I said, knowing in my gypsy bones that whatever she had found had to do with Kathy Harper.

In the next breath I remembered that Kathy had owned a copy of *Gone with the Wind*.

"This. Here." She handed me an envelope. "Open it."

Inside was the birth certificate of a female child who belonged to Kathy Gordon Harper and David Inmon Harper and a death certificate for that same child, dated two years later. The cause was listed as an accidental drowning. There were newspaper clippings in the envelope that said there had been an investigation into the child's death, that the father was a suspect. Then another article stated the father had been cleared. The child's death was ruled an accident and the case was closed. But there was a glaring piece of information in the newspaper articles that caught my attention and held it. David Harper was the owner of Harper Grocery Stores. I may not have been so well traveled but even I knew of Harper Grocery Stores. There were at least two hundred of them all over the midwest and the West Coast. Their ads were everywhere and their charitable support to end children's hunger all around the world was very well known. The death of the Harpers' child must have been completely devastating to them, especially if there was a cloud of suspicion around it. I got the chills and shivered all over.

"Oh, dear. Are you all right?" Marilyn asked.

"I'm fine. I'm relieved. I'm so relieved you can't imagine. Do you mind if I take these?" I said.

"No, of course not. Did you know about this child? I'm so sorry if I've upset you."

"Don't worry. I'm fine. I knew the child's mother. This may have just given us the last piece of information we needed to solve a very big puzzle."

"Well, good! I'm glad I could help!"

I got up to leave.

"Marilyn? Thank you. Thank you for saving this for me. If you find anything else in the library books?"

"I'll call you right away," she said. "Lisa? By the way?"

I opened the front door to leave then stopped, turning back to her.

"Yes, ma'am?"

"How well do you know Mr. Morrison?"

"Well enough," I said. "Is that handsome devil flirting with you?"

"No, I don't think I would call it flirting exactly," she said, and looked a little sheepish. "But if you're calling him a devil, that must mean he has a reputation."

"Let's just say he likes the ladies," I said.

"Gotcha!"

I hurried back to the office, grabbed my phone from my purse, and called Paul.

"You gotta be kidding me," he said when I told him.

"Nope! Do you want to come over for burgers and watch Carrie's and Suzanne's faces hit the floor when I tell them the news?"

"Only if you'll let me do the grilling. I wouldn't want to miss this."

"You are about the sweetest man I've ever known," I said.

"What about the sexiest?"

"Okay, yes, that too! You're so silly."

I stuck my nose in Harry's office. He had been amazed and horrified to hear the story of Wendy Murray and Kathy's estate. He was at his desk.

"Sherlock Holmes reporting in. You got a minute?"

"Sure! What's up?"

I told him the story and showed him the documents.

"Holy crap. That's terrible about the baby, but it's not unusual for the death of a child to cause a divorce. And you know what? I would shake out the rest of Kathy's books and see what else you can find. And I'd put something in the newsletter asking residents to give us anything they come across."

"Of course, and I will, but, Harry, this means we can find *him*! He can identify the stuff Wendy's holding and put an end to that madness! All we have to do is get his phone number or his e-mail from his website. We've found him!" I blushed from head to toe and knew my body temperature had to be over a hundred degrees.

"Want me to look him up?" Harry offered.

"Yes! Please!"

With a few clicks of his mouse, he was there.

"Come see. Is this your man?"

I went around his side of the desk, and there was the face of a man named David Inmon Harper in one of those corporate head shots on the company's website. There was an e-mail address to reach him directly, a phone number for the business, and a street address of the headquarters. Quickly, I copied down the information. I was so happy I was just a blither.

"Oh my God, Harry. This is major. Thank you, I mean, this is incredible."

He sat back in his chair and said, "Gosh, I just love watching grown women get so worked up! Now, get out of here. I've got a mountain of work to do."

"Oh, fine," I said, and turned to go.

"Wait a minute," he said. "What do you think this means for Suzanne?"

"Justice. And it might mean a lot of money, Harry. A lot."

"And here I was harboring the wicked thought that she might be after mine. Shame on me."

"Sure. Listen, I'm making burgers on the grill tonight and I'm saving this news until I get home and they're all there. You want to join us?"

"Paul coming?"

"Yep," I said.

"Oh, what the hell. I can wash my hair anytime."

"You know what, Harry?"

"What?"

"Sometimes you're actually funny, in a 'blond joke' kind of way."

Late that afternoon, I walked my dog, set the table, and got the burgers ready to go on the grill. I decided to call my parents to discuss Marianne and her husband.

"Mom?"

"Well, there you are! Your father and I decided it was best to let you cool off for a few days."

"I don't know. I think I'm still in shock. I can't believe that she really married that stupid idiot. Can you? What could she possibly see in him?"

"Please, I've been weeping since Saturday."

"Me too. And Miss Trudie died. We had to bury her this week. It's just been a terrible week all around."

"Oh, come on. Didn't you tell me she was ninety-nine years old?"

"Yes, Mom. But that doesn't mean I won't miss her."

"Okay. I understand that. But you always have had such a problem with loss. You know that, don't you?"

If I'd been in the room with her then, I might have strangled her dead two times. But she wasn't going to change and I wasn't going to teach her anything. So I let her words slide in through my right ear, out of my left, and visualized them disappearing into dust motes and then nothingness.

"Yes. But now I'm afraid I've lost Marianne again."

"No, you haven't. She's still your daughter and I wouldn't bet five cents on the longevity of that marriage. Your father says it might not even be valid. An Elvis marriage? Come on. I mean, we never saw a marriage license, did we?"

"I had not thought of that, Mom. Did Dad look this up on Google?"

"Google? Siri? Safari? TripAdvisor? How should I know where he gets his information? But he does have serious doubts. What does your handsome boyfriend think?"

Handsome boyfriend. Oh, boy.

"Well, he's not as blunt as Dad, but he thinks her anger is temporary, that she'll eventually calm down. Even my friend Carrie says to wait and see. It's so ridiculous that it's hard to take it all seriously."

"You're right. It seems like the only kind of decision Marianne knows how to make is a wrong one."

"I agree. But here's the killer: Mark! How could he do that to me?"

"Because he's a narcissistic son of a very bad word."

"He sure is. Should I go out there? Should I call him?"

"No, and say what? 'Why did you hurt me?' Are you serious? Leave them alone to stew in their own juices for a while. They'll come around. So tell me. Are you going to be moving again?"

"Not right away. Suzanne wants me to stay. And Carrie got married, did you know that?"

"I don't know Carrie, and so no, I didn't know."

"Well, she's the other friend . . . oh, never mind. Anyway, her new husband has moved in with us now."

"What's this? Are you living in a hippie commune? Let me get your father. Alan! Alan!"

"Oh, Mom. No. Please! It's not like that."

Sometimes she could be so exasperating.

We hung up and I began pacing the floors, with Pickle on my heels, of course. Waiting for Suzanne, Carrie, and Mike to come home from work was like watching a pot of water, waiting for it to come to a boil.

Carrie and Mike had moved all her things and much of his into Miss Trudie's rooms, and it looked so cozy. Miss Trudie would have approved. In the few days Mike had been in residence, I'd decided it was pretty sweet having a man around the house. As long as he was there, I wouldn't have to carry bags of groceries or dry cleaning up the steps. He wouldn't let me. He was a perfect gentleman. But meanwhile, where *were* they?

"Come home!" I called out to the thin air.

I was still staying in my room and Carrie's former bedroom was now designated as the guest room or the snoring room. In other words, now that Mike was here and on occasion Paul, if and when they started honking like rhinos in the wild in the middle of the night, they were redirected to the extra bedroom.

Harry had not yet been awarded sleepover status but it was only a question of time. The longer Suzanne held out, the more creative he became in the ways he tried to lure her into the sack. Last night, he brought her gelato from BeardCats and fed it to her, telling her she was too thin. And the night before, he brought her some kind of French perfume and told her he had dreamed they were in Paris together, drinking wine and eating foie gras, and Edith Piaf was singing "La Vie en Rose" somewhere in the distance. Two mornings ago he appeared at seven thirty and made her banana pancakes while Jack Johnson sang the "Banana Pancakes" song in the background on his iPad. I had no idea Harry Black could be so adorable but I knew he also had to be at his wit's end. Soon Suzanne was going to be on the receiving end of the I'm-a-man-and-I-have-needs-you-know speech. Poor Harry. I really felt for the guy. We all did.

Finally! I heard a car and I snapped out of my fog. Oh, I know, I could've called Suzanne and Carrie at work, but I wanted to see the look on their faces when they heard the news.

"You're not going to believe my good news or my bad news," I said as soon as they reached the front porch.

"What?" Carrie said.

"Give us the bad news first," Suzanne said.

"Kathy Harper had a baby who drowned." I handed them the newspaper articles and the death certificate. "This was found in a copy of *Gone with the Wind* that belonged to Kathy. A resident at Palmetto House found it."

"Merciful God!" Suzanne said. "How terrible!"

"Oh Lord. I wonder if her heartbreak caused her cancer?" Carrie said. "The poor woman!"

Suzanne and I stared at her.

"What? They say there's a mind-body connection between illness and happiness, don't they?" Carrie said.

"Actually, you're right. There is a lot of thought on that. Anyway, here's the good news. I found David Inmon Harper. He's the David Harper of Harper Grocery Stores."

"Get out of town!" Carrie said.

"Where is he?" Suzanne said.

I held up the piece of paper with his contact information on it.

"Let's get this guy on the phone," Suzanne said. "Wait! Is your laptop on?"

"That thing? I should throw it off the bridge. We can e-mail from my phone or your phone right now."

"Wait. It's six here, so it's still four in Minneapolis," Suzanne said. "No, I'm going to take a shot with a phone call. He might still be in his office."

Carrie said, "Who knows? But yes, call him. I hate putting things in writing, especially when I don't know what impact they might have. I mean, maybe he's got a psycho jealous colleague who he's having an affair with, who'd threaten murder and suicide if she thought she was losing him, and a crazy second or third wife at home who'd go postal and set the house on fire if she found an e-mail about his ex-wife on his computer."

Suzanne and I stopped and looked at her.

"You really ought to write thrillers," Suzanne said.

"How do you even think of these things?" I said, and laughed.

"I read the newspapers," Carrie said. "Y'all don't have a single solitary clue about what goes on in the world. I do."

"Right," Suzanne said. "Y'all? What am I going to say to him?"

"Easy," I said. "When the secretary says, 'Who's calling?' you say, 'This is Suzanne Williams from Charleston, South Carolina.' Say, 'I was Kathy Gordon's best friend.' Don't use his name because then the little busybody will tell everybody in the office before he even has a chance to decide how to handle this."

"Good call, Lisa," Carrie said. "And if she says, 'He's in a meeting,' just say, 'Please ask him to return my call' and give her your number. That's all. Keep it real simple."

"Right. Keep it simple." Suzanne took a deep breath. "Okay, I'm doing this."

She pressed the numbers into her keypad and put the phone to her ear. Sure enough, a living and breathing secretary answered. We nearly fainted.

"Good afternoon. This is David Harper's office. How may I assist you?"

The connection was so clear that Carrie and I could hear every word without even putting Suzanne's phone on speaker.

"I'd like to speak to Mr. Harper, please?"

"May I say who is calling?"

"Of course. This is Suzanne Williams calling from South Carolina. Please tell him that I was Kathy Gordon's best friend."

"Hold please and let me see if he can be reached."

"Sure," Suzanne said.

The hold line was playing a droning, looping commentary on how important fiber was to our diets while Suzanne was nearly hyperventilating from nerves.

"Are you okay? Do you want me to talk to him?" I asked.

"No! No! I want to do this," she said.

Minutes passed. Just when it seemed that Suzanne had been on hold forever, the secretary picked up again.

"Mr. Harper will take your call now. Mr. Harper? You're on with Suzanne Williams."

"Mr. Harper?" Suzanne said.

"Yes? How can I help you, Ms. Williams?"

"Well, I'm afraid I'm calling with some very sad news. Kathryn Gordon Harper passed away a few months ago."

"Oh. I'm very sorry to hear it. When my secretary said that you said you *were* her friend instead of you *are* her friend, I knew. Kathy was a very special and very lovely woman."

"Yes. Yes, she was. I was her friend and she also worked for me."

"I see. Well, Kathy and I divorced a number of years ago."

"Yes, I know. I'm the executor of her estate and I've seen the decree. I apologize for the fact that it took me so long to contact you. We had a hard time piecing Kathy's past together."

He was quiet then and we all knew he was wondering if Suzanne knew about the baby.

"What do you mean? She was your friend and she never told you she had been married?"

"No, she didn't. Mr. Harper?"

"Call me David, please. I guess I shouldn't be surprised."

"Then call me Suzanne. I knew Kathy when I was a little girl. She used to babysit for me. Then she left Charleston, moved to Minnesota, I moved to Chicago, and we never heard a word from her. When she came home she refused to discuss her years there with anyone. By then her parents were deceased and she had no siblings, but of course you know that."

"Yes. Suzanne, may I ask what the cause of death was?"

"Cancer."

"Cancer. Oh, the poor girl. My God. Well, cancer is tragic enough, but I'm glad it wasn't an accident or foul play. I'd have a harder time accepting that. She had enough tragedy in her short life. Well, how terrible. She was way too young to die. I'm so, so sorry to hear this. Tell me, what can I do?"

"Well, I have her ashes and I thought you might want them, or if you don't, maybe you'd have a better idea of how to dispose of them. She told me to just spread them around my herb garden, but that didn't seem dignified enough for her."

"I know exactly what to do with them, and yes, I would like to have them."

"I think it's legal to ship them through the post office. I can check to see what the requirements are, if you'd like me to do that?"

"Let me just look at something on my calendar." There was a pause. And then he said, "I thought so. Okay, I have to be in Atlanta to look at a property on Monday. I haven't been to Charleston in years. So, if it's convenient for you, I can fly in Monday night?"

"That would be great," Suzanne said.

"And maybe I can buy you dinner in return for all the trouble you've been through?"

"That sounds very nice. I actually have some questions I'd like to ask you to put some things to rest."

"Sure. I'm happy to share anything I know that might help. I'll call you Monday?"

"Yes. Thank you, David. Here's my number."

Suzanne gave him her number and pressed end call.

We looked at each other and started jumping like the Masai, hugging and screaming.

"Woot! Woot! We're gonna kick Wendy's ass! Oh yeah! And get a pound of flesh for Kathy!"

"Have you ladies lost your beautiful minds?" I heard Mike say.

Paul, Harry, and Mike were standing in the doorway.

"I *could* medicate them," Harry said to the other guys. "But I like my women frisky."

"You're so terrible, Harry Black!" Suzanne said. "Just wait until you boys hear what we have to tell y'all!"

The story came pouring out over the smoky grill and iced tea and beers all around. We decided we were going to make dinner for David Harper when he arrived on Monday.

"I mean, I just can't see me taking Kathy's ashes to a restaurant in a shopping bag or something," Suzanne said.

"And I'm not so sure I'm happy about you having dinner with

some guy with a lot of money who might be single," Harry said.

"I'm not flighty, Harry," Suzanne said. "You should know that by now."

"Well, anyway, y'all," I said. "What are we going to do if he says the letter opener, the magnifying glass, and the furniture actually belonged to Kathy?"

"Good question," Carrie said. "What *are* we going to do?"

"First, let's see what this guy has to say," Paul said. "Then we can figure it out."

"Yeah," Mike said. "No point in paying the toll twice."

"But," I said, "shouldn't we have a vague idea of what we'd do? I mean, we could go to the police and file a complaint. We could go over there and confront Wendy again, which is a good idea if you have a taste for high drama. Or we could ask the police to get a search warrant and go there with him, maybe? How does this work on the cop shows?"

"Not only do I not know how this works on TV," Paul said, "I have no idea how it works in real life. I don't know any real criminals and I hardly watch television. Besides, I don't really like hostile confrontations."

"Me either," Mike said.

"Me either," Harry said. "I mean, I say use diplomacy first."

"Wimps!" Carrie said, and laughed.

"We are not!" Harry said. "Gentlemen don't go getting themselves into a common brawl."

"Well, that settles it," Suzanne said. "I guess we'll just have to wait and see what David Harper has to say."

When we were cleaning up the kitchen Suzanne said to me quietly, "Are you okay? You don't seem like yourself."

"Oh, Suzanne. It's my daughter. She got married to a druggie by an Elvis impersonator in Vegas."

Everyone stopped talking, waiting for me to tell the story, but I was choking back tears. Between what I was able to say and what Paul and Carrie filled in, the whole story came out.

"Jesus," Harry said. "This is why I'm glad I never had any kids."

"I was there," Paul said. "Lisa's not exaggerating."

"Don't worry, Lisa," Mike assured me. "It won't last."

I gasped.

"That was a little cold," I said.

"I'm sorry," Mike said.

"It's okay."

"Well, if you ask me, this justifies a common brawl!" Harry said. "We'll go to Colorado and wring this guy's neck if you want us to, won't we, gentlemen?"

"Oh, hell yeah!" Mike and Paul said.

"Not necessary," I said, and smiled. "But thanks."

"Honey," Carrie said. "I think what Mike means to say is that almost half of the marriages in this country end anyway, even when they seem like they should work."

"Well, I'm not happy about it," I said.

Everyone agreed. How could I be happy about this?

Over the weekend Carrie and I helped Suzanne unpack and arrange the huge collection of Kathy's snuff bottles along the edges of the glass shelves in Miss Trudie's breakfront. The stacks of plates that stood behind them were pretty boring and the little bottles breathed new life into the display. We were sprucing up the dining room and indeed the entire downstairs for David Harper's arrival. Mike and Harry replenished the bar and Paul claimed to have found some great wine on sale at Bottles. I ironed eight white linen napkins and placemats with spray starch. Carrie polished all the silver in the house—there wasn't much, only two candlesticks and some flatware. I spray-waxed and dusted all the furniture. Mike swept the porches and the steps. Suzanne brought in flowers for the whole house and put an arrangement in every room.

"These little bottles are so pretty," Carrie said. "It's easy to understand why she collected them."

"Good thing they weren't Wendy's taste," I said.

"I know," Suzanne said, putting a low arrangement of flowers in the center of the dining room table on the freshly laundered linen runner. "That would just be one more thing to arm-wrestle her over. What do you think about this? Too long?"

Carrie and I stopped and considered Suzanne's centerpiece.

"I think it's breathtaking," I said.

"I'll bet all those little bottles have a meaning," Carrie said.

"Probably. So, what do you want to make for dinner Monday night?" I asked.

"I don't know," Suzanne answered. "I was thinking about just shrimp and grits and a green salad. I know we just had gumbo last week but you can't get fresh shrimp in Minneapolis."

"That sounds perfect," Carrie said.

"Plus, I don't know how to cook anything else," Suzanne added. "And I can't keep turning the reins over to Paul. It doesn't seem fair."

"Do you think Paul cares?" I said. "He loves to cook."

"You'd think the king of England was coming to dinner," Harry said, passing through with groceries for that night's meal.

"Queen," Suzanne said. "Queen of England. Her Majesty, QE Two still reigns."

"Right," Harry said. "And it's such a disappointment to Prince Charles."

"I think he's reconciled to it," I said.

The banter went on like that and would continue until Monday night, when we hoped to get some answers. It seemed that since Miss Trudie's funeral, the six of us were spending an awful lot of time together. But the boys were as bought into the mystery as we were. Besides, there was safety in numbers and we were getting to the bottom of it together.

CHAPTER 19

Take That!

When David Harper called Suzanne on Monday, she convinced him the better plan was to come out to the beach for dinner and to meet all of us. He thought it was a fine idea and agreed.

"How very gracious of you, Suzanne. I'd love to see the Isle of Palms and meet your friends."

"And they want to meet you too. We were so fond of Kathy."

"Well, believe me; it pleases me to no end to know she was so loved."

It was a little after seven in the evening and the light of day was fading. Although summer was technically over, the days and even the nights were still balmy. Carrie and I were standing on the porch together when David Harper pulled into the driveway in a black car with a driver. We'd been poised for his arrival since four in the afternoon. The living room and the dining room sparkled. The rich patina of Miss Trudie's treasured silver candlesticks and flatware placed on crisp white linen and fresh flowers in every pastel shade you could name were beautiful and inviting.

Suzanne was in the kitchen, fussing over the hors d'oeuvres. She had made silver-dollar-sized crab cakes to serve with hot pepper jelly on top. Suzanne wasn't much of a gourmet but she'd been poring over recipes all weekend and she said this seemed easy enough to make. Harry was helping her set up the bar. Mike and Paul had yet to arrive.

Anyway, David Harper got out of the car and turned to have a glance at the ocean before he came toward the house. You could tell from the fit of his suit that he was a wealthy man. I held my breath for a moment but Carrie's gasp was audible. He looked like a movie star and a diplomat rolled into one.

"I'll go tell Suzanne and Harry that he's here," I said, and hurried to the kitchen.

"Well, helloooo there!" I heard Carrie sing out, and my first thought was, Well, that's it for Mike Kelly.

Some marriages have a short shelf life. Maybe Carrie could smell marriage, but I could smell flirtation. When Carrie's hormones kicked into gear it was something akin to witnessing the eruption of a small, polite geyser. Not Old Faithful, which would probably involve some really vulgar body language like twerking. My friends' and my twerking days were behind us, so to speak.

"He's here," I said to Suzanne.

"Great," she said, and grouped some items on the counter as she put her dish towel down. "Lisa? Would you?"

She pointed to the crab cakes and I knew she meant for me to please put the platter together.

"Sure!"

"I'm squeezing limes to extract their magical and life-changing juices," Harry said. "Tough job but somebody has to do it."

"And this job requires a doctor who's really an alchemist?" I said, and laughed.

"Or a mad scientist. This is my chemistry project for the evening."

"Ah, I see."

I began arranging the tiny crab cakes on a white ceramic platter and put a small dollop of jelly on top of each one. I wasn't a chef either, but I could manage this. Next I unwrapped the slab of pâté that was sitting there on a plate. I put a smallish cube on plain water crackers, mashed it with the back of a teaspoon, topped it with a drop of Dijon mustard, and stuck a sliver of a cornichon into the mustard. I only knew to do this because all the ingredients were there, waiting to be assembled, and they were segregated from the pepper jelly so there would be no confusion. Wisely, Suzanne was taking no chances with my culinary skills.

Harry and I hung back while she went to the door, because there was no reason to bombard David Harper with all of us in the same moment. On an odd note, Harry Black was really growing on me. My fondness for him was on the rise because of his affection for Suzanne. I wanted him to win her heart. He was certainly a lot more personable outside of Palmetto House, but I should have expected that. There was a difference between the guy in the white coat and this one in the madras plaid shirt and khaki pants. To my relief he had curbed his excessive use of scent. And he was a stand-up guy, pretty much, except when it came to delivering bad news.

I could hear Suzanne talking as she and David approached the kitchen.

"Would you like a glass of red wine or white or something stronger?" she said.

"I'm making a batch of Moscow mules," Harry said, and extended his hand to shake David's. "Hi, I'm Harry. And this is Lisa. Would you like one?"

"Sure," David said.

"You can take off your jacket and tie," Harry said, handing him a tall glass. "It can get warm in here."

They shook hands and David turned to me.

"Thanks!" he said.

David struck me as the sort of man who was so polite that he would've accepted any beverage Harry was pouring short of a Molotov cocktail.

"I'm David," he said, and shook my hand. "It's nice to meet you, Lisa."

"It's nice to meet you too. We've all been looking forward to tonight for so many reasons," I said.

He took off his jacket and removed his tie. He also rolled up the cuffs of his shirt to reveal the muscular and deeply tanned arms of an athlete. His dark hair was white around the temples and his eyes were deep blue and framed by eyelashes I'd kill for. In that fleeting moment of first impressions, I was afraid to make eye contact with Carrie for fear that she had already keeled over.

"Why's that?" he said pleasantly.

"Well, because we loved Kathy. And Suzanne, Carrie, and I . . . well, actually, all of us—Paul and Mike aren't here yet—we're hoping you can help us figure a few things out."

"Suzanne said that too. I hope I can help."

I glanced over to Carrie and she was practically frothing.

Oh God, I prayed silently, Please don't let sweet Mike notice.

Speak of the devil? The front door slammed and moments later Paul entered the room followed by Mike.

Paul came right to my side and kissed my cheek. "Sorry I'm late. Caught the drawbridge."

"That rascally drawbridge," I said, and realized how happy I was to see him.

Then he turned to our guest. "You must be David. I'm Paul."

They shook hands and then Mike introduced himself.

I picked up the platter of crab cakes and offered them to everyone. "Would you like one?"

"Thanks!" Paul said. "Mmm! Delicious!"

"Suzanne made them," I said. "Good, aren't they?"

I passed the crab cakes all around and refilled the platter, putting it on the kitchen table for them to help themselves. For some reason, we never managed to entertain in the living room. Maybe it was too staid. Whatever the reason, we always seemed to gravitate to the kitchen. If I ever built a house it was going to be one giant kitchen, with maybe a few bedrooms and bathrooms off the sides.

The conversation was sailing along as we got to know each other a bit. Once we got past the normal niceties, I passed the pâté, and somehow the subject of Kathy and the baby came up. There was no lack of sympathy in the room as everyone had something to say about the terrible heartbreak of losing a child.

"We were so sad to discover the news," Suzanne said. "I'm so sorry."

"It was a horrible accident," David said. "The most god-awful thing I've ever been through. I still blame myself."

"You shouldn't," Carrie said. "Blaming yourself doesn't change anything. I mean, there is such a thing as an accident."

"No, I should've had my eyes glued to my baby and I looked away for three minutes because I was reading the newspaper. Three minutes was all it took to ruin us. Ever since then I've been trying to do things to right some of the wrongs in the world."

"That's a mighty noble mission," Harry said. "I know what you mean."

"Harry runs a senior care facility," Suzanne said.

"And there's a lot of nobility in that, I'm sure," David said.

"Well, beyond keeping our residents as healthy and comfortable as possible, the real mission is to make them feel they still have worth," Harry said. "Lisa knows; right, Lisa?"

"I work for Harry," I said. "And Harry's right. Sometimes it gets complicated, but overall I think we provide more than we're expected to deliver."

We were quiet then because the story of David and Kathy's baby was too painful for any of us to move past easily.

"Anyway!" David said, breaking the silence. "Tell me how I can help you solve your mystery."

Carrie told him the story of Wendy and Suzanne and I filled in the blanks.

"Good grief! Do you have pictures of the furniture?" he said.

"We sure do," I said. "I'll get them."

I went to my purse and dug out my cell phone. Suzanne turned up the heat under the grits and threw the shrimp in the cast-iron skillet with the onions and andouille sausage she had sautéed earlier. The pan sizzled and quickly filled the room with the mouthwatering smells of onions and garlicky butter. She stirred and I scrolled.

"What fabulous dish are you preparing that smells so good?" David asked, and wandered over and stood very close to Suzanne's side, crossing his arms and giving her a grin.

I noticed that Harry arched an eyebrow, and when I looked at Carrie she was sulky. Oh Lord, I thought. I kept scrolling.

"It's just shrimp and grits," Suzanne said. "It's very popular here in the Lowcountry. And I figured it was something you wouldn't have all the time."

"I've actually never had a grit, so I'm anxious to try one," he said.

"Oh, goodness! What a darling thing to say!" Carrie said. "You can't have one grit! You eat grits by the spoonful! Y'all? Isn't he precious?"

Precious. In the interest of peace on earth I said, "So, David? Are you married?"

"No. After Kathy and I lost our baby, I just threw myself into work. I built a business. That's a lot less risky than having a personal life. Right?"

"I guess that's true, but a certain amount of risk can bring big rewards," Harry said.

I knew those words were really intended for Suzanne.

"Carrie and Mike just got married a week ago," I said. Where *was* that picture?

Carrie gave me some stink eye.

"Oh! Congratulations!" David said.

"I performed the ceremony," Paul said.

"Nice! Are you a minister?" David asked, and looked at Suzanne. "You didn't tell me I was having dinner with a man of the cloth."

Suzanne looked at him, clearly wondering why he was paying so much attention to her.

"No, I'm a notary public," Paul said.

"And he's a celebrated architect," I added.

"Is that so?" David said to him.

"In my own small way, I'm trying to save the planet. I build green."

"Fantastic!" David said. "We should talk. I'm planning to put up fifty stores in the southeast. Since I sell organic, it would be great if our stores were as environmentally sensitive as possible."

"I'll give you my card," Paul said, and reached into his wallet, handing him one. "Call me anytime."

"Thanks! I will," David said.

Suzanne was oblivious to David's attention but Harry and Carrie were not. I finally found the picture of Kathy's chest-on-chest and showed it to David.

"Okay, please look at this," I said. "Do you know if this was Kathy's?"

"Let me see? Sure. It was hers."

"I knew it!" I said.

"My goodness! Now what?" Carrie said.

"Is this something her landlady is saying is hers and not Kathy's?"

"Yes," Suzanne said. "It sure is." She spooned the grits into a serving bowl and covered it. "I knew it too."

"Well, that's simply not true," David said. "I bought that with her right after we were married. It's from Kentshire Antiques in New York. I probably still have the receipt somewhere. It was a very valuable piece."

"Sometimes it's easier to be wrong. I'll take that to the dining room," Carrie said, and picked up the covered bowl. "Show him the linen press, Lisa."

I did and he said, "I'm less certain about that, but it looks familiar."

Suzanne then emptied the contents of the frying pan into another serving bowl and covered it.

"Serving spoons, biscuits, and salad are on the table," she said. "Okay! Come on y'all, let's eat before it gets cold. And let's figure out what we're going to do."

"Suzanne?" David said. "You inherited Kathy's entire estate, did you not?"

"Yes, I did. But if there's anything you'd like to have . . ."

We began taking our seats at the table, weaving around Mike while he poured wine in everyone's goblets.

"No, no. Of course she left it to you. And I want you to have everything, but I have a question. Besides all the snuff bottles in that cabinet and the furniture, did you happen to find a letter opener and a magnifying glass? Old? Very ornate?"

I think we all stopped breathing for a moment.

"Yes," I said, "we did. Excuse me. I'll just grab my phone. Y'all start! I'll be right back."

I zipped back to the kitchen, grabbed my phone, and hurried to the dining room. I quickly took my seat and began scrolling through the pictures again. I found the one I wanted and passed my phone to him.

"Is that it?"

"Thank God they're not lost," David said. "By the way, this is delicious. Grits, huh?"

"Yes, it is," Mike said. "Ground cornmeal."

"Like polenta. It's fabulous, Suzanne," Harry said.

"Thanks. Why? Do they have sentimental value?" Suzanne said.

"I'll say they do. I gave them to Kathy to sell if she ever needed money. They're Fabergé, signed, made in 1896. Those stones in the handles are pigeon rubies. They're worth a fortune."

"What's a fortune?" Carrie asked. "I thought Fabergé only made eggs for the czar?"

"He did, but his studio also made other things like cigarette cases, inkwells, and perfume bottles. I couldn't even begin to say what they're worth. They're priceless because they're so rare. They've been in my family for over a hundred years."

"Well, then we've got a big fat problem," Suzanne said. "Wendy Murray says they're hers."

"Oh, no, they're not. Wendy Murray is a common thief and a liar," David said. "I can show you hundreds of family photographs with them in the picture. Why don't we pay her a call after we finish dinner? "

"Excellent idea," Harry said, not wanting to be outdone in machismo.

"I'm in," said Paul.

"Me too," said Mike.

Who had the longest yardstick? Suddenly we had testosterone raining all around us like manna.

"You ought to check out the value of those snuff bottles too, Suzanne," Harry said. "Some of those things can be worth a lot of money."

"Really?" Carrie said.

"No kidding," Suzanne said. "What is snuff anyway? Is it like cocaine or opium? I mean, they're obviously Chinese."

David wiped his mouth before speaking. "Yes. There's a great history surrounding snuff, which is actually tobacco ground into powder. The Portuguese introduced it to the Chinese at the end of the sixteenth century. They thought it had medicinal properties to cure all sorts of ailments. The more intricate the design of the bottle, the more it's worth."

"Kathy sure had a lot of them," Paul said, looking over at the breakfront. "I haven't had a chance to look at them but I'd like to. Some other time."

"Be my guest!" Suzanne said.

"They're amazing," Carrie said. "So many tiny details."

"People spend money on the craziest things. I read somewhere that some guys paid over three thousand dollars to buy an X-ray of Hitler's brain," Mike said. "Carrie? Would you pass the biscuits?"

She passed them right away and he took one. I wondered if Mike was a little irked with Carrie. I thought her attraction to David was obvious but Mike seemed unbothered.

"Really?" David said.

Mike nodded and slathered his hot biscuit with butter. No, Suzanne had not made the biscuits. She smartly purchased frozen Callie's biscuits from Harris Teeter, telling me how much easier they were to bake. I agreed. Mike passed the basket on to me. I took one and handed the basket to David.

"Don't leave this table without trying one of these," I said. "You can't buy these in Minneapolis."

"Oh, I don't know," he said, and we all laughed.

Hello? He owned a chain of grocery stores. If he wanted them, he could introduce them to the midwest and West Coast and have them any old time he pleased. What was I thinking? I was glad geography wasn't on the quiz.

It was around eight forty-five when dinner was finished. We asked each other if it was too late to take a ride downtown to confront Wendy.

"Yes, it's too late," David said. "But that's why we should go now. I think the element of surprise might work for us, not against us."

"I agree," Harry said. "I mean, should we wait until the sun is shining to be polite? That's ridiculous."

"Let's go," Mike said, and Paul nodded his head.

"I'm ready," he said.

I was plenty nervous but cautiously optimistic because all the men were coming and we had David with us, who, I knew, would take no bull from Wendy. So we left the dishes, squeezed into Gertrude's land yacht, because it was the only vehicle we had that could accommodate all of us, and drove downtown.

We pulled up in front of Wendy Murray's house with the bare yard and got out, gathering on the sidewalk. There were lights on all over the house.

"What's the plan?" I said.

"Who's going to ring the doorbell?" Carrie said.

"You ladies stand back," David said. "Let the men handle this."

David's commanding demeanor took over like Navy SEALs were on the job. We gladly did as we were told. Our last encounter with Wendy had scared the devil out of me. So Suzanne, Carrie, and I stood back while David, Paul, Harry, and Mike banged on her door nonstop until she answered it, only cracking it open ever so slightly.

"What do you want? Go away! Or I'll call the police!" She slammed the door.

"Let us in," David said, "or I'll call the police!"

"You'll do no such thing!" she shrieked.

"Yes, I will! Let us in!" David said.

"Open the door!" Harry said, his courage clearly bolstered by David's.

"No!" Wendy screamed. "Go away!"

"You know what you stole and it belonged to my wife!" David said. "I can prove it!"

"I don't know what you're talking about!" she yelled.

A light went on in the house next door and then another across the street. Noise in this neighborhood was cause for alarm.

"Give it all back peacefully or I'm calling the police," David said.

"You're trespassing! I have a gun!" she said. "And I'm not afraid to use it!"

I saw a light go on in another house on the other side of Wendy's.

"It's probably stolen!" Carrie yelled.

"Hush!" said Suzanne.

Oh dear God, I thought. What are we doing here?

"What kind of scum steals from the dead?" Mike said, yelling.

"Just give us what we came for!" Paul said calmly but loudly.

"No! You can't come here like this!" Wendy screamed. "You have no right!"

"Yes, we do!" David yelled, and he was so loud it made me dizzy.

David Harper was Hollywood handsome but he had a Conan the Barbarian temper to go with his looks.

Just then, the men pushed the door open and got inside. Wendy ran deeper into the house and suddenly I was terrified. Everything was happening too fast.

"Y'all!" I said. "We have to protect the men! Call 911! She has a gun!"

"Come on, Lisa. You know she's lying!" Carrie said.

Suzanne said, "What if she's not?"

I ran toward the door and slipped inside. Suzanne and Carrie were right behind me. We cowered in the foyer. I'll admit it, we cowered, but for good reason. We were honestly frightened.

The men were in the living room and from where we stood we could see David's reflection in the hall mirror as he picked up the magnifying glass with the matching letter opener and tossed one piece to Harry and the other to Paul. Mike grabbed an ancient saber from over the fireplace where it hung, pulled it from its sheath, and pointed it toward Wendy, who had just reappeared with a pistol. She was shifting her aim from David to Harry to Paul to Mike. I don't think she even knew Suzanne, Carrie, and I were there. Carrie crouched and pressed 911 on her keypad and hit send. Then she whispered the address.

"Put them back on the table or I'll blow your brains out," Wendy said. "You're all trespassing and there's not a judge or a jury in this world who would convict me for killing you."

"Listen, put the gun down," David said. "Just put the gun down.

You know what you've done, and unless *you* want to go to jail, you'll put the gun down."

"That's right," Paul said. "The police have been called, and they'll be here any minute."

"No, they haven't," Wendy said, and aimed her gun at Paul. "You're bluffing!"

"No one's bluffing, Wendy. Do what we've asked you to do," Harry said.

"I can take her and get her gun, Harry, if you'll move aside a bit," Mike said.

Suddenly Wendy spun on her heel and fired a shot in Mike's direction. He fell to the floor wounded.

I covered Carrie's mouth with my hand to muffle her scream. There was genuine fear in my eyes and in all our eyes.

"Anybody else want to die tonight?" Wendy said. "I've got a lot more bullets."

"Let's calm down, okay?" Harry said in the voice he reserved for hysterical patients and family members.

"Come on, now," David said, "we only want what's ours. You know that."

"Do I? How do I know that? For all I know, you're here to rape me, rob me blind, and kill me."

"Rape you?" Mike said from his place on the floor.

"Be quiet, Mike," David said. "We're here for these two items and two pieces of furniture."

"What are you saying? Are you insane?" Paul said to Wendy. "We're not interested in you! Put the gun down!"

"Yeah, just calm down," Harry said. "You really don't want anyone else to get hurt."

In our haste we had made no provision in our plans for moving the furniture. In the end, it wouldn't matter, but at that moment I realized we'd done something that was extremely foolhardy all across the board.

I heard a patrol car outside. Two policemen appeared and rather roughly pulled Carrie, Suzanne, and me from the foyer to the street.

"What's going on?" one of the officers demanded.

"Hurry, there's a back entrance!" I said.

"Hurry!" Suzanne said.

"She shot my husband!" Carrie said. "Oh God!"

"Calm down, ma'am. Where's the door?"

Carrie, Suzanne, and I ran into the courtyard with the police while they called for backup. They kicked in the door to Kathy's room, the door to the hallway, and the door into Wendy's part of the house.

"Stay here and don't move," one officer said to us.

There was a loud skirmish, but we couldn't see what was happening.

"Let go of me or I'll shoot you too!" Wendy screamed.

"Like hell you will," a man's voice said.

There were a few more shots fired and a scuffle of furniture being turned over and glass breaking. Finally there was relative quiet. Calls were made for an ambulance.

Against orders, Carrie ran inside the house to be with Mike. I didn't blame her. I would've done the same thing if Paul had been shot. Suzanne and I followed her inside, inching along slowly, wanting to be certain the violence had ended. In the living room, there stood Wendy in handcuffs, being read her Miranda rights.

" . . . and if you can't afford a lawyer . . ."

"Oh God," I said. "What happened here?"

Carrie was on the floor with Mike's head cradled in her lap. Wendy's bullet had gone into his shoulder. There was blood all over them.

Suzanne took one look at Mike and the pooling blood and passed out cold on the floor. Harry scooped her up and laid her on the sofa. A police officer stepped over to stop Harry.

Harry said, "It's all right, Officer. I'm a doctor."

"So what?" the officer said, then softened. "I'm gonna want to see some ID."

"You bet," Harry said. "Carrie, apply pressure to the wound."

"Help's coming, Mike," Paul said, and put his arm around me. "You're gonna live," he said to Mike.

"Jesus!" David said. "That woman's one crazy bitch! You okay, pal?" he said to Mike.

"Yeah," Mike said, "it just hurts. A lot."

"Okay, okay!" A detective showing his badge from the homicide department came in through the front door with three or four or maybe six crime-scene investigators. "Nobody touches anything. Let's turn on all the lights."

I started to reach for a light switch and he yelled, "Not you, ma'am. Please! Let's let *my* people do their job. Thank you. This is a crime scene. Nobody's going anywhere until I get some answers."

Mike, of course, was taken to the hospital, and Carrie, although she begged relentlessly through a flood of tears to be allowed to go with him, was made to remain with us.

Over the next four hours, we answered so many questions our heads were spinning. We finally got our story out and the detective in charge was stunned.

"I've never heard a story like this. And believe me, after twenty-five years on the force, I thought I'd heard it all!" he said.

One officer took Suzanne back to the beach house to get Kathy's will, which would verify her ownership of the items. They believed David that he had in fact given the items to Kathy if she ever needed emergency funds.

"Google me," David said.

The detective's partner did in fact Google David and showed the results to his partner. The lead detective shook his head.

"None of you folks have ever even had so much as a parking ticket," he said. "And this woman pushed you over the edge so easily . . . why?"

David said, "Because a pigeon blood ruby, similar in color but smaller in size, sold last year at Sotheby's in Hong Kong for over seven million dollars. Never mind the fact that signed Fabergé pieces are worth a fortune on their own."

Seven million dollars? Holy hell! Suzanne was rich! We were completely dumbstruck.

"I had no idea!" Suzanne said when she finally found her voice. "David, these belong to you."

"No, they are yours. That's how Kathy wanted it and I couldn't agree more," David said.

She looked like she was going to faint again. So did Harry.

"You people do realize that you should've just come to the authorities, don't you?" the detective said.

"Yes, of course," David said. "But by the time we made you understand the enormity of the crime and the urgency involved, those objects could've been sold to someone on the other side of the world and lost forever. And, these nice folks made me see how unreliable and unpredictable Ms. Murray was. I started the whole thing. This is really my fault."

"No, it isn't," Paul said. "We came here of our own free will."

"Yes, we did," said Harry.

"She's a raving lunatic," I said, "and a liar of the highest order."

"That may be. You all do understand that while the majority of the crimes committed here tonight belong to Wendy Murray, all of you carry some blame? We don't really like our citizens running around and taking the law into their own hands like Charlie's Angels and friends."

"Really?" Carrie said. "What did we do wrong?"

"Forceful entry, for starters? And, you know, this might go to trial? Therefore, the magnifying glass and the letter opener have to be entered into evidence."

"Detective? Does the police department of Charleston really want to take responsibility for holding something with that kind of price tag?" David asked.

The detective thought for a moment before speaking. "To be perfectly honest with you, I think there is no precedent for a situation like this. I'll have to ask the chief. What time is it?"

"Ten after three," Paul said.

"Oh gosh," the detective said, and sighed. "He hates it when I get him out of bed."

The chief of police was consulted and the situation was explained. When the detective finally got off the phone, he looked at us and said we should go home and get some sleep.

"I'm gonna let our CSI guys take some pictures of the magnifying glass and the letter opener, and I strongly encourage you not to come back around here to take anything else."

A man with a camera stepped over and took pictures.

"What about the furniture in the apartment?" Suzanne said.

"We'll get that all sorted out later. Let's see what Ms. Murray has to say when she's interrogated. Here's my card. I have your information. We'll be in touch."

We all went home to the Isle of Palms, except for Carrie, who had us drop her off at the hospital, where Mike had been admitted for overnight observation.

"If everything's okay, I won't bother you until tomorrow. I just want to sit with him."

"We understand," I said. "Give him our love, okay?"

She nodded and hugged all of us.

"We'll call you when we get up," Suzanne said.

As we drove away Suzanne said, "Good thing Mike goes by 'Mike' and not 'John' or we'd be planning a funeral."

"What's that supposed to mean?" Harry said.

"I'll explain it to you another time," Suzanne said.

The moment Suzanne asked David to stay with us at the beach for the rest of the night, he accepted. It was too late to check in to a hotel, or too early, depending on your point of view.

"I think I'm staying too," Harry said.

Suzanne looked at him and smiled. Harry was guarding his territory.

"Oh, okay. But no funny business."

"Who me?" Harry said.

"This is rich," David said.

Finally, Harry had gained admittance to Suzanne's garden, but would he be given the keys to the gate?

"Some of us are late bloomers," Suzanne said.

Later on I was curled up in bed with Paul and Pickle was in

her bed on the floor. Sadly, I couldn't hear any creaking bedsprings overhead but Suzanne and Harry were exhausted. Paul and I were beyond tired too, but sleep wouldn't come. And the sun was just beginning to creep in through the blinds.

"This was some night, wasn't it?" I said.

"You sure run with a fast crowd," he said, and kissed the back of my shoulder.

I smiled, and for the hundredth or so time, I thought about how relieved I was that Paul had not been hurt. Or Harry, or David, or of course the rest of us, really. Poor Mike.

"Did you say something?" I said.

"I said, I need to take you away from here where I can keep you safe."

"What are you saying, Paul Gleicher?"

"I'm saying, marry me."

"We'll talk about it in the morning," I said, and smiled in the dark.

"I love you," he said. "You have to marry me. Or I don't know what . . ."

Then I heard a little tiny snore. He had fallen asleep in midsentence.

"I love you too," I said, and drifted off to sleep.

Epilogue

Suzanne gave Kathy's ashes to David before he left and he said he was going to spread them around their baby's grave site. Wendy Murray's face was plastered all over the papers every day for two months and we sent all the articles to David. Fortunately, all the charges against us were dropped, with a stern warning from the judge.

"I don't want to ever see your faces in my courtroom again. Is that understood?"

Wendy was charged with attempted manslaughter, illegal possession of a deadly weapon, resisting arrest, obstruction of justice, and grand larceny. Through a plea bargain, she was fined twenty-five thousand dollars and sentenced to five years in prison without parole. The judge told her she was lucky he didn't throw the book at her because he could've sentenced her to thirty years.

"I wonder how she's adjusting to the life in the big house," Carrie said, and jangled her bangles.

Yes, Wendy fessed up to stealing the bracelets. Suzanne gave them to Carrie.

"I hope she rots in hell," Mike said.

His arm was still in a sling. I couldn't tell you if it was still necessary but it did wonders for his martyr status.

"Baby, you are so my hero, you don't even know!" Carrie said.

"And you're the love of my life," he said.

"Excuse me!" I said. "There are children in the room!"

Carrie's affection for Mike had doubled, maybe tripled, ever since he took a bullet in the name of righteousness.

Paul and I were sitting on the porch with them, waiting for Suzanne and Harry to arrive. And no, I was not twirling a diamond around my ring finger. Paul and I were in no hurry to get married. We were going out for dinner on Sullivans Island at The Obstinate Daughter, where our love affair officially began. In case anyone was wondering why such a great little restaurant had such a peculiar name . . . well, of course, it's grounded in history. Back in 1776, the Battle of Sullivans Island took place as the patriots on Sullivans Island fought the British in a furious struggle to defend the harbor of Charleston. This victory prompted a British cartoonist of the day to depict and describe a "Miss Carolina Sullivan as one of America's obstinate daughters." And that's really who we were too. Carrie, Suzanne, and even me. We stood our ground when the things that really mattered to us were at stake. And sometimes that resolve came with a price. For me, I was all but convinced I had lost the love of my daughter, Marianne. Every time I brought the subject up with Paul he'd tell me to be patient. On the outside I appeared patient, but on the inside my heart was broken into a million little pieces.

So imagine my surprise when we returned home from dinner and on the front porch there sat Marianne with my ex-husband, Mark. Marianne jumped up from her chair. Her face was streaked with tears.

"What in the world?" I said.

"Momma!" She ran to me, threw her arms around me, and hugged me so hard I felt my vertebrae move.

I burst into tears and so did she.

Paul, Suzanne, Harry, Mike, and Carrie just stood there like a garden row of slack-jawed and awkward asparagus.

"Y'all? This is my ex-husband, Mark, and this is my daughter, Marianne."

"Hello," they all said, and shook hands.

It was an exchange of the most minimal hospitality I'd ever seen them offer.

Suzanne said, "Why don't we step inside and let Lisa have a moment?"

They shuffled off the porch and into the house, but if I knew anything about them, they would position themselves so as not to miss a word.

Mark looked pretty good for someone I hadn't seen in person for decades. Yes, I occasionally watched moments of his reality show out of morbid curiosity. He had on camouflage from head to toe, but other than that he seemed clean. Marianne, though, looked haggard.

"What are you doing here? How did you find me?" I said.

"I knew you worked at Palmetto House, so I went there and one of the nurses gave me the address," Marianne said.

"Where's your husband?" I asked.

"Oh God! Oh, Momma! I made such a stupid mistake—no, so *many* of them. Can you ever forgive me?"

"You're going to say this is my fault. And maybe you're a little right," Mark said. "I'm the one who put her into her business and I'm the one who told her it was okay to marry that idiot. And don't be angry with Marianne. She's a good girl."

"You still haven't answered my question," I said. "Where is he?"

"He had to go away for a while," Mark said. "He got into some trouble."

"What do you mean 'go away'?" I said. "What kind of trouble?"

"He was helping this guy drive a truck into Kansas and it turns out Kansas laws aren't as flexible about certain things as Colorado laws are."

I knew he meant that it was a marijuana problem but I was going to make him spell it out.

"About what?"

"Horticultural issues," he said.

"Horticultural," I said. "Could you possibly be less vague?"

"He took some marijuana plants over the border, Mom."

"How many?" I asked.

"A little over two thousand," Mark said. "If you get busted with more than five it's a felony and you go to jail for twelve to seventeen years. Mandatory. No parole."

"So, like they say on *Law & Order,* what did he get?"

"Seventeen years! Mom! Seventeen years!" Marianne continued weeping and collapsed into a chair, head in hands.

"Yeah, apparently he gave the judge some lip, so the judge screwed him. Asshole."

"Who? The judge or my son-in-law?"

"That's the problem, Mom! We aren't married! We never got a marriage license!"

I sighed the biggest sigh of relief I had ever expelled in my entire life. In my mind my sigh had leveled the sand dunes across the street.

"The judge, of course," Mark said. "He basically ruined this kid's future!"

"The judge ruined his future, did he?" I said.

"So, I brought her home to you, Lisa. We sold her business to some suits from Seattle. She's been crying nonstop, but she's got a fat bank account. You can't be in the hospitality business if you're crying all the time. She was afraid to come back to you on her own. Anyway, I'm sorry because I think I screwed up here somehow. Don't be hard on her. She's hurting."

"You think?" I said. "Mark? You can go now."

"What? You're throwing me out again? It's just like old times!" He started laughing.

"Yeah, I guess I am. Thanks for bringing my daughter home to me where she belongs. It's the first time in your life you've ever done the right thing."

"You were always too judgmental," he said.

Mark gave Marianne a kiss on the head and left.

"Are you going to kill me?" Marianne said.

"Kill you? Are you insane? I'm going to throw you the biggest party I've ever thrown!" I was so happy then I thought my heart would burst. "Come on. Let's go wash your face. I want to introduce you to some honestly wonderful people."

And that marked the beginning of our healing process. There are issues in life on which two people may disagree and sometimes they will never agree. Nonetheless, Marianne's adventure had certainly posed an interesting question. In this life, you have to develop good judgment. You're not usually born with it. In fact, the question got all of us talking about morals, ethics, and values. And indeed, Paul and I harked back to the thirty-six questions and remembered that we didn't care so much about money and fame but that we wanted our lives to have meant something. We wanted to be remembered well. Marianne agreed with that.

Suzanne welcomed Marianne into the fold like a long-lost niece, and day by day there was mounting evidence that Marianne's wounded pride and broken heart were on the mend. In the first weeks of her homecoming we had lots of family dinners, which created a forum for interesting discussions. We talked about self-recrimination and how much of it was healthy. We talked about trust and what love really meant. We talked to her about redesigning her life and letting go of the past. Her past wasn't a total disaster because while she was in that quagmire she had learned to run a business.

Everyone was very kind to her, offering advice when she asked for it, giving her space when that seemed like the thing to do. Oddly, none of my friends had children, so Marianne suddenly had an abundance of would-be parents wanting to direct her to more worthy pursuits. I was so grateful for that. She was most interested in Paul's career and he had taken a definite shine to her.

"She's smart like hell," he said.

"Thanks. Now, if we can put those brain cells to good use?" I said.

One night at Paul's condo over a bowl of his delicious Bolognese, Marianne said, "Well, if nothing else came out of living in Colorado for a while, I sure came to understand that we're screwing up the environment all over the place."

"Well, maybe you can do something about that," Paul said. "Would you like to come to work with me for a week or two? You might learn something."

"Really?" she said, and for the first time since she'd been home, I saw a glimmer of excitement in her eyes. "Yes, I would love to do that. I mean, I think I'm retired from tourism. I'm gonna have to find a new future."

I didn't say one word. Not one word. I just smiled.

As you might imagine, one week turned into one month, and Marianne was becoming an environmental disciple.

"If you're thinking about doing this for a career," Paul said to her, "you really should think about going back to school."

"What?" I said. "I can't afford—"

Marianne cut me off. "Don't worry, Mom. I can pay for school. The one good thing that came out of my adventures in hell is money. So, Paul? Where should I go?"

"Well, I'd apply to a few places and see who bites," he said. "Meanwhile, I can keep you busy. It won't hurt to have an internship in the field on your résumé. And I can give you a letter of recommendation. Especially to Cornell. Listen, you might have to go back and take some undergraduate courses to get your transcript in order."

"Thanks. I wouldn't mind that. Hopefully a good transcript will temper the rest of my sordid past, right?"

"Right, but I wouldn't call it sordid. Look, you're young. You're supposed to try different things. And you learned how to run a successful business and I'm sure you learned some other things as well."

"I sure did," she said. "But I also took a mental thrashing in a lot of other areas."

"That's okay, sweetheart," I said. "We all live and learn."

I'd been spending more and more time downtown with Paul and Marianne was staying in my bedroom at Suzanne's and taking care of our dog. It was right before Thanksgiving when Paul told me he wanted to show me something.

"Come with me," he said.

We went up in the building's elevator to the ninth floor.

"What's going on?" I said.

"Well, there's a two-bedroom condo that's become available and I was thinking it might be good for us. Let's have a look."

He had the key and opened the door.

From the minute I went inside my eyes were drawn to the huge windows. There was an unobstructed view of Charleston Harbor and the Ravenel Bridge. French doors opened onto a small terrace. There were no exposed pipes or snaking metallic ductwork, but there were beautiful moldings and a fireplace with a mantel that was kind of grand. I ran my hand across its smooth cool surface.

"The fireplace surround is limestone. It's about two hundred years old. The previous owner brought it over from France."

"This place is a little palace," I said, wandering from room to room. "This kitchen's gorgeous, isn't it?"

"Yeah, and look at this."

He opened the door to the pantry closet, lifted a fake jar of mustard, pressed a button behind it, and the wall swung back to reveal a hidden wine cellar.

"Behold! The cave! Is this about the slickest thing you've ever seen?"

We laughed from the surprise of it. And it was beautifully constructed.

"No, you're the slickest thing I've ever seen!"

"Well, anyway, I was just thinking. If you won't marry me, at least we can shack up in style."

He pulled me to his chest and kissed me.

"I'll marry you," I said.

"You will?" He looked at me suspiciously.

"Yes, of course I will. Just not tomorrow. But you know I love you, right?"

"And I love you too. Listen. Lisa. Your daughter needs a stable environment," he said. "She can't stay at Suzanne's forever. It's like living with *Bob and Carol and Ted and Alice*. She needs her own home."

He was right.

"My daughter is an adult," I said, admittedly stretching the truth. He stared at me. "My daughter is almost an adult. Okay. I'll think about it."

"Well good, because I close on this place in thirty days and I just accepted an offer on my condo downstairs."

"You knew I'd love this place, didn't you?"

"Yes, I did. If I can't sway your heart with words, I had hoped a place like this for us and for Marianne would do it."

He was right again. I loved Paul like I'd never loved anyone in my entire life. And the big glaring lack in my life was a stable home.

"You win," I said. "Want to get married on New Year's Eve?"

"Sure! But why New Year's Eve?"

"Because every year we'll have fireworks to celebrate? I don't know. It just seemed—"

"Brilliant! It's brilliant! And now I don't have to return this."

He dug into the pocket of his pants and pulled out a sparkling diamond ring. He blew off the lint and dropped to one knee.

"So? Shall we make this official?"

"Oh, Paul!"

"Will you?"

"Yes!"

He slipped it on my finger, stood up, and then he kissed me in such a way that I was glad we were alone.

"Here's what you need to know about your ring," he said.

"What? It's gorgeous!"

"And it's a quarter of a carat bigger than Carrie's! Ha! Ha!"

"You're so wicked," I said.

"And I already asked your father's permission," he said.

"Really? How did that go?"

"He said, 'Please! Marry her! Her mother and I can't go on worrying about her going through life alone! It's killing us!' "

"No way. Did he really?"

"Of course not! He said he'd be honored to have me in the family. What else was he going to say? Besides, they're so happy that your daughter is back home and in a good frame of mind. They kept thanking me as though I was responsible for her turnaround."

"Maybe you weren't completely responsible because we know the devil stepped in to snag Bobby. But you surely made a valuable contribution to the cause."

"I'm just glad we got her back on the right road."

"And I'm so grateful that you're so accepting of her."

"Listen, I don't have to raise her. You already did that. This is a relaunch situation. We're just gonna relaunch her in the right direction and it will all work out fine. I love your eyes. Have I told you that before?"

We went over to Suzanne's late that afternoon with champagne and there was much celebrating and toasting. Marianne was thrilled for us. She threw her arms around me and then Paul.

"Dad!" she said. "No, really. What am I supposed to call you?"

"How's 'Paul'?" Paul said. "That's what you've always called me, isn't it?"

She giggled and hugged me again. I had my little girl back and we were going to be a family. A good solid and reliable family with the paperwork to prove it.

Harry said, "Well, I hope this bodes well for me. Congratulations, you old dog!"

He shook Paul's hand and gave me the most polite kiss on the cheek.

"I'm really happy for you, Lisa," Harry said.

"Thanks, Harry."

Carrie said, "Now, let me have a good look at this ring!" She stared at it and then she stood back and wiped her eyes. "I'm just so happy for you, Lisa. Paul's such a great match for you."

"Thanks!" I said. "He sure is. He's that fairy-tale guy on the white horse."

As it turned out, my parents were spending Thanksgiving with my brother and his wife in North Carolina, so we passed that holiday with our core group of friends plus Marianne. My parents promised to come for Christmas and stay through the wedding. My brother, Alan, and Janet, his wife, would be there for the wedding as well.

Over Thanksgiving dinner Paul said, "Hey, Marianne? I spoke to the dean of admissions at Cornell. They got your application and transcript. You only have to take six courses to be able to apply to an architecture graduate school. What do you say to that?"

"Really? I say, hello, Ithaca! Wow!"

"Thanks, Paul," I said.

"Or, you could take the courses at Auburn," he said. "I looked at their curriculum."

"No, I want to go where you went," she said.

"Okay, then, we'll figure it out."

I was worried that Marianne missed her almost husband, Bobby, because every now and then she looked melancholy, but she hardly said a word about him.

"So, what are you thinking, baby?" I said when I saw that sad look in her eyes.

"I'm thinking what a fool I was to love someone like Bobby."

"No, no," I said. "You never have to apologize for loving anyone."

"Well, I'm totally over it now. Did you ever fall in love with a jerk?" she said.

"Do you really want me to answer that question?" I said.

Then we laughed and laughed.

"Oh, Mom! Dad *is* such a jerk, especially when you put him next to Paul."

"Well, I wouldn't say that, but at least with Paul I don't have to sleep with one eye open."

On another afternoon, I saw her on the little terrace at our new home, her book left open on a chair. She was staring into space.

"What's going on in that pretty little head of yours?" I asked.

"Shakespeare was right," she said. " 'All that glitters is not gold, often you have heard it told, many a man his life has sold . . .' *Merchant of Venice.* I almost sold my soul."

"But the important thing, my little scholar, is that you didn't."

Suzanne sent pictures of her letter opener and magnifying glass to a store in New York on Fifth Avenue, right across from the Plaza Hotel, that specialized in sales of Fabergé anything. They found her a private buyer who offered her a price that was so astronomical she couldn't even bring herself to repeat it. But it had to have been wildly generous because I came over one day in early December to find men on ladders painting the house and another crew of men digging out a spot for a swimming pool.

"I want you and Paul to be married here and I can't have a wedding with the paint peeling right off the house," she said.

"Oh, Suzanne! You are too nice to us!"

"You know it's my pleasure. Hey! Who's performing your ceremony?"

"He didn't tell you?"

"No, who?"

"Why, Harry is! He's becoming a Universal Life minister!"

"I'd better check my lightning rods!" she said, and we laughed.

And so on New Year's Eve I married Paul with my daughter on one side and my dog at my feet, right in the middle of Miss Trudie's living room. When Harry said, "You may kiss your bride," I could almost hear Miss Trudie warming up the keys to play a medley of love songs and "Auld Lang Syne."

My mother and father had prepared a buffet dinner of an enormous fish covered in aspic and stuffed with crabmeat, Hoppin' John rice, and a collard-green salad.

I really hated collards, just like I hated kale, but I didn't say anything about it because no one asked me what I wanted for my wedding supper in the first place. Except for Carrie.

"Shall we talk about your wedding cake?" she asked.

"Surprise me," I said, knowing she'd do something outrageous.

She'd had our cake made by a pastry chef she knew and it was mouthwateringly delicious.

"What's in this?" I asked. "It's familiar but it's not."

"Krispy Kreme donuts and Grand Marnier," she said, and we laughed.

"How'd they get donuts in the cake?"

"I don't know. Maybe she cut them up in little tiny pieces?"

But back to my mother and the nasty business of collard greens?

"We're having them tonight. It's close enough to New Year's Day," my mother said. "Don't worry. I've got a big ham and more collards for tomorrow."

In the Lowcountry, New Year's Day dinner was ham, collards, and Hoppin' John rice made with field peas. As you know, traditions here are sacred.

"Thanks, Mom. I wasn't worried for a minute."

"I'm just so happy you snagged Paul before he got away, aren't you? And I'm so glad Marianne didn't come home pregnant. What would we have done then?"

"You're right," I said, because any other answer would only result in memories of the day I didn't want to have.

The fireworks started at ten. We all went outside to the porch to watch them. Whistling rockets and crackling comets lit up the dark winter sky. Firecrackers and cherry bombs were exploding all over the neighborhood and then more fireworks, ones that bloomed like flowers and others that burst into wide open feathers and plumes of color high in the air. It was the most gorgeous display I'd ever seen, or maybe it was just my excitement.

My folks were the first to leave, followed by my brother and his wife. We hugged and kissed each other and there was another round of congratulations. Finally, it was time for us to go home to our new condo.

"I'm staying at the beach tonight," Marianne said. "You know, to give you kids some space."

"Thanks," we said, and thanked Suzanne again and again.

Paul said, "So, what about you and Harry? Are you ever going to marry the guy and put him out of his misery?"

"I don't know," she said. "We'll see. I kind of like being single. Y'all let me know if it's worth it, okay?"

"Okay."

"Hey, Suzanne?" Harry said, coming up behind her. "I've got some questions I want to ask you. There are only thirty-six of them."

It was probably just a matter of time before we'd have another wedding.

Before we got into our car to go downtown, Paul and I walked over the sand dunes to have a look at the ocean and to share a few moments that were only ours. We could still hear the pop of a few remaining fireworks in the distance, and across the water we could see the waning ones light up the sky.

"Tomorrow is a new year," he said.

"Tomorrow starts a new life," I said.

"Come on," he said. "I want to take my wife home. It's cold."

Home, I thought.

There were two stars in the sky that were brighter than all the rest. I couldn't stop looking at them.

"Do you see those two superwhite stars? Were they this bright earlier?"

"I don't know," he said. "Why? What are you thinking? Someone's looking down here at us and smiling so brightly that they're twinkling?"

Kathy Harper. Miss Trudie. It would be wonderful to believe that. Even more wonderful to know it.

"Well, why not? This is the Lowcountry. Magical things happen here all the time."

They really do.

ACKNOWLEDGMENTS

Using a real person's name for a character has been a great way to raise money for worthy causes. And in the pages of *Carolina Girls* four generous souls come to life as my characters. I have met these folks only ever so briefly, so I can assure you that the behavior, language, proclivities, and personalities of the characters bear no resemblance to the actual people, especially Mark and Marianne, who I hope are really good sports. So special thanks go to Mark and Marianne Barnebey and Jack and Mayra Schmidt for their generous support of the Manatee Library Foundation. I can't remember having more fun raising money and I hope y'all will get a big hoot out of seeing your names all over these pages. And special thanks to Carol and Alan St. Clair for once again supporting Bishop England High School in Charleston, South Carolina. And special thanks to my good friends Margaret Seabrook and Judy Koelpin for appearing in these pages as nurses and for our shared love of Johns Island tomatoes. I could live on them! More truth: Roy and Mary Anne Smith do not have a reprobate for a daughter and, in fact, to the best of my knowledge, they don't have a Debbie among their offspring. They are lovely and upstanding citizens in every single way. I hope y'all will be pleasantly surprised to find yourselves in this drama. It was fun being reminded of you each time I wrote your names!

And make sure you do stop in for dinner at The Obstinate

Daughter on Sullivans Island. Say hello to the executive chef, Jacques Larson, and tell everyone who works there that I sent you. I really love this charming place that sets the scene for Lisa falling in love with Paul . . . this brings me to Paul, named for the real Paul Gleicher, a superbly talented architect in real life as in these pages, who is married to the real Lisa Sharkey. Together they penned a fabulous book about eco-friendly architecture called *Dreaming Green*. If you want to learn more about living green, this book is a great resource. And you know, Lisa, I wanted to call this book *Lisa Sharkey Takes a Bite out of Life,* but Carrie said no, she didn't think so. Well, fine. Anyway, I've made your namesake a fallen vegan, backsliding yoga devotee, donut-addicted, dog-loving geriatric nurse. She's my favorite character next to Carrie. Oh, and Miss Trudie, who's named for no one. And Suzanne, who's named for Suzanne and that's all I'm saying about her except that I'm crazy about her and she knows it. However, Mike Kelly is real and wonderful but not as goofy as the character named for him. And Mr. Morrison, guess which one, among the many that I know, is not, in real life, an old codger chasing skirts in a nursing home. He is a brilliant and dignified gentleman. And may I just say to my dear friend Kathy Gordon: Sorry, babe. I didn't mean to kill you off, but hey, that's how it goes in fiction land. I shoulda sent flowers! Ha ha! And, your husband, the lovely gentleman that David I. Gordon is, should rush right to the store to buy you a letter opener and magnifying glass just like Suzanne's.

Clio and Alicia are two of the finest women on the planet and would never behave as they do here. Ben and Giles would never support it, and Clio and Alicia wouldn't be so awful in the first place. So, to wind up these true confessions, a certain shy character took a walk and was replaced by her mother, Wendy. No last names necessary. You all know who you are! And I hope you both laugh at the antics of this wicked, treacherous woman, who's definitely not a belle! A true belle would've used the sword.

Thanks to Dianne and Cecil Crowley of The Tavern and Table in Mount Pleasant for the restaurant tip on how your waiters take their orders. I had dinner there and ordered exactly what I ordered in these pages. It was absolutely divine. And the *panna cotta* was out of this world! And some serious bowing and scraping to Arthur Aron, PhD, for his marvelous research into how and why people fall in love and how to expedite the process using his thirty-six questions, which went viral after they were mentioned in an essay in the *New York Times*. I even have the app. What a world.

Special thanks to George Zur, who is my computer webmaster, for keeping the website alive. To Ann Del Mastro and my cousin Charles Comar Blanchard, all the Franks love you for too many reasons to enumerate!

I'd like to thank my wonderful editor at William Morrow, Carrie Feron, for her marvelous friendship, her endless wisdom, and her fabulous sense of humor. Your ideas and excellent editorial input always make my work better. I couldn't do this without you. I am blowing you bazillions of smooches from my office window in Montclair.

And to Suzanne Gluck, Alicia Gordon, Tracy Fisher, Catherine Summerhayes, Clio Seraphim, Siobhan O'Neill, and the whole amazing team of Jedis at WME, I am loving y'all to pieces and looking forward to a brilliant future together!

To the entire William Morrow and Avon team: Brian Murray, Michael Morrison, Liate Stehlik, Nicole Fischer, Lynn Grady, Tavia Kowalchuk, Kelly Rudolph, Shawn Nichols, Frank Albanese, Virginia Stanley, Rachael Brenner Levenberg, Andrea Rosen, Caitlin McCaskey, Josh Marwell, Doug Jones, Carla Parker, Donna Waitkus, Eric Svenson, Dale Schmidt, Austin Tripp, Lillie Walsh, Michael Morris, Gabe Barillas, Mumtaz Mustafa, and last but most certainly not ever least, Brian Grogan: thank you one and all for the miracles you perform and for your amazing, generous support. You still make me want to dance.

To Buzzy Porter, huge thanks for getting me so organized and for your loyal friendship of many years. Don't know what I'd do without you!

To Debbie Zammit, it seems incredible but here we are again! Another year! Another miracle! Another year of keeping me on track, catching my goobers, and making me look reasonably intelligent by giving me tons of excellent ideas about everything.

To booksellers across the land, and I mean every single one of you, I thank you from the bottom of my heart, especially Patty Morrison of Barnes & Noble, Vicky Crafton of Litchfield Books, and once again, can we just hold the phone for Jacquie Lee of Books a Million? Jacquie, Jacquie! You are too much, hon! Love ya and love y'all!

To my family, Peter, William, and Victoria: I love y'all with all I've got. Victoria, you are the most beautiful, wonderful daughter and I am so proud of you. You and William are so smart and so funny, but then a good sense of humor might have been essential to your survival in this house. And you all give me great advice, a quality that makes me particularly proud. Every woman should have my good fortune with her children. You fill my life with joy. Well, usually. Just kidding. Peter Frank? You are still the man of my dreams, honey. Thirty-two years and they never had a fight. It's a little incredible to realize it's been only thirty-two years, especially when it feels like I've loved you forever.

Finally, to my readers, to whom I owe the greatest debt of all, I am sending you the most sincere and profound thanks for reading my stories, for sending along so many nice e-mails, for yakking it up with me on Facebook, and for coming out to book signings. You are why I try to write a book each year. I hope *Carolina Girls* will entertain you and give you something new to think about. There's a lot of magic down here in the Lowcountry. Please, come see us and get some for yourself! I love you all and thank you once again.

ABOUT THE AUTHOR

New York Times bestseller DOROTHEA BENTON FRANK was born and raised on Sullivans Island, South Carolina. She resides in the New York area with her husband.

Dorothea Benton Frank's most recent bestseller, *The Hurricane Sisters,* debuted at number three on the *New York Times* list, where it remained in the top twenty for six weeks. It was also a *USA Today* bestseller for four weeks, debuting at number eleven.

A contemporary voice of the south in the ranks of Anne Rivers Siddons and Pat Conroy, Dorothea Benton Frank is beloved from coast to coast, thanks to her bestsellers, including *The Last Original Wife, Porch Lights, Sullivans Island,* and *Plantation*.